The Secret Diary

of

Anne Boleyn

ROBIN MAXWELL

Scribner Paperback Fiction
PUBLISHED BY SIMON & SCHUSTER

SCRIBNER PAPERBACK FICTION
Simon & Schuster Inc.
Rockefeller Center
1230 Avenue of the Americas
New York, NY 10020

First Scribner Paperback Fiction edition 1998
Published by arrangement with Arcade Publishing, Inc.
SCRIBNER PAPERBACK FICTION *and design are trademarks of Macmillan Library Reference USA, Inc.,
used under license by Simon & Schuster, the publisher of this work.*

Manufactured in the United States of America

9   10   8

Library of Congress Cataloging-in-Publication Data
Maxwell, Robin, 1948–
The secret diary of Anne Boleyn : a novel / Robin Maxwell. — 1st
Scribner pbk. fiction ed.
p.   cm.
1. Anne Boleyn, Queen, consort of Henry VIII, King of England,
1507–1536—Fiction. 2. Great Britain—History—
Henry VIII, 1509–1547—Fiction. 3. Queens—
Great Britain—Fiction. I. Title.
PS3563.A9254S43   1998
813'.54—dc21   97-53056
CIP

ISBN 0-684-84969-0

For my mother

*G*OD'S *DEATH!*" roared Elizabeth. "Will you not give me one day's respite from this tiresome pestering? You make my head ache."

The Queen's councillors could hardly keep pace with the extraordinarily tall and slender woman now moving in great strides across Whitehall's wide lawn to her waiting mount.

Her chief advisor, William Cecil, a stern and steady man of middle age, was torn between admiration and despair of his new young queen, now attired in a purple velvet riding habit, her gold-red hair flying long and unbound behind her. Headstrong and stubborn did not begin to describe Elizabeth Tudor at twenty-five. Reckless she was, lacking in anything vaguely resembling restraint, with a razor wit and a bawdy tongue unfitting England's monarch. But, he was forced to admit, her intellect was broad and magnificent. She spoke six languages as fluently as her own and was easily as magnetic as her father Henry VIII had been in his long and turbulent life. If only, thought Cecil, she did not take such perverse delight in outraging the great lords whom she had appointed to counsel her. Cecil chanced her further wrath.

"I beg Your Majesty to give the archduke Charles more thought. He is, besides being the best match in Christendom, said to be, for a man, beautiful and well-faced."

"And, more important," added Elizabeth with a decidedly lascivious leer, "well-thighed and well-legged."

"I'm told his stoop is not noticeable when he's on horseback," added Lord Clinton, hoping they were gaining some ground. But Elizabeth stopped in her tracks and turned on them so suddenly that the councillors collided with one another like players in a stage comedy.

"And *I* am told he's a young monster with an enormous head! Good Christ, the pitiable choices for husband you offer give me scant cause to change my state of matrimony."

"Prince Eric is a . . ."

"Lumpen Swede," finished Elizabeth.

"But he's very rich, Your Majesty, and generous to the extreme."

"But that ridiculous delegation who came simpering to court in their crimson robes with velvet badges of arrow-pierced hearts . . . ?" Elizabeth rolled her eyes. "You ask me to consider the French king who has stolen Calais, our only remaining port on the Continent . . . and Philip, my queen sister's swarthy Spanish widower, who is a devout and unwavering *Catholic?!* Come now, gentlemen, surely you can do better than that."

"Are the English suitors more to your liking, then?"

"The English suitors?" Elizabeth's eyes seemed to soften, and a hint of a smile tilted the corners of her scarlet mouth. She turned and continued at a more leisurely pace toward her fine chestnut stallion trapped in a footmantle laced with gold, and toward the tall well-built young man of confident posture and athletic grace who stood beside it, reins in hand. Cecil regarded Robert Dudley, the Queen's Master of the Horse, with quiet annoyance. It was surely Dudley who brought the smile to the Queen's lips and the almost languorous sway to her walk as she crossed the remaining distance to her mount.

"Indeed," she purred, "I do like my English suitors far better."

Cecil could hear the councillors grumbling discreetly at the sight of Robert Dudley. This arrogant nobleman's outrageous pursuit of the Queen and her even more scandalous acceptance of that pursuit were creating an unwholesome climate that imperiled Elizabeth's chances of marrying honorably here or abroad. For Dudley, believed by many to be the Queen's lover, was a married man. Cecil pushed out of his mind the thought that Elizabeth's wanton behavior was her way of insuring that she would never have to marry, but could instead keep a series of lovers throughout her reign; worse, that the Queen might be showing a streak of her mother's nature. The Boleyn blood was tainted with perversity. As it was, everyone — from Elizabeth's royal advisors who supplied her with endless choices for matrimony, to her childhood mistress Kat Ashley who begged the Queen to come to her senses, to her loyal subjects who petitioned her daily — was demanding that for her honor's sake and the welfare of the kingdom she marry and relinquish the reins of government to her lawful husband.

Elizabeth approached Dudley, who, rising from a deep bow, stood straight and manly, his strong features and clear-eyed expression forcing even Cecil to admit the horsemaster was a fine figure of noble virility. Dudley locked his gaze on the Queen's. With no thought to the disapproving stares of her councillors, Elizabeth reached up and with careless intimacy caressed Dudley's cheek, drawing her long white fingers down his face, slowly tracing the sharp line of his jaw and chin, ending with a tiny tickle in the hollow of his throat.

"How does my great stallion?" she asked, suppressing a smile. Perhaps the outraged sniffs and sharp intake of breath from behind prompted her to slap the chestnut steed's massive flank with a resounding thump, affording her stunned councillors the distant but grateful possibility that the Queen's remark was not the grossly vulgar one they suspected.

She turned to Cecil and bestowed on her advisors a warm, playful smile. "My lords Clinton, Arundel, and North, I do greatly appreciate your clement advisements and take them to heart." She allowed Robert Dudley to boost her onto the horse, and sat tall and regal in the saddle looking down upon the men. "My choice of husband and king is one not lightly made, requiring much reflection. So you will forgive a poor weak woman's hesitancy to commit. But I do promise this. When the decision is made, you will indeed be the first to know. Good day, gentlemen."

With a swift kick her horse was off. Dudley, inclining a mockingly respectful head to the councillors, leapt upon his own horse and sped off after the Queen, who had already attained a full gallop.

Cecil and the other chagrined advisors turned and, without meeting each other's eyes, began a slow and troubled walk back to the royal palace.

It was late in the afternoon when the first sunshine pierced the overcast, falling through the cottage window in a golden swath across Elizabeth's pearl white and naked breasts. Dudley, reclining close beside her propped upon an elbow, traced a lazy path around the small dove-soft mounds with a rough-skinned but gentle hand. He grazed the rosy nipple and it moved beneath his touch. An unexpected sigh escaped the mouth whose painted lips had by now been kissed clean. Her eyes fluttered behind the lids and opened slowly.

Elizabeth and Dudley had had a hard ride through green April fields and come at last to the royal hunting lodge, a rough and tiny timbered house at the edge of Duncton Wood. The pair had entered laughing, breathless from their exertions but with the blood racing in every extremity, and had fallen into passionate embraces and kisses, and, as had been progressing in the months preceding, to several intimacies.

"You take some liberties with your queen, my love," Elizabeth murmured with just a trace of sharpness.

Measuring his words and finding room for boldness, Dudley replied, "I mean to take more, Your Majesty."

Her protracted and steady gaze was surely meant to cause hesitation. But Dudley was a man aroused and almost past caring. Elizabeth's sleeves and bodice lay undone around her reedlike torso, but the skirts and petticoats of her velvet riding habit were still intact upon her hips and legs, though rumpled and softened by the steamy vapors of their afternoon's embraces.

His wandering hand caressed Elizabeth's waspish waist and the hot, moist ridges of her spine. He pushed his fingers down beneath the lacy underkirtle to find the soft vee between her buttocks and, with this grasp, pulled her hips against his. She gasped in sudden pleasure and, so emboldened, with the skirt all loosened from above, he groped to find her mound of maiden hair.

"Robin, stop."

He answered her command with one fierce kiss covering her mouth. She moved beneath him, but not in ardor. She pulled her face away.

"Don't stop me now, Elizabeth."

"Yes, stop I tell you, stop!" Her voice had changed, had lost its silk. Her body's softness turned to rigid wood. Dudley's features flushed with helpless rage. He pulled his hand reluctantly from the Queen's great skirts.

Elizabeth watched Dudley's beautiful face as he struggled to control himself. His naked desire for her body which she loved and feared had changed, with her command to stop, to sudden fury and then to something different, more difficult to discern. She was queen. He was her subject. His eyes showed the confusion of this awkward state. She was, she knew, the only woman in England who had the power to command a man this way. This exultant strength was new, for her coronation had been only three months before, and Robert Dudley had been her dear friend since early childhood. Once she'd become queen, his loyal affections had taken on a fervent quality which she had found altogether irresistible. She had with an imperious flourish named him her Master of the Horse, and he had ridden proudly behind her in the coronation procession for all the world to see. Most believed them already intimate to the fullest degree. But Elizabeth had withheld the ultimate favor.

"Robin, love . . ." She stroked his hot, damp cheek.

"Don't call me love," he said with a sullen gaze.

"I'll call you what I will," she said in tart response. The light was fading fast and they both knew their precious private time would soon be ending. Elizabeth sat up, pulled her bodice back together, and fumbled with the many closings. "Come, help me with this now." She teased him with a coquettish grin and despite his pique he was, as ever, completely charmed by this frail girl. His clumsy fingers pushed the tiny pearl buttons through their satin eyes. Once his fingers slipped purposely, brushing her now corseted breast with his hand.

"Your councillors are wild with fear," he said. "They think you mean to marry me and make me king." He sat up, pulling closed his shirt and vest, not looking her in the eye.

"And what, pray, would they have us do with your good wife?"

"Wife? Have I a wife?" he joked.

She stood before him, forcing their eyes to meet. "If you and I were wed, would you forget me so easily?"

He saw that he had blundered, not simply making light of his own loveless marriage but recalling the coldbloodedness with which her father had discarded his wives, including Elizabeth's mother. But this girl, his queen, his love Elizabeth, drove him mad with her changeability. At times she opened to him like a flower to sunlight, laughing, teasing, making wicked plans in much the way they had done as children. In those times they were as if intoxicated, crazed with delight in each other's company. She had even contemplated marriage to him. Sometimes she pushed him to be strong with her, to dominate and be her master. Then with the swiftness of a summer storm she turned dark and harsh, playing upon his insignificance, toying with him as she would a chess piece.

"I have too many suitors, Robin — princes, kings, and emperors — to think of you to marry." She said this flippantly, but he sensed a softening in her. He watched her move as she put on her velvet jacket, saw the shoulders droop just so, the eyes unfocused, the forehead tight and strained. Wishing to bring her back to mildness, he pulled himself erect and made his stand, looming tall above her. His voice a mellow purr, he tilted up her head to his.

"Do you not think you have some loyal subjects of your own to make an heir for the English throne?"

"An heir?" Her eyes flashed and seemed almost to snap. "An heir, Robin? Is this the issue here? Not love but royal offspring? 'King Robert, father to many sons, high ruler of England and, oh yes, I'd forgotten, husband of Elizabeth.'"

"You twist my words, you take me wrong!" he cried.

He'd chosen ill and blundered yet again. Elizabeth crossed the rough-hewn floor and made for the cottage door, her face flushed crimson. Her succession to the throne had been a ghastly road littered with the dead. Robin Dudley was her love, not her lord. To talk of heirs now in moments sweet as these was a noxious thing. She pulled open the door but Dudley slammed it shut.

"Let me by."

"No, Elizabeth."

"I command you!" she roared.

Dudley saw the purple pulsing veins beneath the parchment skin of Elizabeth's hollow temples. He saw that she was about to cry. He dropped to his knees before her.

"Your Majesty . . ." He could not go on for a moment, terrible emotions overwhelming his reasonable mind. He raised his arms a supplicant and encircled her waist. Despite the many layers of cloth and corset bones he felt her trembling. "Oh, forgive me, please."

"Robin, rise. . . . I did not mean for you —"

"No, no, let me speak." Though his head was bowed he spoke with such intensity that every word was sharp and clear. "I knew you as a child, Elizabeth. Born a royal princess, then cast aside as bastard by a father who wanted only sons. Sent from court to live in obscurity and in poverty. You suffered without his care. But in that nursery schoolroom where my father sent me, I found a jewel. A brilliant mind, a glowing soul, a lovely face as pale as a Yorkshire rose. I loved you even then. We were brother and sister, friends, schoolmates. We laughed, we wept, we helped each other through some times, did we not?"

Dudley did not raise his head to receive the answer, but he knew his words were being heard. The talk of older days and childhood had stopped her trembling, and her breathing eased and slowed.

"This frail, sweet girl survived a tender brother's reign and death, a bloody sister's rule and demise . . . to become Elizabeth the Queen. The girl is gone, but in my mind not the playmate, not the sister, not the friend. They remain. But now I feel a greedy passion for the woman's body. This creates a deep and terrible bond, each to the other. True, I am married to Amy Dudley by the law. But to you I am married by my heart and soul and mind."

"Robin . . ." Elizabeth's voice was soft now, but he commanded her to silence with his eyes, holding her gaze with steady intensity.

"Let me say this. I am yours completely — subject, vassal, obedient servant. If you would have me as your husband, you will still command me and I will have attained a heaven on earth. If you choose a consort not myself, for reasons of alliance, I will understand and serve you. If you choose another man for love . . . part of me will wither and pass away. But hear this, Majesty. No matter what you choose to make of me, I will always love you as I did when first I saw your lovely self, and I shall fight and die, be torn asunder limb from limb, to save this land and your own right to govern as you will."

Without warning Dudley tore his shirt and vest open and laid bare his chest. With a flash of gleaming metal he had slashed it with his dagger.

"God, Robin!" Crying now, Elizabeth fell to her knees, pressing her fingers over the wound to stanch the crimson flow. "I would not have you die for me. I want you to live for me . . . make love to me. Make love to me, now."

Robin Dudley had nothing to do but obey his queen.

※

It was already dark when they clattered through the Whitehall Palace gates and brought their steaming horses to a halt at the torchlit front portico. Guards and footmen snapped to attention but lowered their eyes as Dudley helped Elizabeth down off her mount, their bodies sliding together before her feet touched the ground. She wore his long cloak which he now wrapped protectively around her. She knew her men were watching them from under lowered lids, and with a sudden care for propriety she formally offered her Master of the Horse her hand. With one knee dropped to the ground, he took her fingers and kissed them.

"Majesty, I am ever at your service."

She reached down and touched his shoulder, then turned and swept past the guards who flanked the massive palace entrance. She strode past the tiltyard and through the Privy Gallery leading to the state apartments. Though the hall was torchlit and eerie, Elizabeth felt not at all alone, for the eyes of her York and Tudor ancestors watched her proud passage. She always sensed the weight of lineage and authority, which seemed at times to pass directly through her thin alabaster skin, adding potency to her claim to the English throne.

Before ascending the back stair to her apartments Elizabeth took into one hand a torch from the wall to light her way, and with her other hand lifted the skirts above her ankles, for the rough stone steps could be treacherous even in the daytime. The going was narrow and gloomy and the torch cast weird shadows on the walls. With the smell of damp in her nostrils and the feel of Robin still about her, Elizabeth suddenly found herself transported to another time not five years before, stealing down another dank, gloomy stair late at night, hand gripping not a torch but a single candle for fear of being caught in a dangerous and clandestine act.

She was a prisoner in the dread Tower of London, accused by her half sister Mary, now queen, of conspiracy against the crown. Terrified and weak, for she was not long out of her sickbed, Elizabeth had been passing her long days of incarceration studying and translating her beloved Greek texts. But if truth be told, the self-imposed tasks had done little to distract her mind from the cruel fear of her own untimely death. This terrible place had seen far too many executions. Seventeen years past her own mother had died here, and in recent times her father's fifth wife, her cousin Catherine Howard, had lost her life. Only months before, another cousin, the sixteen-year-old Jane Grey, queen for nine short days, had had her head hacked off on Tower Green and it had been remarked, Elizabeth remembered with a shudder, that the neck had spurted more blood than any imagined could be contained in so petite a body.

Elizabeth stole carefully down the narrow stair of Beauchamp Tower, cupping the candle with her other hand to make the light as dim as she was able. She knew that things would go hard with her if she were caught, and worse still with the kindly warder who had taken pity on the fragile girl who was his charge. Or perhaps he saw her not as a traitor, thought Elizabeth cynically, but as good King Harry's daughter and a future queen who, when she sat on the throne of England, would long remember the kindness of her old gaoler. In any case he had conveniently looked the other way, and now Elizabeth was blissfully free from the eyes of her keepers for the first time in more than two months.

Halfway down the tower stair she froze in her footsteps as she heard a piteous low moan, distant and hollow. For a moment she thought she had imagined it — nay, hoped she had imagined it — for it was the terrible sound of a man whose existence was an extended agony. Many prisoners were not as lucky as herself, but shut up in windowless cells, dark and cold with only mouldy straw for a bed, racked joints aching, skin raw and pustulent with vermin bites.

"Dear God," uttered Elizabeth over and over, trying to shut the sound from her ears.

Just as she reached the second landing a hand suddenly shot

out of the shadows and clamped around her wrist. She gasped, turning to see Robin Dudley, his bold handsome face lighting up the gloom of the tower stair.

"Elizabeth, thank God!"

With a great heaving sigh, for there were no words to express the profound relief or the terrible rush of love she felt for her old friend, she sank heavily against Robin's broad chest, and his strong arms enfolded her trembling frame. Hot tears spilled from her eyes to dampen his cloak and she was racked with sobs. He held her fast and spoke in hushed and hurried whispers, for they both knew this stolen time would all too soon be ending.

"Are you being well treated?" he demanded.

"Well enough." She sniffled and finally found her composure. "And you?" She peered at him in the flickering candlelight. "Robin, you're so thin." She touched his hollow cheek.

"The food they bring is decent, but I've suffered from a flux these last weeks." He did not say, but Elizabeth guessed the recent execution of his father and elder brother had sickened him.

"I'm so sorry about your father and John. How are the others?"

"My brothers are all right. Prison is not so foul a time when spent in the company of your family. I'm kept a solitary prisoner, though, in a cell of my own on the floor below them."

The Dudleys had been imprisoned for their role in their father's arrogantly self-serving and ill-fated plot to place Lady Jane Grey on the throne so that his own son Guildford, Jane's husband, could be crowned king.

"Perhaps," mused Elizabeth aloud, "that you alone of all your brothers proclaimed Jane queen, there in the marketplace of King's Lynn, angered Mary sufficiently to make your confinement solitary."

"No matter," said Dudley, reluctantly releasing Elizabeth from his embrace and holding her at arm's length. "Tell me how *you* are. If ever there was an unjustly confined prisoner 'tis you."

It was true. Her own imprisonment was the result of young Thomas Wyatt's rebellion which, riding swiftly on the heels of Dudley's uprising, stood in defiance of Mary's betrothal to a foreigner, Spain's Prince Philip.

"But is it not easy to see how Mary might believe my complicity, Robin? The plot's express purpose was to depose her and place *me* on the throne."

"Will she not listen to reason from her reasonable sister?"

"I have written letters, I have begged audiences, and none of them have been answered or granted. That wretched Spaniard de Quandra has always hated me. He poisons her mind against me. But they will never find honest proof of my involvement in poor Wyatt's scheme."

"Who needs honest proof?" muttered Robin morosely. "We are more like to die on the falsely uttered word of an enemy than from any truthful accusation."

That dreadful low moan rose again from the bowels of the stone prison, echoing up the dark stairwell as if to remind the two young prisoners of their own fate. And the rapid scuttering of rats at their feet made them shiver with cold disgust.

Elizabeth was suddenly gripped by a not unreasonable terror. "Should we put out the light? If they catch us meeting like this, it will be the end of us."

Dudley leveled a sharp, desperate look at her and then blew out the candle. They were plunged into a darkness like a curtain of black velvet that, paradoxically, did not muffle but rather magnified every sound. Even their breathing seemed loud enough to bring about detection, and so they drew close once again.

Elizabeth was all at once acutely aware of the nearness of Robin's body, the humid warmth of his breath on her cheek, the hand that snaked around her waist, joining them like flowers along the same vine. But it was the sharp tingling between her thighs that startled her most fiercely, causing her face to flush so hot that she imagined Robin could see her glowing in the dark. This brought an instant rush of shame and guilt. Elizabeth blurted, "How is it with Amy?"

She imagined she felt Robin's grip of her waist loosen momentarily, as if the question about his young wife had stirred guilt in him as well. But his voice was steady when he answered.

"They allowed her and my brothers' wives to visit us a fortnight ago. She fears for my life, and" — he paused as though he had begun a thought he did not wish to finish — "she misses me very much."

Again Elizabeth was thankful for the utter darkness, so that her friend should not see the lines of emotion that must certainly be etched upon her face. Jealous, she said to herself incredulously. I am jealous of Amy Dudley!

"Elizabeth," she heard Robin whisper. "Elizabeth, I feel such a traitor to say this, but aside from relief at seeing a friendly face and a gratefulness for the food and gifts Amy brought, I was not much moved by her presence. I dared not admit that I rarely thought of her or pined for her, and I could hardly bring myself . . . to make love to her."

Elizabeth could not immediately find a reply to Dudley's startling admission, for it was relief she felt and a strange joy at his miserable confusion. She remembered how, only three years before, she had stood witness at Robin and Amy's spring wedding. How adoring the couple had been each to the other, and how well matched they seemed. At the time Elizabeth had felt only happiness for her childhood companion, though she now remembered a brief but sharp pang when she saw Robin kissing his pretty young bride. Had the emotion been jealousy, she wondered now, still groping for the right words to comfort Robin.

"Perhaps your lack of desire was the unhealthy effect that captivity had wrought upon your body and your mind," Elizabeth offered, feigning confidence in the idea.

"Then why," asked Robin, tightening his grip of Elizabeth's waist and pulling her so close that their bodies melded together all along their trembling lengths, "why do I dream incessantly of *you*, see your face in my mind's eye, long for nothing more than the sound of your sweet voice that might soothe my soul? And why, Elizabeth, do I want your body lying next to mine in the dark?"

As he spoke Elizabeth felt that she had stopped breathing altogether, afraid that the faint hiss of her breath might cover the sound of even one of Robin's precious words. She had lifted her face to his and despite the deep darkness had no trouble finding his hungry lips with her own. And there they had stayed, all pain and fear and guilt forgotten, locked in each other's arms until the frantic whispered voice of her gaoler had come from above with the first thin light of the morning.

Now, in her own palace of Whitehall, Elizabeth reached the

dark warren of private rooms and anterooms where the doors of her Great and Privy and Withdrawing Chambers stood guarded each by two armed yeomen. She came like a whirlwind through her bedchamber door, scattering her waiting ladies like so many brittle leaves. "Go, go now. All of you." She kept the cloak pulled tight around her, hoping her brusque manner concealed her fluttering heart and shaking legs. With a great perfumed commotion of rustling skirts and petticoats, the ladies one by one curtsied and filed out.

It was thankfully quiet but Elizabeth was not alone. Katherine Ashley stood very still near the fire, her arms crossed below her breasts, a grim look upon her careworn face.

Elizabeth was queen, but she did not yet dare order Mistress Ashley to leave her. Instead she moved across to the fire, trying to ease her nervous smile, and turned her back on Kat. Wordlessly the older woman reached up and removed Dudley's woolen cloak from Elizabeth's back and hung it over her arm. As Elizabeth turned to face her lady of the bedchamber she said quietly, "Have no worry, Kat, the blood is not mine."

Despite the warning Kat's eyes widened at the sight of the dark brown smears that streaked Elizabeth's velvet riding jacket. Wordlessly the older woman covered her eyes with a creased hand and tried to calm herself. Her worst fears were coming to pass. The young princess, her charge from earliest childhood, was now a defiant queen. In that one brilliant moment, ten thousand candles illuminating Westminster Abbey, when the crown of England first rested heavy on that beloved child's head, everything that Kat and Elizabeth had between them changed irrevocably. And yet, she thought as she lowered her trembling hand from her face and looked into Her Royal Majesty's eyes, nothing had changed. Nothing at all. She reached across and began unbuttoning the velvet jacket.

Elizabeth's rigid posture relaxed, her limbs went flaccid with Kat's familiar ministrations. She knew her servant could smell Dudley's scent rising off her clothing, her body. She knew Kat was straining now, searching her mind for the proper words to convey her worry, her anger, without breaching the new etiquette between them. When Elizabeth was a young girl, a princess sent from court with little chance of reaching the throne, Kat had shown a loving but strict discipline. Her protective instincts were almost feline with their necessary fierceness and loyalty. She'd always spoken plainly, even harshly if the situation demanded. For the girl whose own blood relatives had all but abandoned her, Kat Ashley and her husband William were the only safe ports in the terrible storm of her young life. And now Kat was wretched with anguish.

"Will you bathe?" she asked with quiet restraint.

"Not tonight," replied Elizabeth. She wanted desperately to keep the last vestiges of Robin Dudley with her for as long as she was able. Kat was folding the Queen's clothing carefully as she helped her out of each piece. Elizabeth, now in only her French lace undergarments, shivered and moved closer to the fire.

"May I speak?" asked Kat in a stony voice.

"When have I ever been able to stop you, Kat?"

The older woman held out a yellow satin dressing gown. Elizabeth slipped her arms through the voluminous sleeves and pulled the soft fur lining around her. Suddenly she felt weak. She slumped into the highbacked chair and looked up at Kat, who was looking down at her own hands.

"Madame," she began, "you are my life and I love you as if you were my own flesh. That is why I say you must put a stop to the terrible things that are being said. They are saying that you and Robert Dudley are as good as married. And tonight" — she looked away, unable to meet Elizabeth's burning eyes — "I know that this is so. I have known this man since he was a boy in your nursery and I know his family. All of them have been executed for treason to the crown."

"Robin Dudley is loyal to this crown!" cried Elizabeth.

"He is a man with ambition in his blood. I cannot say he does not love you, Elizabeth, but like all the rest of them he loves the dream of power more. I do not trust him. He is a married man!"

Elizabeth looked away. For a time this afternoon she'd been able to forget this truth, or maybe in the flush of her newfound strength believed it did not matter. But with the coronation just three months behind her, there were already scandalous rumors simmering about herself and Robin. Still, she thought to herself, she had no worry of pregnancy, as she did not bleed with the moon's cycle as other women did. And she was the reigning monarch. She could do as she pleased.

"Do you not see what is plain?" said Kat. "Are you so blinded by lust that you do not comprehend the future of this action? You are losing respect, Elizabeth, from your councillors, your court, your subjects too. If they withdraw their affection, alliances will crumble. You know as well as I there are other rivals to this throne and if your claim should weaken, do not doubt that blood will spill. Innocent blood, and it will be on your head. I swear to you if I had known it would come to this I would have strangled Her Majesty in the cradle!"

Elizabeth trembled with the fervor of Kat's terrible oath. But the older woman was not yet finished. She knelt and took the Queen's hands in her own. "Marry, Elizabeth. I beg of you, commit yourself to a worthy suitor befitting your rank — foreign, English, it matters not. Marry. Bear Tudor heirs or chaos will prevail!"

Elizabeth smoothed the spotted skin of Kat Ashley's hand. "I know, Kat, that these are the outpourings of a good heart and true fidelity. But listen now. In this life of mine I've had so much of sorrow, tribulation. So little joy. I have earned what happiness this dear man gives to me." Kat started to object, but Elizabeth placed a finger on the woman's lips as if to seal them. "Say no more. I am queen and I do as I will. If indeed I have found pleasure in such a dishonorable life, then there is no one in this land, this wide world, that can forbid it."

Thoroughly defeated, Kat pulled herself to her feet and looked down upon this willful woman who confounded and constantly amazed her. She had done her best and had failed to move Elizabeth's mind.

This mysterious girl, her pale red hair framing a face of pure ephemeral innocence, was going to be the death of her.

※

"My lords." The Queen exploded into her Privy Chamber with the force of a catapulted arrow, skewering each of her councillors with a piercing stare. None of them, save William Cecil who had dealt with Elizabeth for several years before her accession to the throne, could yet make sense of this formidable and beguiling monarch.

"The news from the Continent is good, Your Majesty," spoke Cecil, opening their morning council. "The French have come to an agreement with us on Calais."

"Excellent. Then they are returning our port city, the one my illustrious sister Mary lost, that which has always been ours, to us?" demanded Elizabeth.

"Not precisely, Madame."

"Well then, how imprecisely do they propose to handle this?"

"They will hold Calais for at least eight further years," explained her principal defense advisor Lord Clinton.

"Eight," mused the Queen. "A lovely round number. Turned on its side, *infiniti*. Mayhaps that is how long they propose to keep Calais."

"At the end of eight years, if they do choose to keep the city, they will pay five hundred thousand crowns to us."

"A goodly sum," said Elizabeth. "Though it is *now* that we need the money in our pitiful treasury."

"Majesty, chance exists that Calais may be returned to us in the future," added Lord North.

"More important," interjected Lord Clinton, "the threat of invasion from the French through Scotland is no more. And for now your young Scottish cousin Queen Mary does not press her claim to your throne. And that is excellent news."

"Indeed it is," said Elizabeth with a tight smile. "A realm gains more in one year's peace than by ten years of war. So says my lord Cecil."

The councillors relaxed and smiled amongst themselves.

"So we have peace," said the Queen. "But in the meanwhile we have, by your counsel, unnecessarily bankrupted our treasury in preparation for war."

"Not so, Your Majesty," retorted her uncle Lord Howard, the greatest soldier amongst her advisors. "The fortification of the northern border castles and the munitions from Flanders were worthy expenditures nevertheless. We will be prepared for unforeseen future hostilities."

"*Si vis pacem, para bellum*," interjected Lord North.

"If you wish peace, prepare for war," echoed Elizabeth.

"Precisely, Your Majesty."

She turned back to Lord Howard. "However, it still seems to me that my uncle does not trust his own treaty."

"I have little trust that such zealous Catholics as Mary of Scots and her French mother-in-law will scarce abandon for long all ideas of overpowering Protestant England and overthrowing its heretic queen. But for now, the treaty pleases me, as I hope it pleases you, Majesty."

Elizabeth scanned the faces of her privy councillors and sensed that they were in sore need of approbation. She was hard on them, she knew — volatile, unpredictable, exasperating. She reveled in chaos and it amused her to use their foibles and weaknesses to lay little traps for them, playing them one against the other.

"Yes, I am pleased, my lords," she said and graced them with one of her warmest smiles. "Even if only for the present we are spared the ruinous cost of war, we should all be grateful." She turned to Cecil. This was the one man she trusted completely. He was honest where she was devious. He was clear and dispassionate while she flew into fits of pique and created hugely dramatic episodes simply to enliven an afternoon. "You will furnish me with the details of those negotiations in our private council, William."

"As Your Majesty wishes," intoned Cecil and inclined his head in a bow. He never ceased to be amazed by the woman who was suddenly the Queen, the frail, incandescently pale girl who had overnight assumed a frighteningly assured command over her men. In such moments Cecil knew unequivocally that the old rumors — the ones surrounding her mother Anne Boleyn's trial for treason and adultery, the ones claiming Elizabeth had never been sired by Henry at all — were completely ridiculous. Even a fool could see her father in the girl. Not just the fine russet gold hair, the aquiline nose, the sunburst smile, but the same inborn imperiousness, perfect authority, and pure animal magnetism. Too, he thought ironically, Elizabeth like her father possessed that rare quality that inspired men and women to cleave to her with passionate love and unshakable devotion, despite her inexperience and sometimes callous insults.

Elizabeth, who had been pacing incessantly as much from an overabundance of nervous energy as to warm her body in the morning chamber's chill, now sought the highbacked chair with its crimson cushions and drummed her fingers on the carved wooden claw arms. "Shall we move on?"

"The time has come, Madame, to take the Acts of Supremacy and Uniformity before Parliament and write them into law."

"Like your father you shall be named Supreme Head of the Church of England," announced the Lord Treasurer, the Marquess of Windsor, a sweet-faced old man whose head seemed balanced precariously in the folds of his starched ruff.

"I prefer 'Governor' — 'Supreme Governor,'" said Elizabeth. "And my late brother Edward's Prayer Book? Will it be reinstated?"

"Immediately, Your Majesty," replied Cecil. "And services shall henceforth be conducted in English."

"God be praised," said the Queen.

"We propose also that attendance at mass should be a crime punished by imprisonment," Cecil went on. "Repeated thrice, punishable by life imprisonment."

"Is this not inordinately harsh, my lords, and far too similar to Roman persecution? On the Continent a new Dominican Inquisitor has been named, and Jews are again forced to wear yellow squares on their backs. I do not want it said that *our* reformation tends toward cruelty."

"'Tis far less harsh than your sister's burning of Protestant heretics during her reign," answered Lord Clinton.

Elizabeth noticed Lord Arundel, the only remaining Catholic in her Privy Council, wince at the reference to Mary's outrageous and deadly persecution of adherents to the New Faith. Many good men, women, even children had died horribly in the flames, among them her mother's good friend Archbishop Cranmer.

"I have been witness to my brother's Protestant fanaticism, which was as repugnant as my sister's Catholicism. The realm is in need of healing and unity, and a middle road in the matter of religion will engender both. And whilst I have no patience with saints, indulgences, and miracles, we shall seek outward conformity, without forgetting that each man's belief is a matter most personal. I have no wish to open windows in men's souls."

"Your Majesty. There is something else we must needs discuss," Cecil began, as gingerly as a man entering a roomful of angry boars.

Elizabeth, knowing full well the subject of his digression, covered her smile with a fist pressed to her lips. "And what could that be, my lord Cecil?"

"Your marriage, Majesty. It is of the utmost importance. A foreign alliance —"

"Do not speak to me of a foreign alliance!" Elizabeth leapt from her chair in a swirl of rustling brocade and wafts of heady perfume which left her councillors dizzy. "When I took the throne I was hailed as a queen of no mingled blood of Spaniard or stranger, but born mere English and therefore most natural. What you want from me is a child of my body, is it not? An heir. Well, do you not believe my subjects wish for a true English prince?"

"But, Your Majesty —"

"I should be better off marrying you!" She twirled to face her Lord Steward. "Indeed, the Earl of Arundel wishes me to believe *he* is the best match in all of England." She turned again and came eye to eye with the old Marquess of Windsor who had served under both her father and her brother. He was bent and frail, but when the Queen ran her ivory fingers over his grey beard he smiled like a young boy in love. "If my Lord Treasurer were a younger man I could find it in my heart to have *him* as my husband!"

"Forgive me, Madame, but you jest upon a most serious subject," said her chief counsellor.

"If I did not know you better, Lord Cecil, I would think you subscribed to the common belief that beauty is nature's gift to woman in compensation for her deprivation of brains —"

"Your Majesty —" he begged.

"— or to the writings of that pompous idiot John Knox who holds that for a woman to rule over men is as reasonable as the blind leading the sighted."

Elizabeth was no longer smiling and an angry flush had spread across her pale cheeks. "I have told you and I will tell you once again. I will act in this matter as God directs me. Besides . . ." she said, regaining her composure as handily as she regained control of an unruly gelding, "I am already married."

Her councillors froze. Hardly a whispered breath could be heard from the lot of them. Had the worst happened? Had the Queen secretly married Dudley? Elizabeth raised her right hand, brandishing the heavy gold and ruby coronation ring at her councillors.

"My husband is the Kingdom of England! Good day, my lords."

❦

She had never seen anyone quite so old. When Kat Ashley showed the bent and hobbling woman into the Presence Chamber, Elizabeth found herself staring. The hair under the cap was thin and dull grey and the face impossibly wrinkled, like an apple left to dry in the sun. The ancient's gown was frayed, faded, and altogether out of fashion, hanging loosely on her bony frame. Nevertheless Elizabeth felt quite certain this was a highborn lady. The woman's deep and well-schooled curtsy despite painful joints was further proof of her nobility and training.

Elizabeth's curiosity piqued, she dispensed with formality and said, before the woman had even time to rise, "Speak. Tell me why you have come."

The woman was now upright but the great widow's hump forced her to throw back the aged head at an extreme angle in order to meet the Queen's steely gaze.

"We must speak alone, Your Majesty."

Kat spluttered at the outrageous demand and with her eyes implored the Queen to allow her to eject the woman. But although the old lady's overproud demeanor seemed at odds with her shabby appearance, Elizabeth sensed a strange importance in the occasion. She dismissed her lady, and Kat, red-faced with annoyance, swept out the door.

"I have something once belonging to your mother," the crone said.

"Tell me your name, old woman, and let us dispel all secrecy. I may have interest in what you bring, but little patience."

The woman stared unflinching into Elizabeth's eyes. "Lady Matilda Sommerville, Your Grace. And perhaps patience will, like creaking joints, be acquired with age." As the Queen gazed at the crone unsure whether she was amused or infuriated, the woman reached deep into the folds of her skirt and extracted a worn old book, then hesitated.

"Let me see this book," commanded Elizabeth tersely.

"It is not a book, Your Majesty."

"Come now, I can see with my two eyes that it is."

Seeming to know precisely the limits to her own insolence, Lady Sommerville hobbled forward and, with gnarled fingers splayed at an unnatural angle, held out the claret leather volume. She came as close as she dared to the Queen and whispered, "It is a diary. Your mother Anne Boleyn's diary."

At once the skin on Elizabeth's body began to crawl and her heart heaved. Her mother! She had almost no memory of her mother and in truth had not even uttered her name aloud for more than twenty years. She willed herself to calm and took time before she spoke.

"A diary? And how, may I ask, would the lady Sommerville come into possession of a queen's diary?"

The woman's rheumy eyes lost their focus, as if she had left this time, this place. "I had the great honor of attending your good mother before her death," she said with quiet pride.

Though logic demanded that the woman's story be viewed skeptically, and the article in her hand subjected to extreme scrutiny, Elizabeth reached for the volume with uncharacteristic openheartedness. The leather under her fingers was coarse, and the faint odor of parchment and vellum wafted into her nostrils.

The old woman was watching the Queen with eyes filled with calm certainty. The young monarch must know she was telling the truth. She would not be punished.

"Sit," Elizabeth said, more an invitation than a command. "Tell me about my mother."

Lady Sommerville gratefully lowered herself onto a chair and arranged her legs under the voluminous skirts in a way that gave her the least pain.

"My uncle, Lord Kingston, was constable of the Tower of London in your father's reign. My relative had been a great soldier who fought bravely in the battle of Flodden, where he was gravely injured. He oftentimes said he wished he'd died there in glory, for a cripple he was all his life thereafter, and a bitter man. Good King Harry rewarded my uncle with guardianship of the London fortress, and though it was a great honor, he was unhappy with his post. The grey walls filled him with gloom, the cold mists from the river ached his poor bones, and the great royal armory inspired longing for battle on open fields, the clash of metal on metal." Lady Sommerville's voice was gaining strength and confidence as she warmed to the memories and lived again as a young woman.

"Kingston was in attendance when your mother, already five months pregnant with you, came for three days of happy confinement in the Tower before her coronation as queen. He served her grudgingly, having been, like so many Englishmen, a loyal supporter of your father's first wife Katherine, foreign though she was. But valuing the safety of his family if not his own skinny neck, he bowed before the new queen and made her stay most comfortable. Three short years later she was back, disgraced and charged with treason and witchcraft. He remembers her arriving on the barge, her face grey and sodden as the sky was. She stumbled as she walked through the river gate into the Tower courtyard, and he caught her arm. She smiled, he said, grateful for any small kindness then, for she had been shown none for so long and had no friends, only enemies."

Elizabeth found her hands trembling and held the diary tightly to quiet them. For she was a part of this story of doom. It was not just the memory of the Tower, that bleak hell where she herself had been imprisoned for months when her half sister Mary, as queen, suspected Elizabeth of plotting her demise. No, it was more than that. This old woman dredged the dark depths of Elizabeth's beginnings and her mother's end, all woven intricately together like a fine tapestry. Till now she had little allowed herself to dwell on Anne's life or her death.

The promise of her own birth had been Anne's great hope — a male child, the heir that Katherine had not been able to give Henry. She knew also that her own sex had contributed to Anne's death. If she had been born a boy, her mother might still be alive today, might still be queen.

"Continue, Lady Sommerville. You said you attended my mother at her end."

"My uncle needed women to serve the Queen in her terrible confinement and few were willing. Your mother was much reviled, Your Majesty." The old woman lowered her eyes, ashamed to speak this truth to Elizabeth.

"She was, indeed. 'Nan Bullen the King's whore' they called her." Elizabeth's mouth quivered and a surge of pity swept over her in a great wave. Like her mother she had been the object of hatred and jealousy, rejected and, even as a princess, called ugly names. A few short years ago, until her succession was realized, she had been nothing more than Henry's bastard. Elizabeth's chest hurt. Her throat felt dry and tight.

"I loved your mother," said Lady Sommerville quite unexpectedly, "from the first moment I laid eyes on her lonely soul."

Elizabeth searched the old lady's lined face for any flicker of emotion to match her words. But there was nothing more than the shriveled lips moving, conveying a precious secret between two women of noble blood.

"She was delicate in stature, her wrists as tiny as a switch, and that long swan neck. . . ." Lady Sommerville went on. "And graceful, so full of grace that you overlooked the sallow skin, the eyes almost too large for their sockets. Her voice was lovely, sparkling and gay, despite her terrible circumstances. And such wit. Your mother made me laugh, she did. We laughed together, just her and me, for no one else would share it. The other lady keepers stared and whispered, and my uncle became very cross with me. But I said, bold as a man, 'She's still the Queen until she's dead. She commands me, not you.'" The old lady stopped and smiled privately, perhaps remembering that moment of brave resistance, then went on.

"Each night of the weeks she was there she let me brush out her long dark hair. Like thick silk it was, and black as a raven's wing. That was when she would cry, your mother. Angry bitter tears. And soft whimpering ones as well. Once she said, 'Henry loved to brush my hair.' That was all. 'Henry loved to brush my hair.' The only other time I saw her cry was when they executed her brother — watching his beheading from a Tower parapet. The deaths of the others, the men accused with him of debauchery with her, did not affect her so. But she loved her brother George." Lady Sommerville looked into the Queen's eyes. "Your uncle."

"Yes, my uncle." Elizabeth tried thinking back. Did she remember George Boleyn? Handsome in his portraits, charming by his reputation. No, she had no memory of him, nor of her grandfather, Thomas, who traded his daughter for ambition and abandoned her for expediency. Even her mother, Anne, was an ephemeral vision, a faint scent of spice, a lilting laugh. But always her face was suffused with a light so bright that its details were all but obliterated.

One of Elizabeth's childish mementos was a fine linen kerchief embroidered with her mother's *A* and her father's *H* entwined like embracing lovers. Later, when Anne was gone and forgotten, supplanted by Jane Seymour, all linens, carvings, paintings, and crests with that bold symbol of Anne's success were destroyed or discarded, replaced by the new queen's *J* entwined with Henry's *H*. All through her lonely and miserable childhood Elizabeth kept the kerchief, an illicit treasure, in a tiny chest that contained what poor jewels she'd been given, and other trinkets of little value. As she grew older the box of trinkets was pushed to the bottom of a wooden chest, and her mother's memory faded like a painted fan.

"Tell me about the diary."

"I knew nothing of the diary until the day your mother went to her unhappy death. She was agitated on that day, as workmen had been outside her prison window sawing and hammering the platform upon which she was to die. Her last pleas to your father for clemency had come to naught, and she was out of hope. It seemed for a time that all grace had left her. She was clumsy, tripping on her skirt and wringing her hands. She would rake her fingers across her face and through her hair, muttering, 'God forgive me. God forgive me.'

"I felt sick at my stomach and light-headed. She was pitiful and not the queen I knew she'd want to appear before the audience of her execution. So I rallied myself and went kindly to her, asking if she did not want me to brush her hair. She looked at me then and it appeared something inside of her settled. She grew very calm and said, 'Yes please, Lady Sommerville, I would very much like that.'

"I did the long slow strokes she so enjoyed, patting the hair down gently behind the brush, and then she asked if I would put it up and fasten it off her neck. It was when she said that I began to cry, for I knew her reasoning." The old woman unconsciously touched the back of her own neck. "They'd imported a fine French executioner, but she was afraid of pain and wanted no hindrances to the sword's clean cut."

Elizabeth found her eyes were wet, but she made no move to hide the tears from this woman, her mother's friend in life and death.

"When her hair was done and I'd helped her into a soft grey gown, she came to me holding that book. She was very calm by then and the terror had gone from her eyes. 'Take this,' she said. 'It is my life. Give it to my daughter, Elizabeth. Give it to her when she is grown, when she is queen. She will have need of it.'

"I'm ashamed to admit, Majesty, I thought then that Henry's daughter from a wife he so despised would never rule England. But I loved your mother, who was going to her death, and I said it would be my honor. And so it is my honor, these years hence, to give you this diary."

Lady Sommerville rose painfully from the chair. Elizabeth put out a hand to steady her and their eyes met and held.

"Your mother died with grace, Your Majesty. She died a queen." Lady Sommerville curtsied low and, taking Elizabeth's white bejeweled hand, kissed her ring.

"Thank you, kind lady," whispered Elizabeth. "You should be proud that you have fulfilled the promise you made to my mother so long ago."

The old woman smiled and gazed at the Queen's pale face.

"You have your father's eyes, Elizabeth, but it is your mother's spirit shining through them."

Lady Sommerville turned and hobbled out the door, not bothering to close it behind her. Kat and several younger waiting ladies were poised there and came fluttering into the chamber. Elizabeth, as if in a sweet dream she wished undisturbed, raised a hand and bade them depart.

The Queen, who throughout Lady Sommerville's entire story had clutched the diary in her hands, now studied it carefully. It was old. The claret leather was fading to pink and the binding was fragile. There was little left of a gold leaf border, but once, she could see, it had been a very pretty book indeed. As though she were handling the wings of butterflies, Elizabeth opened the front cover. There in stylish penmanship in large black letters on yellowing parchment was the inscription

The Diary
of
Anne Boleyn

Elizabeth turned the page.

4 January 1522

Diary,

So strange, a book of empty pages. I have never seen in all my life a thing so very odd or very wonderful as this parchment diary. For different from a book that I might read whose author offers up to me like some rich meal, his thoughts and words and deeds, this empty volume defies and mocks me, begs of me to make its pages full. But full of what?

Thomas Wyatt, giver of this gift, insists that I am able, offering as proof that I've acquired, he says, the habit of writing in several languages, that I'm adept at conversation, full of witty anecdotes, delightful stories of the French Court. These are compliments, to be sure, from a gentleman to a lady but they hold a draught of Truth. In deed Wyatt, gift in hand, had found me in the tiny day room set aside for Queen Katherine's waiting women, quite alone and sitting at the writing table quill in hand, a letter to my Mother almost done.

I turned to see him, smiled an honest smile. For Wyatt is a great man among men. A writer, in deed the finest poet in Henry's English Court, handsome in the extreme, very tall and vital. He is said to be, save royal blood, Henry's equal and is in fact the Tudor King's good and constant companion. Since my cold and miserable homecoming from the French King's Court this gentleman has singled me from other ladies, showering me with more favors even than my fair Sister Mary. He flatters me boldly in his poems which are the cause of much admiration and some jealousy. But even this had not prepared me for so unusual a gift.

"Few men and fewer ladies still, commit their words in such a way," said he. "But in my mind there is none I know whose thoughts and dreams, whose wit and history should better grace these pages." He said he found this courtly life too close and gregarious for easy fostering of solitary thoughts, but bade me remember that we are always alone, even in the midst of others. And then he said, "If you find a way to write with open heart to Diary, a friend with Truth, no detail spared, your tome like Petrarch's works will contain the scattered fragments of your soul."

I was clean amazed. Thomas Wyatt, clever man, had offered up like some Yuletide walnut pressed within the soft sweet flesh of a date, an arch challenge hid within the kindest compliment. I knew then that despite small opportunity in a waiting ladies life for such work, that *I must write* and coupled with a careful plan, conceal my act of privacy. The carven chest I carried home from France has lock and key and there my journal intime shall find its safe repose.

Wait! I hear the laughter of approaching Queen and ladies echoing down the passage. They come returning from some amusement, so I must end and join amongst them. Till then I shall remain

Yours faithfully,

Anne

15 January 1522

Diary,

I've feigned a head ache and stayed behind, the others gone to see the bear baiting in the castle yard. I sit just near the window in my tiny room with quill in hand and think upon my daily life to find that Time has little changed my gloomy mood. Since my return from France to Henry's dull provincial Court I wait upon his pious Queen, carrying her woollen sleeves or soiled linen thro dark and narrow passages, the grey damp rock walls chilled by English mists that rise up from the Thames. They chill my heart as well and I find my self adrift in longing.

Had Father not been called home from France, all cordial diplomacy with them in ruins, then I should be, as in my dreams still am, dancing nightly in Francis' glittering Court. *There* was glamour, brilliance, beauty and there was wild and wicked amour. That devilish King (though to be fair Henry's person compares in size and majesty and virile handsomeness) has a thing of which our Sovereign never dreamt or wished to have — bawdy, splendid love of lust which he does grant to each and every member of his elegant entourage.

'Twas in France I spent my youth and education from early nursery days, close companion to the little lame Princess Renee. High arched windows of the royal palace welcomed in a kind of crystal light that made blaze each color to most extreme brightness. Every wall was hung, every nook was stuffed, every floor inlaid with priceless treasures — tapestries, paintings, statues and metalwork to tease and please the senses. Great philosophers, writers, scholars flocked there from every port. We would dine in the company of the great poet Marot, gaze for hours at da Vinci's Mona Lisa brought by that fine Italian gentleman to grace the King's own hall. Ah, the time, the place, they linger in my mind. I have a memory — a moment in a perfect day within a life a world away. I will tell it full and let you see, my Diary, what life had been not long ago for Mistress Anne Boleyn.

. . . I hurried down the sunny palace corridor to meet Josette where at our fitting she had promised me to tell a tasty bit of gossip. But then I saw King Francis approaching like a torch carried thro the black night, his own loud and bawdy presence outshining his many jewels. The men of his French Court glittered in his reflected brilliance, strutted with certainty and impudent grace embracing his every word, flattering his every elegant move, quenching his every whim.

They drew nearer. I boldly met the French King's eye and held his blatant gaze before dropping the lowest of seductive bows. I arose and knew that all the courtiers were admiring me, caressing me, undressing me. The King, his men and I exchanged some words — a compliment on His Majesty's latest Italian plunder, a jest at another lady's expense, a greeting to my Father the Ambassador, an invitation to play at cards. I tilted my head, flashed my eyes, smiled a teasing smile. Years of cultured coquettry worked a spell, for I knew that they were thinking, "This is Anna de Boullans, sister to Marie the infamous English mare. This one is young, still unsullied. Here stands a pretty world of possibilities and potential seductions. Let me smile the most handsomely, pose the most brazenly, cause with my wit the brightest laugh. Let me be her lover first and win from my King, if indeed he does not bed her before, his deep and salacious admiration. Let me be the one to share with His Majesty — for it is his greatest pleasure — the titillating details of our passionate liaison, the very words spoken in heated embrace."

So with sly innuendo before I took my leave I pretended to yield to thoughts of lasciviousness and goad them on to fantasy, with me at its delicious center. They knew not as they sauntered on to their next small amusement that I was whole as ever in body and maidenly resolve. Virginity was mine for I was well taught in this matter.

I saw my sister and the names she was called. Mary was a true beauty, but she was dull minded, led only by the reins of desire and that day's aggrandizement. She thought of nothing past the one night's conquest.

I learned, too, from the Queen we served, Claude — dowdy and chaste. All Claude's ladies scorned her ways and flaunted her husband's escapades. To most she was of no account. But not to me. For what I saw was that she was *Queen*. She wore the Crown, held the King of France between her thighs and passed thro them Royal Princes who bore his name. The gilt and witty ladies of Court in silken gowns, ablaze with jewels and hotly pursued . . . had nothing. Neither love nor name nor lasting glory. I played their game. Laughed and flirted, pretended to debauchery, drank from a goblet etched inside with salacious scenes . . . and did not blush. I kept my counsel. I was but fifteen.

The sunny French corridor filled with sparkling music and

a scent of rich parfum drifted to me and by. I touched the colored marble of a naked god upon a pedestal. I gazed upon his stony sheath of maleness, and thought of flesh. His thigh was cool, my hand upon it warm, nay burning hot. I deep inhaled. . . .

Rude shouts and the scream of a dying dog in the courtyard. My sweet reverie shattered, brittle ice upon the window glass. I am in England. But I am sick in my heart and lonely for that golden life. I wish I were in France.

Yours faithfully,

Anne

ELIZABETH SAT MOTIONLESS, stunned by the revelations of the diary. What strange and singular fortune had placed this document in her hands, that she should now be made privy to her mother's most intimate thoughts, and a world almost forty years past.

Elizabeth felt as though she had suddenly found entrance into a secret chamber long sealed — as a tomb — in which hidden were mysteries dreadful as they were fascinating, dangerous as they were important. She searched her heart, but found nothing that might be called love for the shadowy personage who had been her father's mistress for six years, his wife and queen for three. Elizabeth had, since childhood, built up around her heart thick walls to protect it against Anne's shameful memory. Her bitterness at the traitoress's death and its tainting of her own life was the mortar.

The crown had been Elizabeth's for so short a time. And she was beset by the gravest of decisions every day which affected not simply her life but all of England, all of her subjects. If indeed the fates had chosen to bestow the diary upon her at this crucial moment, she thought, she would be foolish to accord it anything less than the utmost attention.

A sharp knock at the Presence Chamber door startled the Queen. "A moment more, Kat!"

Her mind raced. Against all odds her mother had kept secret the diary throughout her life. Now no one but herself and Lady Sommerville knew of its existence. Elizabeth determined in that moment that no one else should ever know. She would lie to Kat about the reason for Lady Sommerville's mysterious visit. And she would hide the diary away under lock and key. In the most public of lives, it would be her most private secret. Elizabeth concealed the claret volume in a pile of state documents before calling her waiting ladies back into the Presence Chamber.

"With whom is my next audience?" she inquired mildly of Kat.

"Lord Braxton and his son. After that is your morning consultation with Lord Cecil. And then a sitting for your portrait, Madame."

"Very good. I'm going to my apartments for a moment," said Elizabeth, scooping up the documents and moving toward a concealed door, the back way to her rooms.

"Now?" cried Kat. "Lord Braxton has been waiting. And Lord Cecil . . ."

"Let them wait," said Elizabeth, clutching the diary to her breast and disappearing through the door.

⚜

Kat Ashley hummed absently as she poked at the fire in the Queen's bedchamber. Elizabeth was irritated with her own nervous pacing and clammy hands which now worried a silk tassel at her waist.

"What gown will Her Majesty wear for the evening's entertainment?" asked her waiting lady.

Elizabeth knew that her answer would elicit a flurry of unwanted questioning. Still she said, "I won't be joining in, Kat. I want to be alone this night."

"Very good. I'll have them bring our supper up. We'll eat it by the fire."

"No, Kat, I mean to be quite alone."

The lady blinked, not yet comprehending Elizabeth's words. The Queen was never unattended. Kat herself slept on a pallet at the foot of Elizabeth's bed. She, at the very least, should stay and —

"Just bring some candles now, all you can find. Light them round my chair."

"Candles?"

"Make it bright as you are able."

"I don't know what's got into you, Elizabeth."

"Please."

There was no sense in arguing with the Queen when she had made up her mind, decided Kat. No sense at all.

⚉

Elizabeth sat in her highbacked chair, flickering candles creating a halo of golden light around her head. The only sounds were the wind in the chimney and the crackle of burning wax. After Kat and her ladies had gone, leaving the Queen in blessed silence, Elizabeth had removed a small key hidden in the lining of a silver box and opened the heavily carved Italian chest that sat under the window. From amongst the delicate folds of her own christening robes she then pulled her mother's diary. It had taken almost a week for her to find this moment of privacy, though the thought of the secret book had played at the edges of her mind every hour of every day since old Lady Sommerville had brought its mystery into her life.

The trunk, scented with lavender, was packed with neatly folded linen and garments, some of them hers, some of them her brother Edward's, some of them her father's, which she kept as mementos — all that was left of her family. Pulling aside an embroidered tunic and a pair of leather hawking gloves, Elizabeth had found the small wooden trinket box she sought, the painted and gilt Bible scene on its lid long since worn away. Seeing the box released a flood of childhood memories, disjointed images from the nursery, from Hatfield Hall — some warm, some painful, all as much a part of her as her next breath.

The lid removed, all inside was immediately visible, a worthless jumble of paste jewelry, the vaguely heart-shaped stone a romantic young Robin had given her, an enameled thimble for a tiny finger, a mouse's skull, a faded bluejay feather. And her mother's handkerchief.

Elizabeth disentangled the square of fine linen from the other contents and held it in her hands. It was stained yellow with age and the lace edging was ragged in places, but the embroidered *H* and *A*, her parents' initials, were yet lovingly entwined for eternity.

Now the Queen sat with the diary resting in her lap, the handkerchief a bookmark, and opened the book to the third entry. She squinted at the script on the page. She would have to read slowly, for her vision was weak and such strain readily brought on the headaches that caused her much misery. With chances for privacy so scant, she knew that reading the diary would take some time. But Elizabeth minded not at all. She would simply savor it like a rich wine, for Anne's story, she felt, must be a piece of the riddle that was her destiny as a woman — and a queen. She began to read.

4 April 1522

Diary,

Such a Sunday it has been! Chapel done, an early summons from my Father brought me to the countinghouse where he was near finished with the feast plans for the Cardinal's visit. I approached him where he sat behind the green baize table in a tête à tête with the Cofferer, an ugly man who from the corner of his lecherous eye surveyed me foot to head. I wished to go, for even then the Cardinal's barge approached, but I was forced to stay, quiet and obedient till time permitted a daughter's audience with her master.

He finally spoke to say that Sir Piers Butler had been made Lord Deputy of Ireland and I should make haste to my betrothed to add congratulations on his father's appointment. At mention of James Butler and his kin I felt my face go hard, but quick replaced it with pleasant smile. I do fear his warlord father known to murder relatives, and loathe the wimpish ass of a son who likes me not much better than I like him. Yet James, when haggling and dowry are concluded by Father and King and Cardinal, is meant to be my lawful husband. You see my Father's Father owns vast Irish estates, but our cousin that vile Piers Butler has prevented we Boleyns from ever occupying those lands. My marriage then to James, 'tis thought, will end old disputes resolving matters, bringing peace to all. I shall travel to wild Irish lands to reign among the savage barefoot peasants there as Lady Butler. So they say I shall. So they say.

Dismissed and free at last I rushed away and stopped before the great bay window seeing Cardinal Wolsey's gilt and painted barge gliding thro the marshy river edge to meet the palace landing stage. My heart leapt and I wondered should I go and calm myself, sit demurely within the chamber of the Queen, or should I fly cross the palace lawn to greet the one I love?

Then thro window glass I saw a flash of scarlet taffeta and then a great and ponderous form. Wolsey, red of hat and glove and gown, magnificent in his obesity preceded by his yeomen bearing all his Cardinal's stuff — silver crosses, pillar, hat, Great Seal of England. From out the palace doors with pomp and circumstance marched King's officials wreathed in golden chains whose tall white staffs they thumped importantly. I knew if here was Wolsey, sure his household followed close behind. And then I saw a figure plainly clad and lovely to my eyes — Henry Percy, thin and shy with kindness like a halo round a clear and rosy face. My heart beat wild within my breast. Even from a distance and tho he saw me not at all, I felt his love and knew he wished to break away and come to me.

So making haste I fairly ran thro the halls and up the stairs to Queen Katherine's rooms where other ladies did attend Her Majesty. I watched the flutter — the waiting women, cooks and maids fussing, tittering, joking every one. The Queen was breaking fast and tho weary eyed, showed gentle cheer this Sunday morn. The two days last were spent, as always Friday and Saturday are, upon her knees on hard stone floors in chapel, fasting, asking God's forgiveness for sins which, to all else, are goodly deeds. I wondered if the habit of St. Francis worn hid beneath her queenly gown did chafe, or give her comfort sorely needed.

You see, tho husband Henry loves her still he takes pleasure in their bed no more. For that he seeks none other than her waiting lady my Sister Mary! A French King's whore, now mistress of Great Harry. I bade Mary tell me how she casts her spells, for truth be told tho she is beautiful, the Court is filled with lovely ladies. She smiled a wicked smile and said to me, "With men it's how you hold them — tight, then loose, then let them go to grab and hold again."

But truly, I have no need for such games with my love, for he is mine and I am his, as clear as these words are writ upon this page. But I digress. Back to that Sunday . . .

The ladies of the Presence Chamber stilled, for suddenly a

male commotion down the hall and coming near was heard. And then they came, a rush of rough and ready gentlemen, all kisses, bows and compliments. Ladies paired with men to play and sing and flirt an afternoon away. Among the gents, a mild breeze amidst the storm, was my love. At first no words were passed between us. Instead he found two pillows, an empty window seat and placed the cushions there. He took my hand and brushed it softly with his lips, then led me to our little nest.

I swear my heart was beating so, I feared I would not hear his words. He was kind and generous and so unlike the lecherous gentlemen of the French Court that my studied charm had long ago dissolved beneath his warming stare. Whate'er his awkward faults I easily forgave. But my eyes could see a pall darkening sweet Percy's spirit, so I questioned him of it. I wished I had not asked. For the sad tale he told was that in recent days, added to my poor betrothal to James Butler, was now his *own* betrothal. He was tied to Lady Mary Talbot and for this marriage many reasons, all but love, were given.

'Tis nothing strange in such negotiations, for in our world love of the romantic kind is but another name for foolishness. And love within a marriage — the only kind permitted — is no more than duty. But in my heart I decry such principles as these, and so to my sweetheart I raged at this abomination of our separate betrothals, and swore against those who would keep us parted.

"The Cardinal and King stand with my father on this," whispered Percy. "What am I to do?"

Softer still and trembling said I, "Defy and marry me!" I saw his face go pale in fear and dread.

I asked if he did not remember the King's own sister Princess Mary. I myself had been in her retinue of waiting ladies when she sailed for France to marry old King Louis. I told him of the great love Mary shared with one Lord Brandon, Duke of Suffolk, and how for reasons of alliance, that love was pushed aside. Obedient servant to her brother and her country, the Princess knew that she must sit upon the throne of France as Queen. But before she sailed upon that cold and blustery day from Dover shores — for I was there and saw her with my own two eyes — Mary pleaded that if Louis died that she'd be free to marry Brandon then. Henry gave his promise that this could be, and we set sail. I told Percy how with three short months as Queen, the old King died and waiting not for Henry's word, she and Brandon married *secretly,* then returned to England bonded thus. And how Henry raged and hurled abuse and sent them both from Court disgraced. "But soon, my love," I said, "he brought them home forgiven, and here they live today."

"Your point?" asked Percy, much confused.

"That our good King has beating in his breast a tender heart which knows how lovers feel, and will forgive us our defiance as he did his sister. And if our King shows clemency, then, too, Cardinal Wolsey and our parents must do the same. And we will have won a rare and wonderful thing. A marriage of love."

He laughed in terror and delight and grasped my hands. "Sweet, sweet Anne, I have never known a woman such as you. My feeble words tell nothing of my longing, so let my arms, my lips, my body tell you instead."

"And like the Princess and her Brandon shall we defy and marry?"

"Yes, yes!" he cried. Curious eyes of ladies, gents and Queen did turn upon his oath, so we returned to calm and proper converse. The morning went to afternoon all sweet and full of soft endearments, promises and plans. Much too soon a call was heard that all of those returning to the Cardinal's house must go with haste or miss the tide.

I did not wish to lose him withal, so walked with him out to the misty river edge. Cloaked in darkness we kissed. O, it made grow a great fire in my loins, shook my legs and arms and seemed to melt my very chest! We clung and touched, my hand found his hardness and his my breast. I had dallied some in France but this flame, this sweet desire was new to me.

Then the torches lit the scarlet Cardinal down our way and we were forced to separate. Hasty goodbyes, quite dignified under his master's ice cold stare. But it mattered not at all, for we were betrothed by our own hearts. This promise shall stand, and by the by in fullness of time Lady Percy I shall be.

Yours faithfully,

Anne

22 November 1522

Diary,

How do I begin? My heart is broke. My life is done. Percy, gentle love of mine is banished North, his Father's wrath a smothering shroud. I too am sent from Court disgraced, and languish now in my family home at Hever in the Kentish countryside. How came this all to pass, you ask?

When last I wrote the world was bright with possibility. The English Court felt more like home and France a lovely memory. Life was gay. Presiding like a living God our King Great Harry, hale and hearty made the ground to shake beneath his feet. In shimmering satins dripping gold at revels he led the leaping dancers like a stag. He rode robustly, jousted hard, yet sang and played, composed sweet verse and made the Court a wondrous place.

I served the Queen and spent the summer days in restless pleasures, hawking, riding, dancing, finding secret time alone with my beloved. O, together we did make a dazzling light and walked upon the air. Our various and false betrothals seemed a distant dream forgot. Our marriage was in all but law a fact and soon we would be joined, we knew.

And then like deadly lightning from the sky came Cardinal Wolsey, thundering wrathful with clear intent to kill our love. Summoned, Percy went to stand before the portly priest whose bulging angry eyes pierced my lover's calm and left him shaking like a sapling in a gale. "Desist," he said, "and leave the girl alone." Of common birth was I, not good enough for he. Our mutual contracting he fumed was "a dire breach, angering fathers, God and King." Henry sought alliance between the Talbots and Northumberlands whose binding gave his northern borders strong defense. So Wolsey, courting favor with the King, smote us vilely, making two of one, tearing beating hearts from loving breasts.

Percy wrote (in secret missive, since we were never let to say goodbye) that he defended me, my birth as high as his, refusing to renounce our vows. I shuddered when I thought of him, a tender boy come toe to toe with such a fearsome enemy. And so did Wolsey curse my wretched love and send him home to his furious father. Our pledges made in honesty were rent apart, infringed, dissolved as tho they'd not existed.

For my part, Father called me to his rooms and thrashed me soundly. That hot pain was sweet and mild compared to nev-erending separateness from my beloved. Stinging from his blows I did not weep but stood my ground and held his marble eyes.

I said, "Great Cardinal Wolsey thinks he's won this game with me a helpless girl who cowers neath his lash. But let me say one thing to you, an oath, that if it ever lays within my power I shall do the Cardinal as much displeasure as he has to me."

My Father stood shocked and still at my outrageous words, a young girl presuming to threaten so high a man. Then Father banished me from Court and sent me packing home to distant Hever Hall where I now write.

Life is dull in Edenbridge, the days are empty as a sodden field at dawn. The flowers have no smell, the birdsong grates my ear, I lose my self within the green hedge maze and wish that I could fade to nothing. A letter came a day ago to say that Percy and the Talbot girl had married. I did not cry, for all my tears were spent. Instead, like sick and festering pustules bursting forth, new hatred exploded within me for Cardinal Wolsey, and I set a curse upon his head.

I'll have his soul, be that assured. When? How? I cannot know. But Anne Boleyn shall have her day.

Yours faithfully,

Anne

25 March 1523

Diary,

I am wearied beyond imagining. Each and every day we sit, my good Mother and my self, before the hearth as Chaplain Parker drones the Psalms and Scriptures and we stitch, stitch, stitch upon an endless tapestry. I swear if I embroider one more hoof of unicorn or wing of mythic dragon I shall scream! How does my Mother live so dull a life? Week after month after year rising early to oversee the baking, brewing, cheese making. Seeing every servant stay full occupied, collecting feathers for our pillows, candle making and prayers, always prayers.

I see behind her clouded eyes a dying fire that once burned sharp and bright, but here among the bumpkins and the sheep, the endless fields broken by a pallid stream they call a river, my Mother's dreams are extinguished like the candles in a chapel, one by one by one. She will not speak of it but I believe there once was affection between her and my always absent Father. Not a love match altogether, but once married they were glad of it. Elizabeth Howard proud of a husband not highly born but bold, who saw the world as his for taking. And Thomas Boleyn glad of a wife who raised his fortunes, a kindly heart and pretty face who proudly gave him one child a year and did not die. Who saw to fields, accounts and manor with an even temper, bearing lonely years in blessed silence.

My Mother, like some domestic tutor, impresses me with virtues I must learn if I would marry well. Chastity, of course, and modesty I can abide. But humility and evenness of temper, in truth, are words that do not describe my self. She sees my sullen pain and tells me, "Do not brood so. You will be called to Court again. Go, take your hound Urian. Hunt, tend the gardens, ride to neighbors, pluck the lute." But nothing changes such a leaden prison. Early to bed for saving candlewax, early to rise for household chores. The days drag on in deadly measure.

They say that with my love of Percy I invoked King Henry's wrath and that his wrath is death. But this banished life he's sent me to is worse than death. I nightly climb the dark narrow circle of stairs to my stone bedchamber, and with every step curse his name and Wolsey's too. Lying on my stiff pallet, the moonlight cannot find its way through narrow window holes to cheer me.

I wrote twice to Percy, each time hiring secret couriers to carry the missive to his hands in Northumberland. I waited endless weeks that went to months for his replies. My heart grew still by measures till one grey morning when hope finally died, so died my heart. It withered then and turned hard like some sweet fruit that once past ripeness dries and goes to leather.

The quiet as I lay abed is terrible to me. Beyond these walls are only blackness, meadows, cattle, trees. No chambers gaily candlelit with gentlemen and ladies amused by jesters, jugglers, fools. No fêtes, no masques, no dancing, music, lovers loving. I sometimes think that I shall go mad with the quiet and the dark and the loneliness. O sweet Percy lying cold and comfortless in your married bed, are we not cruelly punished for loving truly? I swear I will not have my Mother's helpless fate. I swear it on the stars.

Yours faithfully,

Anne

6 June 1524

Diary,

A celebration! George my brother rode home to visit Hever Hall and stayed a fortnight and a day. He is a charming boy who ladies love with handsome grace and reckless wit, and for these things I love him dearly too. Our Mother came alive with him at home, the only living son, adored and he adoring her. Special meals were made and we three sat for hours to gab, drink, make music, play at games.

But when I could I'd steal him far away, and we would ride for leagues, Urian running at the horses hooves. We'd take the hawks and hunt or walk the grassy path beside the River Eden, and idle days away. Full of gossip, current courtly jests and puns, he amused and filled me full where I had been bereft.

One day we lay beneath a shady elm, the hound lazy at our feet. He told the news that stirs our family's fate. Our Sister Mary is still mistress to the King. "She does our family proud," said George, a wicked grin upon his lips. "The saying has it that with Mary Boleyn, a King and his codpiece are always parted."

"And how grows our good King's manly accessory?" I asked gravely.

"Large as a pie plate, sister, and embroidered with the Tudor crest, all swords and stags and pomegranates."

"Pomegranates!" We laughed together till our eyes were wet.

"I swear that girl is bold," he said and made a crown of wild daisies for my head. "She's looking well. She glows in jewels and fine gowns he heaps upon her every day."

"And what of William Carey? How does our brother in law enjoy his cuckolding?"

"As tho it happens every day, his wife made the King's whore. I would think him wise if he were making use of it, seeking favor in return for use of Mary. But he does nothing."

"A pity," said I, thinking now upon my sister's fate.

"No pity really," replied my brother. "From Mary's lot I've been shown some favor from the King. A manor house is mine. Small but very sweet. But our Father, he is in very great favor. A ceremony making him peer of the realm was held together with one making Henry's bastard by Bessie Blount the Duke of Richmond. 'Twas a sweltering hot day, but the new Royal Palace at Bridewell was very grand — all trumpets and golden canopies. Of course the main ceremony was for the child, but it was a great day for our Father. Very great in deed."

"I suppose he was given money too." I felt my mouth go hard.

"A pension of a thousand crowns. What is it, Anne? You look as tho a cat had crossed your grave."

I said nothing then. My Father's fortunes risen over Mary's debauchery was natural to George. To all men. And should have been to me. But I was sickened. I thought, but did not say to him, "A woman is a castle or a piece of land, most valued, oft admired, improved upon. Then she's sold or bought for fortune's sake, for heirs, a bribe, a prize, a debt repaid. Her flesh, mind, aching heart forgot, nay, considered not at all!"

I stood and made to go. But George begged me stay. The sun was warm, he said the castle dreary. He promised he'd braid my hair. I forced my heart to calm, to brood in secret and let him soothe me with his idle talk and gentle ministrations. We spoke of my own banishment's end, a return to Court.

"The Percy thing's forgot and now with our family on the rise I see you back within the year."

"Please, Christ, let it be so."

"Thomas Wyatt asked me of your health the other day. He said a curious thing. Reminded me to bring you quills and ink. Who is it you write to? Wyatt? He's a married man, and that is trouble you little need." I must have blushed because he asked, "Not Percy, Anne?"

"Certainly not Percy. 'Tis poetry I write. Wyatt gave me most encouraging words before I went away, and so I try my hand at verses."

"A woman poet, what a thought! Will you let me see the verses? You know I write my own."

"No, no!" I cried, saying they were badly writ, not worth the parchment used. Then I changed the subject, said 'twas getting dark and we had a far ride to home. He helped me up and put his arms round me then and held me with a brother's sweet embrace.

"I brought the quills and ink for you," he said. I laid my head upon his comfortable shoulder thinking that here was one man in all the world who loved me for my self. Too sad. Too sad. Too sad.

Yours faithfully,

Anne

4 July 1524

Diary,

Last night as I prepared to lay me down to bed I heard a quiet footstep near. I found it was my brother George with candle torch who crept the circular stair to my chamber clandestinely, a gift in hand. Unwrapt, I saw the reason for his secrecy. He'd brought to me a most heretical tract, Erasmus' "Praise of Folly" which savaged Pope and Church and Clergy for corruption, priestly greed and lechery.

I thanked him soundly. Books to read are scarce in country

life and one so bold as this a prize. George lamented that he'd failed to place his hands upon the newest scandalous tome, William Tyndale's translation into English, of the New Testament.

"The books are burned at St. Paul's Cross," he said, "the author persecuted, running from our own King. The volumes that miss the fire, I'm told, are passed from hand to hand. The Church, in deed your good friend Wolsey, tracks these copies down searching house to house." He spoke in even lower tones. "All known literates are suspect, and rewards offered to informers."

"I do not understand," said I. "In France I read the Christian Gospels translated into French. No ban there exists. In deed 'twas encouraged by the King's own sister and my tutor in such things, the Duchess Alençon."

"You forget our King is, in Rome, the Pope's own shining star. He's named Defender of the Faith against all Protestant heretics."

I begged my brother that he get me Luther's tome. 'Twas dangerous, he said, for Henry hated Luther, writing out against the German's works, defending Catholic sacraments. Luther all outraged had called our Sovereign a "lubberly ass, that frantic madman, King of lies."

I laughed out loud at such audacity. George put a finger to my lips, afraid and whispered, "We are still good Catholics, are we not?"

"I suppose," said I. "We go to mass, take communion, confess. But brother, listen." I drew him very close. "Have you no love for these Protestant ideas? That God and man can speak together without authority of priests? I tell you now it suits me well, this New Religion."

His hands in mine were trembling with my words. "They still burn heretics," said George.

"I will be cautious, say nothing aloud to bring us harm. I promise you." His trembling ceased, his posture eased. "But get me that Tyndale Bible when you can."

He laughed and said, "Nan, you are a vixen. You'll be the death of me, I swear."

I bade him go, then put the volume in my hiding place behind a loose stone. I longed for daylight. A book to read! Treasure good as gold.

Before I laid me down I went to bended knee, the bedchamber my chapel — blasphemy — and called to Jesus Christ my Lord in supplication to save my miserable soul . . . and soon to bring me back to Court.

Yours faithfully,

Anne

ELIZABETH FOUND HERSELF TREMBLING as she closed her mother's diary. Coming back into her own world from Anne's was not unlike a barge gliding out from under the shadows of London Bridge into the blinding daylight. But tonight, with many of the candles Kat had lit round the chair having flickered out, the room was dark and gloomy outside the small halo of remaining light, and her eyes were fatigued.

Kat had become suspicious of these strange sessions. The secrecy irritated the Mistress of the Maids, for Elizabeth had never kept a secret from Kat since earliest nursery days. She'd complain about the Queen looking tired with great dark circles under her eyes after a night awake, or when Elizabeth remained silent about her solitary exercises behind closed doors, mutter quietly about evil habits and the Devil's work.

Pinwheels of light swam before Elizabeth's eyes and pain swelled in her head. When she stood she was gripped with a terrible nausea that made her clutch the chair for support. It was surely the onset of one of her bad headaches.

"Damn head!" she hissed. Her forehead was clammy and she was not at all sure she could make it to her bed. If this was the effect that reading her mother's diary had on her, thought Elizabeth, it would take forever to finish it. But the idea was driven from the Queen's mind as a bolt of pain crashed through her skull. She had barely the strength to call for her ladies to help her before the spinning lights inside her head grew dark.

6 November 1525

Diary,

I have not writ in so long, for all reports from Hever would have talked of nothing more than ennui. But now I am gratefully received at Court again, back in service to the Queen. I sleep in close quarters with Her Majesty and other waiting ladies, in all we are seven. The time is lively spent with our King setting the daily pace — we never seem to sleep. Falconing, hunting — Henry is said to tire never less than eight or ten horses on a day — he wrestles, jousts. And watching him play at tennis is the prettiest thing in all the world. His favorite foe is Thomas Wyatt in whom he's met his match. We sing, play on flutes and virginals — my pretty voice is popular — and dance most evenings. The Queen's years are showing next to Henry's own vitality. Mayhaps his wandering eyes and hands and heart dull her spirit, for it seems her ladies shine more brightly than does she.

My Father, raised to lofty heights, has new permission from the King to bring his household to the Court and live. My Mother, therefore with him has apartments in the palace, a rare favor, which I think she's glad of. Two pretty panelled rooms with fine carven cupboards filled with plate and silk hangings o'er a great bed. No more dreary Hever, endless days of stitching till the fingers bleed. Beautiful still, my Mother takes her days in quiet grace. I see her watching from afar as younger women play the courtly game. Me she watches closely saying little. 'Tis clear I am my Father's charge, and he has plans for me. Plans he'll not divulge.

Cardinal Wolsey, gaining power, wealth and property with every passing day thro Henry's faith in him, never sees me, even when I'm in his sight. He remembers nothing of his punishment to Percy and to me, nothing of the pain he caused. But I remember, O do I remember! Poor Percy, he is banished still. I must admit my heart's grown ever colder since the loss of him. I have many playful suitors. They mean nothing. I will let my heart feel nothing. It is my part, I know, to play this game but I am not required to feel, and to be sure there's no one who will care. I'm a pretty ornament, some property to buy and sell. So I'll not give my heart to any one.

Last night at supper hour there was amongst the rabble at a lower table some old hag whispered to be a witch. When the meal was done, dogs scavenging scraps beneath the groaning board and all the nobles gone to evening's amusement, I found the woman and begged to bend her ear. She looked at me through clouded eyes whilst her hands still stuffed a pouch with bits of food the dogs had not yet found.

"What d'ye want m'lady?" She smiled, if you would call it smiling, teeth beneath her lips black and rotten, her breath a putrid stench. "A spell, a potion, something magick that will hold your beauty everlasting?"

I gave no answer but instead I put my hand in hers and turned it so the specially long and pointed sleeve did fall away, and she could see the little extra flesh and nail they call a finger.

"Six fingers!" she cried and grasped my hand most greedily. "You must be Mistress Anne Boleyn." It startled me, I tried to pull away. She held it fast. "You're famous for this little finger. Aye. They say 'tis a Devil's mark."

"The same as this wen upon my neck," I whispered and pulled my choker down so she could see the raised brown spot the necklace hid. "What think you, old woman, am I a witch like you?"

She took no notice of the wen, instead stood staring at my hand in some long silence. The waxy smoke of candles stung my eyes. Her fetid breath was too much to bear. More silence, then I cried, "What say you! Tell me quickly, I'll not stay much longer."

"Hold, Mistress, I am reckoning, reckoning, how much I can afford to pay for this small finger."

"What, buy the finger!"

"Oooooh yes, Lady, cut it off, 'twould hardly bleed and 'twould look so lovely in a jar," she whined, "alongside unborn bats wing, pregnant toads, the like."

"Certainly not!" I cried and pulled my hand away.

"Did you not ask?"

"I asked you your opinion on it, on me, not to be some ghoulish surgeon."

"My opinion," she placed a bony finger on my cheek, "is that the Lady Anne has powers like a long and yellowed scroll as yet unfurled. And if she choose, she shall make a brilliant and an infamous career." She shoved a wrinkled hand at me, palm up. I quickly filled it with a coin, then turned from her, caught my breath and took myself away. Brilliant and infamous. Her words rang so loud all day and evening within my head that I needed singing with my sister ladies to drown them out and give me peace.

Yours faithfully,

Anne

20 April 1526

Diary,

Having heard that Thomas Wyatt's named the Master of the May Day Revels I rode out this day, very fine and warm, upon my favorite chestnut mare to Shooters Hill behind the Greenwich Palace. There, from deep inside the forest were the sounds of sawing work and hammering, so I unhorsed and went on foot down wooded paths to find so strange a scene I scarce believed my eyes.

The rustic home of Robyn Hoode and his band of Merry Men was being built by royal carpenters, a rough banquet table set amongst the alder grove, a full jousting field was cleared with viewing trestles set in branching trees. I found Wyatt sitting, back against a tree with quill in hand, inscribing dialogue for Sherwood Forest's Masque. His brow was furrowed deep, a frown upon his handsome face.

"Come, Thomas, you should have no trouble thinking up an outlaw's words. You're one yourself."

"Anne, you took me by surprise!" He sprang to his feet but I pushed him back, sitting down beside him on the ground. "I've come to ask a favor, sir."

"You know your wish is always my command, so pray what favor have I granted you?"

"That I'm Maid Marion in this masque. I've always liked

her character. I think I'd play her well." He smiled, but his look betrayed a sullen mood. "What is it, Thomas, tell me? You look poorly. Are you ill?"

"No, Anne, not me. What worries have I, sitting in a wooded glen with such a lovely lady scribbling fanciful words for a pagan fertility rite on a sunny April day? 'Tis my friend Henry there, in dreary council rooms who broods on grave and worldly matters now, and every day grows sadder still."

In truth I'd noticed the King's listless mood, so different from his usual rough gaiety, but made little of it.

"What ails him then?"

"Do you really wish to know?" and looked at me peculiarly.

"Yes, I do."

"It's not the kind of gossip ladies care to hear." By now the man was teasing me.

"Do tell me, Thomas, or I'll box your ears!"

"Well then," he said and settled back against the tree, "do you remember, or were you even born when Henry took the throne? How he shone then, like a star. The young King who, eager as a lion for war, invaded France in glittering armor, driving knights who fled from fields at the Battle of the Spurs. What glorious feats of soldiering! He captured towns, then treated enemies with such good grace he earned the name Great Harry. O, Anne, he was marvellous, and thought he would continue thus and one day conquer all of France. His Great Enterprise — so he called it — proceeded with, he hoped, the help of Queen Katherine's nephew, Henry's staunchest friend and ally."

"You mean the Emperor Charles of Spain," I said. "The Queen is very fond of him."

"And he has used her in years past like an ambassador between the two. But now you see, Charles has armies larger than our Henry ever dreamed, and invaded France himself. King Francis is his prisoner."

"So I've heard. But what does it mean to Henry?"

"The Emperor no longer wants a part of Henry's Great Enterprise. He has plans to conquer all the world alone. And this after Henry'd given half a million crowns to Charles for his adventures."

"So he is betrayed."

"Yes, but there is more. Henry will not give up his dream of conquest, and therefore let Cardinal Wolsey set a tax on all his subjects. The Amicable Grant he calls it, but the people call it injustice, and rebel. Tax collectors in the country — your father's one — are met with loud resistance, sometimes force. The rabble fall upon commissioners and will not pay for Henry's war, but worse, heap scorn upon the King and Cardinal Wolsey. So coupled with a traitorous ally, Henry faces open rebellion amongst the folk who loved and cheered him most."

"I see why he is troubled, and Katherine also. She's torn between beloved kin and husband now."

"But Anne, Katherine is the problem, too. In taverns and in garrisons rumors abound that King Henry's marriage is accursed. He has no sons, Princess Mary is his only heir, and there are mutterings that incest is the cause."

"Incest?!" I spoke the word so loud that workmen stopped and stared at us. I moved closer to his ear. "Incest? How do you mean?"

"Katherine — you must know this — was married first to Henry's brother Arthur. But he was weak and died ere the marriage was consummated, so said the Queen, and she was believed by all. Since the match with Spain was so important, and because the Princess Katherine then was fair and sweet, Henry wed her happily. All was well for many years, but now with Katherine past the time for bearing babes and Henry sonless, talk's begun. Is God punishing him with a marriage barren of sons because he'd taken his brother's widow as a wife?"

"'Tis a cruel thought," said I, thinking of the great love Katherine bore the King.

"You know, Anne, that Henry is conversant with the Scripture and he has found there in Leviticus a plain answer to his tragedy. It says that if a man shall take his brother's wife, it is impure, he hath uncovered his brother's nakedness and they shall be childless. Henry's begun to feel this tainted union will come to be his own undoing."

I was breathless. All that Wyatt said was finding place inside my head like pegs in perfect holes. I thanked him, saying that no one ever had spoke so plain and clear to me of weighty issues, timely news. I kissed him quickly, then taking from my waist a little lace and jewelled tablet, thrust it in his hands as a gift from me. He took the jewel and hung it round his neck.

"I'll wear it near my heart," he said and kissed me. The kiss was lingering and might have led to sweeter things, but I pulled away and said, "Come calling when you've writ a poem for me in it, it won't be hard . . ." I kissed his ear and smiled most wantonly. "Or will it?" Then lifting skirts and petticoats to show a bit of stockinged foot and ankle to his admiring eyes, I leapt away and into the wood.

This night, by candlelight I found a quiet room and came to think. These things that Wyatt said, tho not my usual thoughts, do feel of some import and so I set them down in black and white in great detail, all the words I can remember. Time will tell if they are so, or nothing more or less than idle castle gossip.

Yours faithfully,

Anne

2 May 1526

Diary,

When yesterday I dressed for May Day Revels, never did I dream the night would end with such portention. My frock — Maid Marion's I mean — tho simple was quite elegant. Rough silk overdress in creamy white, fawn panels, sleeves embroidered thick with rosy trimming. The tight bodice cinched my waist to nothing, exposing bosom, shoulders, back.

I let the Queen and other waiting women go ahead, claimed I'd left my headdress in our rooms and waited, watching courtly lords and ladies in their old style finery saunter down the garden path toward Shooters Hill. Hanging back I saw two hundred archers dressed in verdant velvet, line the forest path. Soon, I knew, Lord Benton playing Robyn Hoode would come with outstretched arms inviting all present "Come into the greenwood and see how outlaws live."

The Court assembled at the entrance of the wood and as rehearsed, the archers pulled back bows and let their arrows fly. But then when Robyn Hoode himself appeared a great cheer went up when it was known the outlaw was not Lord Benton, but the King himself! Great laughter and good cheer as Henry welcomed all and led them to his rustic grove. I waited then till all disappeared within the wall of trees. Waited till I heard the music wafting on the wind and knew the masque begun.

As I hurried down the path I knew the other ladies would be whispering, "Where is Anne? She may not come. Who will play Maid Marion?" The time was ready. Robyn Hoode had battled sword and dagger with the Sheriff's men and climbed the tower where Marion would soon her self be revealed. I circled round, climbed the wooden stair to where the platform stage was set, pushed aside the startled lady who would take my place, and made my breathless entrance on the stage.

Delighted gasps heard all round at my appearance, then suddenly I found my self face to face with His Majesty. He loomed so large, those blue and laughing eyes so bright, the smile so dazzling I felt the breath go out of me. He spoke his lines of love to Marion with bold and clever grace, and I spoke mine with equal elegance. Then he swept me up within his arms, my feet did lose the ground. I know 'twas in the scripted play this close embrace, but I swear I felt the cod beneath the codpiece stir and when he kissed me, that too was most sincere.

The masque went on to its finale, all were rejoiced, the actors gracious cheered. At play's end the King was swept away by courtiers, the next event the joust to be prepared. I joined with other ladies at Queen Katherine's side and felt her dark eyed searing stare. She must have seen the play was something more, her husband's wandering eyes, his arms round my slender waist unlike her own thickening one, and hated me. But she said nothing, just went among her waiting ladies to the tiltyard hung with waving banners all of rainbow hue.

My heart was beating fast, my mind aclutter and confused. Were the King's attentions truly meant for me? Impossible, I thought, my Sister Mary'd warmed his bed not six months past. Twenty crashing trumpets and as many drums intruded on my fantasies as the joust began. Sound and colors, men in flashing steel on quivering horseflesh. The King astride his steed approached the Queen and as her favorite received, as custom told, her gossamer scarf for luck. But there within his gaze I saw nothing for his wife, no love, no care and in hers a pain so bright it hurt my eyes.

The joust began, all knights and soldiers taking part, each great and ghastly charge with screams and cheers and curses, crashing armor, terrible falls and trampling hooves. Thomas Wyatt challenged Henry and was unhorsed. Unharmed, in good cheer to be beaten by his master, they strode arm and arm from the jousting field.

At the banquet in a festooned chamber made of woven alder boughs and fragrant flowers, I was seated next to Wyatt who was very well and jolly in the candlelight.

"Tell me, when did Henry steal the part of Robyn Hoode from Lord Benton?" I asked.

"When he found 'twas you would play Maid Marion. When the masque began and you were nowhere to be found, 'twas clear he was distracted."

"And when I suddenly appeared?"

"Anne, I needn't tell you what he felt. I'm sure you felt it too."

My cheeks burned red. I grabbed the goblet, drank some wine to cover my embarrassment and changed the banter then to something less unwise, and Thomas did oblige.

But later when I took my rest from dancing in the cool darkness of the woods beyond the torch light, this night's mystery and adventure full unfolded. I'd bent to fix my slipper when I felt a pair of manly hands behind me covering my eyes. He was tall with broad shoulders and I thought it Thomas Wyatt.

"Have you writ your poem to me?" I said flirtatiously, then stood and turned to him. And for the second time that day, surprised, I found myself within the King of England's firm embrace.

"Poem?" He was smiling down at me. "So you require a verse extolling all your beauty and your charm?"

So strange. After that exchange all manner of emotion welled up within my breast and limbs and head. Fear, then courage, desire, then loathing, sweetness, bitterness, memories of past and thoughts of future, too. In that small moment when silence hung between his last words and my next phrase I felt a calm descend like some winged angel o'er my head. Courage slew fear and then I spoke.

"Haven't I virtues enough to make a pretty verse of me?"

"More than enough." His eyes bored into me.

I gently pulled away beyond his arms. "Well, begin."

"What?" he said confused.

"Begin the poetry. I'm waiting, Sire."

He laughed out loud at my audacity, calling me a demanding wench, but took the challenge up like a leather gauntlet thrown upon the ground. He began:

"As the holly groweth and never changeth hue / So I am, ever hath been, unto my lady true."

"Yes, go on."

"As the holly groweth green, with ivy all alone / When flowers cannot be seen: and the greenwood leaves be gone . . .

"Now unto my lady promise to her I make . . . From all others only to her I me betake."

"Excellent, Your Majesty!" said I and clapped my hands.

"Now do I get a kiss?"

"You've had your kiss already, on the stage."

"Then I'll have what comes after." He pulled me back into his sturdy arms.

"Stop it!" I cried and wrenched free.

"You tell your King to stop? How dare you?"

My heart was pounding in my chest. "For his own good," said I, "protecting him from certain incestuous liaisons."

Even in the shadows I could see his face go flush with rage. "Incestuous?!" He seemed stricken, confused. Was I speaking of his sore and sinful marriage to his brother's wife?

"May I speak plainly, Majesty? My Sister Mary not so long ago shared your bed," then whispered, "bore your child. For me to do the same it seems . . . incestuous."

Relieved and gathering his wits he said, "You are far too bold, Mistress Anne. You speak here to your King."

"And you to a virtuous maiden who full intends to stay one, Sire." Then I curtsied low, looked up at him and smiled most gracefully. "But I do enjoy your sweet attention."

He grasped my hand — by luck the five digit one — and kissed it, lingering with his lips to my fingers. Then without my leave he pluck'd my garnet ring from me and placed it on the smallest joint of his smallest finger.

"If I cannot have your heart, I'll have this instead," he said and turned to disappear amongst the forest shadows like a ghostly stag.

Tho hours remained of May Day Revels I was lost amidst such reveries and possibilities, that time flew and I'd returned to bed not knowing how I'd come. I lay in darkness hearing all round me waiting ladies whispering gossip of the evening past, but I had one thought only. One thought which left me trembling and sleepless till the morning came — the King of England was pursuing Anne Boleyn.

Yours faithfully,

Anne

17 July 1526

Diary,

In my vast confusion this day I find myself at once bereft and joyful. Good friend Thomas Wyatt's fled to exile in Rome, self imposed but necessary. And Henry King of England's wooing me. The two facts intertwine like thorny brambles twisting round my self. That it has come to this I am amazed.

'Twas not so long ago Wyatt filled my head with courtly politicks and I, grateful, made a gift to him of a small keepsake — a jewelled tablet on a lace. And soon thereafter Henry at the May Day feast stole my ring and placed it on his little finger. 'Tis hard believing that these two gentlemen have almost come to blows for these small trinkets sake. The story goes like this.

Henry and his favorites, Wyatt among them, played a game of bowles the other day. The two were on opposing teams when Henry claimed a good cast — someone else's — as his own. Wyatt, with his Grace's leave, objected. Then, it's said, the King quite *pointedly* pointed with his little finger, the very one on which my ring was worn and said, his eyes on Thomas, "Wyatt, I tell thee it is mine. I tell thee *it is mine!*" The King, though certain in his words, did have a smile upon his face and Wyatt thought his humor good and so replied, "And if you give me leave to measure it, Your Majesty, I hope it will be mine." Then just as pointedly he took from his neck the lace with my jewelled tablet, stooped and made to measure up the cast. Henry, seeing my token in Wyatt's hands, took the action as a challenge o'er my affections. Like some petulant child the King then kicked the bowl and said, "It may be so but then I am deceived!" and angrily departed from the game.

Before I'd even heard the tale and ignorant of my role within it, I was summoned to the King to speak in private. Though since the May Day Revels he had made it clear he fancied me with sidelong glances, partnered dances, and singing harmonies, we'd been most public. Now I entered his apartments which were more grand and glorious than I'd ever seen or dreamed. Great bowed and mullioned windows caught the sun from three sides setting the room in a blaze of light, chests and tables carven and gilt, the monstrous overmantel lined with two dozen silver jugs, a silken tapestry magnificent in size and brilliant color stitched of St. George slaying a green dragon, a great canopied chair and in a corner several musical instruments. The King all in white velvet and silver thread was, too, illuminated by the sun and some internal fire which shone out thro his eyes. My heart was pounding neath my bosom which I do admit I carefully displayed. But on this day a vast expanse of creamy parfumed skin did little to repell the anger blowing off the King like some scalding summer wind.

"Do you take me for a fool!" he cried. A vein throbbed his scarlet forehead and I could not pull my eyes away from it. I did not know my crime but he was there for telling me. "You dare play with your King's affections on the same court with Thomas Wyatt?! Have I not raised your father into high position . . . ?"

My limbs grew numb with my Father's name spoken so.

"Have I not helped to pay your brother's bride's dowry, honoring your family once again? Is this the way I am repaid?"

My arms and legs were ice, my heart set beating like a drum, but my mind was racing fast and clear and I could see *the King was courting me,* not capriciously but in most earnest fashion. What was his game? He'd had my Sister. Some said he'd had my Mother, too. Father and Brother were in his thrall. Was he on a dare to conquer all Boleyns? I wondered when it'd started and I suddenly saw my love for Percy as a bone in Henry's throat. Should I grovel as was done by all, or should I play the game? Was I most desirable as Wyatt painted me in verse, a fleeing deer in some enchanted forest? I thought then, Yes, be elusive as the wind and he will seek but never hold me.

"Wyatt stole the trinket from me," I lied, then boldly said, "just as you took my garnet ring. You both are acting like my heart was stolen, too. It isn't so in either case, tho I do love Your Majesty as loyal subjects love their King."

"I want you, Anne." His voice was a passionate growl. I knew he was deadly serious, so I laughed gaily as I was able.

"If this is how the King treats with a woman he wants, then I should hate to see how he treats with his enemies."

"Well I, I . . ." he stammered, stricken dumb at my impertinence.

"By your leave, Majesty," said I, wishing no further discourse — and curtsying low, quickly left him standing there, a look of great surprise decorating his handsome face.

I fled back to the Queen's apartments, shaking in my soul. What am I to do? I had spoken the truth. I do not love the King the way a woman loves a man. But if I know him, he will not finish till he's caught the wind and held it in his hands.

I asked my Mother's counsel, but she looked sad and only murmured, "He is the King, he is the King."

My Sister offered this advice. "Take him, let him have his time with you. He'll give you pretty dresses, many jewels, a bastard if you're lucky. You'll be the King of England's mistress, Anne, a proud title for an untitled, skinny girl." It made me cross, this brainless answer from a brainless whore.

Then I went to see my Father who'd called me to his room. He looked very grand, his satin doublet gleaming black and regal gold, stylish French cap laid flat against his silver hair.

"You're favored by the King," said he, "so it seems." He put his arm round me, something he'd not done since I was small, and smiled. 'Twas nothing loving in the gesture, tho. I was not fooled.

"Play him, Anne," he whispered low, so low you'd think the Devil at his back was listening in. "Did you hear me?" I had not yet answered him.

"Yes, Father, your advice is very clear."

"Will you do it, then?" He gripped my shoulder with his bony fingers, squeezed it tight. My Father'd long been my lord and only master, but now within my mind I saw my Father and my self, on some timeless future path. But where he always seemed to take the lead he stumbled now and fell behind.

"I'll do as I will, Father," said I.

His eyes flashed with fury, but this I ignored with some new and dangerous courage. Then I removed from the vise of his fingers and left the room without a backward glance.

Yours faithfully,

Anne

24 August 1526

Diary,

His Majesty pursues me still and I resist. He is a man in love, he says, giddy with it. It seems so. His dark mood is gone, reborn to manly vigor. In his Kingly role he moves aggressively again, his brilliant statesmanship restored. He speaks to me of family, his children and their marrying. His bastard son by Bessie Blount he sometimes thinks of wedding to his lawful daughter Mary. Anything, he says, is better than a woman ruling England. Women are not strong enough to keep the peace.

Thomas Wyatt, my tutor in such politicks, is gone from here, his exile and discomfiture on my behalf known to all. I wish that I could see my friend again, making him my teacher in this circumstance of Henry's appetite for me. I do not know why such a desperate passion's roused in him. This man, a *King,* has made himself my slave. He thirsts for the very sight of me, moans like a heartsick calf that he's enchanted and bewitched and begs me day and night to be his own. He brings me tokens, flowers, bits of gilded ribbon, writes me songs and sings them in a trembling voice.

Mayhaps I know this feeling after all. Was it not thus with my own love for Henry Percy? If it is so, if the King truly loves me, what am I to do? I do not love him, have no wish to follow in my Sister's path. But my family — there's the misery. If I hold myself aloof, reject the King's advances, invoke his wrath, what of my Father's hard won high position? My Brother George is newly made cup bearer to His Majesty. Will my Mother languish once again in distant country houses?

But if I declare more affection than a subject loves her King, I'll find myself his mistress and for that I do not have the stomach. I must find a way to hold the King at arm's length or bring disaster down upon my head. O let me think! Here at Court there is so little time for solitary thoughts. No place for peaceful contemplation. Always chattering ladies, entertainments, meals and duties to the Queen. And this golden haired giant who seethes with love pursuing me both night and day. I will, I must find a way.

Yours faithfully,

Anne

13 October 1526

Diary,

I am saved for at least a time. The answer to my quandary came within a dream. In the night I dreamt of olden times, a lady in a tower — a wife — and the Knight who loved her, not her spouse. The lady's face was sometimes strange, sometimes my own. She spoke in rhymes I wish I could remember, but they were gone when I awoke. More important was the scene the lady and her admirer played, watched even by her husband who nearby sat upon a cushioned chair. It was the game of Courtly Love. The young man, her servant in all things professed his passion, sung her songs, paid her compliments, gave her tiny tokens, expressed his soul's obedience to her. She teased, flirted, swooned to hear his amorous verse. That was all. They never bed. A kiss upon her hand, his head laid upon her knee, a fond caress, 'twas all that was required. Courtly Love.

When I awoke I pondered on the dream and saw its possibilities. 'Twas a dangerous game to play upon a King, I knew, but I had little choice. And so it began with Henry making his advance. I boldly joined the dance with laughter, smiles, allowed a brief caress, matched him wit for wit, pun for pun. I teased him, confounded him, roused him to a pitch and frenzy, then retreated and, feigning modesty, told him virtue did forbid me to continue or to love a married man. The King was like a tripped horse. He blustered, fumed . . . then laughed delightedly. He liked the game! So I sent him on his way and when next he came to me we played again but differently — new verses, duels of wit, a kiss I let him steal. But my evasion was the final act, and when the curtain fell I'd managed once again to keep the King at bay. Let us see how long it lasts.

Yours faithfully,

Anne

12 November 1526

Diary,

I am much exhausted by this Sunday's adventures and the odd games I'm forced to play to keep the King at arm's length. It began in early morning when all of Court had gone to Mass. There I knelt beside the Queen whose loud fervent prayers drowned out all others. Her eyes were bound upon her rosary, but Henry's eyes — he knelt across the chapel in the King's Pew — were fastened hard on me. I chanced a smile cross the crowded room and he returned it, beaming broadly, most unfit behavior for a King engaged in God's prayers. I shot a fierce and stern expression, scolding him. He laughed aloud! All heads turned to him and he covered his laugh with a fit of coughing which surely no one believed.

Later as we filed out of chapel he sought to walk beside me and whispered, "'Twas a harsh face you made me, Lady."

"I was but practicing. 'Tis the one I'll use, a mother, for my naughty son."

"Son? Do you plan to have a son?"

"Many sons," said I. "One for each day of the week." My smile was pretty as I dutifully followed my Queen and her women to their breakfast, Henry watching as I went.

Late morning, crisp and cold found the King playing with his lords at the newest manly game called Barriers. In this contest each combatant, wearing special breast plate and helmet, does mock but furious battle on foot, carrying two headed swords and seven foot lances. I and several ladies — tho not the Queen for she was once again in chapel — watched the competition, clapping at the derring-do, gasping at its violence. Henry, as in all such endeavors, ruled the field. 'Twas not that he was King and his men deferred to let him win. He truly was the best. He fought the boldest fight, vanquished most enemies.

Between bouts he came to field's edge where I stood shivering amongst the ladies. Heat rose in a mist from his body. I could see his breath which came hard from exertion. His eyes were shining and he asked me wordlessly for my favor. All the other ladies watched this exchange with some interest, but no one dared speak or even whisper. I handed him a lace handkerchief which he put to his nose and sniffed the fine French parfum. He beamed happily, then strode back into the field my champion, and thrashed his men soundly in my name.

Game finished, ladies left and I found him following after me, armor clanking.

"Mistress Anne!"

I turned, smiled. "You played well, Your Majesty. You may keep my handkerchief."

"I would have kept it, had you never offered."

"What a knave you are!" I cried.

"I deserve a trophy for my efforts. I beat them all." He

pulled off his breast plate and I fought to keep myself from staring at that impressive chest.

"But can you beat *me?*" I asked.

"Beat you!" The King laughed so heartily that his belly shook.

"I don't mean at Barriers, silly fool."

"What is the challenge then?"

"Chess," said I.

"Ah, chess. A woman's game. But one I play as well as any other. I accept your challenge. The gaming room one hour after dinner's done."

"I will be there."

And so I was. I'd changed my gown to one I knew he liked, for he had paid me several compliments of its color — deep russet red — and how it set my eyes to their greatest advantage. 'Twas cut low at the bodice. I knew I would be bending o'er the table as I made my moves, and hoped the sight of my pert duckies might confuse that razor mind to my advantage. My hair I wore long and flowing down my back. I'd lightly touched my lips and cheeks with some vermillion creme. And finally with a thin lace, fastened carefully the pointed flap of my sleeve round my fifth finger, hiding that sixth finger from his sight.

The King arrived not in his usual manner — all bluff and blustery, arrayed in gaudy layers of fur and jewels and finery. He came quietly in soft voice and subtle smiles. He wore pale hose and a flowing linen shirt under a doeskin doublet. No cap. He was freshly bathed and there was no sign of his morning's exertions. His hair gleamed gold in the afternoon sun. All in all a fine picture of a man.

We set comfortably down at the board and with few words began the game. I moved at first boldly and he, surprised at this tactic, did the same. We played in earnest silence. I took his knight. He took my bishop. Pawns were lost on both sides. Then I hesitated. Pretended confusion. Covered that confusion with bravado. The ploy worked well. Thoughtful and intense he took steps to trap my queen. I sighed loudly, bit my lip. So convinced was he that I had faltered, and overconfident in his position, he never saw my feint and when I whispered "checkmate" he froze.

"Checkmate," I said louder this time. I tried to make him meet my eyes but they were glued to the board, trying to make sense of his defeat.

"This cannot be," he mumbled.

"But it is. I have beaten you, Your Majesty."

"No!" He shouted and pushed back his bench so hard it fell on the floor.

"O, don't act the spoilt child, Henry. 'Tis only a game."

"And you're only a woman!"

"A woman who has beaten you." I laughed hoping not to sound cruel, but to dispel his fury. "Come, I must have a reward for my victory."

"A reward! You should be thrown in the Tower of London for treason against the King."

"Majesty!"

"All right. What do you want?" he asked with a petulant sneer.

"A kiss . . . ," said I. "A kiss from the loser." His eyes flashed dangerously, for I was pushing the barriers of his good humor. But his anger melted against the strange heat of my unusual demand. He moved to embrace me, but I held his arms.

"No, Henry. I mean to kiss *you*."

O, he was a man inflamed when I pressed myself against him, found his lips with my lips and used my tongue in the French fashion to search his mouth for all its intimate sweetness.

Sometime during that kiss his arms did go round me and so 'twas not an easy thing to break the embrace. But once it had been accomplished and we stood again in two separate places, our breath coming hard, he smiled.

"The winner of this round," he said and bowed low to me. "Mistress Anne Boleyn."

For all my taunting words and clever teasing I swear I feel no winner, but just a girl in deep water closing o'er my head. But I remain.

Yours faithfully,

Anne

HE GREAT LIVING SNAKE was three miles in length and made of a thousand clanking, rumbling pieces which sent a long, thick cloud of dust into the sultry July afternoon. In its escape from the heat and filth and pestilence of London, the royal summer progress into the Kentish countryside — Elizabeth's first as queen — had been underway for less than a week, but already the heavy and overladen carts and wagons, herds of livestock, and multitudes of pack horses carrying the baggage, goods, and furnishings of the entire court, had torn up the highway and wrought havoc — albeit a welcome one — on tiny farm communities along the route.

James Thomas, his plump wife Joan, and seven of their wide-eyed children had, with the permission of their landlord, stopped work for the better part of the day. Now they sat on blankets with pots of cheese, loaves of hard bread, and jugs of ale — a proper picnic — to watch, enthralled, the endless parade which was without question one of the greatest spectacles of their lifetime. The goods and cattle trundling down their rugged road were only the beginning of the remarkable pageant, for when they had passed, leaving their dust and droppings, then came the equerries and road masters carrying carved and painted coats of arms and brilliant banners which did not flap in the breeze so much as hang limply in the wilting heat. Guards and yeomen on their prancing horses surveyed the way before them. Gaily bedecked young maids of honor rode next, cheerfully holding handkerchiefs to their noses against the choking dust, followed by a company of liveried guardsmen, riding tall and alert in their saddles.

"Look here," James Thomas instructed his family, for he had once in his childhood seen such a progress when Great Harry was king, and he had never forgotten the wonder of it, or the order of the thing. From the rough carts and herds of cattle, to stately carriages of ladies and gentlemen, the Lords of the Council, and finally to armored regiments of guards announcing that the royal personage was not far behind.

"This'll be yer Queen comin' now. Stand up, all o'ye," he instructed, pulling them to their feet. "King Harry, he rode on horseback so I did get a good look at him. Aye, he was handsome and very tall and broad, too. But a woman now, I think she'll not ride out in the stink and dust, but in a carriage."

But James Thomas was wrong and happily so, for he and his family could now see, past the guardsmen, a fine jennet mare ridden by a red-haired woman who, resplendent in silver and brocade, sat high in her saddle and seemed to emit a kind of sunlike brightness all round herself.

"There she is!" cried Joan. "The Queen." James could hear the children muttering, "The Queen, the Queen," whilst the eldest boys commented on the fine horseflesh and trappings.

"Why, she's tall like Henry, and fair like him," said James Thomas, amazed.

"A good thing," whispered his wife, as though the pale-faced woman waving and smiling at them as she passed could possibly hear. "With a mother like that 'tis a blessing she takes after her father."

Elizabeth, eyes burning with the dust and bright sunlight, her mare bouncing under her, was appraising the Thomas family at the very moment they were appraising her, silently thanking her good subjects, as she had thanked God, every day since her accession, for bringing her to the throne.

Her thoughts scattered with the sudden boisterous commotion of Robin Dudley, who reined his enormous stallion to a breathless halt next to the Queen as though he had this very moment returned from a great battle.

"Majesty!" he panted, his forehead beaded with sweat.

"My God, Robin, what have you been doing up ahead? Vanquishing St. George's dragon?"

"I rode the distance to Canterbury to inspect the evening's lodgings."

"And then rode back again! Why didn't you stay, silly?"

His eyes shone as he caressed her face with his gaze. "Because I couldn't wait to see you, my love. It would have been hours. I too much like seeing you on horseback — the Queen on her summer progress. So proud and magnificent."

"And with a desperately sore bottom. Stop them up ahead, will you, Robin. I want to get down and ride in the carriage awhile."

He smiled at the familiarity with which they spoke, now that they were lovers. "Will you be stopping to visit the weavers' cottage in Oxted?" he asked.

"Are they expecting me?" She sighed, exhausted.

"They are."

"Then we shall not disappoint them." Shielding her eyes from the brutal sun she peered out at the green rolling farmland dotted with sheep. It was the first time Elizabeth had seen this region of her country. "Robin, do you really think the people like this business, the whole court descending on them like a great plague of locusts?"

"'Tis a monstrous burden in some ways, but it is an ancient custom — country hospitality. And we do bring our own wine and beer, after all," he added with a crooked smile. He took her hand then, unmindful of the stares of the coach drivers behind them. "They love you, Elizabeth. Your people want to see their new queen. And I wager they like what they see."

Dudley spurred his horse, rode to the head of the liveried guard, and ordered them to halt, allowing the train of supplies and cattle before them to plod ahead. Elizabeth let herself be helped from the saddle by one of her equerries. Her legs were rubbery from the long ride, and as she walked back to the ornate Dutch-made carriage, she slapped dust from her heavy brocaded riding skirt. Inside the carriage Kat Ashley dozed against the rose silk cushions, a thin film of perspiration lending a sweet shine to her lightly wrinkled face. Elizabeth's old and trusted servant Thomas Parry sat across from Kat hunched over a large account book, squinting at a column of figures. He sprang to help the Queen into her carriage.

"Madame, have you done riding for the day?" he inquired.

"Yes, Thomas. From the feel of it, maybe forever."

Unconsciously examining the Queen's face for signs of serious fatigue or illness, Parry handed her a flask of clear water. Elizabeth drank deeply until it was empty. Parry, like Kat Ashley, had been in Elizabeth's service since her early childhood. His wife, Blanche, had rocked the Princess in her royal cradle. Now the young queen collapsed wearily next to Kat, glancing affectionately at the older woman.

"She couldn't wait to be gone from that stinking, flea-infested house, but I think she hates the traveling more," whispered Elizabeth, hoping not to wake her waiting lady.

"Well, she'll be having to get used to it, will she not? July to November, every year from now on," said Parry.

"I expect I'll get to see a lot of my kingdom."

"Aye, you will do that." Thomas Parry smiled at the thought. Elizabeth's kingdom. How close she had come to losing it all before it could be hers.

Elizabeth, too, was remembering — the dangerous tribulations that she and Kat, Thomas and Blanche Parry had shared and suffered. She had thought much on those times in recent days, since reading Anne's diary describing the early months of Henry's enforced courtship of her mother.

What choice has a young girl when a king or nobleman forces his affections on her, what choice but to submit? thought Elizabeth. A woman had no escape. A hart — a hind — pursued by the hounds. A woman's mind confused by the rigid teaching that a man must always have what he desired. That a woman's wants meant nothing, nay, less than nothing. Her mother pursued by Henry. Herself, but a girl, pursued by Thomas Seymour.

Lord High Admiral. The name and the image of him flew into her mind unbidden. She could see him clearly, handsome and swaggering with his long red beard and iron-hard arms.

Thankfully Parry had gone back to his accounts, so he did not notice Elizabeth's face flush with the simple thought of a man dead more than ten years.

She closed her eyes. She could smell him ... oh God, taste him ... could even now hear that rich voice booming "By God's precious soul!" in a jovial oath that pierced the dull haze of sleep a moment before the heavy bedcurtains were ripped open and Thomas Seymour's overlarge presence filled her sunny apartments.

"Rise and shine, Princess. 'Tis too fine a day to lay about in bed."

Elizabeth had flushed scarlet as she sought to cover her small naked breasts with the lawn sheets and squirmed lower under the covers, unable to speak for sheer embarrassment.

"Admiral, for shame!" cried Kat Ashley springing from her pallet at the foot of Elizabeth's bed. Seymour, barelegged in his nightgown and slippers, had already leapt into Elizabeth's four-poster and was tickling the thirteen-year-old girl until her shrieks of helpless laughter echoed through Chelsea Manor. Kat rushed to the bedchamber door and slammed it, then stood arms akimbo over the writhing tangle of bodies and bedclothes, trying to decide how to end this outrageous display.

But as she watched the pair of them, the large, handsome red-bearded man and her dear Lady Elizabeth, she felt her sternly pursed lips soften into a smile. They were a pretty couple, far prettier than the one Seymour made with his homely middle-aged wife, Catherine. Kat wished desperately that she had never harbored such scandalous thoughts, but she had to admit that Elizabeth and Catherine were not the only women in this household that Thomas Seymour had bewitched.

Seymour rolled onto his back and lay smiling up at Kat. "Come woman, dress your charge quickly. We hunt this morning."

"Out of the bed now," she ordered him, finally finding her voice which, she lamented, was less one of authority than playfulness. "All right, Elizabeth," she added. "Up you get."

"Make him leave."

"Out," Kat told Seymour. "The Princess needs her privacy."

"I'll turn my back," he replied and stood facing the heavy velvet arras. "Go on, I won't peek."

Kat and Elizabeth exchanged a dubious look.

"I'm not leaving, so make haste, ladies."

With an embarrassed giggle Elizabeth jumped out of bed,

winding the thin sheet round her, and stood as her waiting woman hurriedly slipped a cotton kirtle over her reed-thin frame.

"Wear the russet jacket and the black brocade skirt," he snapped as though he were still at sea barking orders to his seamen.

As Kat laced her into a bone corset the Princess wondered if her stepmother knew where her husband was, if she knew what a fool he was making of her. Elizabeth tried to push all thoughts of the mild-mannered Catherine Parr from her mind, for she loved the woman dearly. Indeed, Catherine was the only mother Elizabeth had ever known. A slap to her petticoated buttocks made Elizabeth squeal with surprise. She turned to see Thomas Seymour grinning impishly at her. But before Kat could push him away he had kissed Elizabeth's flushed cheek and given her waiting woman's thigh a good pinch.

"Beautiful," he said, looking Elizabeth up and down in a quick inspection. "The stables in three quarters of an hour, no later!" He bounded out the door, leaving the two women floundering in the wake of his audacity.

Now as the royal coach rocked and rumbled over the pitted road Elizabeth conjured the memory of her adored stepmother Catherine Parr. Elizabeth had been nine when Henry, by then an old and sickly man, had married Catherine, his sixth wife. Finally relieved of any illusions of marrying for love or producing more male heirs, he'd been content with a woman whose holdings would strengthen his northern borders, one who might offer him some comfort in his old age. And comfort she gave him, sitting for hour upon hour with his sore leg propped upon her lap, arguing companionably about philosophy and religion. When Henry chose Catherine, she had been for many years central to a coterie of steely-minded, forward-thinking noblewomen who, by patronizing the great scholars and tutors of the Continent, brought the teachings of humanism and religious reform to court and wielded the first real, if limited, power over kings and princes that Englishwomen had ever enjoyed.

But, Elizabeth mused, her adoration for Catherine Parr sprang from something far deeper than respect, for she had within months of her coronation not only soothed the raging spirit and pain-racked body of her husband but plucked the long-estranged "bastard" child of Anne Boleyn back from lonely exile and into the warm bosom of the royal family. Henry once again showered his red-haired girl with affection and allowed Catherine to oversee Elizabeth's brilliant classical education. The Queen in one swift maneuver had bestowed upon her stepdaughter her life's most precious gift — the restoration of Elizabeth's place in the royal succession.

Four years later Henry had died, leaving his widow the richest woman in England. Elizabeth's home was with the Queen at Chelsea, and she and her younger half brother, Edward — now king at age nine — were comforted by Catherine's kind ministrations. But then within three months of Henry's death everything changed again. The dowager queen had fallen hopelessly and passionately in love with Thomas Seymour, uncle to the young king and Lord High Admiral of the Navy.

In those bewitching days the house at Chelsea had fairly thrummed with sensuality and Elizabeth found the high-spirited courtship of Thomas and Catherine unfolding before her girlishly romantic eyes. There was laughter and music and merriment and kind affection shown all round — an utterly intoxicating existence for the studious and modest young princess. Elizabeth watched fascinated to see the once demure and utterly serious-minded Catherine dissolve into a giddy, lovestruck girl. And so when Thomas Seymour's pursuit of Elizabeth had begun in earnest, she had been entirely unprepared to distinguish assault from innocent good fun.

Thomas. In the gardens offering her delicate bouquets he'd fashioned with his own thick-fingered hands.

Thomas. In her bedchamber merrily pestering her every morning.

Thomas. Romping round the schoolroom like a silly boy as she tried to study.

Thomas. Teasing her. Chasing her. Touching her.

She had finally become unable to hear the man's name without blushing furiously. It was commonly taught that infatuation was itself a form of unchastity, and that a maid should not be proud that no man had touched her body if men had pierced her mind. And Thomas Seymour had more than pierced her mind. Like a fortress with its walls breached, he had invaded and entirely overrun it.

It did no good to confide in his new wife.

"How can you think such things of Thomas!" cried Lady Catherine Seymour, absently twisting the pearl ring on her finger round and round and round. "He's playing, Elizabeth. He is a spirited man, and he loves you like a father."

"But, Mother, the servants are gossiping. Kat says my reputation —"

"Kat is a foolish woman!"

Elizabeth was worried about her stepmother. Something, she knew, was terribly wrong. Catherine was not herself. The queenly confidence and serenity that had suffused her whole being were gone, replaced by a strange nervous discomfiture. She had done nothing to curtail either Thomas's early morning visits to Elizabeth's bedchamber or the rumors. They were beginning to spread even beyond Chelsea's walls.

"Listen to me, Elizabeth," demanded Catherine. "You must learn the first rule of a royal household. You are the princess. They are the servants. All their scandalmongering can do you no harm." Her voice, once so calmly modulated and assuring, had a new edge of shrillness. And the words she spoke . . . Even a child would know they were illogical.

"You always told me that a girl's modesty —"

"How dare you turn my words back on me!" Catherine shrieked. "Go now, leave me in peace and let me hear no more of your complaints about my husband. I've had three others before him, and I can tell you I have had more joy from Thomas Seymour in one year than from all the other three in a lifetime!"

﷯

Elizabeth squinted at her volume of Cicero in the muted afternoon light of the deserted schoolroom. Her beloved tutor, Asham, had taken suddenly ill with a flux and retired to his bed for the day. The other learned virgins of Lady Catherine's household had leapt at the opportunity for a day off from their lessons, but Elizabeth was well into her translation of the Roman statesmen's observations on the last days of the Republic. It was only her studies that gave Elizabeth any relief from her troubling thoughts, for these days Catherine had actually taken to joining Thomas Seymour in his early morning escapades, jumping into the bed with him and tickling the Princess unmercifully. And just last week the dowager queen had held Elizabeth's arms while Thomas had inexplicably slashed her gown to ribbons with a long knife.

It was all so confusing, thought Elizabeth. Why was Catherine acting so queerly? Could it be because she was finally pregnant with Seymour's child? The news filled Elizabeth to overflowing with equal measures of love and joy for Catherine — mingled with wholly unmanageable jealousy and terrible shame for her torrid secret fantasies about the husband of the woman she loved most in the world. She prayed fervently and daily for guidance, but found little help from God. So she turned back to her books.

Elizabeth was so involved in her translation that she never knew Thomas Seymour had entered until he quietly spoke her name. She turned, expecting the usual teasing playmate she had known, but was met instead by a sober and mannerly gentleman. Elizabeth searched Seymour's face and was alarmed to see tears threatening to spill from his eyes.

"Lady Catherine? Is she ill?" Elizabeth clutched Seymour's hands. He shook his head but offered no explanation for his miserable demeanor. "What then? Tell me, you must tell me!"

"I've had no courage, Elizabeth," he finally said, never letting go of her long white-fingered hands. "But I must say it now or go mad. I am afflicted with a terrible love for you which makes my marriage to the Lady Catherine no more than a painful drudgery."

Elizabeth felt as though the breath in her body had ceased altogether. She could not move. All words, all thoughts had flown out of her head with his declaration, as in a great commotion of swallows exploding from a cathedral dovecote.

"I married her for I knew that you would be left in her care after your father's death," he said quietly. "And I wished only to be close to your sweet presence. I knew no other way to make that so."

His tears washed his cheeks and his face gleamed with them, but Elizabeth was surprised to find only angry words spewing from her mouth.

"I may be nearsighted, but I am not blind, sir. You want me not for myself but for my royal blood and my nearness to the throne!"

As she accused him bitterly, Elizabeth wondered from what place these ideas had sprung so fully formed, for she had never before given conscious thought to such things.

"You don't love me. You don't love me!" she cried, praying with all of her soul that Thomas Seymour would quickly and vehemently deny her accusations, prove her harsh assessment altogether wrong. She had not long to wait. He'd fallen to his knees clutching her skirt in his hands.

"Do you think so little of me, Elizabeth, that you could have so low an estimate of my sincerity?" He gazed directly into her eyes and forced her with his will not to turn away. "And do you think so little of yourself? For with such sentiments you disparage your worthiness as a woman who could be adored by a man like myself. Do you not see how lovely you are? How desirable? I think . . . ," he went on, great passion causing his voice to quiver, "I think I shall die without you."

She was lovely. She was desirable. She was a woman, no longer a girl. And this beautiful man, he loved her. Loved her. An unbidden sigh of joy and relief escaped Elizabeth's lips. It was this sigh that the High Admiral took as his leave. He rose to his feet, swept the Princess into his arms, and kissed her deeply and soulfully as a man who loves a woman is wont to do, and as a young girl only dreams of being kissed. Elizabeth was drowning, tossed about in a great wave of sweetness and passion. Drowning. Dying . . .

"Oh God!"

Hearing these words as though from a great distance, Elizabeth struggled to pull herself from the deep. She opened her eyes to find Lady Seymour, bloated with pregnancy, slumped heavily against the schoolroom door.

Elizabeth and Seymour stood apart then, trembling and mortified. No one spoke. Elizabeth hardly breathed for the unbearable, unutterable shame of it. The silence was finally broken by two starlings squabbling on the window ledge. Elizabeth chanced a look at Seymour. His eyes were alive, darting. Inside his head, she could see he was forming his arguments, his excuses, his lies.

Catherine, mustering what dignity she retained, had turned and walked away. And Seymour, with no more than a stricken look at Elizabeth, followed.

Elizabeth's waiting lady opened one eye to find herself sitting across from Parry in the stuffy coach being bumped along the dusty road. "Aaugh, haven't we yet arrived?"

Parry signaled with his eyes that they were not alone.

Instantly Kat straightened her posture and forced a smile onto her face. For although the woman was as intimate a companion to Elizabeth as any person alive, she retained always a strict code of etiquette, and a firm sense of her place as servant to the Queen. "Your Majesty . . ."

"Have you had a good nap, Kat?" inquired Elizabeth.

"I wouldn't call it good, jounced as I was to Kingdom Come and back. But it passed the time well enough. Come, Parry, what have we in the basket to eat? I get hungry when I sleep."

"When are you not hungry, Mistress Ashley? I think one of those legs of yours is hollow."

Kat swatted old Parry with her fan and he pinched her bony knee in return. Elizabeth watched their antics, two old friends as easy with each other as they were with their charge, once princess, now queen. There was a time when things had been far from easy for all of them.

"So, you all sing the same song?" growled Lord Tyrwhitt.

Elizabeth refused to let her inquisitor see her trembling, though it pained her to think of Kat Ashley and the Parrys prisoners in the Tower, being likewise interrogated. This Thomas Seymour treason conspiracy had enmeshed them all.

"We do, Lord Tyrwhitt, for the song is the truth and so we cannot forget the words."

"I will ask you again, Princess. Had you any knowledge of the High Admiral's plot to kidnap your brother the King and foment an uprising?"

"And I will tell you again. I knew nothing, and my servants were ignorant of his rebellion as well."

"But you were to be his wife and the successor to the throne. Did you not realize that your marrying without written and sealed consent of the Council is strictly illegal and would have forfeited you your place in the succession?"

"I had no plans to marry Thomas Seymour." She struggled to keep her voice calm and steady, as her thoughts were not.

Marry a man who had betrayed his own wife and caused Elizabeth to betray her as well?

Marry a man whose sinister influence had sent Elizabeth in disgrace from her stepmother's house, the shame of which had destroyed her own health, and now placed her and her servants in mortal danger?

"But your man, Thomas Parry, spoke with Seymour on several occasions about that possibility," insisted Tyrwhitt.

"They spoke only of land, some his, some mine, which lies in close proximity. 'Tis a far cry from talk of marriage."

Tyrwhitt leaned very near Elizabeth, his face so close to hers that she could smell on his breath the stink of stale beer and onions.

"Rumor has it that you are even now pregnant with Seymour's child. Surely you plan to marry him?"

"That would not be possible," she said, defiantly holding Tyrwhitt's gaze. "The Lord Admiral is not at liberty, but a prisoner in the Tower of London." Elizabeth summoned the memory of Thomas Seymour's rugged face and tried to imagine what terrible passion had possessed him that he should steal into the royal palace and shoot the King's favorite watchdog in trying to reach her brother. She wondered what Seymour was now suffering in his captivity. Were they torturing him as they had already threatened to torture Kat and Thomas Parry for statements that would link the Princess with the traitor?

"What is your knowledge of the men and arms that Seymour had amassed in the West Countries to feed his rebellion?"

"I have no knowledge! How many times will you torment me with the same questions?"

"Until I have the truth from you," he spat.

Elizabeth felt her spine stiffen. Her words were clipped and icy as she spoke them.

"Lord Tyrwhitt, I had always believed you to be a toward and intelligent man. But to treat with someone who might one day be your sovereign as you would treat with a lowly beggar on the street, is nothing less than stupidity."

Elizabeth saw hatred flare in Tyrwhitt's watery blue eyes. To be spoken to thusly by a fourteen-year-old child — and a girl — was an outrage. But, Elizabeth mused, if ever there was a legacy from Catherine Parr it was her keen grasp of diplomacy. When to practice restraint. When to remain silent and protect one's loyal friends. And when to speak out with eloquence and fearlessness.

"I would caution you," she went on, "to have a care, my lord, for I am my Father's daughter and I have much of his anger, as well as his long and terrible memory for enemies to the crown."

⁂

Elizabeth's Master of the Horse galloped up to the carriage and rode alongside as he spoke through the open window.

"Your Majesty. We approach Oxted. What is your pleasure?"

"I wish to see as many of my subjects as is possible. And I wish them to see me. What preparations are made there?"

"The usual. Streets have been swept clean. All prostitutes and idiots are gone out of sight, the gallows taken down, houses and shops and public buildings freshly painted and decorated. And great crowds in the village square await your arrival."

"Send word that I'm coming into their town," she said to Dudley, "and that I await their sight with great pleasure."

"Yes, Majesty."

"And, Robin, have my horse brought round. I shall ride into the village."

Dudley smiled then, a smile so warm and proud that her queenly demeanor threatened to waver. He spurred his horse and disappeared. Her darling Robin. So loyal. So trustworthy.

So unlike Thomas Seymour. . . .

Seymour had died on the block. Elizabeth still trembled as she remembered how narrowly she had escaped with her life. Lady Catherine had not been so lucky. Three months after Elizabeth had been found in Seymour's arms and sent away in disgrace, Catherine had given birth to a little girl. She had sickened in childbed, but Thomas had delayed summoning a doctor for three days. The once regal dowager queen had grown frantic, perhaps suspecting that her wayward husband wished her to die. As her fever spiraled she'd given furious voice to her sense of betrayal, charging him and all those round her bed of caring nothing for her and laughing at her grief. Thomas, it was said, had lain down beside her to quiet her with gentle communication, but she had pushed him away, blaming him for keeping the doctor from her. Her fever had worsened still and she'd died two days before Elizabeth's fourteenth birthday. All the harsh deathbed accusations had been put down to the ravings of a delirious woman. But Elizabeth's grief for her stepmother was compounded by suspicions. It was contended that Catherine had regained her senses enough before she'd died to dictate a new will "in good mind and perfect memory and discretion" which bequeathed all of her great wealth to her husband. The deathbed declaration, though not signed by Catherine, was nevertheless hurriedly approved and accepted. Overnight Thomas Seymour had become a very wealthy man.

The Seymour affair had been Elizabeth's first lesson in the treachery of ambitious men. She had forgotten Thomas as one forgets a painful dream in the light of morning, pushed him far from her thoughts all these years past, till her mother's diary had plucked the images and memories from the furthest recesses of her mind.

Now the sound of church bells chiming out a welcome could be heard in the distance. Elizabeth imagined her entrance into Oxted. It would be the same as it had been in all the other towns and villages along the progress route. There would be speeches of welcome, plays and pageants and music, sweet children singing songs and reciting verse, all in her honor. She would stop and talk to the crowds, make a kind speech of her own, listen to a serious grievance or two that the town fathers might take this occasion to air. While her purveyors were buying provisions from local farmers and merchants she would visit the weavers' cottage, then perhaps choose a likely-looking house — grand or humble — and without warning ask for entrance, there requesting a small plate of food or a cool drink from her deeply honored but frantic hosts.

It was lovely to be bathed in so warm a wash of affection, and though she was weary and sore the Queen found her heart beating faster, anticipating her joyful entry into the village.

Not queen for six months yet, thought Elizabeth, and already I am greedy for the love of my people.

The bells chimed louder now and Elizabeth could see the first crowds of townsfolk, women in their Sunday finery, farmers with scrubbed faces, little children perched high on the shoulders of their fathers and brothers straining for a glimpse of Great Harry's daughter, their new and precious Queen Elizabeth. Yes, she thought as she smoothed back her unruly curls and straightened her jacket, she would give them a good look at Great Harry's daughter. A very good look indeed.

But on the morrow when she came to Edenbridge and her mother's home of Hever, the eager onlooker would be herself.

25 March 1527

Diary,

Sometimes I think my life, the one I live out breath by single breath is but a dream, the vague and swirling scenes of night are the reality. This day is such a one. For Henry, King of England has proposed to me that I should be his wife, the lawful Queen of England!

He'd pursued me and I'd resisted, made my self a quarry worth the hunt. I'd retreated home to Hever Hall where his letters sent by royal messenger followed me. Letters full of passionate oaths of love to be his mistress. He, claiming to have been "struck by the dart of love for more than a year" and apologizing for pestering and boring me. I wrote back refusing him, quoting his own Grandmother, Elizabeth Woodville who, whilst hot pursued by his Grandfather wishing to bed her said, "I may not be good enough to be your Queen, Sire, but I am far too good to be your mistress."

I'd used the wiles I learned in France, coquettry to drive him mad with wanting, tho honestly 'twas just a game that came most naturally to me. Mayhaps somewhere in my fondest dreams I saw my self as Queen . . . but they were fantasies! Now he claims the fantasy as true.

Having sent no messenger or warning here, Henry rode this early morning up to Hever moat and crossed the drawbridge into the cobbled court with clattering hooves that woke the house. He demanded immediate audience of my self, and in a rattled state I threw around me sundry robes, washed my face, chewed a mint twig to clean my teeth. Gathering what small dignity was possible at that ungodly hour I went to greet my King. He was in a wild state, mud splattered, red faced and almost shouting. He grabbed me, pulled me close to him, kissed me roughly on the mouth. He stank of sweat and smoke and horses, but his unbound passion was strangely sweet to me, so reminiscent of another Henry that I felt my own resolve melting neath his touch. He began to pace and stabbed his finger in the air to make his point.

"I have had enough of this accursed marriage!" he cried. "God's angry hand has smote my sonless matrimony long enough."

"But Katherine —" I began.

"Katherine is my sister in law. My brother's wife. Family to me and under canon law within forbidden degrees of affinity!"

"I do not understand how you can seek a separation from the Queen."

"The Pope will help me willingly. I'm Defender of the Catholic faith. Clement's granted other dispensations, voided royal marriages where problems of succession rose. He must only be shown the error. He will help me!"

"If anyone can make him see reason," said I most cautiously, 'tis you, Henry."

"And Cardinal Wolsey, he will help in this matter."

"What will Katherine say?"

"She will agree. I'll make her understand that we've been living in a sinful state these many years. And pious as she is, she'll take the holy vows and henceforth be a bride to Jesus. O Nan, Nan, Nan!" he cried like some mad creature. "Can you not see that I am sick with love? I cannot sleep. I cannot eat. I cannot rule my kingdom any longer. All I do is think about having you. I must have you! If I cannot, I swear I will break the world in two with my own hands!" Then he fell to his knees. "Marry me, marry me. Bring me sons and break this wretched curse upon my life!"

I stood still and silent as a statue as my mind flew wildly

from post to pillar. Good Christ, I thought, this man at my feet would depose a Queen for me, send her to a nunnery! Thro old Wolsey he would argue with the Pope in Rome to have me. How that would gall the Cardinal! So now beyond the title and the value of the King's own love, I could smell the odor of some sweet revenge in this.

"Say yes, Anne," cried Henry. "Say yes and be my Queen!" But as I stood in Hever Hall, a King kneeling at my feet, the morning sun warming the air and the stone beneath us, I felt such a chill foreboding draft, like some evil wind, that the answer froze within my throat. My hand went to my neck as if to coax it out, but it was useless.

"I shall have to think on this," said I. "Ponder your proposal, let you hear my answer when it comes to me to know."

He was speechless that I'd not leapt upon his offer. And if truth be known I'd shocked my self. But something odd, something cold held me paralyzed. I bade him go and that he did, muttering some low curses after womanhood. And that is where I stand even now, looking for a sign to show my future clear to me — doom or glory if I take this path with Henry. So I wait.

Yours faithfully,

Anne

9 April 1527

Diary,

I have just now returned from Canterbury with George, tho I spoke not at all to him on our ride home, for I was speechless. Speechless and trembling in my soul. I have had my future laid down before me like a midsummer's feast, and its glorious bounty overwhelms. Unless the Saints lie, I am to be Queen of England and will bear Henry's desired son. This I know to be true, and where once I foundered in a sea of fear and indecision, I now stand saved, feet planted firmly in the soil of English destiny. *Queen Anne.* This is how I know.

Henry pressed and pressed, showering me with promises and kisses. "I will marry you," said he, "marry you and put aside Katherine." The words tho pretty did ring false to me, for Katherine, of most royal Spanish blood, is loved by all and so devout she must have God's ear. But Henry was persuasive. This man who wages war with Emperors and fixes laws upon the land and counts his neverending gold, this man on bended knee was seeking to convince a lowborn girl to be his wife.

I was wild with indecision. Paced the hedge maze hour upon hour thinking on my destiny. Could I trust the fates and place my life within his hands? Or was it deadly folly to be playing such a game?

George, palace gossip in his ear, hurried home to be with me. I was glad to see that face, the steady brow, the warm brother's smile.

"Let us go and pay a visit to the Holy Maid of Kent," he said. "She can tell the future, so they say." I had heard of her, this peasant girl who counselled Kings and politicians, whose visions oft came true. And she was cloistered now in Canterbury not far from here.

'Twas east of Kent, a full day's ride on sodden country lanes. What sights, sounds, smells! The next day's market found a stream of farmers wives with loaded baskets filled with cabbages and artichokes, turnips, crayfish, peas and gooseberries. Cowbells clanked, oxen and their creaking carts sunk mid wheel into mud. Shepherds, sheep, goats, pigs, a rude horseman splashing as he flew past. Young peasant girls with muddy feet laughing, jostling, rough men who eyed me sulkily. Wet leather, damp wool in my nostrils. Then the spire of Canterbury Cathedral o'er a distant rise. More country folk now making rude camp outside the city wall, awaiting dawn's first light to sell their wares.

We rode in, found the Convent St. Sepulchre, asked to see the Holy Maid and were directly taken down a dank and narrow passage. I saw the women there, the sisters — some seemed holy, others simply noblewomen discarded by their families, left to rot. Those girls' eyes followed after me, jealous of rich clothes they'd never wear again. Stale, starched loveless lives hidden 'hind the cloistered walls.

A plain door was opened. There she was, the peasant girl made nun, upon her knees her back to me. The door closed. We were alone within her tiny cell. Grey stone, and no adornment here, no tapestries to warm the chill, no rugs or rushes underfoot. A narrow bed. Rough linen. No cushions on the chair. 'Twas dim in there except for light from one small window falling on the crucifix hung upon the wall, an altar where now the habitant of this spare room was kneeling, praying fervently. I'd made ready all my queries. She was still, had not stood nor turned to me when I heard a whisper.

"Anne." She knew my name!

"Holy Sister," then I said, "I have come to seek . . ." She turned, fixed her eyes on me. Those eyes, O Diary let me never see such eyes as those again! Molten gold, darting here and there. Terrible, terrible and mad. I saw the form beneath her novice robes, Elizabeth Barton, just a peasant girl, her skin still ruddy from sun. In fields, in muddy bogs her trances came, they said. She'd fall upon her knees and visions — Heaven, Hell, Purgatory, the souls who wandered there — were shown to her.

She spoke my name again, a childish voice both pure and sweet, she took my hands within her rough and callused grip. The bitten lips moved silently. A prayer? Divine words by God inspired? An answer to the Devil squatting on her narrow shoulder? I must have stiffened, for she said, "Be not alarmed, good lady, your destiny is set. Your life is here before my eyes. Wish you that I tell the seeing?"

"Yes, yes!" I cried. I wished to hear, yet something in me wished to go before the fateful words were spoke.

She closed her troubled eyes, lips drained of color, twitched, then uttered, "Ahhhyeee . . ." 'Twas not a word, 'twas more a breath, a lingering sigh. "I hold the hands . . . of a Queen."

My knees went watery but I held and stood against the tide. "Tell me more."

"Oh yes, there is more. A Tudor son shall rise up from your belly there to shine as England's brightest star, and will not set for two score years and four."

"A Tudor son!" I cried. "A son for Henry. Are you sure?"

The girl's eyes opened wide — a yellow stare — she could not see me, that was clear.

"I am tired," she moaned. I helped her to a comfortless chair. She was blind, pitiful, trapped still 'tween two worlds. "Go," said she. "Be the Queen. Be the Queen."

And so I went and travelled home, no words to share with my good brother. Too afraid to speak the prophesy. But now here within my grey stone room I find I'm ready to believe it true. The Nun of Kent did know my name and with no questions asked, could tell my life to me. My fate is done. Tomorrow I will write to Henry, tell the King the words he longs to hear. I'll be his wife, Queen Anne, and have his son.

Yours faithfully,

Anne

25 April 1527

Diary,

I have writ assent to marry Henry in a letter and have sent therewith a jewelled brooch to seal that new agreement. 'Tis a picture of a lady in a stormtossed sea. This lady I perceive as me, who knows the perils of such a promise 'twixt our selves, and still braves that violent sea in some flimsy ship named Love.

Love. I declared that state to him in my letter. I vowed a love as rare as his, but this was a lie. Tho I could never wish to have suitor more devoted or more passionate, and tho the gift he makes to me — to be the Queen — is more than I have ever dreamt, in my deep heart the place where truest feelings rest . . . I do not love him. My fervent hope, my prayer to God is that the day will come my heart will open like a rose in spring does open to the sun.

Till then, altho I've promised him my self, I still refrained from any pledge of us bedding ere a marriage binds us legally, that tho I most desired him, my virtue would forbid such tender congress. In this matter I spoke half truly. I should desire him. My future husband is a handsome man to any lady's eye — broad shouldered, solid chest and well muscled legs. A good jaw and healthy cheeks. He is fair, golden reddish hair, curly and yet abundant. Fine blue eyes that have a sparkle to them. But best of all, his mouth. Lips full and supple, teeth strong and white, breath sweet. I do enjoy the way he kisses me with that mouth — hard, insistent, soft then playful, and the way he smiles and laughs with it. I think that when he does, he is most beautiful of all men that I have known.

I asked my Sister Mary of Henry's prowess as a lover, but she keeps her counsel. So unlike her this closed mouth, so I poke and wheedle, coax and make her giggle but to no avail. She will only say that he's prodigiously endowed. But that's no news to me for I can feel the rod of hardness in our chaste embraces.

Does he love me truly? I believe he does. Will he make me Queen? I believe he will. O, Diary, I am grateful for this place to write in all confidence, for I have no friend whom I may trust with all these wild thoughts, outrageous events. You are my great secret and I shall guard you with my life.

Yours faithfully,

Anne

6 May 1527

Diary,

Having returned to Court I am held in such high estate as not before, this stemming from the King's open love for me and his attentions paid regularly. Most believe I am his mistress in both body and in spirit. None, not even Wolsey, will believe the truth, that I keep us chaste and that when Henry's will be done, I should be not concubine . . . but Queen.

But Queen or mistress, still my fortunes here amongst the highborn lords and ladies have grown substantially. They now come and seek my favor knowing how I have King Henry's ear. They call me friend.

"O Mistress Anne, if you please, my brother's son could use a good word in seeking a position in the Court."

"Good Lady, how lovely you are looking today." (He'll kiss my hand, then.) "May I speak with you about a piece of woodland that is under siege by poachers and needs policing from the King?"

O how I enjoy the grovelling. They must think me very stupid, that I would not remember how not long ago these same grand folks held themselves far above me — I the daughter of a common tho ambitious man, sister to the King's whore.

Yes, even Father's paying homage in his way. Sending every day the jewellers, women to care for my hair, silk women to my rooms. Always miserly before, he makes very sure the King's favorite lady looks the part. He tries to speak of how it is between the King and me, but I will not divulge how our liaison holds together. My Father dies to know. If I were the green girl I was before he'd box my ears, send me sprawling cross the floor, receive timely answers to all that he had asked. But I am no longer that child, and tho it gall him, still he holds me with a certain reverence, a fear. How very sweet this is.

Most strange to me is how Katherine, whose waiting lady still I am, regards me. She is neither deaf nor blind, must know my place in Henry's heart, yet treats me kind as ever. As I tend her daily needs I watch her closely, realize that here lives the woman who in all the world loves best the man who loves me. She cannot know what he intends for her, cannot know. For even if she knew his depth of love for me, she would see me only as a mistress, nothing more. For Kings, by ancient custom, are allowed that pleasure. Sometimes I feel a pain for her and stand inside her mind. She loves the King as I loved Harry Percy, maybe more since I was just a girl and Henry's been her beloved for many many years. I was made to watch, altho from far away, as Percy wed and bed another, as she must every day endure her husband's infidelity.

I should not think too long on this nor on my vast disloyalty to my Queen, or I will loosen my resolve. I must stand with Henry in his firm belief that England's greatest need is an heir, a boy, a son that I will give him, not his barren wife.

Too much of late I give myself to worrying. It seems that time goes by and naught is done regarding this divorce. I know the King is elsewhere occupied. The French envoy that's here to make a treaty tween France and England (and war upon Charles the Emperor) is foremost on his mind. Each and every day he and Wolsey sit for hours scheming, making plans and then convene for meetings of diplomacy with Frankish ministers for argument and bargaining.

When Henry comes to me in evenings after these dealings, I see the strains that crease his brow and hear the weariness within his voice. If he and Francis do not join in force against the Emperor, this man will surely rule the world. Already German lands and Spain are his. Charles holds as hostage Francis' two sons as he once held the King of France himself. Some evil trade — his freedom for his sons' imprisonment.

What an irony. France and England, ancient enemies, now made to join their forces or face defeat. Little Princess Mary is to be a pawn in these bargainings. She'll be wed to one of these captive sons when he is freed, combine the might and majesty of two lands in matrimony.

I often wonder how these things will change when I am Queen, mother of Henry's son. But for now I know the politicks must still proceed like all is well with King and Queen, else the chink within the armor will mean death to all the bargaining. I will keep my silence, trust that Henry's word is good.

Yours faithfully,

Anne

20 May 1527

Diary,

Patience I own was never my foremost virtue and it has vexed me sore to see my fate taking second seat to French and English bargaining. But negotiations finally done, a banquet and a celebration in the French envoy's honor then was planned, the likes of which had not been seen since the famous celebration — the Field of Cloth of Gold. I made my own plans, stood for hour upon hour in fittings for a gown that would outshine all others. I accosted my father for several jewelled necklaces, bargained with a parfumier for an essence said to work exotic spells.

In recent days I had befriended Maurice Mamoule, then secretary to the chief negotiator Vicomte de Turenne. He remembered me, a scrawny girl of twelve in Francis' Court and was delighted now to see how I'd risen in my influence, tho he believed as all believed that I was Henry's whore. This did not lower me in his eyes, coming as he did from so debauched a Court, rather raised me high in his regard. He'd kept me well informed of all the goings on, and in the few days before the banquet, said official rumor in his circles held that Henry might discard his wife. I bade him tell me more. The French envoy believed, as Wolsey hoped (for Wolsey championed France) that Henry's choice would be my French childhood playmate Renee, a Princess born and raised. My heart leapt. For word was out that Henry meant to rid himself of Katherine. And this French princess meant nothing to the King. She was unnaturally short and limped from a deformity. Henry, I knew, would never tolerate so imperfect a mother for his many perfect sons.

So I dressed with joy for that celebration, all in shiny black and deep purple trimmed ermine, causing some stir amongst the other ladies with my gown and jewels and scent, whilst making way with them at Katherine's side to the feast. What a day and night we had. Henry was magnificent in slashed yellow silk and diamonds, far too large for life, voice booming welcome to his guests, smile telling all of his French success.

The tiltyard was more grand than I had ever seen. Very long and hung with gaudy tapestries of purple fruit and flowers, cabinets filled with gold and silver plates and goblets as if to say, Look, here is our wealth, you are well to throw your lot in with us. First there was the jousting, very fierce and spirited, infused with dreams of future wars it seemed to me. Then several masques, one in which the Princess Mary played a central part.

She looked frail, younger than her eleven years inside her gilded garments, the thrall of rubies, emeralds, pearls. Her small voice faltered not at all, she spoke her lines with utmost dignity, so unaware her usefulness as royal pawn was coming to an end. At the banquet King and Queen presided grandly side by side. I watched and saw the love that flowed a river from Katherine's source to Henry's raging sea, but never did one drop of that ocean's love return to her. His eyes followed me. I was careful, taking my attentions elsewhere from the King. But each and every time I chanced to look his way, there were his eyes trained upon my self. Others saw him watching me. Katherine pretended not to see.

Just past midnight all the Lords of France emerged, now dressed as Venetian noblemen in royal blue and black velvet. The music filled the fragrant moonlit garden and the dancing was begun. First dance Henry bade Vicomte de Turenne to pair with Princess Mary. She bowed most gracefully and took the floor with him. Her mother glowed with warm Spanish pride. You could see her then expecting Henry to take her own hand. But in a trice her smile turned bitter. For Henry'd made his way cross the floor to none other than my self, and then for all to see extended out his hand. As terrible for my Queen that moment was, was wonderful for me. I met his eyes, thanked him silently with all my heart and took his hand. He held firm and as we moved to center I could feel no trembling there, just strong resolve. We took up the music and leapt into the galliard — a perfect moment — he'd publick made his love for me.

Yours faithfully,

Anne

N THE FLOOR-TO-CEILING LOOKING GLASS of the Queen's bathing chamber, Elizabeth watched in reflection as two of her ladies dressed her gleaming hair, braiding the red-gold locks with strands and clusters of tiny black pearls.

"Open, Majesty," ordered Lady Sidney, and Elizabeth obeyed, grimacing with lips pulled back like some growling beast so that her maid could clean the royal teeth with her enameled gold pick.

"Do you wish to be powdered this evening?" inquired Lady Bolton, holding out a pot of finely crushed eggshell and alum.

"I think not," said Elizabeth, accepting from Lady Sidney a crystal cup filled with marjoram water. She rinsed her mouth and spat into a bowl. "I am still young and fresh-faced enough to go without, am I not?" the Queen demanded, knowing full well that her ladies would spring to praise her youth and beauty in a boisterous chorus pleasing to her ears.

Elizabeth stood, shook away the ladies fluttering about her, and strode into her bedchamber where Kat and several more waiting women had laid out on her sprawling bed of multicolored wood this evening's attire. An array of fabulous jewels sat upon her silver-topped table and her favorite chair was strewn with a choice of delicate slippers. Throwing off her dressing gown, she stood quite still while the ladies carefully built the foundation of garments onto her, much as a manservant might build onto his master a suit of armor. First the stomacher was laced onto Elizabeth's already thin frame, flattening her belly and breasts into a V-shaped board.

"Have I a new pair of silk stockings?" asked the Queen, and instantly Lady Springfield brought forth two fluttering thick ribbons of fine knitted silk.

"Does Your Majesty like this new Italian fashion?" asked her maid of honor as she stretched the hose up one and then the other of Elizabeth's alabaster legs.

"I do love pretty things," replied Elizabeth, wriggling to let Kat slip the heavy purple velvet overgown over her head and begin fastening the row of a hundred pearl buttons at her back. "But dressing is not a passion with me, so much as an act of state. The French envoy is come to ratify our peace treaty, but this is also the first occasion on which they will meet me as queen, and so my person must be as magnificent as the glory that is England."

The Queen thought but did not say aloud that this week's lavish entertainment also carried a deeper meaning. For not only had her mother Anne been raised and educated in the court of Francis the First, but the friendship of the French had been her mother's great hope during the long struggle of her father's divorce from Katherine of Spain. They could not forget that Elizabeth was the daughter of Anna de Boullans, renowned for her great beauty, gaiety, charm, and sophistication. While the English might despise the Great Whore, her mother in the French perception was a figure whose attributes were to be emulated and hopefully surpassed.

As the purple velvet sleeves heavily embroidered in silver and gold were laced to the overdress, Kat held out two jewel-encrusted watches for the Queen to choose between.

"The flower or the ship, Your Majesty?"

"Neither. I'll have my father's brooch."

"As you wish." Kat needed both hands to lift the giant sapphire stone ringed with diamonds and rose rubies. As she clasped it to the center of the quilted purple bodice, she whispered to the Queen, "Ask after your cousin Mary and her husband newly made king."

"And what should I ask?" Elizabeth sounded mildly amused at Kat's typical impertinence. "Whether she is enjoying married life with her childhood sweetheart and her overbearing mother-in-law de Médicis? Or whether she's with child, a French prince who might one day lay claim to my throne?"

Kat wound strand upon strand of gleaming pearls round Elizabeth's throat, wrists, and waist. "You make fun of your old companion," sniffed Kat, "but that young Scots queen is your father's own niece, and must needs be closely watched. Now that she is queen of France as well, she will be trouble for you, mark my words."

"I always mark your words, Kat, but I think tonight is no time for such converse about my cousin Mary. Tonight is a time to celebrate a hard-won peace. Do you not agree?"

Kat looked away peevishly, but Elizabeth pulled the lined face to her with a finger under the chin and grinned, finally coaxing a smile out of the older woman.

"You look radiant, Majesty," said Kat with a final and imperceptible adjustment to the Queen's costume. "The night will belong to you."

Elizabeth glided out of her bedroom into the paneled Great Chamber where, already on his knees in advance of her entrance, was Robert Dudley lowering his head in further obeisance. "Your Majesty."

She stretched out her whalebone white hand to him, but so covered in great rings was it that he was only able to graze her fingertips with his lips. "Rise, Robin. Let me look at you," she commanded.

Instantly Dudley came to his feet and rose like a great sturdy tower in front of her. Tall as the Queen was, she had to look up to her Master of the Horse.

He really does love me, Elizabeth thought to herself. What I see in his eyes is an emotion not easily feigned.

Indeed, Dudley was this evening utterly overwhelmed by the regal presence of his childhood friend. He could not tell if the effect was caused by her pale luminescent beauty, the riot of gold and sparkling gems that glittered in the sunset light, or the hypnotic perfume which she made to waft round herself with tiny flutters of an ostrich feather fan.

"I am speechless, Elizabeth." He whispered these words in the fragile shell of her ear, for such public familiarity with the Queen was forbidden. "I envy the French ambassadors who will monopolize your time tonight."

"Do not suppose I'll have no time for you, Robin," she said, admiring his form in the peacock blue brocaded doublet. "I expect you to partner me in the first galliard of the evening."

"Your wish is my greatest pleasure," he replied and, placing her hand on his arm, escorted her toward the chamber where the French were gathered.

Whitehall had quickly become Elizabeth's favorite London palace, its huge sprawling wings spreading over more than twenty riverside acres. Built over several centuries, it was arbitrary in design, and many portions were antiquated, even falling into disrepair. But Elizabeth loved the stately halls hung with their splendid decorations, and delighted to see the great house teeming with her courtiers and ladies in their finest fancy for the evening's entertainment, all bowing and curtsying low as she passed on her handsome escort's arm. It was excellent to be the queen of England. Right and well deserved. I have at this moment, she thought to herself, not a care in the wide world.

"It makes them cringe when they bow to you that they seem to be bowing to me as well," said Dudley, suppressing a smile.

"You're right, Robin. I'd wager you're the most despised man at the English court."

He chuckled. "No doubt they'll find even more to complain about after this week."

"And why is that?"

"Because I've outdone myself in grandiosity with the preparations. Lavish and magnificent revelries in every respect. Food, decoration, music, masquing. Seeing it, you'll find it hard to remember you're nearly bankrupt," he said with a sly grin.

"Robin!"

"You agree the show for the French is most important," he said quickly to divert the Queen's sudden anger. "And it cost much less than it actually appears. For example, all the flowers were brought from your castle at Richmond, and the game birds —"

"All right, enough!" They'd stopped at the great carved doors of the Privy Chamber attended by what seemed like a small regiment of French and English soldiers. "I need a moment to compose myself."

"You will dazzle them, Elizabeth. You're like a sun that breaks through a gloomy English afternoon."

Elizabeth inhaled deeply as though to fill herself with what courage she yet lacked.

"I'm ready," she said finally, and Dudley motioned for the sentries to open the tall Privy Chamber doors. He watched as she swept majestically into the presence of the French ambassadors and their exquisite ladies, grand in their brilliant silks and broad-beamed farthingale hoop skirts, and accepted one dignitary on either arm — Monsieur de Mont Morenci and Monsieur de Vielleville. There under Holbein's masterpiece, a wall painting of the entire Tudor family, did Elizabeth begin to weave her spell around them all. She had cleverly positioned herself, Dudley noticed, under the huge and unnervingly lifelike portrait of the father she so perfectly resembled, as though to remind them all of her unquestionable royal lineage. Elizabeth was a magnificent woman and queen, thought Robert Dudley as he strode away to attend to the evening's entertainment. He would do everything in his power to secure for himself not only her love but the elusive Crown Matrimonial.

⚜

"I was a prisoner in the Tower of London for two months whilst I was princess, along with several noblemen who were charged with plotting my sister's overthrow on my behalf," said Elizabeth to de Mont Morenci and de Vielleville as they strolled the torchlit Privy Garden just after dusk. "I would surely have been put to death by her had it not been for the loyalty of my subjects."

They approached a large stone sundial set within an intricate fountain surrounded by thirty-four columns topped with gilded beasts carrying the Tudor coat of arms. Surely the garden's grandeur paled in comparison to many of the French palace gardens, but Elizabeth was determined to impress them into believing she was, even in her youth and femininity, as mighty a monarch as her great swaggering father had been.

"It tells time in thirty different ways," she bragged of the sundial.

"Almost as many ways as there are opinions concerning the path to peace between our countries," added de Vielleville with a cynical expression.

"Ah," sighed Elizabeth thoughtfully. *"Quo homines, tot sententiae."*

"Indeed, Your Majesty," said Mont Morenci. "There are as many opinions as there are men . . . and women, so it seems," he said with a respectful nod.

The sound of a dozen trumpets signaled that supper was served.

"Shall we, gentlemen?"

"Tout à vous," spoke the ambassadors in unplanned unison. They all laughed merrily at the good humor they shared in that perfect moment, and as if on cue a rainbow of colored water leapt from the many fountain spouts high over their heads.

Elizabeth led the Frenchmen toward a door made entirely of red-and-white Tudor roses and their leaves. Pushing it open they found themselves in the piazza under the vast windows of Whitehall's Long Gallery. Elizabeth gasped with delight.

The place had been transformed into an enchanted summer glade. Illuminated by torchlight and awash with the gentlest music of lute and virginal, its bower walls were draped with the thickest of silver and gold brocade. But the tapestry for all its richness was rendered nearly invisible by the riot of fresh flowers that covered the walls, ceiling, and ground of the pavilion. Wreaths and garlands of violets, wallflowers, primroses, kingcups, pinks, cowslips, and daffodils hung in vast variety and profusion, twisted and looped, dangled in tendrils and sprouted from supporting beams and arches. Behind the dais was a great mural portraying the Queen on a white stallion, conceived all in tiny tea roses. As Elizabeth entered the bower her slippers sank into a carpet of southernwood leaves, lavender, hyssop, and wild meadowsweet. The mingled fragrances were unimaginably delicious and the Queen, who normally abhorred strong odors, could not breathe deeply enough.

She paused, the French ambassadors on either arm, and together they watched as a sweet and impromptu farce unfolded before them. Each of the French ladies seated at the table took up the space of three people, so far to the sides did their farthingales extend. So the displaced English ladies in a mood of good fun had seated themselves upon cushions among the rushes on the ground where, comfortably ensconced, they were waited upon by the English gentlemen with much laughter and amusement.

There at the far end of the pavilion Elizabeth spotted Robin Dudley, the master showman surveying his fantastical creation. He was her man, she thought, body and soul. Her soldier. Her loyal servant. Her master. This last sent a shiver and a strawberry flush to the Queen's pale cheeks. Suddenly he turned and saw her. Their eyes across the bustling pavilion joined and locked together as a great red hawk and its airborne prey will do in the moment before the death strike. For the love that flew so swiftly from Elizabeth to Robin Dudley and back to her again was as hot and fast and strong as death on the wing.

All at once the Queen was converged upon by a dozen courtiers and ladies come to accompany her to the place of honor under a bower of hanging lilacs almost the color of Elizabeth's gown, and the marvelous sight of her beloved was obscured. No matter, thought Elizabeth, taking her seat flanked by the French ambassadors, this night is young and I shall yet have my way with it.

⚘

The wooden door swung open to reveal the warm firelit recesses of Dudley's private rooms. Elizabeth, in a hooded velvet cloak, stood across the threshold from Robin, his peacock blue doublet limp with dampness from the night of wild dancing, a warm and familiar smile on his handsome face. All the misapprehensions she'd felt about the brazen act of coming to his apartments melted clean away.

"Come in quickly," he whispered, and guided her inside. Gently he pulled her hood away and saw that Elizabeth was gazing around his rooms with a look akin to wonder.

"Is it the modesty of my apartments that gives you so much surprise, or the very fact that you've come to them?"

"That I've come to them," she said and smiled wickedly.

"I think we caused a great scandal already this evening, you and I," he said as he removed her cloak. "It was a state occasion. You should have danced with someone besides myself."

"I did! I danced with the ambassadors. One time apiece. And I danced with Lord Cecil."

"Elizabeth!"

"Well, I don't care. You're the best dancer and I am the Queen. I dance with who pleases me. And besides, it's only the English who took any notice," said Elizabeth, moving into the room. "The French are not so easily scandalized. Did you not see the way Madame de Vielleville flirted with young Lord North?"

Dudley laughed, remembering. "He was tripping over himself, he was so besotted."

"She is very beautiful."

"She is nothing next to you." His eyes softened then and his look upon her lost its sharpness. She saw him raise his hand to her, palm outward, and all at once felt her heart thump back in her chest. To another the palm placed just so was merely a peaceful salute. But to Elizabeth it was an echo from the past, a five-fingered token of childish love, half of a broken circle only she could mend.

Gazing across time she found herself in the greenwood behind Hatfield Hall. There were she and Robin then no more than nine years old, attired for the outdoors, tousled and flushed with exertion. Two brown geldings beneath a canopy of oak nibbled contentedly at the grass and damp moss under their hooves. Dudley was the smaller of the two children, for Elizabeth had always been a tall girl. But the boy's body was solid and strong and moved with uncommon grace. When they rode out from Hatfield as they often did when their lessons were done, racing and jumping rock walls and hedges, Robin spurred his mount with a fierce physical insistence that impelled the beast to great feats of strength and speed. Elizabeth somehow gained the same loyal performance from her steed through sheer force of love and will.

The children, smiling impishly, faced each other with their palms — his left, her right — pressed together. Robin spoke first. "Together we are a steeple."

"Together we are a *clam*," said Elizabeth and giggled. Her favorite quality in her favorite playmate was that Robin Dudley made her laugh and inspired her to bouts of silliness, perhaps the only levity the young princess was permitted in an otherwise tightly laced royal life. All at once Elizabeth noticed that her friend's gaze had changed. Where it had been playful it was now earnest. Where his eyes had darted here and there they were now fixed, seeming to study her in the way that together they would sometimes study the inside of a flower. And when he spoke, his voice too had changed.

"Together," said Robin quietly, "we are a prayer."

The sensation that passed through Elizabeth's soul was as subtle as the touch of a butterfly lighting on the back of her hand. And yet her child's heart was touched and lifted beyond measure. Without words to express her tenderness she simply pressed harder with her hand on his. He pressed back and the moment was magic. Elizabeth was suddenly aware of tiny flecks of dust gently suspended and dancing in the warm air, lit by the dappled sun glinting through the oak branches. She was aware of birdsong so clear and lovely she thought she might cry from the sound of it. And of Robin Dudley whose moist warmth through the blue doublet radiated out to enfold her like two arms. He, too, was transfixed by the strange and wonderful moment.

Then, since they were neither of them able to break from it, nature prevailed and did it for them. A push of wind in the branches above sent a rain of dead, prickly-tipped oak leaves down upon their heads. Surprised, the children laughed and their hands separated. The spell was broken.

"What shall we play at?" demanded Elizabeth.

"I've brought dice."

"I don't feel like dice."

"Shall we catch a frog and examine it?" he offered, half expecting Elizabeth's dramatic sigh of refusal. "All right then, we shall play Queen and Courtier."

"Robin!" Elizabeth squealed.

"What? You like the game. Indeed you play it very well."

"I do like it," admitted Elizabeth. "But we should not play at it."

"And why not?"

"Because . . . it's treasonous."

"Only because it's *you* playing it," he responded mildly.

"Well then . . ."

Robin grabbed a curl that had escaped from beneath Elizabeth's cap and dandled it teasingly. "You don't like the game because you wish to be queen and fear you never will be."

Elizabeth felt her pale face flush hot and red. "I don't want to be queen! My brother is the heir and I love Edward!"

"I'm sorry, I meant no harm, Elizabeth. And it's no harm to pretend, really it isn't." With that Robin, one foot slightly in front of the other, doubled over in the most extreme bow he could achieve, arms swept out from his sides like the wings of a hawk. As he rose he brought them together, fluttering and weaving his hands in a hilariously exaggerated gesture of obeisance which wrenched an unexpected laugh from Elizabeth's throat.

"Your Maaaaaaajesty," he intoned in the most lugubrious voice the nine-year-old could muster.

Elizabeth took up the game. "Sir Dinglebelly," she replied with excessive seriousness.

Robin lifted one eyebrow. "Have you knighted me, then?"

"Oh yes, don't you remember the feast I held in your honor? Your whole family were there, all seated above the salt. Your father was very proud, and your brothers were very jealous."

"Of course, how could I forget such a magnificent celebration? And didn't you grant me six great houses, twenty thousand head of sheep, and a cupboard full of gold plate?"

"Have you forgot the horses?"

"No, Your Majesty! A stable full of them. You have been most generous with me."

"Indeed I have. And what, pray, have you brought me, Sir Robert?" Elizabeth, fully engaged now, turned and swept imperiously away from her friend. "Your queen, aside from flattery, demands gifts, you know. Rich treasures. Fortunes. Rare books. Jewels. Exotic animals."

"Like the green talking parrot I gifted you last week."

"He sings my praises very cleverly," said Elizabeth, spinning the story into an intricate tapestry, pacing under the arch of branches as though it were a stately presence chamber. "God bless Queen Bess," squawked the girl in the imaginary parrot's voice. "You are more fair than the loveliest Tudor rose and smell more sweet, more sweet, more sweet, aarrgh, aarrrgh!" Then she was in her own voice again. "But that was last week. Where is *this* week's offering?" she demanded petulantly.

The little boy grabbed Elizabeth's hand and uncurled her fingers. In her palm he laid an object. It was a stone, not unusual in its smooth blackness, but a small miracle of shape. Though obviously natural and clearly uncarved, it was as perfect a heart as nature could have designed. All pretense of the game fell away as Elizabeth contemplated the perfection of the object and the significance of the gift. For the second time that afternoon she was struck dumb.

Robin Dudley, too, had abandoned the game of Queen and Courtier. "Do you like it?" he demanded excitedly.

"Yes, of course I do. Where did you get it?"

"That's my secret."

"Come, tell me! It's amazing. I must know, Robin."

"I won't tell you." His chin hardened in determination.

"You must. Your queen commands it," announced Elizabeth haughtily.

Robin thought for a moment before jumping back into the fantasy. "I am at your service, Majesty. Your wish is my command. But first, may I not receive a kiss in return for my gift?"

"No you may not!" shouted Elizabeth in mock outrage.

Suddenly in a grandly theatrical gesture Robin threw himself prostrate on the ground and began kissing the velvet hem of Elizabeth's gown. "Oh Majesty, Majesty, let me kiss your hem, your feet, your petticoat, your ankles!"

Elizabeth giggled, and as Robin pulled himself up her skirt to his knees spouting courtly gibberish and various parts of her anatomy and clothing that he might kiss, Elizabeth roared with uncontrollable laughter till tears streamed down her face and they were bent over clutching their bellies and gasping for air.

"Come, let's ride," said Robin when he could finally catch his breath.

"Where shall we ride?" Elizabeth asked, praying for an answer that would crown this timeless moment as it deserved to be done.

The boy looked far back into her liquid amber eyes and saw the challenge that this pale golden girl laid before him. And because he knew her so well and loved her even then, he replied in the voice of an adventurer, a pirate, a king.

"To the future," he cried. "Let us ride to the future!"

Indeed they had, Elizabeth thought, smiling as her mind, like some great invisible bird, soared forward again across time, depositing her in Robin's firelit rooms. Here before her was the same handsome boy, a blue doublet, his hand up, palm facing her.

"Together we are a prayer," he whispered, matching her smile with his own. Slowly she joined her hand to his, pressing palm to palm, fingertips to fingertips. Yes, thought Elizabeth, he was the same boy, the one who could endlessly amuse her, reduce her to helpless laughter. The same loyal and trustworthy lad who, before there'd been any hope of her taking the throne, had sold off parcels of his own land to pay her debts. The brave man who had dared to rebel against her sister Mary, and stood as a rock during their dark days as prisoners in the Tower. And, mused Elizabeth, he was the only one who had ever learned his way through the twisted maze to her heart.

Now her eyes fell on a group of miniatures displayed on a table and she moved closer to see them.

"Your family," she said quietly. All of the Dudleys — save Robin and his brother Ambrose — were now dead. She lifted one of the gilt-framed portraits, this one a distinguished but leaden-eyed man of forty.

"My grandfather Edmund," said Dudley, peering down over Elizabeth's shoulder. "Loyal servant and instrument of King Henry the Seventh."

"*My* grandfather . . ." Elizabeth's voice trailed off as she remembered the stories she had heard about the first Tudor king, who had taken the throne of England by force. The first English king who had realized that money equaled power. And this man whose picture she held in her hand, Edmund Dudley, had been the King's own instrument in attaining a great fortune.

"I have heard," Elizabeth began again, "that Edmund Dudley used, let us say, less than savory methods to enrich the crown."

"Extortion is a generally unsavory practice," agreed Robin with a wry smile. "And he tended to enrich his own coffers quite substantially in the process."

"He was not very well liked?" asked the Queen somewhat rhetorically.

"Despised is closer to the mark. He was in fact likened to a 'ravening wolf.'"

"Did you know him?" asked Elizabeth.

"I did not have the chance." Dudley bent and made the motion of dusting the tiny portraits with his finger, but Elizabeth could see the gesture covered a deep discomfiture in a man who was always comfortable.

"Because my father had him executed," offered Elizabeth.

The slight slump of Dudley's shoulders told her she had struck home. "One might think Henry would have been grateful. He'd inherited four million pounds on his father's death, nearly all of which had my grandfather . . . procured for him."

"It was the beginning of my father's reign. He wanted desperately to be loved by his people." Elizabeth swallowed as she defended her father's murderous behavior, feeling the tug of understanding for the dilemmas faced by a new monarch. "I think he must have yielded to popular pressure."

"But to call it treason . . ."

"It wasn't fair, Robin. But my father, you know, was not well known for his fairness." Elizabeth reached past Edmund Dudley's portrait and lifted another of the miniatures, this one's frame studded with tiny pearls.

"I think you look quite like your father."

"Another traitor to the crown," Dudley intoned bitterly.

Elizabeth stroked his cheek with the back of her hand. "The Tudors and the Dudleys. We are so tightly bound each to the other. So tightly bound."

Now suddenly it was Elizabeth who was uncomfortable. She shook the thought from her mind — the thought that Kat had so insidiously planted there — that Robin Dudley, from a long line of treasonous scoundrels, had "bad blood" running in his veins. She turned and placed John Dudley's miniature back in its place.

"So, do you like my small family gallery?" Dudley asked, moving to Elizabeth's side where he stood near without touching her. A strong silent current flowed between them.

"I do," she said. "But where is your mother?"

"My mother was too modest to sit for her portrait," he answered as Elizabeth moved toward the fireplace to warm her hands. Dudley stiffened. A letter lay open on the mantel and even now the Queen's eyes were feasting on its private contents.

"Dearest husband . . . ," she read aloud and turned to him blazing with challenge.

"Do you in fact keep up a lively correspondence with Amy, so far from court, poor woman?"

Dudley could see a storm of conflicting emotions scouring Elizabeth's face. He wished desperately to answer in a way that would please her. "She attends to household business as good wives do and keeps me in full intelligence," he replied finally.

"Business is it?" Elizabeth plucked up the letter and held it to the light of the fire to read, knowing it was a childishly wicked thing to do, knowing Robin cringed and sweated with every word.

" . . . so I've made haste as you requested and sold the wool directly off the sheep's back, tho at a small loss which could not be helped, so that you might discharge the debt you are so anxious to make good."

Elizabeth appeared relieved and not without contrition as she replaced the letter on the mantel. "Have you need of money? I will see to it that you have all you require."

"I don't want your money. I want you, Elizabeth." He reached for her but she moved away before his hands could grasp her.

"Then you're a fool, Robin. If I offer you titles, properties, gold, then you will take them and prosper. I am the Queen. I cannot, after all, be surrounded by paupers."

He could see the sweetness of the moment slipping inexorably away like fine sand in an hourglass.

"Is she well, then? Amy, I mean?" The Queen's face had grown hard and she touched a throbbing vein that showed purple through her parchment skin.

"Why are you doing this, Elizabeth?"

"*Is she well?*"

"Not entirely. There is a growth in one of her breasts."

It was as if an invisible hand had slapped the Queen suddenly. All imperiousness vanished. She faced Robert Dudley and asked with the look of a guileless child, "Is it bad? I knew a woman once, Lady Windham, who died from such a malady. Died horribly."

"No, my love," said Dudley, putting his arms around Elizabeth gently, "she is not dying," and wondered silently if that was news to make them glad or unhappy.

"Oh Robin, love, why is our lot in life so hard?"

"You well know the answer. But the reason for our misery is, as well, the answer to our darkest troubles. It is because you wear the crown of England. You are entirely responsible and you are all-powerful. You may in all things do as you please. You can raise me or lower me. You can make me king or see me executed on Tower Green. I am your creature, Elizabeth, and my fate lies wholly within your hands."

Dudley released Elizabeth and turned away to hide his wounded eyes from her sight. For all his postures and strutting and confident intimacy with the most powerful woman in his world, he was deeply humbled by the truth of his own words.

"I'm feeling suddenly tired, Robin. Will you forgive me if I do not stay?"

"Forgive you, Majesty?" He laughed softly to himself and turning back to face her, swept into a low and graceful courtier's bow. "If you sent me to hell for eternity I would forgive you, Elizabeth. But I will not let you leave me here tonight without a kiss."

She flew to him then like a moth sucked into the thrall of a great flame. As he crushed her within his arms the two, unsullied by the tortures of guilt or fear or pain, found a moment illuminated by the brilliance of purest desire and tenderest love. She was no longer queen nor he her creature.

1 June 1527

Diary,

A most happy day this, for Henry's taken steps which in their final dénouement allow for us to marry. Most cleverly conceived, this plan has Cardinal Wolsey calling Henry *as defendant* into ecclesiastic court to prove legality of his bond in marriage to Katherine. Is the logic not quite clear? Let me explain as Henry did for me on this evening's visit.

Firstly, Wolsey knew the King desired a legal severance from the Queen, tho he'd been less than forthright with the

Cardinal who still believed the object of a further marriage was not me but the French Princess Renee. So Wolsey, papal legate that he is (that is to say he acts with independent rule from Rome, to oversee the moral virtues of the souls in England) convened today at York a secret court comprising wise, respected churchmen to decide the royal fate. Of course these learned men are cleverly pick'd, among them William Warham Archbishop of Canterbury, whose opinion years ago upon the papal dispensation granting Henry leave to marry Arthur's widow, did then dispute its true legality. Henry says that shortly Wolsey will give sentence of divorce after which the Pope in Rome will confirm this wise decision.

Most important tho, is this convention's secrecy. For if Katherine knows of it she must sure petition both her nephew Emperor Charles and, too, the Pope himself. But all was handled quietly, said Henry, all participants, boats and barges come to Wolsey's landing stage, the prelates retiring to a castle room with neither pomp nor circumstance.

The Pope knows Henry as his friend and champion from early days when the English Prince did most heated battle against Luther. (A small digression . . . I have never spoke to Henry of my love for Protestant ideas. I do not think it prudent now. It does not serve our present cause. But one day when we are man and wife and bound by ties of children and love and time I'll speak my mind . . .) In deed, Henry loves the Pope and may be the staunchest Catholic King in Christendom. And tho this plan is clever wrought and will result in worldly benefit, Henry (quoting always Leviticus) does believe most truly in its Godly course.

Wolsey, for his part in this ecclesiastic court, is held in high regard with gratitude by Henry since instead of looking like a man who wants to shed a wife, the King *defends the accusation by the court* that he and Katherine broke the Church's law and lived in sin. When the papal bull allowing their cohabitation as husband and wife is brought forth to justify his actions, the Cardinal and his men will rush to show its innocent but grievous wrong and then a quick annulment will result.

Henry, on this night, tho tired was flushed with joy, and

feeling hope that this timely legislation will prevail and make us two as one. I pray with all my heart that this is so and I can give the King his son.

Yours faithfully,

Anne

21 June 1527

Diary,

Hope has turned to horror, joy to grief. For madness rules in Rome. German and some Spanish mercenary soldiers of the Imperial army, tho mutinied against the Emperor, have sacked the sacred city in a bloody massacre. Maiming, murdering, looting all the churches' treasuries. Marauding door to door. Priests, Cardinals, tortured, killed. Nuns raped, beheaded. Atrocities beyond imagining. Despoiling relics of the Saints, smashing holy altars. The Vatican made a bloody stable. Pope Clement now hides from harm cross the Tiber in the Fortress of St. Angelo.

And there's the rub. Whilst I mourn for the humanity, still my selfish thoughts prevail. For Wolsey's court and ruling on King Henry's marriage does require confirmation from the Holy Father for its true legality. But now himself a prisoner of the Emperor, he dares not further anger Katherine's kin with such a dispensation that would make her marriage mockery — change a Queen to royal whore, a Princess to a well dressed bastard.

So whilst refusing to admit his failure, Wolsey did adjourn the secret court (secret to no one — Katherine knew of it in hours), then set out all in grand measure, as he is wont, to France where there he hopes to make a pact with France for war with Spain, and aid the Pope, free him if he can. But I suspect, like Henry does, that Wolsey hopes to fail and then achieve instead the Papacy for himself.

I watched by Henry's side as Wolsey's great procession, scores of men in black velvet, church accoutrements, Great Seal of England left the gates of Westminster. He told me then, "The

Cardinal promised me to soon revive my secret matter when the peace is made. Do you think he failed me, Anne?"

I answered, "He's ambitious for himself, remember that. You and I truly stand alone against the world. Whilst Wolsey's indisposed in France we must proceed most independently."

He took my hand, held it to his beating heart. "I must face Katherine. Break with her, no longer live as man and wife."

"Yes, you must," I said and moved his hand to my own breast. He flushed, kissed me hotly. "Go tomorrow," I whispered in his ear. And so he shall and bear the news of their marriage ending, as I steel myself from all compassion of her, or have no way to live with my self.

Yours faithfully,

Anne

6 August 1527

Diary,

I am back at Hever Castle for the summer months whilst the King hunts with all his men in progress thro the countryside. When Brother George took leave of that manly gathering to visit me I learned that I was sore mistaken thinking I and Henry were alone in wishing for our marriage to be done. You see, my family — father, uncle Duke of Norfolk, brother — stay close by his Majesty's side, plotting, scheming, putting forward plans on my behalf (and so on theirs). In deed, their fortunes as the future kin of the King are rising fast. Henry's given them extra lands, titles and more close congress with himself. Like a family of spiders they weave a web round the King, its strong gossamer threads drawing him closer, catching prey to feed his appetites. I do not like this family business, but for now have no choice in it. Tho I rule Henry's heart, men still rule the world.

George brings with him much news of Wolsey, still in France. The pork bellied pig in a red hat — George calls him that — was trying for his own advantage, to devise a papal government in exile, in the city Avignon. As self appointed saviour of the Church he would of course take the part of Pope whilst Clement's captive still. That plan required Henry's leave; but the King sent instead a bull directly to the Pope asking him to grant Henry his permission then for nothing less than bigamy. This letter Wolsey intercepted. George says Wolsey knows now that I'm the object of the King's desire to wed, not his French Renee. He is furious but more than that he's terrified. Terrified and helpless.

George saw the letter Cardinal Wolsey wrote the King. It begged Henry to withdraw the document, protesting that he wished nothing more from life than bringing to a happy close Henry's "secret matter," signed "with the rude and shaking hand of your most humble servant and chaplain, T Carlis Ebor." T Carlis Ebor in deed. Fat fool. I hope he chokes on his syrupy words.

Then George showed me a velvet pouch and pulled from it a rolled document, closed with Henry's scarlet sealing wax. 'Twas a second missive to the hostage Holy Father, he said, to be carried to St. Angelo by our very trusted rector of the Church in Hever, John Barlow. George said we could not open it, but I desired to see the contents of this document which made a case for Henry's marriage to my self. I coaxed and threatened George and on the night before the letter found its way to Barlow's hands, my brother and I crept down the castle stairs into the dark kitchen now deserted but for scurrying rats. We boiled a pot of water and most carefully did steam the letter open and by flickering candlelight read the plan concocted by the King and those who wish to see me Queen.

It did not mention me by name, that's so, but its intent was clear: let the Pope allow Henry's marriage to a woman who might be related in the first degree of affinity. This, George said squinting at the dispensation, referred to Henry's intimacy with our own Sister Mary. Was this wise, I asked George, since Henry's own link to his brother Arthur was the very case for his own marriage's dissolution? George would not say that it was wise or not, just pressed me hard to quickly finish reading.

There next was brought to issue Henry's right to marry a woman who might earlier have been contracted in the state of matrimony to another man (though without its consummation). This was clearly meant for mine and Henry Percy's sake. This clause I felt was wise, for there were those who'd surely use that young contract of love against a royal marriage. I forced my heart then not to quail in thinking of my sweet Percy and our sundered fate. It was in the past, and only the future now remains.

We read the final issue in the tract. I neither knew to cry or laugh and George was simply shocked. It would allow the King to marry someone whom he'd swived!

"This last clause is quite unnecessary," I quipped and started sealing up the document. George looked at me with wicked questions in his eyes. "Listen closely, Brother. I am not the King's lover nor will ever be if not the Queen. I'll not lay down without the Crown upon my head and that's a fact."

"And here I thought the iron spine within this family in our Father's back," he said. Then with candle in hand he led me up my spiral stair to bed. "You do amaze me, sweet Sister."

And truly Diary, I do amaze my self sometimes.

Yours faithfully,

Anne

22 November 1527

Diary,

O 'twas a day of sweet revenge! Two weeks have passed since Court has moved to Richmond Palace and I, the only object of the King's desire, moved with it. There he's doted on my self keeping me close at his side as tho I am some necessary appendage. He speaks freely to his councillors with me there, tho as of yet he does not seek my counsel on the issues of state, but only on the matters of divorce, remarriage and succession to the throne.

News of Wolsey on his foreign mission'd come to us and it was clear his labors there had been for naught. No Papal seat at Avignon had been arranged, nor peace, nor help for this divorce.

Wolsey'd learned of our missive to the Pope and no doubt felt betrayed. Worried, too, that my Father whispered in King Henry's ear a most malicious suit against him self, the Cardinal hurried back from France. He'd come home weak and empty handed and when directly he did ride from Dover straight to Richmond Palace, sent his messenger to Henry asking whether and when the King would soon receive him.

I was standing there with Henry when the Cardinal's man came asking for direction, knowing well the King should see him privately as 'twas always done. Before he'd finished speaking, my mind flew to past betrayals, remembering the Cardinal's most heartless choice of action in the case of Percy and my self. How he'd called me that "foolish girl yonder in the court." Now 'twas he the foolish one, and so I spoke before the King could do and answered with a question to the messenger, in a high and stately air, "Where else should the Cardinal come but here, where the King is?"

The man stood and stared at my audacity to answer for the King, then looked at Henry for more proper a reply. But Henry must have thought my answer clever or was him self annoyed of T Carlis Ebor and spoke, "As the Lady says." With these words the messenger went pale, no doubt perceiving his next chore — to pass the message on to Wolsey. Wrath upon wrath is heaped upon the messenger who brings bad news, 'tis said. So sickened at the thought, he turned and left.

Henry said nothing to my self but neither did he bid me leave for Wolsey's coming. And so when at last the Cardinal came, still dusty from his ride and not much full of dignity he knelt before the King and therefore as I stood at Henry's side — *he knelt before me*. His cheeks showed crimson, eyes cast down to meet the floor, speech faltered trapped between hot rage and fear.

Then he rose and they did speak together of many things, but I swear I could not hear at all, for in my head the bells were chiming loud and happily. The man in red was bettered by a girl and for his cruel deeds he'd been repaid.

Yours faithfully,

Anne

16 January 1528

Diary,

How very strange it is continuing as waiting lady to Katherine. Convention and civility prevail between the King and Queen despite the truth that I must one day soon usurp her. When I look at her, steely eyes ablaze with courage for the fight, quivering nostrils, mouth hard and resolute, a shudder passes thro me. I do admit I lack the confidence that Henry has, of Katherine's surrender to his will. He says he knows her well and that she'll bow to him. I watch her closely but as yet she shows no signs of weakening.

Many nights she bids me play at cards with her and other ladies. I wonder sometimes, are the invitations meant to keep me in her sight and far away from Henry? Last night we sat cross the table, Katherine and I. Her eyes, I saw, would fall upon my hands and she stared quite openly at my sixth finger, impossible to hide. At first this did annoy me, then it made me bold. I used the hand more frequently, with graceful sweeps and flourishes making much of my abnormality, the other ladies holding back their smiles at my audacity. The Queen grew colder still and very quiet. The game continued and in the course of play I dealt to my advantage . . . the King of Hearts. The poisonous card did lay between us on the table, the gaudy painted monarch lying on his back. No one moved. No one spoke. The air was rich with jealousy — hers for my future, mine for her past. The Queen broke the silence then, her heavy Spanish accent brimmed with bitterness.

"Mistress Anne, you have the good hap to stop at a King. But you are not like the others. You will have all, or none." Then she folded up her hand, placed her cards upon the King . . . and left. My heart froze inside my chest. For just then I'd felt the shock of having for an enemy a great Queen in whose veins flowed generations of royal blood. No matter if I marry a King, even when the Crown shall rest upon my head I will never have her majesty, the surety of lineage, superiority.

What have I then? Henry's love? My family's ambition? The promise of a half mad Nun? But if truth be said, what drives me to an unknown fate is my own desire for a better hand than what my life has dealt to me. Katherine sees correctly. I have had the good hap to stop at a King, but with this single card I shall play one grand and dangerous game — win it all . . . or lose everything.

Yours faithfully,

Anne

29 March 1528

Diary,

The humbled Cardinal, after his return, has made most diligent effort for the King and I to wed. My Father, touting his own shrewd perceptions in the case, brought me aside to give me guidance and I bit my tongue to listen. He told me it would serve me well to make the Cardinal my friend. "'Tis still within his power to make or break your fate," he said. The word was that the Pope, of late, had fled from Rome and seeking safe asylum, found the town of Orvieto — plague ridden as it was — a place beyond the arm of raiding soldiers of the Emperor. From here Wolsey hoped the Pope would send a kindly answer to his pleas.

As my father spoke to me of plots and plans I saw he spoke as to a peer, not to his youngest daughter Nan. I swear something moved inside me then, some power that grew with every uttered word. My soul felt very large and still and open like a sunlit field. I was content, magnanimous. And so I thanked my Father for his good advice and promised that in future I would give old Wolsey some respect and love for his part in this affair.

And so I have. He and Henry lately brought to service in our cause two Gentlemen, Doctor Edward Fox and Doctor Stephen Gardiner who on their way with letters to Clement in Orvieto, came to pay me their respect and prove that their employers were most eager for the swift conclusion of the task. They brought a note from Henry to my self which told me he prayed that he and I should have our desired end, which would bring more ease to his heart and more quietness to his mind, than any other thing in the world.

And then a second missive which was a list compiled by Wolsey and the King of all my virtues which shall be read aloud by emissaries Fox and Gardiner to the Pope. This masterpiece of praise made me smile, even laugh with great delight. For I'm a sober maid and meek, have purity of life and true virginity. I'm wise and beautiful with high and noble blood, educated, mannerly and apt to bear a hearty brood.

To grant more hope to hostage Clement, Henry sent a herald to the town of Burgos, that proclaimed a war with Charles the Emperor. 'Twas only an empty threat, for he would never go to war with Spain or Flanders, or surely lose the markets there for wool. But Henry knew the French were making swift advance down Italy and soon its soldiers would free the land and Holy Father too.

So we wait for word. The winter days outside are grim and chill. But here inside the castle walls I'm wrapt warm beneath the cloak fashioned out of Henry's love. There is much hope and even happiness. He holds me almost chastely, so convinced is he we'll have success, soon be wed and quickly bed. But it's more the Cardinal that surprises me. Each and every Monday night when Court is placed in London, Wolsey entertains us lavishly. Great feasts and solemn banquets at his homes of York and Hampton Court. We dine on plates of solid gold, dance and masque and make quite merry, sometimes stay to greet the dawn.

For his kind administration I have sent of late to Wolsey a letter from my self thanking him for his good deeds on my behalf with promises to make a just reward to him when I am Queen. As I wrote the humble words of praise for him I had to stop and ponder at it, when so short a time ago I'd wished him ill or even dead. Am I a two faced girl with wild and shifting loyalties? Or do I truly mean what I have said? I am sore confused at this. I believe a person can change. But who has done the changing here? He seems sincere. And even if his motive is impure (he loves the King and fears his wrath) his actions are the fact. If by his machinations he does make me Queen, am I the one to say I love him any less because he does not love me truly? I think not. And so for now he is my friend, as we wait for news from Italy.

Yours faithfully,

Anne

3 May 1528

Diary,

The doctors Fox and Gardiner, braving tortured seas and flooded rivers finally found the Pope in Orvieto. Their several letters in reply from Clement made us hopeful. The Holy Father, tho pitiful amidst the squalor of his tiny expatriate rooms, did promise them to grant our two requests. One — a trial for the determining of Katherine and Henry's marriage should take place on English soil. The Pope would send his Cardinal Campeggio, a most impartial judge, to serve with Wolsey on the case. And two — that when these priests had given judgement, it would stand as final, no challenge by the Roman Curia or any other hand.

The emissaries' letters told how Clement claimed he'd stand with Henry even if the Emperor complained, and we were full of joy. For these documents, we waited with expectancy all spring. Meanwhile Cardinal Wolsey did continue granting favors to our family — the fair settlement of that old dispute of Piers Butler's northern lands, giving Father not only property but more important the title Earl of Ormond, making me the daughter of that titled man.

In this time of waiting, too, at Greenwich some fell ill with smallpox, and Henry saw fit to move me to some rooms above the tiltyard there to keep me far from harm. This chamber, tho never used for sleeping rooms, was most cheerful — large windows o'er the yard and very sunny. More important was the privacy, so Henry came quite often and we had some merry afternoons. He wrote me songs which then we sang and played on flute and virginal. He spoke to me of battles, clashing swords and armors, his men and their bravery in them. 'Twas strange that when he spoke of these manly things he seemed more like little boy to me than King. I saw some spark of human kindness that I liked and thought, yes, this man who fights like a soldier to be my husband will make me happy. And so we waited for these documents.

Then yesterday as the sun was falling there stood outside my chambers in a golden light a man I hardly recognized. 'Twas Doctor Fox, mud splattered and weary, having come from crossing at Calais and riding night and day in haste to bring us tidings from the Pope. He had brought with him signed documents from Clement giving full permission for the court in England! I gave him wine and meat and bread and sat him by the fire. Then Henry came and as the envoy ate he spoke of all wiles and wise maneuvers Doctor Gardiner made withal the Pope to bring a fruitful ending here. A frightful battle it had been with Clement's strong objections soundly trounced by threats and compliments. Then tearful he'd relented after warnings that his faithful English King would withdraw support from him.

The second document, the one that promised no revoking of the court's decree, he would not sign but gave his verbal promise of the same. It was enough, a cause for celebration. Henry kissed me, hugged me to him, swung me like a child and then embracing Doctor Fox, made many more marvellous demonstrations of his joy.

Late that night with Doctor Fox sent home to sleep, Henry and I held each other close. He kissed my face, neck, naked shoulders. With this marriage so near I felt restraint had slipped away. 'Twas warm between my legs and his strong body melded fast to mine. Pulling down my bodice for his hungry mouth, he found my round white duckies, nipples hard and tight. "Shall I have you, Anne, shall I have you now, my love?" he whispered hoarse and low. I felt "yes" between my thighs, but then said "nay." We'd come so far in chastity. Then he agreed and let me go. With shaking legs and trembling hearts we parted sweetly in good faith that when the Cardinal Campeggio soon arrived we'd have a marriage bed to join within and then to make a son. The spring night comes softly thro the tiltyard windows as I write by candlelight. All will soon be well.

Yours faithfully,

Anne

15 June 1528

Diary,

Jesus help us now, the sweating sickness comes. The Court at Greenwich making plans for its remove to Waltham, fell most silent with reports from London. Thousands dying by the day. Whole families carried off in hours.

I went looking for the King and found him yonder in the apothecary's rooms. Having heard the news, he and old John Coke set to work together, hoped to find some cures. They stood hunched above the trestle strewn with jars and baskets filled with fragrant herbs and strange colored brews. Henry ground a mortarful of stinking flowers as Master Coke whispered potions in his ear.

"Henry," said I and he turned to me. I swear there was a kind of happy look upon his face.

"Come in, Anne, and see what we have made." I moved closer and he showed me what he ground beneath the pestle in his bowl. The paste was greyish green and smelled like a mould. "You see this herbal plaster here? When spread upon the skin it draws the venom of the sickness out."

Then Master Coke held up a beaker in which a tawny liquid stirred. "His Majesty is very wise in things medicinal. He's made here a mixture out of henbane, wine and ginger that a person who's afflicted with this New Acquaintance as they call it, drinks for nine days straight, followed by this other." What he held up then looked to be a half full bowl of treacle.

"Henry . . ." I tried to make him hear me.

"Listen, love," he interrupted. "You must remember in this time of sickness to eat most sparingly, drink less, and take the pills of Rasis once a week. Purge the poisons from your rooms with vinegar and hot braziers burning night and day."

"I've seen this plague before," muttered old Coke, turning to his sorcerer's table. "Ere it strikes with pain in head and heart and ere the sweat begins, a person knows an awful sense of fear, an apprehension if you will. And then it hits you like a club. It matters neither if you wrap yourself all warm, or not. You burn with stinking perspiration from your head and pits and crotch."

"Henry!" I cried. "My maid's been taken ill." He went sober then and pale. "It means I cannot go to Waltham with the Court. I have to take my leave of you. I'll go to Hever. Stay there till it ends."

"A separation now . . . I cannot stand the thought!"

Then John Coke spoke unbidden. "But she must, Your Grace, it is the law. A member of the household —"

"I know the law!" cried Henry, anguished with this reckoning. "Leave us, Master Coke," he said more gently, and the old man shuffled out. Henry stood at arm's length, but he did not reach out to hold me. He looked wholly helpless, as I'd never seen before. "What am I to do? You are my love and I want you at my side . . . but I am King. I have first to save my life."

"I'll go. That's all there is." I turned to leave.

"Take these potions with you, please!"

"Make up a packet with directions and I'll send someone to fetch them." My hand was on the door when I felt his arms around me urgent, trembling. I turned and we were face to face.

"God help us, Nan. Please don't die of this." He kissed me then. Fear had made his sweet mouth bitter.

"Nor you, my Love." He let me go. His eyes were wet. "Godspeed," said I and took my leave.

Yours faithfully,

Anne

23 June 1528

Diary,

I write now hand shaking. This may be my end, for Death stalks the halls of Hever, and I fear He's coming after me. So many gone already. Ere I could take my hasty leave from Greenwich Castle, hundreds died in little more than hours, many from the King's own chamber. Norfolk's ill and the Suffolk eldest son and heir has passed away. The Reaper roamed along the highways, too, from Greenwich all the way to Edenbridge. Haunted downcast eyes of drivers, peasants, maids, carriages closed from view, no friendly greetings on the road. Some putrid bodies lying where they fell, ravens feasting on their bones.

Hever's ripe with death. My Sister's husband William Carey's with his Maker. Father and my Brother George are gravely ill. Mother thankfully is well but with her tending husband and son, she could also fall at any time.

This morning young Zouche, the King's special messenger who's carried all our many letters forth and back arrived to Hever just past noon with a note from Henry Rex. But 'fore he'd left my sight he clutched his guts, his face went white. He begged my leave and sure enough I gave it. But when his eyes met mine I saw them wild with fear, and then we said goodbye. He collapsed outside my chamber and was dispatched within our servants quarters sometime after four.

The letter sent from Henry, wholly well himself and cloistered down in Waltham, sent me hopes this illness passed me by, reminding me of how "few women or none" have got this malady, and that none of our Court and few elsewhere have died of it. 'Tis a hollow hope and quite mistaken. My maid did die. Our cook's helper and my Mother's sister too. I do pray for the King's good health, but feel some bitterness with his cheerful mood. He stays to himself, walks alone in deserted gardens, thinks and writes upon the subject of divorce in hopes of Campeggio's coming. How he thinks of this I do not know, when such woeful pestilence rules our souls. I do sometimes fear the King is bloodless, strange and cold.

Night came round again and halls were left to darkness, no tapers lit by scurrying servants on their evening rounds. I made the rounds my self, for unlit passages are all too sinister and call the Devil's demons there. One by one I set the lamps aglow but there was little comfort — only longer shadows, dark whispering corners, slyly creaking doors. When I finally climbed the spiral stair up to my room I thought I heard the sound of rustling robes and ghostly footsteps following close behind. I turned to face the spectre just to find a skulking creature made of fear. They say the sickness starts this way. There's nowhere here to hide. Diary, Friend . . . pray for me. My life is surely in God's hands.

Yours faithfully,

Anne

God help me I am stricken. I can write no more.

2 July 1528

Diary,

I have met Death and live to tell of it. There is little I remember of my body's illness past the pain like daggers in my eyes and a terrible heat that seemed to boil my blood. I called out for my Mother and her face was the last clear thing I saw in the world 'fore a long strange night descended on my soul. They say I lay abed teasing the Reaper for five days, writhing under the covers, crying out delirious, sometimes joyful, sometimes as tho in mortal combat with the Devil him self.

My Mother, that sweet and ever faithful lady, tells me my disease took a fearful course, for instead of sweating out the poisons, they turned inward, made my body reek with noxious vapors. She despaired of my life and sent for Chaplain Barlow who gave me Absolution, and left having said his own goodbyes to the girl he'd brought before the christening font twenty years before.

As to what I can remember of my unconscious state, there were many colors, very bright and always moving. Sometimes they took the shape of elves all intertwined and dancing in some wild circle. There was music too, a sweet tinkling of fairy bells as if from far away, so very beautiful and merry. But other times a suffocating darkness fell upon me. There was no light, no sound.

'Twas a void so black and crushing I knew then that I had died, gone to Hell, for its bleakness was terrible. God and Jesus did not reside in this place, I knew that surely. And so when again the colors and the sounds burst through this black prison I must then have cried out in joy, for I knew I lived or was on my way to Heaven.

Then, just before I came back to this world I saw a vision of my Mother's mother Margaret, long since dead. She looked beautiful, even with her wrinkled face and hoary hair, for she was dressed very fine and had the figure of a girl. She seemed to be illuminated from all round and the light even seemed to glow within her. She had a great crown upon her head and jewels at her neck and wrists and fingers. Then I saw her belly was no longer slim but like some gentle Madonna, she was big with child. She placed her hands upon her belly and smiled. But suddenly I saw the face was not my Grandmother but *me*. 'Twas then I opened up my eyes and found my own Mother there looking down at me with her sweet smile.

I have been weak as a babe these many days since I returned from my otherworld sojourn, but thankful to God for not only my life, but that of my Brother George and Father who have also made recoveries. Henry sent me his own Physician, Doctor Butts, when hearing of my illness. The King was sore aggrieved that his first physician was absent and could not come to me, but prayed the man he'd sent could cure me. As it was he arrived too late to be of any help with my body's sickness, but brought with him a document from Henry which did my mind much good in deed. 'Twas a letter from the French King confirming his staunch support for Henry's divorce, which is so important. For without the love of Francis our good cause would sure be lost. And a letter, too, from Henry came with Doctor Butts, begging me return to Court the moment I am well and strong.

For now I am content to rest at Hever praying for Cardinal Campeggio's safe passage out from Italy to France and hither then to England, and thanks be to God that I'm alive.

Your faithfully,

Anne

5 August 1528

Diary,

God's Blood! Cardinal Campeggio has not yet left for France and all this time I thought, as Henry did, the man was on his way to bring us our salvation. Poor man suffers from the gout and so remained abed in Italy till its subsidence. Meanwhile French soldiers lose ground daily to Imperial soldiers moving closer to Orvieto where the Pope still resides. What will happen if Emperor Charles should take old Clement prisoner? What then becomes of his new friendship in our cause? Dead and gone, altogether hopeless.

I prod my Father and my Brother, Uncle Norfolk too, for news of war in Italy. Nights I look for sleep but find my self instead in fervent waking prayers, supplications all to God to help King Francis' soldiers, that these men fight with valor, luck and bold intent. That their armor, swords and shields hold strong against the deadly clash of the Emperor's assaults. Henry wishes me to stay with him at Ampthill for a fortnight more, but I declined. I shall go back to Edenbridge once again, for tongues are wagging. Henry, more than glad to see me well again, makes daily scandalous demonstrations of his love and lust for me, and fondles my self publicly. He even bids me make the plans for marriage, but this is folly! Soon Cardinal Campeggio will be well and start his journey here. When he arrives he must have no cause to think the King desires divorce to marry me. I say this to Henry and he laughs and kisses me, made reckless by desire. It does gall me to have to rein him in. So, wearily I pack again for Hever House to wait for some old man's gout to heal and pray for France's victory. I remain in steadfast hope

Yours faithfully,

Anne

19 October 1528

Diary,

I am altogether wretched. As I came in from hunting with Urian at my heels, I passed the kitchen and chanced to hear a whispered conversation tween two maids. 'Twas little more than market gossip but it cut me to the bone. They tittered, joyfully scandalized, how a mistress of their house was subject of the gossip brought all the way from London with the spices and the Flanders wool. "Nan Bullen, the King's black eyed whore" they're calling me. Me, a whore! All this time I have with firm resolve kept intact my maidenhood. My conduct has been strong and chaste — I've kept a lusty King at bay. Does a monarch spar with Pope and Emperor to win a legal wedding for a whore?

But this is idle gossip, nothing but a trifle and a misdemeanor. Worse is that there is no progress in the case of this divorce. Campeggio, finally come to England, pleads endlessly his gouty legs and will not call the trial. Methinks this is a ruse, a poor excuse with full intent of purpose to delay. His master is the Pope and my heart tells me that despite reports that Clement is Henry's friend in this, the man of God is just a man, with fear for his own life and limb. I swear he plays with Henry. And Henry does not know it.

The King came to Hever one week ago. He came with news he thought to cheer me — gave report of how after a fortnight spent in bed at Bath Palace, Campeggio roused himself to seek audience with Henry. How it rained in Biblical proportions as the legate's barge was borne down the Thames to Bridewell. He could neither ride nor walk, and so four men had carried him in a crimson velvet chair from river's edge to castle steps where Henry waited. Old Wolsey in procession with his fellow Cardinal was waterlogged, the mule he rode in mud up to its knees. Inside was a magnificent occasion. A great feast. Some letters from the Pope and many honeyed speeches. Henry dangled 'fore Campeggio's nose the Bishopric of Durham which the legate covets mightily, we're told. But of all this, nothing came! For pleading pain and indisposition, the Cardinal begged early leave and Henry, ever gracious, gave it.

When next day Henry made the trip to Bath to make

his studied theologic case against the marriage, Campeggio dissembled, begging the King consider making good his current wedded state. When Henry did object, firm but most politely, then the Cardinal made a new suggestion, one which Henry liked quite well. Let the Queen retire to a nunnery, was his advice. A pious woman and a reasonable one, she would sure oblige.

Next day, in fact, Campeggio and Wolsey made the pilgrimage to Katherine down at Bridewell, told her that the Pope did wish this happy end for her. The Queen withheld response, Henry told me, several days hence paying a call to Campeggio her self, at Bath. Then did she regale him with so harsh an answer that he was chafed and sore amazed. She told him firmly she would live and die within the state of matrimony into which God had called her. She had had no intercourse with Henry's brother Arthur and was certainly a virgin when she came to Henry's bed. And it was her most resolute decision that she would rather to be torn limb from limb and die several times, than make alteration to her married state with the King her lawful husband.

If this were not enough to make me wretched, a great crowd, angry at these divorce proceedings, came to Bridewell Palace loudly calling out their blessing and their love for Katherine. "Victory o'er our enemies!" they cried. Who else, I wondered, is that enemy but me, their future Queen?

I was in a fury. I tore at Henry like a dog let loose at a bear baiting. How could this tiny woman from Spain prevail o'er papal prelates, courtiers and Kings, I wished to know? How could he allow the sly Campeggio to stall and feign his gout and play him like a deck of cards? The rude legate had not even been to visit me, as Henry'd promised that he'd do.

The King tried to take me in his arms to kiss and soothe me, but I pulled away. He had to see the sense I made, that he was being made a fool. So he smoothed my hair, stroked my hand and promised me he'd see the course went differently. Then rode off with high hopes. I stayed behind and prayed.

A letter came from Henry yesterday. He said he'd writ an order that no crowds could come and gather at the palace grounds again. What thinks he? That since they cannot say in public places how they love the Queen, they do not yet feel it in their hearts? Henry then reported of a meeting that he'd called of all the London Aldermen and Mayor, to his great hall at Bridewell. Here he hoped to gather all their loyalties to the cause of his divorce. He made much deference to Katherine, said how he loved her still, but pricked by conscience and the need for male heirs, did seek a separation. The Aldermen seemed amenable, he said, but when he heard some whisperings amongst these men he added one more thing so they should know his cold resolve. That if he found anyone who spoke in unsuitable terms of their Prince, "there is no head so fine" but he would make it fly.

The final blow, he wrote to say, is that the Queen has found (or mayhaps forged) a copy of Pope Julius' dispensation for her marriage to Henry, given she says, to her mother Isabella on her deathbed. This document, with different wording from the one that Henry keeps, throws Cardinal Wolsey and the King into confusion and anxiety. Now *they themselves* delay the trial!

So the King makes stabs at this beast but does not kill it, barely wounds it. And I am left helpless here at Hever, with nothing more to show for my travails than a weary body, a foul mood and a rude nickname. The future does indeed look bleak.

Yours faithfully,

Anne

2 March 1529

Diary,

I fear your faithful friend's become a shrew. I am crowded with vexations and frustrations that leave me sore and tearful, even causing me to heap my screaming rage upon the King. He holds me tenderly and soothes me with his many hopeful words. To see me in my lavish new apartments here in Greenwich, richly hung with gifts from loving Henry, surrounded by my family and those courtiers who hope to see me Queen, you'd think me only happy, hopeful, merry. But I have many grievances and much cause for moroseness. *Seven months* in England, and the Cardinal Campeggio has not seen fit to open up the court. Seven months of vile procrastination, letters flowing here to Rome and back like some foul and circular tide, filled with pleading, useless logic, lies.

Henry sent a delegation, Warham among them, to the Queen with a harsh report from him. There were rumors, Warham told her then, of murderous plots afoot against the King with Katherine the cause. They'd advised him he should henceforth make him self altogether absent from her presence, both her bed and company, lest he be poisoned by her self or servants of her house. They say she listened with a face of stone and bade them leave. The King placed spies around her then and kept her from all correspondence with Mendoza, diplomat of Spain. Henry too forbade the Queen from seeing her daughter Mary, which admittedly is harsh beyond all reason. And did this break the Queen of spirit or of mind? *Not at all.* Her stubbornness grows stronger every day, and with it loyal subjects' staunch support for this cheerful martyr. Some days in my temper I do wish to claw her pious eyes out one by one! And strangle all the scores of weak livered men who at most can bully her, but neither understand her mind nor steer her from her righteous course.

But worst of all and dangerous to me is that cursed Wolsey's plotting my demise once more. Last week the Dean of Henry's chapel found amongst my things a tract by Tyndale — "Obedience of a Christian Man" — and brought it to the Cardinal's attention. Wolsey took it to the King. 'Tis true that even reading such a book is thought to be a breach of Catholic ethics, heretical in fact. I could see my self with Wolsey standing by, a smile upon his piggish face, whilst I, disgraced, walked in public procession carrying a faggot on my way to prison. I knew that brooding long on this was folly, and in truth I felt more anger then than fear, and swore to George and all my courtiers loud and clear that it should be the dearest book that ever Dean or Cardinal took away from any one.

I went and found the King that very hour and fell upon my knees for kind forgiveness for my act. He'd been thinking, then he said to my relief, that tho he was a loyal Catholic still, he wished to read the book him self and make his own opinion of it, maybe write a treatise of his own. I was saved and most grateful for dear Henry's open mind and heart.

But Wolsey, it is clear, still wishes for my downfall. And at this writing I can scarce believe the King will even have his day in court or take his legal leave of Katherine. Sly fox, this Campeggio who, with long and ragged beard, has claimed he grows it thus to mourn the English Church. I think he never meant to bring us any joy, but only empty promises and lies from Clement. My head aches with anger and this cold and never ending winter. We have not seen the sun in many weeks.

Yours faithfully,

Anne

31 May 1529

Diary,

'Tis a great morning, this. The legate's court has opened and my wedding's now assured. Last night 'twas chilly at my Father's river mansion Durham, when King Henry's gilded barge brought him hither to await the changing tide. He was very jolly, very self assured, having put behind him all of Clement's foul excuses and delays, and with a Kingly hand did call the court himself. This, he said, was necessary to prevent the Pope convening it in Rome, which meant disaster for our cause. So 'tis done, and even now Henry sits at Greenwich Castle waiting for his formal summons from the legates at the Priory of Blackfriars where the court will be.

Last night he regaled us — me, my Father, Brother George — with scholarly epistles he had writ upon the subject of his marriage and divorcing under canon law. Henry has become quite the expert, and convinced the Cardinals will champion his cause. He was full and happy in those hours he spent among our clan, well at ease with his new family, which is how he calls us now and I, his blushing bride to be.

When the tide had turned and Henry's barge departed, I

found my Father standing at the central fire alone and lost in contemplation. I moved beside him, warmed my hands but kept the silence. Our eyes met and in his stare I saw a kind of consternation, even wonder, 'fore he turned his face away. I removed my self and went upstairs where George was also retiring. We met in the passage tween our rooms, candles flickering, voices whispering. Sweet George, now Esquire of the Body of the King and Master of the Buckhounds, I asked him if he understood our Father's mind upon the subject of my self and he said yes, he did.

"Father still grovels to the King, as yet I do. We fear the slight misstep, the word with tone too harsh, too soft, too controversial. But you, Anne, you have him at your feet. I swear he'd wash your dirty linen if you bade him! You scream and curse and make a proper tantrum as you please. You're taken into confidence on matters of importance as a man would be. And now he's brought him self before the Papal Court to ask divorce from Katherine for *your* hand. He's quite beside him self, this King of ours, and you're the only cause. Our father sees this and can neither understand nor be altogether happy."

"Why not happy? His daughter will be Queen."

"'Tis not done yet, Anne."

"But the King believes —"

"The King believes his dreams."

"And I believe them too!" said I most fervently. "Henry rules this land and neither Lords nor Emperor nor Pope nor God him self will keep him from his heart's desire. And that desire is me. How this came to be's a mystery, I'll grant. I used my French wiles, my wit, my reticence that made him want me more, but to be honest, Brother, I know not how his Majesty came to love me with such a raging fire as this. I do know that he burns so deeply that he will move all of Earth and much of Heaven to have me. So be of good faith, George. I will be Queen. You'll see."

He smiled with such hope and sweet affection that my heart swelled with love for him. Tho my father broods upon my fate and lacks true loyalty, I have luck to own a brother such as George Boleyn. And so I wait here in Durham House as Henry waits at Greenwich. Waits for all the English Bishops and the

Cardinals at Blackfriars Court assembled altogether in their scarlet robes and scarlet hats on thrones of cloth of gold, to call him there to make his case that for twenty years past he had lived adulterously.

Go with all good grace and honor, Henry. Shake the world and take the fallen pieces in your hands to make it ours and ours alone!

Yours faithfully,

Anne

21 June 1529

Diary,

The battle has been roundly joined and on this day tho all are bloodied, none are yet fallen. I watched out Durham's river windows as Katherine's barge was taken by the morning tide to Blackfriars for her day in court.

All lined along the river's edge were citizens, women most, who cheered her stately progress on with cries of love and loyalty. I knew they were but a few of many who support their Queen and much hate me. I have heard of all the jostling crowds who stand outside of Blackfriars Hall to wait for her and call her name, give her strength to carry on her doomed campaign against the King.

The day was hellish hot and no relief was found along the river. Inside, the stagnant air was rank with fear. Hours dragged and no word came from Father nor from Uncle Norfolk of the day's proceedings. But when the long afternoon melted into honeyed evening light, the great floating procession then began of divers wherries, boats and barges of the court's participants making upriver back to London. There amongst them was Henry's most magnificent craft which broke away and docked at Durham quay.

Smiling and defiant and in plain sight of all, he strode cross the lawn and I, made brave by that defiance, went out to meet him in my rich sapphire gown, hair unbound and flowing down my back. But once concealed within the house the King's strong posture changed. He seemed to wilt, the smile dropt away replaced by tired anger. I sat this weary soldier down and ministered to him kindly — wiped his brow with cool and parfumed cloths, brought him chilly wine, and kissed him gently.

He smiled a little then, seemed to be remembering why he fought this endless battle, then began to talk about the day in court. He had started with his heartfelt deposition of a conscience most tormented by his own innocently adulterous acts with Katherine, his brother's lawful wife.

"I spoke well and long," he said, "and brought about my arguments to make advantage of my case, but then when I was finished, Katherine stood and with that regal Spanish bearing walked across the silenced hall and fell upon her knees at my feet. She then beseeched me, Anne, for all the love that had been between us and for the love of God in whose name she claimed to speak, to let her have Justice and Right. She asked for pity and compassion being a stranger and a foreigner, and said that she had indifferent counsel. This is true. The two Imperial lawyers she had hoped would come from Flanders to plead her case did never come — they say her nephew Charles would not allow it, fearing for their safety. But let me tell you, Katherine did speak well enough to put any counsel to shame. She said she'd been a true, humble and obedient wife, loving my friends and hating my enemies. And of the stillborn children that she'd had, their deaths were not her fault but only God's will."

Henry stopped then and threw back his head as tho remembering something painful.

"What is it, love?" I asked. "What then did she say?"

"That with God as her judge — God again, how many times did she invoke his name — that when I first took her to my bed she was a true maid without touch of man. A virgin she went to Arthur's bed, and virgin came she away."

"'Tis the opposite fact upon which you wholly base your argument, is it not?" He nodded gravely. "But my Father," I continued, "remembers that he spoke to Arthur the morning after their bedding and Arthur clearly said, 'Bring me a cup of ale, for I have been in the midst of Spain last night!' Others proclaim it true. She was not a virgin when she came into your bed and so your case is justified, no matter how many times she invokes the name of God." He listened to my logic, but still looked haunted.

"You did not see the crowd when she left the hall. 'Twas wholly with her. All the Bishops, clerics, lawyers, Legates sitting stunned and quiet heard the cheering thro the open doors. 'Good Katherine!' cried the people. 'How she holds the field!' 'She's afraid of nothing!' O, Anne, she was marvellous strong."

"And so are you!" I cried and grabbed both Henry's hands in mine. I could see his strained and ropy neck, the unhappy flush upon his cheeks. "She spoke truly, Katherine did, in saying she's a foreigner here. This is *your* country and she was Queen only by your gracious hand!"

"True, true," the King agreed. He seemed to rally at my words.

"Your Tudor blood fought for this Crown and won it. You are the eighth Henry to rule this land, but by far the greatest. No Spanish princess can murder your resolve."

"Nor should a cursed Cardinal!" We both looked up to see my Father enter then, recent from his river transportation and the court. "Begging your consideration," he continued, "your man Wolsey does you wrongly, Majesty. This thing is out of hand and I believe his fault."

"A harsh judgement, Thomas."

"Not harsh, Sire. Too kind. The Duke of Suffolk, sent by you on diplomatic errand into France, quotes King Francis saying Wolsey had 'a marvellous intelligence with the Pope, and in Rome, and also with the Cardinal Campeggio.' Where's the loyalty, I ask you? Even Thomas More, that learned scholar, calls his actions crafty. Says he juggled with you most untruly. The people hate him too, Your Majesty, for taxing them offensively to pay for foreign wars. I say watch him closely, and that other red robed lackey of the Pope, Campeggio."

"Thank you for the sentiments, Lord Ormond, and for yours, sweetheart. But tho you may be right about the Cardinals, I believe within my heart that they will never dare to rule against me. The Pope in Rome is loath to lose his English ally. We have had a hard day, my friends, but we shall prevail."

So, good humor restored, the King dined with us at

Durham. We shared a pleasant meal, laughter. I played the lute. We sang and after when my Father did retire, we kissed and clung together. Henry said 'twas this that made him move all Heaven and Earth. He loves me truly and I search my heart every moment to find the same for him. One day, I know, my love will match with his but for now I make pretence and remain

Yours faithfully,

Anne

25 July 1529

Diary,

Such unimaginable treachery is done by the Pope's hand that I can hardly speak of it. But speak I must for my fate and Henry's are thus entwined. The Legate court has been adjourned with no verdict made at all, neither favorable to the King's divorce nor against it, but simply closed, the case revoked to Rome! A disaster, pure and simple. Katherine has won this battle, for if the case is heard in that place, it will surely be determined in her favor.

How it has come to this is clear and the Queen, tho victorious, is not her self the cause. She is just a pawn of men and war, like me. What has happened is, unknown to us, the French were sore defeated in the Italian field at Landriano by Imperial troops, and a plague did carry other Frankish men away. So as Henry sweltered here in Blackfriars' summer heat waiting patiently for some resolution to his cause, Pope Clement went to Barcelona and signed a treaty with the now crowned Emperor. Then our ally Francis went to make a peace with them in Cambrai. All of this we did not hear. Just the grave announcement of the court's adjournment, told that when it opens once again in Rome, the trial will come to fair conclusion. 'Twas only afterwards that all was clear to our minds. The Pope, now peaceful friends with Emperor Charles — Queen Katherine's kin — will never ever put his name to this divorce.

On that final day of court, supposed day of judgement, 23 July, I went myself to Blackfriars — I could not wait at Durham Hall to hear my fate decreed or I'd go mad — and hid behind a balcony. The Cardinals stood and Wolsey, pale and sick knowing what would come was silent, trembling as the Cardinal Campeggio spoke his righteous smirking speech.

He proclaimed that he did fear God's displeasure and his soul's damnation if he granted any favor to a Prince or high estate, and that he could not give a judgement here. Henry, poised for happy news, was outraged, but helpless as a babe. He strode fuming from the court, shaking the floor neath his feet.

The Duke of Suffolk spoke for Henry then, venting all his fury saying, "By the Mass, now I see that old saw is true, that there was never Legate nor Cardinal that did good in England." Alone in that balcony I admit I cried bitter tears for all that time wasted. All those hopes shattered.

And where was Cardinal Wolsey's great influence in all this? Where in deed. Impotent old fool who caused us to believe most falsely that the Legate court could have a happy disposition here in England. Cursed Wolsey. Ipswich butcher's son risen most glorious and high. His star has lost its luster now. Henry hears me when now I speak badly of T Carlis Ebor. He *will* suffer my displeasure, this wretched Cardinal. He will fall and never rise again. I will see to that.

Yours faithfully,

Anne

31 August 1529

Diary,

The King and I and all the Court are midway thro the hunting progress in the high summer countryside, having made our house in Waltham, Barnett, Tuttenhanger Holborn, Windsor, also Reading. There is some grumbling amongst the courtly retinue when I ride beside the King on my stallion, magnificently caparisoned in fringed and tasseled black velvet, silks and gold. But even more grumbling when I ride pillion close at Henry's back upon his great horse. Common folk who see us thus are scandalized and most believe me his flaunted mistress soul and body.

On this day we rode hard thro green and flowering hills and fields, horns blasting, stag bounding majestic, dogs yapping, wind whipping sunburnt faces. Henry loves the hunt. He is a sight on his white charger, bold and manly, his eyes ablaze with happy fire. All cares vanish under those thundering hooves, and even then is his Great Matter soon forgot.

My hound, Urian whom I'd sent for, brought down and killed a cow today, ripping out its throat. Henry paid the farmer for its worth, but there was more whispering. Urian is the name of Satan's familiar, they say, making me once again a sorceress who has bewitched the King. 'Tis true, he's badly smitten and shows his love to me most clearly. Not just gifts, tho these are many — all my saddles and my harnesses, clothing, bows and arrows, shooting glove, undergarments too. But publicly he shows me great affection, fondling, kissing, petting for all to see.

When we supped this evening in his private rooms before a blazing fire, I told him these demonstrations are unwise. Far away in Rome his men still try delaying Henry's trial for this divorce. The Queen, tho banished now from Henry's eyes, likewise persists with Spanish ambassadors in her favor. Till then, I told him firmly, we must give the look of chastity.

Then when we were done, wine flushed and full, he stood with back to me and stoked the fire saying quietly, and I thought slyly, that some months back Clement told him that if he stayed in married state to Katherine he, the Pope, would grant a special dispensation making my bastard children with Henry legitimate. I could not believe my ears! I stood and made to leave his chamber 'fore he saw my furious tears. He grabbed me, held me at the door.

"Nan, don't go. I never meant that I agreed to this."

"Then why tell me of it?"

"I tell you everything!"

"I believe you like his offer. Keep your Queen. Have me. Have your bastard sons made legal. Keep the Pope your friend.

Yes, Henry, you like it well!" I tried to pull away, but he held me fast and now my tears fell freely. "O God, what a fool I've been. I have been waiting so long who might in the meanwhile have contracted some advantageous marriage and borne children, but no! Farewell to my time and youth spent to no purpose at all!"

His face fell, his broad chin quivered, his eyes were glittering wet. "Hear me now, Anne. I will marry you with the Pope's decree or else without."

I stood like some deaf woman who now could hear. "You would do that?"

"If I must."

I was silent, knowing what this meant to him. Excommunication from the Church. A holy war against all England.

"You see I read your book," said Henry quietly. "Tyndale's 'Obedience of a Christian Man.' "

"And what found you in that book?"

"The passages you marked for my perusal with your fingernail I read and read again." He looked past me, staring at the fire. "'Tis a book for all Kings to read. It says Kings are themselves responsible for not just the bodies of their subjects, but their souls as well."

My tears were drying fast. "Go on," I urged.

"I am an English King, and so by an ancient right am absolute Emperor . . . and *Pope* in my own Kingdom."

"Yes, you are, Henry!" said I. "And if you have a liking for the thoughts within that book, I have another for your own examination."

"What book is that?" he asked, his eyes flashing with a light alike to one I've seen when we are hunting.

"'A Supplication for the Beggars' by one Simon Fish."

"And he says . . ."

"That it is King's work reforming Churches, not the clergy's, for they are wicked and corrupt, and that Purgatory's nothing more than gross invention, made to milk good Christians of their money, believing most erroneously that the sacrificial payments help their loved ones trapped twixt Heaven and Hell."

"'Tis a strange title for a tome."

"Fish writes cleverly, appealing on behalf of all the hordes of English beggars made, he said, because the clergy steals the money they might earn in honest work."

Then Henry's face grew dark and he was overcome with heaviness like Atlas with the world's weight upon his shoulders. "These ideas are right and true, I grant, but they are simply words on paper writ by authors who have only one life to care about. I cannot afford a war with all of Catholic Europe now. I have no standing army nor money to pay my soldiers. All of England would suffer so . . ."

"I know."

"And we have not lost in Rome yet!"

"I know that too."

"God, I love you, Anne!" he cried and held me to his breast. "Stand and fight with me in this and we will win, I know it!"

"I shall, Henry, I shall." I kissed him then and held him. Our battle will be long and brutal hard, but this night I knew his purpose still was strong, but more important I knew he'd seen a path to our goal illuminated by a different light — a light whose source was far from Rome and whose name was Luther.

Yours faithfully,

Anne

27 October 1529

Diary,

'Tis a marvellous occasion. The once great Cardinal Wolsey has fallen and I, "that foolish girl yonder in the Court," have been the instrument of his destruction. He did truly dig his own grave, setting foreign law — the Pope's — above the King's, and thus defying English law of Praemunire. So that one fine morning this week past, the Dukes of Norfolk and of Suffolk strode into York Place and seized his Chancellor's Great Seal of the Realm, divested him of rank and all his lands and worldly goods. Head bowed, tail between his fat legs, he left York Place upon his painted barge whilst London's citizens in boats, at least a thousand strong, did jeer at him and shout they hoped he'd end the Tower's prisoner. His final destination tho was banishment to a cold and distant house called Esher.

My part in this was making Henry see that Wolsey was no friend, in deed was one who brought down upon the King's head no end of trouble and disgrace. Whilst we walked in Greenwich garden with winds blowing leaves in swirls about our shoes, I lectured Henry like some sharp tongued tutor.

"That great loan the Cardinal arranged to pay for your war against the French," said I, "has indebted every English subject in the realm worth five pounds, to you. But worse, your Cardinal's diplomatic blundering has left us now without the French as allies. All his arse kissing of Francis wasted. England's place amongst the European powers lost."

Henry nodded gravely knowing what I said was true and this made me brave to then continue my invective. "You have raised this Priest so high that his wealth is fully one third of your own treasury, yet Wolsey has no country to run on *his* income. Do you know they call your English Cardinal the King of Europe?"

Henry winced as tho I'd struck him, for there ingrained within his seething anger for old Wolsey were both loyalty and love, and thus a pain within their parting. But there was no help for the man. His fate was sealed.

When Wolsey'd left York Place, Henry took me there and we looked amongst the Cardinal's confiscated booty. It was far beyond imagining, the richness and the quantities of things we saw laid upon great trestles and along the walls. Tapestries, dozens upon dozens of rugs, pillows, hangings, sixteen carven and canopied beds, tables, thrones, chests, huge paintings, golden plate and goblets made to serve one hundred, jewelled and gilded crosses, chalices and vestments.

"These are yours now, Henry, and rightfully so," said I as we stared at all the bounty. I could see amazement in his eyes that these lavish treasures now he owned.

"'Tis yours too, Nan," he said.

I smiled a smile he could not see. "A wedding gift from Wolsey, is it?"

He was silent then and sad, perhaps with thoughts of all the Cardinal's good counsel.

"You've done no wrong, Henry. 'Twas Wolsey's time to go."

"Aye, I need a Chancellor now who's no cleric. What think you of my choice of Thomas More?"

I did not speak quickly for I knew the lawyer, learned author of the tome "Utopia" was Henry's friend. He was a man both respected for his fairness and most popular at Court and with the common folk. But thought of his appointment gave me pause.

"He is a staunch Catholic, my love, and opposes the divorce," I finally said.

"True enough. And in that I encourage him to follow after his own conscience. But he shall not concern him self with my divorce, but only other state and legal matters. More has always shown to be my loyal and obedient servant, and only gives opinion when I prompt him to."

My mind went wandering back to when I'd first laid eyes upon the man Thomas More. I stood in Henry's Presence Chamber which rustled loudly with stiff satin and heavy gilt chains clinking gainst great jewelled brooches, where French parfum wafted from every starched lawn fold of every slashed doublet and lacy bodice. Then into this gaudy peacock garden strode a bird of an altogether different feather — a man in black and rough wove garments simply hung upon a slender frame. The eyes were soft, expression kindly.

His reputation did precede him. Henry's friend since childhood and counsellor of many years, he was Katherine's friend as well, host to Erasmus when that scholar came to England, a family man and father. All knew of his long marriage to sharp tongued Alice More, and of his natural daughter Margaret, and his adopted child — again a girl — and their devotion to this man. I could not tear my eyes from that face, imagining sweet words from those lips to his daughter's ears. Soft guidance, tender education in this harsh life. All those confections that from my Father I should never know. A vision came before me of my Father's face — steely eyes, razor slit for mouth spewing harsh advice on my advancement. My worth measured only on that advancement . . . I snapped back to present circumstance, to Henry's question wanting my advice.

"More's reverence for His Majesty is admirable and I'm sure sincere, but he's got a family to support and needs advancement to his career."

"You question his motives?" Henry asked.

"Not motives, but propensity to change his mind. In More's 'Utopia' does he not deal with harsh immovability upon those guilty of adultery or any other sexual sin? The first offense is punished with slavery. The second with nothing less than death."

"'Tis true. But also in his book he does allow divorce is possible. And I believe that all my studied arguments, both rational and theological will turn his mind round eventually. Then he will be a most valuable ally to our cause."

I pray Henry is correct, for we have before us a pitched battle and a terrible fight.

Yours faithfully,

Anne

2 December 1529

Diary,

This grey and blustery day I saw my Brother away to France. On Dover beach in Dover Castle's shadow we stood. The wind was in my unbound hair and also in my skirts. It blew them out like canvas sails, and only George's firm arm thro mine did keep my feet on English sand. 'Twas cold, but we were warm in our affection. He pressed my shivering hands deeper in my red fox muff whilst we watched small boats loaded high with baskets, travelling chests and wooden barrels rowed past breaking waves to where the "Princess Mary" anchored off the white-capped shore.

Our heads close, we spoke of many things. How Henry's love for me had raised our family's rank and fortune — my Father made Earl of Wiltshire and Earl of Ormond, George made Lord Rochford, my Sister made Lady Mary Rochford, and I, Lady Anne Rochford. Too, George was made Ambassador to France and thus, his journey there.

We recalled the great banquet Henry gave at Whitehall for our family to celebrate that raising. 'Twas most magnificent this gathering, with many high lords and ladies as his guests. George said he thought the King's sister, Duchess of Suffolk, looked greener than her chartreuse gown to see me seated high at King Henry's right hand, a place reserved for crowned Queens. Du Bellay, the French Ambassador did eye the night's proceedings closely, and George chanced to see Eustace Chapuys, the Emperor's new spy at Court (and Katherine's counsellor), writing notes of the affair into a small tablet hanging at his waist. Methinks the goings on were made into a missive to his master Charles to use as weapon on his Aunt's behalf.

Many fine and sumptuous courses were set at this meal — roasted goose and hares, mutton, pigeons, quail and venison, butter pastries stuffed with winter berries, vast quantities of sweet wine, and a pear and apple tart so large it hung beyond the table's edge. Musicians played all thro the feasting. Later came the merry making fools and jesters. Still more musicians played when tables then were taken down. We danced, laughed, caroused till morning light shone thro the palace windows. 'Twas such a happy night, some whispered that it seemed as tho it were a wedding celebration.

As we stood upon that winter shore, George and I, there came a lord, his lady and their retinue to make the Channel passage. The lord was handsome, his wife fair, and there behind them came several maids and several daughters. They stood against the wind and shook to think of such a crossing on a wooden ship in choppy seas.

"O George," I cried. "Just now I see a vision of my past! I was a girl of nine. Tall and skinny, you remember."

"I do remember that child. High spirits, wild temper. Her father's willful black eyed girl."

"Were you not with us here on Dover beach that day when our Sister Mary and my self accompanied Princess Mary on her wedding journey to France?"

"I was up in London then."

"'Twas a day much like this. Grey, cold and stormy seas. We all huddled on the shore with several royal ships anchored past the waves waiting for our boarding. That day I laid eyes on Henry for the first time. He was handsome as a god, made King not long before, still happy with his Spanish bride. They'd come to see his sister off, to make her royal match to doddering old King Louis. I saw the young King standing in the sand, tho never did he notice me, a scrawny girl. In those days his eyes were only for the Queen, proud Katherine whose belly swelled large with child."

"I remember Henry in those days," said George. "He seemed overlarge to me, almost bursting from his garments with great vitality and hunger for the world. His childhood had been a kind of prison. Second son, destined for the priesthood, he'd been cloistered in his father's own austere apartments. Schooled well but allowed to speak to no one save his tutors, he walked alone in empty castle gardens. All tolled, a very lonely boy. Then his father died and soon thereafter Arthur died, too. O Anne, young Henry was like a butterfly escaping his cocoon. He emerged fully formed from that quiet state into a wild and brilliant life, as tho he'd been born to it. Great Harry — an apt title for a marvellous man and King."

George turned and took my hands. "He will marry you, I know he'll find a way. I intend to return to see my sister crowned a Queen."

Then a sailor came and bade George climb aboard his tiny boat to row him to the ship, heaving and rolling at its anchor. I kissed him, bade him Godspeed and let him go. He climbed aboard the creaking dinghy and as I watched, a sudden gust took his cap, but his nimble fingers snatched it back. He turned and grinned at me, a little boy again. The warm love in that smile flew across the sand and enfolded me like some great wool cloak. And thus protected I stood and watched as his ship set sail and disappeared behind the grey horizon.

Yours faithfully,

Anne

25 December 1529

Diary,

O am I wretched in the extreme! Hidden away in my apartments I can hear the raucous Christmastide festivities in the great hall of Greenwich — most grand and public celebrations presided over by the King and Queen whilst here in my paltry gathering I'm attended only by my Sister and my Mother, Thomas Cranmer and several loyal courtiers. George is still in France and Father — I think he does not know what loyalty means — feasts beside the King tonight.

I railed loud and fierce at Henry for this miserable arrangement, but he claimed impotence at changing ancient custom.

"Whilst she is Queen," said he, "Katherine must remain my public consort still at Yuletide and at Easter celebrations. Other times, sweetheart, you'll surely be at my right hand. Already we are most scandalous and flaunt our love prodigiously. But on these holy days my subjects would not stand to see you at my side, but would rebel most loudly, Anne. Forgive me, please."

I did not forgive Henry, but sent him from my sight with hot tears rolling down my face. And now I listen to the music wafting from the hall below, see in my mind a thousand candles making bright the festive tables, Henry's glittering guests, their jewels and gorgeous fashions, dancing, laughter and my enemies gloating at my absence.

I laid my miseries on my widowed sister Mary's doorsill. She listened long to me as I lamented all my enemies. First of course the Queen, who in her stolid perseverance and infuriating dignity, repels all Henry's machinations and refuses still to treat me badly. Mary claims that Katherine believes that we will never marry, that if she holds her place with firm resolve and says nothing ill construed or hurtful, day will come when she is reinstated in her place in Henry's heart, her marriage once again whole. The Queen, she says, cannot hate me, that her Catholic faith and pious love will not allow it.

This is not the same for Princess Mary. My Sister clearly sees, as I do, the poison in that young girl's eyes for me. Catholic or not she wishes me dead. And tho Henry more and more despises Katherine, he yet loves his pretty daughter Mary, now thirteen, most clever and well schooled, his Pearl of the World. Until my womb bears our little Prince this frail girl remains his only legal heir.

Lesser enemies but still vexing are Katherine's Spanish waiting ladies. I've said aloud I wished they all were lying at the bottom of the sea. Mary asked was it true I'd told the Queen's maid Maria de Moreto I would rather see the Queen hanged than confess she was my mistress. I confessed yes, 'twas true in deed, and Mary roared with laughter which I joined. 'Twas good to feel the grey cloud lifting from my heart as we dispatched my many other foes with great bawdy jokes and jabs.

Then she asked me what I wished most fervently for. It took me no time to answer. To have Henry send the Queen and Princess Mary far from Court, I told her.

"Let me tell you how to wrest such a favor from the King." She leaned close. "He's a lusty man, our Henry, and all your kisses, fondling and such must leave him most unsatisfied."

"'Tis how I hold him, Sister. In his dreams I am far more than I could ever be in life."

"Give him *something,* Anne, and still keep your maiden flower. Assume the French technique of satisfaction — with your mouth. I swear 'twill please him marvellously well, and you'll be hard pressed to count the gifts and favors granted you withal a night of these embraces."

I felt my liquid humors boil. Was I to take advice from Henry's used and now discarded concubine? Said I to her, "Do you presume to teach me the strategy of love when I'm within arm's reach of England's crown?"

"O, do as you will, little sister. But that crown still rests firm upon Queen Katherine's head, and she will not gladly part with it."

"Henry loves me!"

"Aye, and Henry is fickle."

I wished to slap Mary's pretty face, but I held my hand. For tho I true believed the King's good intentions, yet I sat abandoned and in exile from him self and all the Christmas feasting.

God, I pray my Sister's wrong and that by Christmas next I will be Queen.

Yours faithfully,

Anne

9 June 1530

Diary,

It much pleases me that in recent days I have come to be schooled in the arts of intrigue and politicks and my tutors — Norfolk, Suffolk, Thomas More, and my Father Lord Wiltshire — are the greatest artists in the land. I watch mindfully as they and Henry weave the fabric of government into a fine tapestry, the warp and woof of fiefdoms, subjects, wars and taxes shot with golden strands; embroider it with elegant diplomacy and laws; and stitch together staunch borders with the thread of loyal lords and fighting men.

I was called upon by one Master Cromwell, Cardinal Wolsey's secretary, and that audience has piqued my mind. This little man dressed all in lawyers black — beady eyes, large pointed nose, small mouth set upon a boxy face — came to beg on behalf of his now humble, still banished master a kind word from my self and Henry. As he spoke of Wolsey, very ill of dropsy and despair he said, and in great need of comfort, I sensed within the man a second meaning. 'Twas nothing in the words he said that made me think he was disloyal. Just a glint in those clever eyes, a half smile upon thin lips that told of other purposes and schemes. Perhaps this brewer's son, risen so high, has an admiration for a girl who'd turned the once grand Cardinal to some grovelling supplicant.

This strange man did excite my curiosity, he seems so sure, so confident. But I held my counsel and pretending generosity, gave a small gift to him for Wolsey — a golden tablet that I wore round my waist on which I wrote some comfortable words and commendations. He thanked me humbly, bowed low and then withdrew.

Thomas Cromwell seems to be somewhere near in my future. Time will tell, I'm sure.

In his passionate attachment to my self, the King has found a clever strategy for claiming his divorce. My family's new chaplain, Thomas Cranmer late of Cambridge and a mild and friendly man, made a bold suggestion that *Henry had no need of Rome's approval,* just opinions of divers European theologians saying if they felt the Pope had right, or not, to have given dispensation for Henry's wedding to his brother's wife. Or even could they judge the case at all? This simple idea was like a bomb dropped upon the King's head.

Altogether impressed with this cleric's vision, Henry swore that Cranmer "had the sow by the right ear" and with no delay sent to all the Universities of Europe many envoys, with their pockets bulging full of gold. Their intent — to guide the minds of scholars of the canon law and help them see the logic of divorce from Katherine, and to write their positive opinions on the matter. What I learn from this is that the means are sometimes unimportant if the ending justifies. And this coming marriage of ours is cause enough for all and every type of Machiavellian scheme.

'Tis cause for much confusion too. The town and country folk despise the English Priests and Bishops, but when those very clerics defend within their pulpits Henry's right to seek divorce from Katherine and Roman rule, they're boo'd and pelted with abuse. Even Henry vacillates on issues of heretical intent. First made furious by Tyndale's tract called "Practices of Prelates" that crucified Wolsey and condemned the King's divorce, Henry suddenly then made offer that the author have a seat within the Royal Council, if the man would publicly change his mind!

I swear, sometimes methinks the world is going mad and I with it. But I must hold my course and steady Henry on his, if we are to have our way.

Yours faithfully,

Anne

1 December 1530

Diary,

T Carlis Ebor is dead. Not beheaded as Henry had ordered, but felled by common dysentery on his way to London Tower. I feared that Wolsey's final battle for Henry's love would see him once again victorious. For the King, of late, had been most displeased with his councillors Wiltshire, Suffolk and Norfolk, lamenting loudly that the Cardinal was a better man than all of them together. He'd given back the Cardinal's properties, let him remain as York's Archbishop and given him a pretty present of some £3,000. 'Twas worrying in deed. What if Henry raised again that vicious prelate to his counsel? Wolsey hated me still. In weeks past I had learned thro certain spies of mine that in his absence from the Court, the Cardinal'd been in treasonous correspondence with the Pope, giving his approval to an edict forcing my separation from the King.

The Duke of Norfolk, no doubt within his selfish interests, tho happily in league with my desires, wrested from the Cardinal's Doctor Agostini, a statement that old Wolsey'd asked the Pope for Henry's excommunication unless he sent me from the Court. And worse, the Cardinal plotted a great uprising in which he him self could grab the reins of government. In Parliament, newly called Chancellor Thomas More spoke rancorously about the lately fallen "eunuch" Wolsey and of the King's necessity to purge his flock of all rotten and faulty men. My loud protestations added to More's, and Norfolk's information were far too strong to be ignored. Stony faced, silent, no doubt broken hearted, Henry signed a warrant for Cardinal Wolsey's quick arrest.

'Twas undecided who would make its presentation to the man, and truly there were few who had the heart for such a job. I therefore took the reins and chose the deputy myself. My choice, as sweet as it was bitter, was Henry Percy Lord Northumberland. O sweet revenge! How I wish that I had been a fly upon the Cardinal's wall that night — the eve of what he thought would be triumphant celebration of his reinstatement in the Bishopric of York. Instead, Percy strode into his dining chamber and spoke the words "My Lord, I arrest you now, charged with high treason."

Then under heavy guard, making his way south in foul weather to London and his inevitable execution, slow in miserable progression he sickened and fell. And there at Leicester Abbey Cardinal Wolsey died more peacefully than I had hoped, depriving my eyes the sight of his humiliating end.

Yours faithfully,

Anne

7 February 1531

Diary,

God bless Master Cromwell. In close clandestine consort with His Majesty — he has a room at Greenwich Palace and the King has secret access there — he has struck upon a plan so ruthless, so brilliant and outrageous that an end to Henry's Great Matter is now in sight. What cunning mind has this little man to conceive the King consecrated Supreme Head of the Church of England!

At the Canterbury Convocation, Cromwell stood before the meeting pointing out that English clergymen give their whole authority to a foreign power — the Pope. Then like a double swordsman wielding this fact in one hand and terror in the other, charged each and every cleric on this isle with the ancient law of Praemunire, the same treasonous crime for which Wolsey found himself arrested and brought down. Finally he demanded payment from the clergy, ransom if you will, for King Henry's pardon of them! Cromwell contends that when the Church's back is broken, the Holy Father toppled from his throne, and Henry made Christ's Vicar here in England, the King can then command the highest prelate in the land — Archbishop of Canterbury — him self to grant him his divorce. And we shall be wed. Well, all Hell broke loose within that Convocation. Appalled but helpless in their rage, they tried but failed most miserably to come to some conclusion short of making Henry Protector and Supreme Head of Church and Clergy in England!

Lord Chancellor More was livid at the act. But he has proven impotent in his new role, once wielded like a cudgel by old Wolsey. As I told Henry he would, More never moved from his position on the King's divorce, remaining hard against it. But Thomas More is also Henry's feckless puppet, far too mild and malleable to work against his will. In More's time in office this family man, this person of supposed high principles has persecuted heretics most mercilessly. Stating disbelievers needed no less than full extermination, he showed no tolerance at all. His constant writings on the subject did annoy the King most righteously but worse, when citizens were found out reading Master Tyndale's "Practices of Prelates," those books were tied about their necks on strings and they were made to march thro London streets and later throw the books on burning pyres. He whipped and tortured men and women, threatened burnings too.

Unmoved by his Chancellor's sore discomfiture, the King commanded More to make a speech before the House of Lords and later to the House of Commons, there defending Henry's motive for divorcing Katherine. Anguished and humiliated he argued his King acted not for love of a lady, as some said, but purely out of conscience and for his scruple's sake. More must have choked on those bitter and lying words.

Henry's great act is historic and most frightening to me, for it is for my hand alone that he has snatched the Pope's hat to sit atop his King's crown. I tremble at the thought . . . and yet I smile as well. I remain

Yours faithfully,

Anne

I HOPE I HAVE FOUND that which Her Majesty desires," said Lord Steward Francis Knollys above the loud clanking of heavy keys on the chain that hung around his slender waist. Elizabeth's tall and long-legged cousin topped her by several inches but still had a difficult time keeping up with her brisk pace down Greenwich Castle's long hall.

"My mother was one of your mother's ladies near the end of her life," he said. "It was, she told me, dangerous to show any interest or sympathy for Queen Anne, and most of her things were quietly dispersed or discarded at her death."

Elizabeth felt a small shiver of pain sweep through her body at the thought of a woman once so beloved by her husband, whose memory had been so quickly and ruthlessly forgotten. It was strange and uncomfortable to be speaking openly of the convicted traitoress, one whose name she had barely uttered in her twenty-five years. But Knollys, a Boleyn relative, seemed happy to be able to talk of her.

"Our friend Thomas Wyatt, God rest his soul, always said his father had been in love with your mother. Wrote verses about her. Made the King jealous. He was loyal to her till the day she died."

Her mother's Wyatt, Elizabeth thought to herself, had given Anne not only the diary but the confidence to write in it, and had weathered the King's wrath many times, to live out his life and die a natural death. His son and namesake, a Protestant patriot, had died but a few years ago under the executioner's axe after leading the failed rebellion against Queen Mary's taking a Spanish bridegroom.

"Here, Your Majesty." Knollys had stopped at a carved door at the end of the corridor and now sorted amongst his jangling ring of keys for the one that fit the rusted lock. "There is not much here, but I do believe the contents of the room belonged to the Queen." He swung the heavy door open into a room which, though not much bigger than a closet, must have once been some lucky waiting lady or courtier's private apartment. Knollys pulled aside a heavy arras revealing a filthy window. Dust played along the streaks of sunlight that managed to shine through the glass. "Shall I bring you a torch?"

"No, no. Push open the window. That will do." With a great creaking, the leaded glass was thrown wide and the chamber was now awash in morning sun.

"Thank you, Francis. I am very grateful. You may leave me."

"Your Majesty." Knollys bowed stiff-legged and backed out the door, closing it quietly behind Elizabeth. Finally alone with all that was left of her mother, she found herself looking around greedily, her eyes falling on one object after another — here an embroidered pillow, there a carelessly folded tapestry, a pair of brass candlesticks, a crucifix, a cracked Venetian glass bell.

Elizabeth pulled open the rude wooden wardrobe. Inside it there limply hung a faded overgown trimmed in russet and orange, its tiny waist and bodice giving credence to the rumors of Anne's birdlike frame. Crumpled on the wardrobe floor beneath it were the gown's sleeves, their silk laces still hanging in tatters from the eyelet. Elizabeth lifted one of them and noticed a long pointed flap at the small finger side of the wrist. This was the fashion her mother had inspired to hide that tiny bit of nail and flesh, her "witch's mark." Elizabeth held the sleeve to her face. She took her breath in deeply, for age had muted the odors. Yet there was something left of sweet perfume and a human scent, part spice, part musk. Her mother. Yes. It was so distant yet so familiar. She closed her eyes and tried to remember the face, but all she could evoke was a blinding light, the memory of gay laughter and bits of a French nursery song sung in a rich and lilting voice.

Elizabeth turned her attention to the low pallet now devoid of bedclothes but piled with several wooden crates and a large domed chest painted in the Italian style. She opened the chest to find a hundred dead moths and a jumble of small personal objects, as though they had been hastily hidden away. There was a basket of dainty heeled slippers, a pair of green satin ones fringed with curly lace, another of looped gold brocade, and one of black velvet silk trimmed with silver tassels. In each shoe was the faint imprint of Anne's slender foot, a sight from which Elizabeth found she could not easily tear her eyes.

But there was more. Wrapped in shredded tissue cloth was a moth-eaten red fox muff, a large silver box of cosmetics — ghostly white face powder which had long ago lost its perfume, a pot of vermillion cheek coloring, jars of once oily lotion now hard and cracked. In tiny bags with drawn strings were herbal potions and medicinal concoctions, long since turned to dust. A miniature of an unnamed and handsome man was framed in tiny pearls, perhaps her Uncle George. She found, carefully folded, one of Anne's servants' liveries — a purple and royal blue velvet jacket with the embroidered motto on its breast "La Plus Heureuse." The Most Happy.

She closed the trunk with a thud, again sending dust into its swirling sunlit dance, and pulled the lid off one of the wooden crates. Books. They were Anne's books. These things Elizabeth knew were most precious, for they had formed the substance of Anne's intelligence and beliefs. The Queen took one in her hands and read the gold lettering on the leather cover. "The Noble Art of Venerie or Hunting." There were Chaucer's well-worn "Canterbury Tales," several romances, several books of French verse. Here was a great volume of drawings of all England's flowers and trees and one of medicinal plants and their uses. Then she found a book, the wine-colored leather thin, the binding torn, which bore the title "Obedience of a Christian Man." Tyndale's work. The one her mother had given her father so Henry might read and educate himself about the New Religion. Carefully Elizabeth opened the book and turned its pages as she imagined both her mother and father had done. She stopped, riveted to a nearly invisible line of indentation which ran down the side of a long passage on page seventy-one. It spoke of a King's duty to see to the souls of his subjects. It was the passage Anne had marked with her fingernail for Henry's perusal.

The New Religion. How many had died, Elizabeth wondered, for the right to believe that a man could speak to God directly, and chose reason over faith? If the Reformation had been a road, it would have begun at the city gates of Luther's Wittenberg and stretched across the Continent, winding its way from Germany into every city and village and burgh. Luther, Calvin, Zwingli, like great generals, had led armies of the converted down this road littered with the martyred dead to a revolution that had changed forever the history of the world.

And in England, mused Elizabeth, running her finger down the indented passage of Tyndale's book, a young woman born a commoner's daughter had, to the dismay of the faithful, led her staunchly Catholic king away from Rome to religious independence. To be sure, England's road had been a winding and rutted path. Henry, once the Pope's most cherished sovereign, was far from a zealous reformer. Indeed, until his death he remained a faithful Catholic in every way but one — his lack of belief in the supremacy of the Pope. Had it not been for the blind passion he'd held for her mother, thought Elizabeth, and the political necessity of the male heir she had promised him, England might yet be squeezed within the steely grip of Papal authority.

Her father's infamous conscience, renowned for its insistence that marriage to one's brother's widow was a blasphemy in God's eyes, had not extended to championing the right of an Englishman to read the scriptures in his own language. Though Henry had himself read Tyndale's works, he had heartily condemned that priest's translation of the Bible into English. Elizabeth remembered her tutor telling of how Henry had named Tyndale a felon for merely attempting to have his Bible printed in England, and how the royal agents had persisted in hounding and stalking him as he fled to Europe to find a printer there. Finally in the very year Henry stood before the Canterbury Convocation and named himself Supreme Head of the Church in England, prompting his excommunication, he had ordered Tyndale's execution as a heretic. The man who had once said to a Catholic friend, "If God spare me, ere many years I will cause the boy that driveth the plow to know more of the Scripture than you do," was publicly strangled and burned at the stake crying, "Lord, open the King of England's eyes!"

When her father died clutching the hand of his friend Thomas Cranmer, Elizabeth's half brother the boy King Edward VI had taken the throne and led England into its first engagement with fanatical and persecutive Protestantism. But Elizabeth knew that Edward's minions had stripped the churches less to be rid of their sacred Catholic icons than to pillage them for their gold and silver altar plate and enrich his depleted royal treasury.

Later in her sister Mary's reign, the religious counterrevolution had been nothing short of nightmarish. Ties with Rome restored and the Reformation driven underground, Protestant heretics had died by the thousand, including Thomas Cranmer. Even Elizabeth herself had barely survived those years. Forced to take the mass to pretend her belief, she had prayed daily to Jesus for the strength to go on and one day return the nation to its true destiny. And once enthroned, Elizabeth had accomplished her goal without further bloodshed.

But religion was nevertheless a confusing affair, thought Elizabeth, turning over the pages of Tyndale's "Folly." Even she, with her moderate and lenient views, believed vehemently that priests should remain celibate. How could they attend carefully and uncorruptedly to God's work with women in their beds and children to be raised? And her dramatic nature, she had to admit, yearned for the high ritual, soaring music, and rich vestments of the old faith. It was an issue, Elizabeth finally concluded as she shut the book and tucked it into the folds of her skirt, that was as deep and complicated as the landscape of one's own soul, an issue that would live and change for as long as she reigned and far into the future of England. But it gave her great pleasure and a measure of amusement that the momentous upheaval of church and state, if not originating with Anne and Henry, had indeed taken its greatest turnings around her parents.

Elizabeth closed the wooden crate, shut the mullioned window, and with a satisfied smile left the room of her mother's memories until she should return of another day.

15 August 1531

Diary,

They call me arrogant and cunning. But tell me, what woman lives and breathes who could resist a certain arrogance when, on behalf of her, the very King of England banished from the Court his own wife and Queen? Thank Jesus, this has finally come to pass. In every one of Henry's palaces Lady Anne Rochford now inhabits those apartments that were once Katherine's. How lovely not to feel her icy stares, see that dour and humorless expression, endure on every feast day her stately public presence, pious air. The King is much relieved, for Katherine is fallen from the throne and yet we have heard from Rome of no castigation nor excommunication.

Princess Mary is also driven from Court, Henry forcing her permanent separation from her mother which I thought excessive, even cruel. But Henry says, and rightly so, that both together they are strong and could foment a plot, perhaps an uprising against ourselves.

And what woman with no cunning in her soul would find her self presiding with the King and the Ambassador of France at the banquet high table looking down upon her own Father and the Dukes of Norfolk and of Suffolk, and center of negotiations for her hand in marriage. I suppose I am cunning. But I did not seek this strange and dangerous path. I was just a simple girl who loved a simple boy. But with that love rent from my heart, and Henry's thrust upon me I do admit I changed, hardened, gathered enemies and learned a form of courtly warfare where a less hardy soul would soon fall gravely wounded and die.

Not I. No, not I. This pitched battle for England's crown, once joined, has a single resolution. I will be Queen. Those who struggle by my side will be handsomely rewarded. Those who oppose me will wish they had not done so.

These days the King is like some great bull who sees a lush pasture far afield and trampling opposition underfoot, hies thereto despite all deadly obstacles. Deep felt love for Henry sadly still eludes me, tho my prayers for that love are never ending. But I believe that something close akin to it is forming in my breast.

I would be a cold wanton if I were never moved by such devotion. I think that I shall love him soon.

Yours faithfully,

Anne

29 September 1531

O Diary!

That I write to you at all, this or any other day again, comes of good luck and the loyalty of one kitchen server name of Margaret. Abroad after visiting her sick brother south of London, she made for my Father's river house Durham, through the streets where she found gathered unnatural groups of common people congregating all together. With loud and angry cries against *my name* they called forth from homes and rude hovels all women who hated me and loved the Queen. Hundreds, nay thousands seemed to join together, picking up their brooms and knives, clubs and sticks to stab the air as tho it were my breast or head. "No Nan Bullen. Kill the goggle eyed whore," they shouted.

My servant said she trembled fearfully, was even made to swear against me, lest she lose her life. As she made her way to home, the mob — for that was what it had become — swelled not just with women but with men disguised in women's clothing, also armed with murderous weapons. And this mob began to shout my whereabouts at Durham House.

Margaret wished to run here with news but feared her actions most suspicious to the angry crowd, and so was forced to find her careful way thro streets now surging with the murderous throng, ahead of them to my Father's house.

The day was warm and I was with my Mother in my bedchamber being fitted by our silk women for several gowns for Court. Father was away in France and Henry, on the hunt, was also far away when Margaret, red and sweating, panting like a hound burst thro the door spitting out the news.

"Begging your pardon Lady Rochford, but a great mob is on the way and they mean to do you harm!"

My Mother's eyes met mine. "Go!" she said to the silk women, and to Margaret, "Tell the other servants to quickly drop all work and take their leave. All but Master Richardson. Tell him meet us at the river door."

I'm shamed to say that I was at first paralyzed with fear and I had only presence of mind enough to grab this diary and hide it neath my skirts 'fore my Mother's sure hand guided me down stairs and to our steward's helpful care. Richardson was strong and calm and with a haste I hardly fathomed, hurried us cross the broad lawn where a poor boat was floating at the dock. Then I heard a sound which came upon the wind. A sound I knew, yet could not place. I stopped to listen, my feet rooted in the warm grass and tried remembering.

My Mother called, "Anne, come quickly!" I knew the sound then — a low roar growing louder. The roar was voices, many voices, and their shouts were murderous voices in my name, clattering weapons, heavy marching bootsteps coming closer, closer . . .

Richardson grabbed my arm and pulled me to the boat where my Mother's terrified eyes greeted her pathetic daughter. As we rowed away we heard glass shatter, dull clubs beat on stone, saw the hateful mob storm my Father's house, horrible strangers pour from our back doors onto the river lawn. Wretched women ran to meet the shore, all their angry faces, upturned brooms and staves, screaming curses that the boat should sink and shrieking hopes that I might die.

I am lodged now in Greenwich and write with trembling hand by candlelight. I am not a perfect soul but I swear I do not warrant such venom. I pray God loves me and sees my goodness.

Yours faithfully,

Anne

14 May 1532

Diary,

A great war pitting Henry and Cromwell gainst the English clergy and Thomas More has been joined and won. Henry had taken issue with the Church's loyalty to Rome which stood before their loyalty to England and the Crown. Within that thinking the Pope was their true King and Henry but a pawn. The Bishops Tunstall and Fisher defended most staunchly these ancient edicts and this enraged Henry. Tho he worried that his subjects held the Church laws sacred, and feared for those laws' banishment as in the days of Thomas Becket, Henry and Cromwell lately went to Parliament with this case and the lords of that body supported their cause. Parliament's "Supplication Against the Ordinaries" took exception to Rome's ecclesiastic courts and canon laws which, writ in Latin, imposed upon the English harsh measures, all without their consent.

Under canon decree a man tried for heresy, a crime punishable by death, may have brought as witnesses against him vile and dishonest men who may wish him harm, whereas in our English Common courts, witnesses must prove their own honesty and good intentions 'fore they speak against the accused. Henry's own Chancellor More, as staunch a Catholic as lives, supported these most unfair prescriptions in his writings with the assertion that heresy is so evil a crime that no law could be too harsh if it succeeds in its purge of heretics — for souls are far more important than civil law.

In deed, More seemed to be provoking something more than opposition to Henry's moves against the Church, but to the King's divorce as well. Did he not know or care that Henry's wrath is death?

Cromwell and Henry laid siege to the spineless clergy with bullying and threats and they, weak and frightened for their properties, and unwilling to stand as martyrs, surrendered to the King's will once more. A document named "Submission of the Clergy" was offered up to Henry's eager hands by England's cowardly prelates. It effects great change within the Church, conceding to the Crown their ancient liberties and their authority. No laws henceforth can ever be made without royal consent, and even Convocation shall never meet without the King's permission.

'Twas a great day for Henry and for Cromwell and, too, my self for in so stripping Rome's Church of its power, this brings Henry closer to divorce, and my self unto the throne. Chancellor More, soundly vanquished, did on the day following the Submission of the Clergy, in the garden of York Place, yield up to Henry the Great Seal to tender resignation, and retire from his public office. And Henry, now full master of his Kingdom and the Church, accepted it.

Yours faithfully,

Anne

20 August 1532

Diary,

Could any woman boast more or bitterer enemies than do I? Common, noble, men, women, young, old, clergy, even children. As I rode out with Henry one day last week a boy, not fully ten, did run across our horses' path hurling insults at the "King's whore" and disappeared twixt high grown fields. Henry made to have the ragamuffin captured, punished, but I asked leniency for him. Too young to know the import of his words or their result, said Henry, he will grow into a man who'll hate me when I'm Queen. But on my wish he let the child go.

More disturbing is the Duchess of Suffolk, Henry's sister, who doubtless does remember me a mere child, her waiting lady's Sister when she journeyed to France to marry old King Louis many years ago. Now her brother wants to wed me, raise me far above her, making me *her* Queen. She snubs me openly, her venal and barefaced insults made of little more than jealousy. She was Queen of France for three short months, then in secret married Henry's best friend Charles Brandon for love. Now the love's gone sour. He treats her with brutality, contempt. She is his property.

But my Aunt, the ill tempered Lady Norfolk, lately showed a most outrageous hatefulness to me, taking much offense at my raising in position. True, the pedigree that Henry had commissioned for the Boleyn lineage is clearly false. This ornately gilt and richly painted family tree is rooted all in lies. My earliest forebear was one Geoffrey Boleyn, a wool merchant first known on English soil a hundred years ago — not as Henry's heralds writ, some venerable Norman lord come to England five hundred years before. But despite my warnings and my pleas, knowing this invention would incense nobility whose pedigrees were truly pure, Henry insisted on this deceit and thus displayed the proud and painted document within the halls of Court. Most ladies whispered, keeping their cruel jests at my expense behind their fluttering fans. Not so the Duchess Norfolk. She marched grandly in, looked upon the document, took it up within her hands and rent the thing in two!

No wonder that Henry's health does poorly. He's turned forty now and the years show upon his face and form, both of which are grown substantially in bulk. His face, no longer boyish, is a careworn mask of misery. A great pustulant ulcer on his thigh causes more pain than a man should bear. His head aches constantly. He hardly rides at all.

I have tried to minister to Henry. Gone to see apothecaries, even women known as witches for the cures for all his ills. One potion of calendula and slippery elm made some fair improvement on his festering leg for several days, but soon it stank with poisoned blood and pus again. When he moans with head ache I take his head between my hands and knead the temples, smooth the furrowed brow. He whispers piteously, "Ah, Nan, your cool fingers, cool hands." In these times when he is my prisoner, I do feel affection for the man. If truth be told I fear Henry too much to love him truly, love him in my heart as I once loved sweet Percy. To hear me lash the King with my sword tongue you would never know I quake at his approach. For I know his capabilities, the inner fire that goes to madness. In his soul I see a battleground, frightened demons in his head who rage perpetually gainst the angels of intelligence, of reason and of poetry. Only Wolsey knew this much about the King . . . and he is dead.

All others see him as he bids them do, most magnificent in deep slashed doublet, wide shouldered crimson silks and satins, furs and gilt, a great God Poseidon, earth shaker, storm bringer. He means for all to fear him thus, and when they do he then despises them. I fear the mad King but must transpose the fear to taunting laughter, harsh words to match his own. He does not see my great performance, thinks that save for royal blood I am his equal. Perhaps 'tis only equal in the way the hart is equal to the one pursuing it, with horse and hound until the hart's own death. But this equality I know to be the reason he does love me. Why he'll move the Seven Hills of Rome to make me Queen.

Yours faithfully,

Anne

2 September 1532

Diary,

I thought I had in entries past made catalog of enemies complete. But one has come from so far afield (perhaps so low) that even I was taken by surprise. Henry's made clear to all that we shall marry, and those who wish our wedding never comes to pass do try in every way to make impediment to it. Some argue that the King's marriage to the Queen is fair, legitimate and can't be broke. Some say divorce is wrong, against the will of God. Others argue that I am most unfit, neither high born nor do I bring much advantage as a foreign princess would.

But suddenly here dances Lady Northumberland upon the stage of royal politicks. This bitter, festering sore of a woman, the wife long estranged from my dear Henry Percy, comes forward with a damning letter — one averring Lord Northumberland admitted precontract of marriage to me. This, if proven true, could make invalid my wedding to Henry. Well, the charge is true, its facts writ upon these very pages long ago. Tho 'twas just a promise made between two lovers one day to marry, this is called a precontract, and bound us legally. But I was loath to let this wicked hag burn my glorious bridges all to ash. So I acted boldly.

First, I my self took the offending letter to the King and said to him, "This thing is patently untrue. 'Tis spoke by one who wishes only harm because her husband never loved her . . . for he loved me. In youth we shared a true and deep attraction, but I swear we never were betrothed nor were we lovers of the sort implied, before the Cardinal Wolsey parted us. I beg you, call the man accused of this lie before your self and let him speak the truth." The King, who fervently wished the lady's letter false, agreed and sent for scribes to write petition to Northumberland.

Meanwhile I called my messenger who carried my letter quickly to Percy, asking for a secret meeting in a place we'd met so many years before. Under covering of night, veiled and in disguise, I made my way past sleepy palace guards to waiting carriage which, with I a solitary passenger, clattered thro the winding cobbled streets deserted but for scavengers and filthy prostitutes. I'd not seen Percy close at hand for many years. I now recalled his face, that sweet expression on his rosy unlined brow, and how it made my heart work an unsteady rhythm, made my feet skip quick and lightly where my sweetheart always was.

The carriage put me down at Rosewood Publick House — a tavern, rooms upstairs. Time had not allowed reply from Lord Northumberland and I could only hope he would appear. Inside I asked a slovenly porter in which room I'd find Master Longheart (a nom de plume we'd used in passing youthful love notes). The ale soaked fellow leered at me, the creases of his coarse face caked with grime. "What'd'ya want with one like that?" he muttered most impertinent.

"Tell me where he is," I shrilled insistently through heavy veils.

A stubbly chin pointed up the stairs. "Number three."

The door opened 'fore I knocked. He'd heard my footsteps in the hall. Smoky lanterns lit the tiny room, sagging bed, the sagging man who'd bid me enter there. Ah Lord, I cannot paint a portrait of that ravaged face and piteous soul without a fit of weeping. Tho he'll not admit the fact, the man is ill. He has that lifeless color — grey with feverish red veined patches, sunken eyes. Naught was left of that lovely boy except his kindly eyes which now held my own. "Anne. Come in," he said raspy throated. Then he closed the door.

We passed no more than one dangerous hour there together. First we spoke of sweet times past, the truth of our adventures, the strange path my life had taken, his forced and loveless marriage to the shrew who sought my destruction now, and of his summons from the King. Percy knew that there was one and only one answer to be given Henry — and that a lie. The King wished no truth be spoke if that truth would keep us two apart. So as friends with no apologies, Henry Percy and my self agreed to be united one last time — and disavow our heart's true marriage to the other.

When he spoke to Henry and the Parliament I was watching from the balcony. Poor Percy seemed more shrunken, grey and old than he had been but several days before. Hoarse voice steady, he denied our prearrangement thrice, as Judas did three times deny his Lord. Satisfied, the Parliament and Henry said "Stand down" and that was simply that.

Yours faithfully,

Anne

6 October 1532

Ah Diary,

An autumn idyll, this. Floating on a lazy gilded barge down winding River Thames past farms and fields and villages, the drifting yellow afternoons are sweet and warm. No prying eyes nor peevish voices rend our peaceful hours. The King of England and Marquess de Pembroke ('tis my new title naming me the highest peer in all the realm save Henry and the Dukes of Norfolk and Suffolk) travel this liquid road toward Dover for the Channel crossing to Calais. There as planned we'll meet the

High King of France and he shall stand as witness to our marriage. God be praised, we shall finally be wed!

Once the Archbishop of Canterbury, Warham, died of much advanced age and left that most important office free, Henry's mind seemed to open like some spring flower, all possibilities bursting forth, seeds of optimistic change flying out to fill the air. Even dour courtiers who feigned excuses so they could stay behind on this, our wedding journey, failed to dampen Henry's mood. My doubts of marrying not on proper English soil where Queens are wont to be married and crowned, Henry laid to rest, assuring me that Francis' firm support was worth its weight in gold to us, and I'd be crowned in England later. Nor even did the talk of plague in country towns along the river route deter his happiness. Instead he made a whirl of preparations — sent for armies then, of jewellers, silk women, lace makers, furriers — providing me with my wedding chest.

We boarded the Royal Barge at Greenwich. Wooden wardrobes filled with clothing, crates of hangings, rugs and golden dinnerware, even Henry's great Bed of State was broken down and taken with. Our friends and favorites — George and Mary, Henry Norris, Francis Bryan, Thomas Wyatt — now travel overland with many hundreds more (our retinue) to meet us at Dover for the crossing. My heart drums with pleasure and anticipation. My mind is rife with thoughts and plans and dreams about to be fulfilled.

In the glittering water I see a waking vision. A thousand candles burning in Winchester Cathedral — a christening. There before the font am I, Queen of England, the tiny babe swathed in silk and lace cradled in my arms, his sweet face a miniature of Henry's. I see his father smile at us — his wife and lawful Tudor Prince — all pain, all anger now erased, all but love forgotten. Beyond the King I see his once resentful courtiers now filled with praise and joy — yielding fealty to the Mother of their future King. And there behind all these phantom figures stands my Father. That hard face molded soft, lips bowed into a smile, eyes moist. He is proud of me, my life, my royal child.

The vision dies. A cloud has blocked the sun, extinguished all the glittering candles made of river glow. In the shadowy waters now I see a different fantasy. There stand my staunchest foes. The ghost of Cardinal Wolsey, tho restored to red robed dignity and clutching silver cross and miter in his hands, stands bathed in hellfire's flames. His lips move, uttering curses on my head, but he makes no sound at all, impotence and silence his damnation. I see Katherine and Mary and, too, the evil tongued Duchesses of Norfolk and of Suffolk. They are grown old and quite repulsive, bent with humps upon their backs, skin mottled, teeth black. Shrill cackling voices.

Now the sun bursts forth once more cleansing my mind of this pustulant dream, flooding it with bright hope. Mayhaps I'll learn the lesson that befits a Queen — magnanimity, generosity of spirit to my enemies — and find that well of kindness from which all acts of goodness spring. Or mayhaps I'll not.

I must end my mindful wandering to meet with Henry for a sunset supper on the deck. He has promised a surprise and so I shall soon write again.

Yours faithfully,

Anne

7 October 1532

Diary,

My hand trembles as I write today. But it is not the morning damp and bitter draughts that chill the chambers in this barge and shake the quill within my hand. Rather, and to my complete surprise, it is a deeply felt emotion that is rattling both my body and my soul. That emotion? Love. Sweet and most sincere stirrings in my heart and loins for my betrothed. A miracle both hoped and prayed for now becomes a living fact.

If one would hear of our night together, of Henry's surprise to me, he might surmise that this is not true love I feel, but only gratitude for generosity. For last night when I appeared on deck to sup, laid upon the trestle was neither mutton, tarts nor

roasted hare, but piled all of Katherine's jewels, the family treasure — bracelets, necklaces, brooches, ear bobs, rings and small ti-
aras made of pearls and emeralds, diamonds, rubies, sapphires —
all sparkling in the dying orange sun. He stood proud behind
them, eyes dancing, waiting like a little boy for my shocked expression, cries of joy. But I was speechless, paralyzed.

"Well," he said. "What say you, Nan? I fought for these
with Katherine as a mastiff fights a bear." I know that he expected warm embraces, kisses, extravagant praise for so wonderful a gift. But all that I could do was laugh! A laugh lacking all
control and very loud in deed. I promise, my mirth was not at
Katherine's discomfiture, but more as tho a cork was pulled from
some great cask of pain within my soul. All fears, hatred, ugliness of six years past were spewed forth upon the sound of my
laughter. It proved contagious, this rush of hurt dispersed, and
Henry joined me with his own brand of great and hearty loud
guffaws. We found we could not stop, were bent double, it ached
our sides until clutching one another, tears streaming down our
faces we slowed and stopped. Saw each other's eyes. Kissed. First
briefly, lips wet and salty, then longer, deeply. I felt my heart
pound a fierce rhythm in my chest. Heat moved from thigh and
belly to my groin. Knees turned to jelly. And unbidden, my
mind whispered in repeated chant, "I love you, Henry, love you
Henry, love you . . ."

Great unutterable joy welled within myself. I clung to this
man, this faithful friend whose large love had borne him, tho
not unscathed yet whole, thro storms and raging seas, all that he
might marry me. So sudden was my hunger and my need to
cling to him, 'twas he that made an end to our passionate embrace.

"Nan, Nan," he whispered. "Let us stop or you will never
see our wedding night a virgin." He released me, a look of wonder in his eyes for truly he had never 'fore this moment felt such
fervency in my many kisses. "Here, put this on." He bade me
turn and placed a heavy necklace on me.

"Let me look at you." Hands upon my shoulders, Henry
turned me to him. In his eyes I saw reflected there the sparkling
water, dying sunset light, glittering gems upon my throat, but
most importantly . . . my love. I know he saw that love and he

smiled warmly. "I am the most happy man in all of England," said the King.

"And I," said I, "am the most happy woman."

Yours faithfully,

Anne

18 October 1532

Diary,

What gay, delirious nights and days. Clothed in gowns and royal jewels, surrounded by a dazzling entourage, I bask in rounds of banquets, masques and balls in my honor. A strange and lovely place is this Calais. French soil, English rule, the last of Britain's Continental land, it's made me more welcome than my land of birth has ever done. Leaving the Exchequer where we're lodged luxuriously, in grand procession through the ancient walled city on our way to St. Nicholas to hear the mass, crowds cheered Henry and my self. Children gave me flowers, men and women both smiled at me sincerely.

I have lately quieted my raging heart which threatened bursting when upon arrival back in Dover Towne before our crossing, news came that Eleanor, the Queen of France (and my old mistress) had, with all the other highborn ladies of the Court, refused to receive me, or stand with Francis at my wedding. I do understand Queen Eleanor's position. She is a sister to the Emperor and therefore Katherine's kin. But Francis' sister, Duchess Marguerite of Alençon, has no excuse for this insulting stance. As a girl in Francis' Court I served her loyally and with great affection, learnt not only strength of mind from her but talent for a bawdy and outrageous style that men so love. Too, she strayed from strict convention, entertaining Lutheran ideas within the Catholic Court. 'Twas none but Marguerite of Alençon who gave me leave to read the tracts in which King Henry later saw a way to make the Church his pawn. This grievous rebuff felt the bitterest betrayal, tho not half so vile as the French King's offer — better called an insult — to bring the Duchess de Vendôme with him instead. This woman is notorious for her tarnished reputation — a courtesan! These arrogant women of the French Court, they forget I know them well, licentious and lascivious, the lot. I'd like to know which among them could have held their King's lust six years a hostage? I'll wager none.

On hearing this hurtful news I held my tongue. I stood, head straight and high, never letting reckless temper get the best of me. I bade Henry tell his cousin Francis leave the Duchess de Vendôme at home and come alone — his own presence meant the most to me. Henry, used to seeing wild tantrums, saw instead a Queenly dignity. Most proud and happy, he said that nothing now could stop him from his course. With Francis by his side our marriage shall proceed.

Yours faithfully,

Anne

22 October 1532

Diary,

Pails clanking, whispering as they work, my maids fill a metal tub before a blazing fire in my bedchamber, lighting several braziers to warm the chilly room for my bathing. I know Henry's Master of the Body does the same in his adjoining room in the Exchequer.

I can already hear how my ladies shall gossip when I release them from their chores. "The King and Marquess de Pembroke both have bathed," they'll say in muted tones. "They'd dined and drunk a bit — we smelt wine on her breath, you know. 'Twas early still when she returned to her apartments and told us that she'd bathe. When we went looking for the copper tub, Exchequer stewards told us Henry's men had likewise sought a tub for him. Lady Anne was singing, in a happy mood when we returned with it. We warmed the water properly, sprinkled it with scented roses, essences and oils and helped her in. There's not much to Lady Anne, you know. Quite skinny, little breasts, long and slender neck. You'd wonder what the King saw in her, you would. Anyway, once bathed she had us place her fresh and parfumed body into thirteen yards of satin, black with velvet trim — a most magnificent nightdress Henry'd had her made — and had us next undo her long black hair and brush it till it matched her gown. Then she bade us go. She means to bed the King this night," they'll whisper scandalized neath their hands. "Five days before they're wed. All these years a virgin. Why not wait? I'll never understand."

I shall explain the why and wherefore of my strange decision. I've writ of my new discovered love for Henry and of the great round of celebrations 'fore our wedding, hosted by Calais. This night is one before the King rides to Boulogne for meeting Francis, jousting, wrestling, feasting with him and later then for bringing him hither for our wedding. Henry and my self decided we'd dine privately on this occasion, for on his return and with the marriage, all manner of excitement will ensue, and privacy must needs elude us.

So early in the evening I dressed prettily and went thro the secret door twixt our chambers to his room. He'd had a lovely supper laid upon the board before a blazing fire. Dismissing all his gentlemen he pulled the cushioned chair for me him self, and poured some wine into two jewelled goblets. He bent and kissed my neck.

"Two great Kings will stand at your wedding, Anne. What say you to that?"

I caught his eye and held it. "I say two are fine . . . but one would nicely do." He liked the compliment and smiled, then took his chair cross from me and drank deeply.

"Is that to say you care little for Francis' blessing on our marriage?"

"Not at all. But you have lately found your true power over clergy, Cardinals and Pope. Why share it with another man, even if he is a King?"

Henry thought on this awhile, then smiled — a cool thin

smile like some crescent moon — and said, "I like your thinking, sweetheart, like it well. Here, drink!" We touched goblets.

"To the greatest King of all who fears no man — Henry."

He swelled with pride and seemed, if it is possible, larger than he was, and glowed with spirit so fine and grand that my heart fairly left my chest. I loved him so in that moment, Diary, this man who'd moved the very world for me.

"Let us sup and drink hearty, love," said I. "Then in your great Bed of State you may have me soul and body."

His crescent smile froze in place.

"Now? Here? Before our wedding night?"

"All of those." I took his hand in mine cross the trestle. "Henry, for six years we have broken every rule there is, save one. I say we break them all. What say you?"

He was on his feet in dizzying time and swept me up and covered me with many kisses and a litany of words, all my name, "Anne, Anne, Anne . . ."

And so to separate rooms we made our way to bathe, our two baptisms before the fire. Then we shall come again together for the granting of two dreams. I have always dreamt of marrying for love. Henry wants a son. Let it be so.

Yours faithfully,

Anne

23 October 1532

O Diary,

I swear that God in Heaven mocks me! What other thought is there to have, remembering this night past? This night which prophesied glory, promised fine reward for six years thoughtful sacrifice and two heroes of restraint. Henry, great King and very soul of virile manhood, when confronted with the object of his most sincere and ardent of desires who lay with open arms to hold him, loving lips to kiss him . . . failed. Completely failed.

Mayhaps 'twas too much French wine. He'd drunk at supper, then continued in his bath, I think to gird himself with courage for the moment in which so much importance was imbued. Mayhaps the strain of all the years, our journey to Calais, his poor health were there to blame. Mayhaps — and this I fear the most — he looked at me naked and abed and saw his once fleeing prey no longer some sprightly object of pursuit, but just a soft trapped victim, doe eyes begging for a gentle death. Saw this and went cold. Even Henry's terrible need for sons could not, in that moment, light again the huntsman's fire quenched when I surrendered.

There was nothing to be done. No coaxing, teasing, holding tenderly to wait for desires yet to be aroused. I wished he'd been enraged, railed against this monstrous moment, as one strong passion sometimes births another. But he was shattered, broke beyond repair. His great bulk at once seemed shrunken, he could not meet my eyes which brimmed with tears — not at my own disappointment or sore surprise, but for my love's miserable pain.

So our night of celebration and rebellious union — Henry the King and Anne Marquess de Pembroke soon to be the Queen — did we spend apart, I lying rigid in the great canopied Bed of State, he slumped in a chair by the window waiting for the day.

I must have finally slept for when morning's light pushed open my eyes the King had gone from his apartments. I did not call for my ladies, but struggled my self to don voluptuous lengths of my black satin nightdress. I put on a false face — languorous and satisfied — as one would don a holiday masque to fool all, of my true identity. Returning to my rooms with good cheer I asked my ladies of the King's movements. From their humble, downcast eyes I saw that Henry had donned the masque of some triumphant lion, and now all knew with certainty that this liaison was un fait accompli, my future as their Queen assured. They said my bridegroom'd ridden for Boulogne with a great complement of soldiers at first light.

My heart is heavy as a stone. What vengeful God repays such valiant efforts with so dismal a reward? I must needs pass these next four days in close and private company with this secret. No one can know of Henry's declination. No one at all. I believe his loss of strength is temporary. Mayhaps he needs the golden binding legal marriage brings to harden his "resolve." But sadly, I believe that in that black moment of failing, a monstrous thing was born within the King that no future potent joining with this writer can erase. Like some diseased seed in hard winter earth planted, it threatens with the rain and sun of coming seasons then to sprout and grow into a hideous twisted vine that chokes all joy from life, all life from love.

But nothing's served by so many haunting ruminations. My happy masque shall cleave to my face till its image in the looking glass will fool even my self. My back's a steely rod, my gaze holds steady on the coming years. All, for better or for worse, shall be revealed.

Yours faithfully,

Anne

28 October 1532

Diary,

Here still in Calais. The rain pours and the wind blows. We are yet prevented from our crossing home to England. Much has happened since last I writ both in circumstance and change of heart. In Henry's absence on his journey to Boulogne to fetch the King I waited, battling despair, gathering strength from friends and family. George and Mary, so gay to be in France again, did organize a picnick outing on a windy day along the wild coast. Thomas Wyatt, faithful and consistent friend, still pays respectful court to me and wrote a verse for this occasion, telling of his passion for my self both unrequited and now finally quenched. It reads:

> Sometimes I feel the fire that me brent
> By sea, by land, by water and by wind,

And now I follow the coals that be quent
From Dover to Calais against my mind.

One cold afternoon Thomas and I sat before a fire alone and
filled the day with quiet reminiscences. Ten years now since I returned to English Court from France and he made gift of you,
my Diary. He did inquire had I filled the book, and I told him
that I had writ verse and several memories, but not much more.
Tho staunch a friend is Thomas Wyatt now, the cynic in me
never wants all the truth of this book's contents known.

The Kings arrived the day before my promised wedding
day with garish pomp and circumstance but I, for reasons both
of dignity and protocol, absented my self. Henry came to greet
me privately on his return. Neither he nor I spoke of his sad failure on the eve of his departure, for he bore a grievous new report. In his four days visit to Boulogne the King had there
withdrawn support for our marriage. News had come from Aus-
tria where Charles' troops had soundly routed Turkish foes. A
resounding victory for Katherine's nephew has now left his
troops wanting another battleground. And if Francis gave his
blessing to our marriage now, he felt, the Emperor — sore
vexed — would press his troops against the French.

I knew not what to say. This seemed a cruel insult to our
marriage, a foul and final obstacle in one long road littered with
the same. But something from a well of calm and reasonable
thought prevailed in me that day. For once I saw these circumstances as nothing personal but simply facts of politicks, Pope
and Kings. *I felt a Queen* and so did act as one, offering Henry
neither tears nor tantrums, but instead a quiet compromise. I
told him, "Sweetheart, did we never speak of how our marriage
would be better made on English soil? Those subjects who bear
no love for me would like nothing more than some wedding
they could say was false and never legal. I am happy, I swear I am,
to wait and wed on more familiar shores."

Henry was quiet and seemed to be digesting these thoughts
as tho they were some great and ponderous meal. In this time
there came a knock upon the door that proved to be a man who
was the Provost of Paris him self. He had come on Francis' bid-

ding, bearing me a gift from him — a large and brilliant diamond in a purple velvet box. The Provost gone, the gem (which Henry took to be worth fifteen thousand crowns) sparkling between us, the day seemed suddenly much brighter. We agreed between us that tho Francis was an ally still, he needed further wooing, and this I surely could provide. Then Henry faced me placing both his hands upon my shoulders, and looked into my eyes. He made to speak, lips parted . . . but no words forthcame. He dropped his hands and left me then, he said to see to business. I felt his words, if uttered, would have spoke of this Queenly bearing lately forged in me, and of his pride in it.

So, 'twas time to make my plans for meeting Francis. I knew it must be splendid, a most glittering occasion. He was wont to have magnificent accoutrements — brightest music, sweetest wine, most sumptuous food, richest hangings, costumes elegant beyond imagining. All this I would provide and more, for we must say to Francis with our hospitality that we bore him neither anger nor ill will for his support withdrawn, that it would serve him well if, tho publicly he turned away, that in his private dealings he should be our good and faithful friend.

The night that would have been our wedding celebration, Henry and King Francis dined together at the Staple which I'd taken great pains to decorate most lavishly. Boards and cabinets groaned with weight of Henry's golden plate. Walls were covered, every inch, with jewelled tapestries and every corner glittered, filled with tapers in encrusted golden candelabras. Fine musicians imported from Paris played the latest lilting tunes and when the two great Kings were drunk with food and wine and hearty laughter, all doors flew open. There in a shower of fine glitter, eight masqued ladies emerged dancing to a sprightly tune. Their gowns, exotically designed, were all of gossamer and cloth of silver, crimson tinsel satin laced with knitted gold. Each mysterious lady chose a French guest as partner for the dance. One of them was Francis, looking most outrageous in his violet cloth of gold and collar made of diamonds, pearls and emeralds large as goose eggs. Then on cue all dancing ladies pulled away their masques and did reveal themselves. The French King's partner was my self.

His eyes lit with laughter and surprise. I saw that he admired my audacious entrance and this clever conceit. We leapt and twirled and I could see that Henry, watching from his place as host crowed with pleasure at the sight — High King of France paying court to his sweetheart. Later in a private conversation with the King we spoke of many things. Some memories of my years at his Court, much flattery both I to him and him to me, some serious words that touched on stately matters. He apologized to me (imagine that!) of his public disavowal of our wedding and made his explanation which I, with royal grace, accepted. In place of support he offered up delicious plots whereby using French Cardinals of Tournon and Grammont, he'll trick Pope Clement to delay his final judgement of Divorce which looks to favor Katherine.

The night was splendid, most successful, Henry quite beside himself. I strove to make advantage of his happy mood and when we did retire that evening late I went unbidden into Henry's arms and there found excited welcome. 'Twas marvellous this unexpected bedding, rough as well as tender, hurtful tho but sweet. My body and my womb accepted all of Henry Rex and his most passionate affection showed itself to me. The night moved into day but we never strayed far from that Bed of State. Then the storms began and made our crossing back to England altogether impossible.

We were glad of it. All meals were thus delivered to our bedroom door. No one did we see for three full nights and days. We laughed, sang, played duets, ate, drank, bathed together 'fore the fire, and made plans as well as love. Finally, two hours ago Henry pulled his clothes round him saying he had better make arrangements on our crossing, for the storm was soon to pass. He kissed me once and smiled. More satisfied a man I've never known. Then he left me here alone . . . and I write.

My fears have mostly gone. My marriage is assured and if there is a God in Heaven I will, from these lush days, soon quicken with a son. I see the future bright in front of me, for love blesses this union, and like a beacon it will shine to light our way forever more.

Yours faithfully,

Anne

3 January 1533

Diary,

Praise Jesus, the prophesy comes true. I am carrying Henry's child! Since returning from Calais I had prayed daily on my knees for such a timely miracle, for with the holidays approaching and great affairs of state intruding, the King and I found little time and less of privacy for love. All at Court knew that we had finally bed together. My good friends prayed with me for some happy result of that tempestuous confinement in Calais. My enemies trembled at the thought.

I hardly breathed as my days of monthly bleeding came and passed, and openly rejoiced with each and every queazy rumbling of my belly. I craved crisp apples by the basket, tho till now had never liked the fruit at all. My breasts swelled spilling out my bodices. My face found roundness filling out its angles. I told Henry nothing, wanting sure proof of my condition. But when the date of the second bleeding'd come and gone I went to him — 'twas two days after New Years — said there was a gift I somehow had forgot, and handed him a pretty box of cloth of silver. He looked weary with all manner of weighty business laying heavy on his heart. "I have nothing for you in return, sweetheart."

"O, but Henry," said I, "this gift is one I give in return for one you've given me." He cocked his head, observed my mysterious smile, then opened up the box. There amidst much gossamer tissue lay a tiny lace christening cap that I'd embroidered thro with gold and royal purple thread. He stared at it, his cluttered mind taking several moments to make sense of it.

"Is it true?" he whispered low and almost disbelieving.

"I am pregnant with our son, Henry. Our son."

He grabbed me, crushed me to him crying out my name. He kissed my mouth, cheeks, eyes, throat. I felt hot tears upon my breast, his body heaving with great sobs and whispering, "Thank you, thank you, thank you." Finally he pulled him self erect. His cheeks were glittering wet, his eyes beacons.

"There's much to be done," he told me, "for this boy must be born to a Queen."

I took his hand in both of mine and kissed it.

"My Lord, 'tis I who thank you most humbly."

Then he left me, striding forth with such strength and un-afraid, and all for putting England's crown upon my head.

Yours faithfully,

Anne

16 January 1533

Diary,

Beneath the Court that's made of Lords and Ladies, mem-bers of the Parliament, Counsellors, Chancellors and Bishops lies a Secret Court, a clandestine government of but a few who truly rule the state. These days it is the King and Secretary Cromwell who tell the sun whence to rise, the tide to ebb. These two plot and scheme endlessly, Henry giving further weight to Cromwell's thinking every day. To be sure he is clever and gives full support to our marriage.

This strange man, tho neither large in bodily stature nor ac-quired of gaudy accoutrements like Cardinal Wolsey — fine houses, marvellous jewels, lavish revels — seems to me much greater somehow. An air of vast and dignified importance sur-rounds his modest presence. I know 'tis ambition great as Wolsey's that lights the fire behind those beady eyes. He makes no mistakes, for he's learned well from his own master's demise. I see Henry leans upon the man as he did the Cardinal, and I wonder at it. Will Cromwell, so high in favor now, with the va-garies of time and circumstance, ever fall so low as Wolsey did? Nevermind, for all matters of importance, save one, are now forgot. That matter, Henry tells me, is like a coin with one side our marriage, the other side his divorce from Katherine.

Cranmer, ambassador to the Imperial Court in Spain, was quick called home for his consecration as Archbishop of Can-terbury. In the meanwhile Henry's Roman agents procured from Clement papal bulls necessary for that consecration. The Holy Father must not know that Cranmer's new appointment has one purpose only — to grant the King's divorce — before the Pope grants those bulls, or all is lost. Clement still believes, as Francis promised him, that Henry will abide by his decision on the question of his marriage in a court in France this spring.

So all talk of marriage, pregnancy and coronation are hushed and stilled. This cold and quiet month of January passes ever slowly. Each morning I wake praying there to be no blood between my legs, no miscarriage to defeat so meticulous a battle scheme.

My Father, one of very few who knows my condition, came to visit me in my apartments which boasted all of Henry's gifts — fine rugs upon the trestles, quantities of gold plate, a new gaming table all inlaid with blue tiles. He looked grim and said little as we stood by the fire, so I teased him.

"You have a sour look about you, Father. Have you too many grandchildren already?" He would not answer, would not meet my eyes. But I would not be silenced by his silence and continued pressing him. "Tell me, how was your mind changed on this marriage? Why do you oppose it now?"

"I never wanted it."

"You did! 'Twas you who placed me, still a girl, under Henry's hungry eyes. You who dressed me, coiffed me, served me up like some fancy French delicacy on a silver tray! You wanted him to want me!"

"But not to marry!"

"But why? I'll be a queen, Father. Queen of England."

His mouth shut tight as a clam. He looked as tho' he'd swallowed some bitter potion. In the hearth a hot coal snapped and in that sound, that moment, I knew my father's mind.

"I'll be above you, will I not? I'll be *your* Queen. You will have to bend your knee to your youngest daughter. It galls you, does it not?"

"Beyond measure," he whispered fiercely.

"This was your arrangement, Father, and now you do not like the price."

"Do you deny your own ambition?"

"Yes, I do!" I cried. "When I was just a girl come home from France I had no ambition save one — to marry a sweet boy for love. Then you and Cardinal Wolsey took the gentle flowing stream that was my life and dammed it, blocked and changed its natural course, so when undammed by Henry's most persistent love for me, it became a flood, a raging torrent with a new and treacherous course — its own. A course that drowned Wolsey and now threatens swamping you as well."

I saw his eyes cold and steely hard. "Hear me, Anne. You play a game more dangerous than you care to know. You toy with Kings and Bishops, even Rome. You make fools of men. And other men will die in your name. You will come to no good end, I fear, and you will bring this family down as well."

He took his leave abruptly, leaving his youngest daughter fraught as much with fear as with arrogant rage at her loveless Father.

Yours faithfully,

Anne

27 January 1533

Diary,

The quill trembles as I write, for I have wed the King of England. Six years have come and passed since this marriage was proposed. Six years! I wonder at all the mountains that were made to move for this rare occasion, tho 'twas nothing like I had imagined my wedding would be, done in hurried secrecy in the wee morning hours as all slumbered unaware.

Secretary Cromwell, Henry and my self conceived the plan together whereby all witnesses — there were but a few — Father, Mother, George, Thomas Wyatt and his sister Margaret Lee — were roused from sleep and summoned by our secret messengers to quickly dress by torchlight. Using every quiet discretion they were bid to creep like thieves thro deserted palace halls to Long Chapel where Henry, Cromwell and myself were waiting. In hushed voices, shivering against the cold, we begged their patience and good graces, telling them nothing of our plan. 'Twas not till Thomas Cranmer arrived looking most somber and official that they knew the purpose of this gathering. He bade them all come close to witness a solemn marriage of the King and Anne Boleyn.

'Twas a brief exchange of simple vows. The sound of our voices echoed in the empty chapel. I heard my Mother weeping. I dared not meet my Father's eyes. Henry was in bad humor, stiff with fear and I think anger that our wedding lacked a proper celebration, but was instead this poor and fugitive ritual. As Henry placed the ring upon my finger, the chapel door creaked loudly. 'Twas only a draft that moved the door but the King's eyes darted like a hunted beast and he cursed softly. I wished to soothe him so I took his rigid hand and placed it on my belly.

"No need to worry now, my love. 'Tis done," said I.

Cromwell came forward with his congratulations, then demanded we give up our rings to him for safe keeping. Till Clement's bulls arrive and Cranmer's consecration, this union must stand secret. Then one by one we left the chapel, going our separate ways. I hurried to my apartments. The passages were dark and bitter cold, but I was warm and not alone. I felt the babe that slept within my belly, part of me. I wondered, Can he dream? Does he share my dreams or I his? When my fool makes me laugh, does he feel the warmth and goodness of that laughter?

I regained my rooms and crept past my still slumbering ladies to my cold and lonely bed, and slept the first time a married woman.

Yours faithfully,

Anne

24 May 1533

Diary,

This night I bide happily confined within the London Tower walls as all Queens and Kings have done before their Coronation. 'Tis true that Henry's love and my own persistence made this day possible, but Thomas Cromwell's great scheme must, too, be given credence. Its final machinations I will now relate as History, for this marriage of a man and of a woman does now begin to grow as one more branch of England's ancient tree of lineage, and must deserve such recognition.

My secret marriage stayed a secret till the bulls from Rome arrived and Thomas Cranmer saw his consecration as the highest Bishop in the land. But before he swore allegiance to the Church, and according to the King and Cromwell's clever plan, this good man in front of several witnesses did take a most extraordinary oath, protesting that he'd always pay allegiance to his King and Country first. Then in Parliament a bill was quickly passed that gave supreme authority in all matters spiritual to this Archbishop of Canterbury, forbidding all appeals to Rome. My brother George was sent abroad to give the French King news of our marriage. Francis relayed his generous blessing and his sister Marguerite, who only months before had snubbed me in Calais, sent her kindest greetings to us both. All was ready then.

Henry made announcement of our wedding to the Parliament, and word was sent by royal envoy to Katherine. She remained, as always, stubborn and unyielding. "I am still the Queen," she told the Dukes of Norfolk and of Suffolk, "and shall be until my death." Most recently, I'm told, she had new liveries for her servants made embroidered with Henry's H and her K entwined. I feel nothing for the woman, Diary, not sadness, not anger, not pity. Just the wish that with some magick spell like Merlin's, she might simply disappear. Truly her presence here in Court grows dimmer by the day, the voices of her faithful, while persistent, are little more than sullen whispers now. Still she irks me.

But I digress. The final matter of Katherine and Henry's divorce was brought forward just six days ago in the priory of Dunstable. Archbishop Cranmer there and then, according to his new authority, judged the marriage invalid, giving both parties freedom again to marry. And just one night ago, that same Bishop in a high gallery in Lambeth Manor, gave further judgement that my marriage to Henry was most lawful. And all was ready for my Coronation.

The first day of it dawned blue and perfect. All superstitious rumors boding ill of this occasion — a fish ninety feet long found beached on a northern coast, or of a great comet with a tail like a hoary old man's beard — I ignored. I woke in Greenwich Castle to sounds of distant cannon fire. My ladies pulled me from bed to dress me in a gown of cloth of gold with pearl encrusted sleeves and bodice, and one extra panel o'er my swollen belly. My hair was brushed slow and long and left unbound except a thick diamond circlet from which a gold and gossamer train there fell.

Margaret Mortimer was looking out the window at the river and cried, "Look, 'tis a great red dragon spewing fire from its mouth!" And in deed it was, come floating on a barge attended by several terrible monsters and wild men casting fire and making a great racket. This splendid barge led a small armada — several hundred crafts all bright with colorful flags, tinkling bells and music down the Thames to fetch my self. And so amidst this floating spectacle was I was borne upriver to London Tower, whose mighty guns were set thundering to greet me.

A crowd had gathered at the somber stone fortress' water steps and when, escorted thro the postern gate I saw as people parted, a lovely sight that was my husband Henry smiling, arms outstretched receiving me. Locked in his warm gaze I closed the distance tween us. They were sweet steps to be sure, but sweeter still was when I came within his reach and he laid both hands on his son inside my belly and kissed me reverently. That public display of his love did more for my heart than I can say.

Then old Lord Kingston, keeper of the Tower, strode cross the green courtyard and with Henry escorted me to the Queen's apartments, all restored and new for this occasion. I could not discern whether Kingston's sour face resulted from the pain of his poor crippled body or his well known love for Katherine, and this wrenching task he must endure as my host. But he has so far proven gracious, and no thing mars this pleasant confinement three days after which I shall be reborn a royal person.

Yours faithfully,

Anne

30 May 1533

Diary,

Is it true? Dare I write the words? I am crowned Queen of England. Queen Anne. Anne the Queen. Anna Regina. The words placed together do seem right and fair. My heart now beats a normal rhythm, but in those hours of pageantry and celebration I feared several times that it might burst from equal parts of joy and terror.

Saturday morn saw me conveyed thro crowded London streets hung with all manner of silks and velvets, bright colored banners flapping in the breeze, and fountains gushing forth with wine. Gentlefolk hung from their open windows and commoners, constables, crafts and aldermen were there to see the dazzling procession. There were blue and yellow velvet clad Frenchmen riding splendid palfreys, great Ladies in crimson chariots garbed in crimson, Lord Chancellor of England, London's Mayor all dressed in high ceremonial. With my belly proudly swollen for them all to see, I sat most regal in white tissue trimmed with ermine borne upon an open litter, under canopy of gold cloth held aloft by four knights marching beside me. Finally thirty divers gentleladies and the King's own guard came bringing up the rear.

'Twas a marvellous sight, tho to be honest few who watched cried out "God Save the Queen" or even lifted off their caps to me. My fool teased them crying, "I think you all have scurvy heads and dare not uncover!" and only just a few then obliged. But this was no surprise to me. I know the people bear me little love. More probably they looked to see my sixth finger as I waved to them, or the wen upon my neck they think is some witch's mark.

But 'twas not till the following day that I was taken into Westminster Abbey for my Coronation. This moment, most solemn and triumphant, saw the haughty Duchess of Norfolk carrying my train, the Duke of Suffolk who had tried with all his might to see this day would never come, carrying my crown before me to the altar where stood Archbishop Cranmer. There I knelt and lay prostrate on the flagstones before I rose for my anointing. Henry, God bless his soul, stood to one side in shadows that he could not be seen but by my self, and sent me looks of encouragement to shine alone. I heard little of Cranmer's Latin blessings, ancient rituals of coronation, but felt the sweet weight of St. Edward's Crown upon my bare head, the chilly golden sceptre in my right hand, the warm ivory rod of royalty in my left. Thus crowned I walked the few steps to my gilded velvet throne alone, turned and sat.

I looked out upon that sea of faces who were now my subjects and in that first moment as Queen, felt an awful fear. I wished to smile but I felt my features set hard and rigid as a statue of ice, the sceptre and rod too heavy, and I imagined they might slip from my shaking hands and clatter to the floor. Then all those sour faces would begin to laugh at me, "Anne the imposter Queen — a common girl, a whore who tries to make her bastard our King." But then — and this moment will remain with me forever — I felt the blessed child kick within my womb as if to say, "Mother, have no fear for I am here with you." That sign from within, like a dazzling summer sun, gave off such a fine heat that my rigid features melted and I smiled. I knew it was a smile so radiant and full of love it gave illumination to that gloom filled Abbey and those angry faces, and shone out the painted windows to all of London proclaiming my right to sit upon this throne.

Yours faithfully,

Queen Anne

HE CASTLE WAS SO QUIET that as Elizabeth closed the diary in her lap, she could hear the sound of blood pounding in her own ears. A small smile came to the young queen as she thought, I was with my mother at her coronation. Indeed, a kick from her own tiny unborn foot had given Anne the courage to face the world as queen. Yes, she realized quite suddenly, her mother had been courageous. Had stood fast. *This* was where Elizabeth had gotten her courage, and not, as she'd always believed, from her father. From earliest childhood Elizabeth had been told her mother was a traitor, and that all traitors were cowards. The pain of this knowledge and of Anne's reputation as adulteress and whore had shaken the child's delicate soul and caused the little princess to cease thinking about her mother altogether, and speak her name never. But now Elizabeth could see that Anne had done something wonderful. Something miraculous. She had prevailed against the impossible. She had held off the fervent advances of the King of England for six years in order to wear the crown and ensure her child's legitimacy.

Elizabeth had been reading the diary in stolen moments for months now and its words and history had moved her, educated her, sometimes angered her. Here within these last passages were memorialized her mother's painful making from commoner to queen, the ceremony that seemed more a funeral than a pageant, and the hatred of the people, her subjects, when at last she wore the crown. And these words thrust Elizabeth into memories of her own coronation.

Becoming Queen of England, even born a king's daughter, had been an uphill battle. As a little girl she lived always in the shadow of Edward the heir apparent with no champion. Her father, though kindly, had little time for the high-spirited red-haired child who was no doubt a bitter reminder of his most passionate and now lost love. Even though Elizabeth had spent her childhood far away from court — out of her father's sight and mind — when Great Harry had died, it was for her as if the sun had set and never risen again. Her friend and brother Edward's brief and turbulent reign, the grasping men who sought to control him, all were dead and gone in the blink of an eye.

And then there had been Mary. Next in line of succession, she had grabbed the throne with the talons of a hungry hawk. Her early childhood as Henry and Katherine's only heir had been sweet and mild. But Anne Boleyn had come into their lives and poisoned it all. The cold dance of Mary's bitterness and hatred revolved around Elizabeth's mother and, to a slighter degree, the little half sister herself.

In fact Mary had shown remarkable restraint toward Elizabeth during her own brief reign. Plots were ever afoot to rid the country of the Catholic queen and raise to the throne the popular princess who looked so startlingly like the young Harry, and all of Mary's advisors had urged her to eliminate the "little whore," the Protestant heretic and possible usurper of her crown.

Elizabeth stood from her chair and felt weariness drag down her fragile shoulders under the heavy ermine wrap. She blew out the candles one by one and climbed into her vast canopied bed. The hot bricks Kat had placed beneath the covers had long ago gone cold and she curled into a tight ball for warmth. But sleep evaded her as memories of the tortuous road to her own coronation swam before her eyes like a dreamy theatrical play with herself and her family the players.

The year that Mary became pregnant by her beloved Philip had been for Elizabeth one of the lowest times of her life. With a legitimate heir to the throne about to be born all hopes that she would ever be queen were dashed like a gull's body on a rocky shoreline. She'd been called from her long exile to attend the Queen during her lying in at Greenwich. She knew her presence would give Mary and her councillors much perverse joy. They would gloat watching Elizabeth's claim to the crown deflating as the Queen's belly grew rounder by the day.

One might have thought that Mary's most blessed and fecund days would soften the monarch's vicious treatment of Protestant heretics, but this had not been the case. From her lying-in chamber the Queen, in a murderous frenzy, ordered the burnings increased, as if she required every infidel in England eradicated before her child was brought into the world.

During that confinement Philip had taken a keen interest in his twenty-one-year-old sister-in-law. They had spent many hours together discussing marriage prospects for Elizabeth, all of which would have added to his already substantial power in Europe, and all of which Elizabeth charmingly but emphatically rejected. She remembered finding the Spanish King broodingly attractive, somewhat shorter than herself and always rather unwell, suffering from a persistent and painful stomach disorder. But he'd taken an obvious delight in this robust girl whose wit and scholarship contrasted with his older wife's dour piousness. Elizabeth guessed that Philip's interest in her was at least partly practical. Mary could easily die in childbirth, and if he wanted to keep control of England, he would certainly seek to marry his wife's sister. But Elizabeth also thought, remembering those days as they waited for Mary to deliver the son the midwives had promised, that Philip had more than a practical interest in her. She was very sure he had fallen in love with her and would have preferred sharing England's throne with herself.

But Mary's child would not be born. The long awaited date arrived and passed with no sign of the Queen's labor. Mary sat for hour upon miserable hour amongst cushions on the floor watching in sadness and horror as her belly began to grow smaller and flatter. And as it deflated, Elizabeth's power and importance began to grow in inverse proportion. It was clear that Mary had suffered a false pregnancy and that, indeed, the aging queen might be barren after all. Mortified at her failure, Mary had risen from her lying-in chamber and announced her court would be moving to the palace at Oatlands. Elizabeth had been summarily dismissed and sent back into exile.

On their separate journeys Mary and Elizabeth had ridden out among the people and discovered that Mary's hold on her subjects had faltered. No one under thirty was a Catholic anymore, and the Queen's murderous treatment of the heretics had angered the populace. The disappointing false pregnancy was the final blow which, like an executioner's axe, had finally severed Mary from the hearts of the English. The gaudy procession to Oatlands, Elizabeth was told, had found along the road many somber faces and forced shouts of "God save the Queen." But Elizabeth's modest caravan back to Hatfield, where country folk had lined the rutted roads to warmly greet her, had shocked the Princess with the profound truth that the common people of England loved her deeply, saw in her the female embodiment of their beloved Henry VIII, and believed her to be their next queen.

In the following year all that was left was for Mary to die. In the end it was her very womanhood that slew the Queen, her female organs rotting inside her. A self-interested Philip had done his part, convincing Mary in her last excruciating days to name Elizabeth her successor. So when the royal messengers rode into Hatfield with the long awaited news, Elizabeth had been more than ready for her queenship. Ready and eager.

My poor mother, thought Elizabeth. Hardly a soul willingly bared his head in her honor at her spring coronation. On Elizabeth's own day, in the dead of winter, thousands of caps had been doffed and thrown high in the icy blue air. The people had enveloped her in love that glorious day. The spectacle had surpassed even Elizabeth's imagination. Streets thronged with celebrants. A thousand horsemen in proud procession, her gold brocaded litter, beloved Robin riding his white stallion behind her, great cries, prayers and good wishes, tender words that came in wave after comforting wave. It had been a time of purest joy.

"God save Your Grace!" they had cried.

"And God save you all!" she had called back to them, her heart bursting. At every stopping point along the procession's way there had been a small pageant, a recitation spoken, a song sung. And at each Elizabeth had listened carefully and joined in with the cele-brants so that by the time she had moved on to the next, she had given each of her subjects a tiny piece of her heart. The promise she had made to a wildly cheering crowd of Londoners at Cheapside, that she would be good to them as ever a queen was to her people, had thrilled her no less than it had her listeners, because Elizabeth saw clearly that it was to her people and her people alone she owed her ascendancy. Without their love, she felt sure, Mary might have been so bold as to see her executed for heresy. Without their love she would never have felt the crown of England on her head.

Elizabeth's eyelids finally felt the weight of sleep pulling them closed.

That love was what my mother lacked, thought Elizabeth just before sleep took her. Anne was simply misunderstood. Misunder-stood to death.

4 June 1533

Diary,

This summer is the sweetest of my life. The long days at Windsor are warm, the air fragrant with cut grass and roses. Henry chose to make no hunting progress this season so he might stay close by my side, tho he rides out often of a day to shoot or hawk, but then returns by nightfall bringing me natural tokens of his affection — bunches of my favorite violets, baskets of juicy blackberries, an owl's feather, a loveknot of plaited grass woven thro with pussy willows and wilted lilies. The King is most proud of my good belly, and I daresay a woman could be held in no higher esteem than I am by him.

I've been given from Katherine's wardrobe a great quantity of jewels, silver cups with covers, pots, beds and stools. Thro the men of my own Privy Council I may now collect revenues from my many rich estates. And Henry has honored me further as a *femme sole* which allows for me conducting my business without his interference.

Happily we have heard grumblings from neither Rome nor the Emperor Charles. They must comprehend that one tangles with Henry at ones own peril. Francis remains our friend and sent a delightful wedding gift — four mules and a fine litter in the Italian style, all richly carved and gilt, hung with antique tapestries and lined with royal purple velvet cushions filled with eider down. The accompanying letter said he hoped that his gift was worthy of so beautiful a Queen.

My apartments are day and evening scene of every kind of merrymake. Music, dancing, gaming and masques. I have a new fool — a woman, of all things! She does make us laugh with her pranks and clever observations. There are many romances amongst my pretty maids and their gentlemen with their small intrigues and giggling plots. In all I keep a virtuous and peaceful household. All quarrels proscribed, I've forbidden my servants frequenting infamous places or keeping lewd company. My ladies, never pampered or allowed licentious liberties, are kept from idleness, sewing for the poor and daily attending divine service. Methinks sometimes I've grown overserious, but now with Henry named Supreme Head of Church and State this Queen must set a most Christian example. And, too, God does bless true believers with male children, so I shall conduct my self most morally and obey his laws.

One young courtier does move my heart. He is Mark Smeaton, a fine musician and singer. He is handsome with an honesty and grace that brings my mind to young Percy as he was when I first loved him. Mark pays me far more homage than is due even a sovereign, and it feels to me like a courtly form of love. He sits at my knee, plucks the lute and sings romantic ballads sweet as God's angel. I should not encourage him, but his devotion does so touch my heart that I often call for his presence in my smallest gatherings. Even Henry loves Master Smeaton, shows him favor as a father might a son.

I am in fine health with high color in my usually sallow cheeks. The boy turns and kicks most heartily, and none dare talk of miscarriage or stillborn babes. But to be truthful, I've had some fear of my own death in childbirth, and so sent a message to the Nun of Kent inquiring of her intelligence once again. In her prophesy that told of my Tudor son and his long and prosperous reign she never spoke of me or my life. And so I would call upon her to see again with those terrible eyes my fate as well. For if I were to die, there are some plans I might have in that event arranged, and certain letters writ. But the good sister, so it seems by correspondence from her Abbess, stays in strict seclusion seeing no one, all worldly matters deferred to spiritual ones. Thus my fate will only be revealed in its slow and timely fashion, and I will live with my impatience.

Yours faithfully,

Anne

12 July 1533

Diary,

Finally word from Rome has come and it is very bad. Two days past when Henry rode out to hunt I felt uneasy. Once gone I worried he might be in danger and my fears prophetic. I swear that since this pregnancy I have another sense past sight and hearing, a kind of knowing without reason. So Henry rode out and when night fell he did not return, but neither did I feel him ill or injured. As I was being put to bed the Earl of Shrewsbury arrived to say that having ridden farther than expected, his Majesty would stay the night at Buckdon Lodge, hunt another day, returning after that. A cold thrill ran thro me and I asked the man if the King was well, and if his hunt had been successful. The King was very well in deed, replied Shrewsbury, and as for his accomplishments, the stags had been elusive and he had as yet caught nothing. I slept, tho not soundly and passed the following day in a strange state.

That night the King returned with several men in a loud and jolly humor. But when he came to my apartments and with smiles and great embraces asked after me and our son, I felt unspoken pain, illness of ease. I pressed him once and he claimed that he was only tired from the distance ridden. But I bade him sit, put my hands to his temples to stroke his brow and pressed him again, but carefully. He let out one long sigh which collapsed his large body into a sagging mass. He made to speak but no words came. His great ringed hand covered his eyes and with a dull voice he spoke my name.

"Anne . . . I have not been hunting."

"Where have you been?"

"At Guildford with the men of my Privy Council. I did not wish to worry you, sweetheart, but truth is we have heard from Clement on the matter of my divorce."

"He will not grant it?"

"Worse. He has annulled our marriage and declared all issue from your body illegitimate. If I do not separate at once from you and reinstate Katherine by September . . . I am excommunicated. Archbishop Cranmer too." Another sigh escaped him and he seemed suddenly small.

I knew that I should make my self smaller still, so I knelt at Henry's feet. When I spoke, the words echoed in my head as tho it were a hollow shell.

"Were we not expecting as much, Henry?"

"We were, of course we were. But knowing a great storm is on its way does not blunt the damage it does when finally it arrives. Fields and crops are still flooded, trees still uprooted, beaches washed away, people left dead." He shook his head, a confused man. "I was not expecting to feel so . . . empty. The Catholic Church has been mother to me for all my life. I have been a most faithful son, and it has given me great succor."

With this I could not argue, and I knew it unwise to speak harshly of a man's mother to him, even if he had spoken harshly first, so I said nothing.

"Now the ungrateful son will cut off his mother's head and replace it with his own." He looked at me with desperate eyes. "She left me no choice, Anne, she left me no choice!"

I gently took his hands. "Listen to me. Some mothers refuse to let their sons grow to manhood and assume their Godgiven rights. And Henry, as King of England you have ancient and sovereign rights. If she will not let you take them freely, you must take them by force. For the good of England!"

He was nodding silently, in uncomfortable agreement.

"Is there nothing can be done?" I asked.

"My canon scholars suggest going over Clement's head, appealing to a general council. But this would just delay the judgement."

"Could not Francis help you? He has the Pope's ear. And what does Secretary Cromwell say?"

Henry laughed coldly. "He says the same as you do about my rights as King coming first before the will of the Church. But sometimes I wonder at the man. I think he has no fear of God in him."

"I think Master Cromwell fears God as we all do, Henry. He simply does not fear the Church. And in this I believe he is wise."

Henry smiled a strange smile and touched my cheek gently. "My Lutheran wife. She has stolen me from my mother, lured me away with many promises greater than are in Heaven."

My body shivered when he said that, for I'd always believed 'twas I who was stolen. But I kept my counsel and did not contradict him, for I knew I had made a promise whose fulfillment was worth the loss of the Mother Church. Our son. His little Prince. And the unbroken succession of great Tudor Kings.

Yours faithfully,

Anne

5 August 1533

Diary,

I am betrayed most foul, and my betrayer is Henry. So unexpected, this miserable deed, for my husband had been so kind and recently sent to my apartments in Greenwich where I would soon hie for my lying in, a splendid bed of state, picked for me by him from his treasure house, all hung with crimson satin, fringed with gold. And on behalf of me, to Katherine's great annoyance, he asked from her that some linen be surrendered to me — one very rich triumphal cloth from Spain which had swaddled all the royal babes in their baptism.

But on Wednesday last, whispered gossip found my ear of Henry's escapades with Elizabeth Carew, my own waiting lady, a girl of great beauty but little mind. Evil intentioned lies, I thought, and cleverly timed with me ponderously heavy and wretched, my usual razor tongue filed smooth by approaching maternity. It seemed not possible, for Henry had possessed my self, body and soul, for not yet one year. One short year after so many, fighting side by side like soldiers in a great crusade.

But when at Sunday mass thro muffled bells and rustling taffeta, I chanced to hear it whispered how many nobles — my enemies by name — were assisting that affair, it dawned suddenly as truth to me. I knew it meant nothing to my high position, for I am secure, the crown firm upon my head. His was conduct neither wrong nor even remarkable by royal standards. But still the thought of Henry's passion spent on someone not my self withered the new and fragile love I bore for him. All those years, pain, struggle squandered in the arms of some artless girl.

I strode to Henry's chambers, strode as well as one grotesquely bloated, face and belly, can and flew at him in reckless rage. "You whoring swine!" was what I cried when I slapped his cheek which came up hot and angry red. He was stunned, my faithless lover, husband, King. He looked at me with deadly calm, but his eyes told the truth of ugly rumors, and my own eyes stung then with acid tears.

"Where is the sweet and tender man who promised everlasting adoration, he who signed his letters 'Henry seeks no other'?!" I made much of turning this way and that as if to search for such a man. "Where is he then, for I see only a beastly, two faced traitor here!"

Henry's gaze, returned with such contempt, surprised my self, for I expected some measure of guilty remorse. Instead he fixed me with a steady stare and icy cold reply. "You will shut your eyes, sweetheart, and endure as those better than your self have done. You ought to know that I can at any time lower you as much as I have raised you." He touched his reddened cheek, then put his giant hand around my throat. Gently, dangerously he held it so. I scarcely breathed. "Queen Anne," he whispered I thought contemptuously, and dropped his hand. "Go."

I stood my stubborn ground and met his eye. "I'll go,

Henry, but know that you have grievously offended your faithful wife, mother of your son." I turned and proudly quit his chambers for my own where I have nursed my private grief. For there is no one save you, Diary, who knows the fathomed depth of this betrayal. I am quite alone.

We have not spoke now for several days, I to Henry, or he to me. The child kicks hard against my belly and in this pain I find solace, for if the King's love is gone, this tiny child beneath my heart will remain a golden cord between His Majesty and me — shining, unbreakable and forever.

Yours faithfully,

Anne

29 August 1533

Diary,

It has been a glorious day! All drums and happy trumpets, banners flapping in a gentle August breeze, I took my place upon the royal barge. Henry, good cheer and kisses (all arguments forgot) was there to see me off. His embrace was warm and strong. He whispered in my ear, "I love you, Nan. We are one in this boy," and placed his hand, a blessing upon my belly. Several "hurrahs" and he was gone.

The moment was mine alone, more lovely somehow than my Coronation, trees swaying on the banks, the River Thames all green and rippling gold. The flooding tide lifted us and bore us down the winding course toward Greenwich, now all lined with common folk. They waved but did not smile. I wished they would have smiled at me, their Queen, her belly bulging with their Tudor heir. But most are loyal still to Katherine and her girl. They will change when he is born, I'm sure and love me then, cry aloud for Queen Anne's long life and happy health. Greenwich Castle's brickwork wall and battlements were glowing red in sunset light when we arrived. Many Lords and Ladies waited on the shore in all their finery, come to help me take my chamber. This ceremonial had been prescribed many years before by Henry's father, first Tudor King. Mayhaps since that Crown was won through battle, not bloodline, he had wanted a ritual made of his children's birthing.

The great river of all History, thought I then, ran beneath this royal barge and Henry, I, our child like tiny streams, had emptied into this and evermore were part of it.

With quiet pomp and muted revelry was I conducted to the chapel where my good friend Cranmer waited. I took Communion and these nobles did pray with him as he asked aloud that God send me a great hour. As we left I saw the Princess Mary, thin and stiff, her dark eyes following my progression. I smiled kindly at her as I went by, for I felt full enough of love to offer her some, but I could see she took the gesture as a taunt. Never mind, I thought, she wishes me and my child dead.

The gathered Lords and Ladies then escorted me to my Chamber of Presence, served me spice and wine and toasted to me heartily. My brother George was one amongst the men, bursting with much pride and happiness for me. I took his hand and whispered, "Loyal brother, think you that this will turn the tide with them and me?"

"I do," said he. "When you are mother to the one day King it will be as if a veil were torn from all their eyes, and they will finally see the sweet woman who is my sister."

I almost cried, such was the wave of grateful love I bore for George. But then before the tears began to flow, he and my uncle Lord Rochford each took a hand and led me to the door of my lying in chambers, bade me good luck and left me there. All gentlemen retired and my ladies followed me in and closed the door behind. As law prescribes from now till after birth I cannot leave these walls, and will see these cloistered women only.

The privy place was dark and airless, heavy tapestries covering walls and roofs and windows, all save one. I saw the narrow pallet bed where birthing's done, the extra braziers to heat the room, bottles of parfum to cover the sticky smell of blood, and shuddered at the pots and basins, piles of linen torn in rags, a great array of midwives knives and dangerous instruments.

The other chamber was a far more cheerful place. My Bed of State was greatly carven and richly hung. I moved ahead in time and saw myself receiving high born visitors, a proud mother, sitting up amongst the fine lawn sheets in a mantle of deep crimson velvet furred with ermine. And when they'd paid respect to me, they'd view the little Prince asleep in his lavish Cradle of Estate, four pummels of silver and gilt, a cloth of gold and ermine lined counterpane.

They say my labor soon begins. I pray with all my heart for bravery, to not cry out, to steel myself against the pain. For there are those who wait outside this chamber door who long to hear me shriek in agony, they hate me so. Please, God, make me strong in my great hour and make my child a fine and healthy son.

Yours faithfully,

Anne

8 September 1533

Diary,

I have a daughter and she is named Elizabeth. Her birth, terrible and bloody, the witchlike midwives murmuring musky spells between my outspread thighs, had been a dark dream. My prayers for a son, sung over and over like an unheard mass were lost amidst my cries and curses. The crimson curtains of my stately bed hung damp, no breeze ruffling the rank and steamy air when in strode Henry, all smiles, the smell of celebration ale upon his breath, come to see his little Prince. He did not see my ladies cowering, whispering in fearful tones as they hid their faces, lest he see them and later remember them as accomplices to this evening's crime. He only heard the lusty cries of his heir long wished for.

"Where is he, Anne? Where is my son?" The months, nay, years of strain were gone from his bloated features. He looked just then young and princely as he had when first he'd woo'd me seven years before. "Show me my son." He looked round the room then, from lady to lady, stared at the gilt cradle and felt a cold and fearful draft at his heart.

"You have a beautiful daughter," I said with what small fraction was left of my courage.

"A daughter," he whispered. "A daughter?!" His eyes blazed with murder — my own, the child's. I feared he'd take the tiny wrinkled babe and crush her head like some ripe melon. Smash her body against the bedpost till it was still and limp. His unspeakable anger was a terrible silent wave rearing up to crash down upon my bone weary shores.

"You," he shrieked, "are a liar, liar! You promised me a *son*. For this whimpering cunt I have put aside my pious Queen, the love of my subjects and Rome! You, Madame, will pay for this girl!" And he strode, scarlet and sweating, from my chamber.

A son. That simple promise to Henry which kept alive our dream, our love, is to be my own great undoing. But O, some promises are hard to keep. Some promises are best never made. Some promises are lies we never meant to tell.

My mind spins like a paper wheel. What of the Nun of Kent and the "Tudor son" she clearly foretold arising from my belly? A *son,* she said, who would illuminate the British lands. Did I understand wrongly? Meant she by her words a heavenly orb? Could that "son" have blinded me to her true meaning? When I, no more than a skinny girl, stood in that spare Christian cell, the oracle's half mad eyes darting this way and that, the prophecy spilling from her bitten lips, did I long to hear with so terrible a need that I took the meaning I sore desired? It must be so, for that soothsayer does never swear falsely. I am such a fool!

When they'd bathed and swaddled the newborn, tightly bound so only the face was seen in yards of cloth, they placed her in my arms. I looked down to see this creamy pink creature of my own destruction. She was wailing, toothless, struggling to be free from muslin bondage. Her eyes flew open and then I did gasp to see . . . they were Henry's eyes! Henry's angry eyes.

Elizabeth, O God, you are your father's child. My womb, my blood, my prayers but your father's rage. Will he let you live? Will he let me live? My innocent child, my daughter, what terrible world have I brought you into? These breasts of mine cry for you and in this dim warm moment I long for nothing more but to lay you down upon my heart and let you feed upon my mother love. But now she comes, your wet nurse, large and soft and comforting, and she wrests you from my aching arms. It is with a humble smile she takes you from me, but she knows with proud certainty that *she* will feel your mouth suckling, she will count your fingers, toes, comb the flaxen silk upon your head, dry the tears I'll never see. No, they'll not let me near you, child, for you will be a Princess reared. There'll be curtsies, not kisses. Embraces through yards of stiff satin. Courtly speech, no tender words of love.

O Elizabeth, tiny and squalling, I hear you in the next chamber. Hear you, feel you, remember you still in my belly. I'll ask to see you and they will bring you to me this night, but tomorrow you'll be gone, sequestered in the royal nursery, so far away from here down dark and draughty passages. No crying infant let to mar Henry's festivities, Henry's council meetings, Henry's lovemaking. Less and less will I see you. My breasts will dry and cease to ache for you. I'll be made to sing and dance, chatter lightly with my ladies, play at cards. Be the Queen and never hold you.

I read once of a nameless but remembered Roman noblewoman, jailed in some black prison. Starved by her captors who meant to kill her this way, she was kept alive by her own daughter who came to visit daily, and fed her in secret. This good child, herself a new mother, every day hidden by the folds of her dress, pretending embraces, suckled her mother at her own milk heavy breast. The old woman never weakened nor died and when the guards discovered the ruse they were moved, perhaps by maternal memories, and freed her. Mother and daughter, daughter and mother. Cherished, cherished the other. O, Elizabeth . . .

Henry hates me now, says I've duped him, shamed him. All wild and grandiose tournaments and feasts for his little Prince's birth are quashed, redrawn into a quiet round of toasts to the health of the Princess and prayers for my womb's quickening with the desired son. And we will try again to make that son, your father Henry and your mother Anne. Rage with our bodies, one against the other and pray with every thrust that when next I come to this lying in chamber, it is with the promised boy.

But we will fail, always. I know this with a terrible certainty. The mad nun foretold my Tudor sun and when I look into your eyes, your father's eyes, I know that sun is you, Elizabeth. You will shine on all the world with your light and glory, despite your father's fury. Of this I'm sure.

My future flies at me like some dark shrieking wind. I am lost, child, but you are found. And you shall be Queen.

Yours faithfully,

Anne

12 October 1533

Diary,

Of late I have had an unhappy education. A pregnant Queen will be lied to for her health, nay the health of her child. I was kept ignorant of a great scandal — the Holy Nun of Kent at its center. She has been speaking out against me and the King, saying we shall come to no good end, with plagues upon our house, and that Henry's marriage to Katherine is good. His Majesty is angry in the extreme, and Cromwell has had the nun arrested for treason. The Secretary has drawn up a list of her supporters and all tremble at the thought of their name on that list. There is talk that she will confess to corruption, that she has been led astray by divers courtiers, Thomas More amongst them.

I flop like a gasping fish on the sand. What shall I think of her? Has she lied or does she confess to escape a traitor's death? Has she never had a true gift of sight, and were her words to me those years ago the ravings of a mad peasant girl made prophetess by Bishops hungry for miracles?

I believed her then, but I took her words the way I wished to hear them. Elizabeth will yet rule, I know this in my heart, tho my firm hand is necessary in the keeping of this promise. My husband the King has grown plainly weary of me, and I have no strength to rekindle his love. He is pleased enough with his little daughter, speaks to me of an Act of Succession which will promise her place on the throne before Mary, but only after the sons he thinks I will bear him. So I am mild and kind to Henry these days, and give him great encouragement in that law's passage. The ones who hate me more than ever smirk and whisper that I follow at Henry's heels like a dog. This knowledge gnaws at my guts but I must grovel, for I feel in my heart I will have no sons with Henry and I must preserve Elizabeth's crown.

'Tis strange to think on Elizabeth's coronation day, for now she is so tiny and soft. Pink and gold, sweet eyes that recognize me as her mother, recognize my body as her home, tho few are the moments I may hold her close, and never may I lend her my breast to suck. But she knows me, folds comfortably into me, smiles at me. I love this child with a heart that needs no urging, like the one that loved young Percy, but greater. Whenever I am seated I call for her to be brought to me on a velvet cushion that is placed at my feet. All my ladies think she is beautiful, the flaxen ringlets, the warm satin skin that smells so new.

I begged Henry that we might dispense with convention, allow our Elizabeth to stay with us where we reside and not be sent from Court to her own household far away. But he scoffed at me.

"I like my daughter well enough, but she is a daughter, Anne. Do you not think you should spend more effort on making us sons than mooning over this girl?" He was cold when he said that, and empty . . . like a hedge maze in winter. I knew repeating my plea was useless, but I hoped his fickle mind would turn and he would relent, allow me the comfort of my babe.

"Royal children are sent to their own household when they are but three months old," I said. "These rules are made by men who know nothing of a mother's need to hold her child, Henry."

He turned on me then, roaring like a baited bear. "This is the ritual of Kings, Kings! And you shall forbear to contradict them, Madame!"

I fell to my knees and kissed his hand to calm him, murmuring apologies. I am ashamed to be brought so low, but I will not endanger Elizabeth with my arrogance.

Yours faithfully,

Anne

LIZABETH SAT STUNNED and staring blindly at the halos around the flickering candles, tears coursing down her cold cheeks.

"Mother," she whispered. She sighed, expelling all the breath she had in her body, and felt hardly able to draw another in again. The revelation had shaken her very soul. *Her mother had loved her.*

Adored her. Fought to keep her by her side. But it seemed to Elizabeth, reading between the words, that this consuming mother love had taken Anne quite as much by surprise as its disclosure had taken Elizabeth. Anne had for so long fought for the crown, struggled to love Henry, and defended herself against her enemies that the child who would be born to her had become in her thinking the desired Prince.

What a great love it must have been, thought Elizabeth, for her mother to have overcome the catastrophe of Elizabeth's femaleness. Or was it, she wondered, quite simply what motherhood meant? A child is born of your body and you are helpless to do other than love it whether it be male or female, docile or a shrieking horror, beautiful or monstrously deformed. But Anne, it seemed to Elizabeth, had felt more deeply, fought more bravely, groveled more pitifully, and believed in Elizabeth's destiny more stridently than any mother was wont to do for a *daughter*.

She had loved her.

And what of Henry, her faithless father? What was she to think of him? It was wrong to vilify him, she knew. He was the King and, according to unwritten but age-old English law, he had the right to a mistress, whatever he felt for his Queen.

He had died the year Elizabeth was fourteen, and by that time he had been transformed from the gloriously handsome, hale, and merry King whose likeness graced portraits, tapestries, jewelry, furniture, and coin to the obscene mountain of flesh whose eyes were mere slits in a bloated, lecherous face. And who, for his great size and diseased leg, had to be carted about from room to room on a litter carried by six men. She had seen him for what he'd become and knew that he had cared very little for her. Elizabeth had been only a valuable political asset to Henry, a princess to marry to a foreign prince, and he had rarely bothered to see her over the years.

Whenever she had been called to audience with him, her child's heart had quivered with fear such as most men reserve for their day of judgment before God. She dared not meet his eye, for she knew that always he required complete obedience and submission to himself. That was a child's unalterable duty to a parent. And of course Henry was king and well acquainted with mindless obedience from his subjects, no matter how high or noble. She would, during such audiences, fall many times to her knees and remain entirely silent at his feet, breathing in the stench of the rotting flesh and putrid bandages of his sore leg. He would forget sometimes that his daughter was there, moving on to other business and only releasing her from prostration when her knees were bruised and she was faint from the noxious fumes.

And yet, Elizabeth mused, she had always somehow loved her father, admired his power and the loyalty he inspired in his subjects. And she reveled in the parallels that many of her courtiers drew between his character and physique in his younger days and her own. She had always found a way to forgive him his trespasses, his ignorance of her personal existence, his dark and vicious tantrums. His murder of her mother.

Stop, Elizabeth commanded herself silently as she replaced the diary in her locked chest. She could think on this no longer. It was quite enough for one night, to have learned that she had been cherished by her mother. Something inside the young queen felt to be expanding, growing like a seedling breaking through soft earth, unfurling its tenderest parts and reaching for the warm sun above.

And as the morning light crept in through her mullioned windows, Elizabeth Tudor, daughter of Anne Boleyn, found herself smiling.

※

"Your Majesty!"

Elizabeth turned to see her royal secretary William Cecil rushing to catch up with her as she moved down Richmond's Long Gallery, taking the only exercise she would manage on this cold and rainy afternoon. Cecil unashamedly plowed through the crush of her waiting ladies who surrounded her like a flock of gaudy birds, and strode along at her side.

"Good day, my lord. I hope you're well. I did miss our morning conference."

"Debate with the privy council was heated and we only just concluded, Your Majesty."

She gestured with her finger for him to begin the report, but he demurred, casting a disapproving glance at the twittering ladies.

"You have my complete attention," said Elizabeth.

But Cecil was stubborn and refused to speak whilst among such a flighty audience.

"Very well." She turned to her ladies and dismissed them with the most subtle lift of her chin. They dispersed and almost magically disappeared. She and Cecil were finally alone in the long hall which echoed with rain pattering on the windows.

"Let me guess," began Elizabeth. "Scotland. You want me to throw more of my money at the Protestant rebels."

"It is imperative," pleaded Cecil.

"I've sent too much already. I'm very poor, Cecil. And I doubt the French will take kindly to my openly opposing their allies."

"Then you wish the Catholics to rule the country?"

Elizabeth sighed with exasperation.

"Then send your troops and make a stand."

"No. I will not."

"You are wrong, Madame, and entirely ill advised in this decision!"

Elizabeth stopped and wheeled on her councillor with the intention of chewing the head completely off his neck. But his look was so sincere and so determinably *right* that she paused. William Cecil was the most conscientious of her advisors and the most prodigiously well informed. Her former steward was a staunch Protestant and had somehow managed to make himself indispensable to her Catholic sister Mary during her reign while remaining faithful to Elizabeth.

She realized that he *always* took this position in support of English intervention with the Scots. He had believed in the rightness of it since the 1540s when he himself had fought at the battle of Pinkie.

"I am not inclined to agree with you just now, Lord Cecil. Speak to me of it in a week or two."

"In that case, I shall resign my post," he said suddenly.

"What!"

"That is how strongly I feel. It would be a mistake of unparalleled proportions, and I could no longer call myself your advisor if you insisted on pursuing such a disastrous course."

Elizabeth stared at her secretary, searching his face for even a glimmer of indecision. There was none. Not the smallest particle of doubt.

"Very well. See to the details and make full report to me."

"Thank you, Your Majesty. I promise you will be glad of your decision." He turned to go.

"Do you also promise that when we are finished paying for a foreign war we will have enough money for our own government?"

"No, Madame. But I will promise that your northern borders will be safe from a Catholic invasion in future."

"Well, that is something," said Elizabeth tartly. "That is something."

2 December 1533

Diary,

I am sick with an anger that lives like some black rat gnawing at my belly. They have taken Elizabeth from me, taken her to Hatfield where she'll live with strangers who'll soon become her family. I am the Queen and I am helpless in this unnatural matter. Torn from my child, trapped within cold tradition — rules made by men with no care for women's hearts.

Miserable too is my hatred grown blacker every day for the Lady Mary. How wretched was my luck that, finally past the dreadful battle with her mother Katherine, I should have no respite, none at all. For like a dragon rising from the ashes of its slain predecessor, Mary looms large, fangs bared, burning eyes fixed on the crown she claims as hers. She defies her father, sweetly stubborn as her mother has done, but defies him all the same. When told she was no longer Henry's heir, her title Princess of England stripped away and now simply Lady Mary, she replied that she knew of no Princess of England save her self and refused to answer to any name but that which she had earned rightly in God's eyes and under English law.

This girl, just seventeen, flirts with treason, for she knows these words and quietly rebellious deeds inflame the population who still hate me, the Great Whore, and Elizabeth, the Little Whore, and would gladly see this Spanish bitch upon the throne. O Diary, I have prayed fervently that my subjects come to love me and my child. But they are too perverse. When I give generously to the poor in every town into which we move our Court — £10 for a cow to feed their children when several shillings would make that purchase possible — it is said the witch tries to buy her subjects' love. And tho the people hate the scurvy Pope and clergy, rail against corruption and indulgences, they would have a Papist Queen again and long for Catholic ritual. I do not understand!

Here at Court the Lady Mary has her loyal followers as well who, given half a chance, would raise a traitorous banner in her name for all those common folk to follow. There is always whispering that speaks of my well deserved downfall. And this low gossip lives always with Mary at its center. Somehow the girl's spirit must be bent or broken, but I fear Henry's plan for this will come to a bitter end. He has ordered Mary hie to Hatfield, take up residence there and serve as Maid of Honor to her half sister Elizabeth. I asked the King, Why place a viper in our daughter's nursery? But he dismissed my worries, seeing Mary only disobedient, never dangerous.

Mayhaps I see enemies lurking behind every tree but I feel

Henry's scheme and his dismissal of my fears as some mild revenge upon myself. Revenge for his humiliation that a daughter, not a son, was born. For tho he pursues this Act of Succession into law, he remains distant from me, coming to my bed only as need prescribes. I would in deed be blind if I did not see the way his eyes devour my pretty maids, or deaf if I did not hear the bitter tone he uses when he calls me his Queen.

The love for Henry which I nursed to feeble life now withers on its slender vine, for it was fed most volubly by his great passion, and not from some inner well within my self. The lack of that love from him to me which I took as my daily measure for so many years, leaves me hollow and bereft. My friend and brother George is still away, Ambassador to France. And now my child is taken from my arms. Here am I left among the wolves at Court who, given any chance, would tear the very flesh from my bones.

I must be strong, inhale some courage and begin again. My enemies shall not have what they desire. I have struggled for this place and name and will not be moved to doubting it. Queen Anne am I. Let them try to shake me from this throne. Let them try.

Yours faithfully,

Anne

7 April 1534

Diary,

I am pregnant once again. Henry is delighted with the news and hopeful for his son. But wary of another disappointment, he is ever distant, mildly cruel. Whispered gossip has him sleeping not with courtly ladies only, but with low prostitutes that he visits in the town. I worried of the poxes he might bring to our bed, and so designed to take my self to a crone I'd heard had cures better than any apothecary's medicines.

On this year's first spring day I dressed modestly and making no commotion of my going, sent for a plain carriage and usual driver. Companion for the journey was Purkoy, a pup given me by cousin Francis Bryan as a gift. Small and comfortable in my lap, he lets me pet him endlessly, his velvet fur between my mindless fingers. He follows loyal at my heels, a sweet and childish subject who loves me blindly.

The sun shone hot upon my shoulders at the palace gate. Several people stared but no one spoke to me and merely bowed for my passing. But when the carriage came my good driver'd been replaced by some liveried stranger, tall and coarsely handsome — John he said his name was. His smile as he helped me in was half a leer, and I hoped he was a good man who loved his Queen. But using some precautions I determined he should never see the crone I visited for he might, if his loyalties were elsewhere placed, believe me conspiring with witches and begin malicious rumors — for I know this is how ugly gossip starts.

So we rode out that fine warm day, John the driver, Purkoy and my self — flew clattering down the cobble streets, then narrow alleys to a small tenement house in ill repair. Purkoy tucked under my arm, I took care when I knocked, that John should not see the wrinkled woman who opened up the rude and creaking door.

"You're welcome, good lady," said she and beckoned me inside. 'Twas not the dark and morbid place that I'd imagined, nor what was grimly promised from the street. Sun shone in thro garden door and windows casting light and shadows on the trestle tables piled high with drying flowers, herbs, and even living insects inside jars. More plants hung, heads down from ceiling beams, throwing fragrant odors from them, and something burning in a pearly shell gave off a sweet smelling smoke that hung in curls above it. A grey parrot with a crimson tail and curved black beak sat perched near the window without a cage. Head cocked, the bird barked like a dog and set poor Purkoy trembling in my arms.

The old woman did not know my true identity, for tho kind she did not bow or grovel to my self. I was happy for the masquerade, for all things and people have a way of changing with that intelligence. So I hid my hands lest she see that famous finger and know me, and I was henceforth just the Lady Anna.

"Put your dog down and let him go sniffing, Madame. He'll find lots to please his nose in here." I put him down to roam. "Then what'll ye have today?" said the crone, her brown spotted hands already back to grinding yellow seeds within a wooden mortar. "Something for your pregnancy?"

A laugh escaped me, for there was no way that this woman could have known my new condition.

"That is not my need, but can you tell me if 'tis girl or boy?"

"Naaa, that is past my knowing. I may be a good physician in my way but I'm no seer, no Madame, that I'm not."

I took the same liberty as Purkoy, eyeing all manner of strange bottles on the shelves, their contents some familiar, some exotic, some dry, some in liquid brew — all piquing my curiosity. I saw a yellow broom flower that Henry's wont to drink distilled in water against surfeits of the stomach, and barbere berries, good for diarrhoea and fevers.

"My husband is straying from our bed. I fear infection from it."

"Aye, a good fear to have. Does he show signs of illness — red rashes on his body, palms, soles, a raw sore on his member, loss of hair on face or head?"

"No, none of these."

The old woman looked at me, made examination of my face, seemed to search my soul with her eyes.

"You're no longer young, but a pretty woman still. Why does he stray, do you suppose?"

My laugh sounded bitter to my ears. "'Tis a long sad story for a cold winter's night," said I.

She smiled, showing a surprise of still good teeth, small and white.

"Perhaps you'll come back and tell it to me. And I'll tell you one, too. Old as I am, men still confound me, the way they find and quickly lose love. If they could only love their wives as they do their mothers."

She shook her head, then bade me come into the light. I gazed out the window at her tangled garden as she made examination of my hair, nails, skin, eyes, breath. She raised her stiff arms so that I should do the same, and then she felt my breasts.

"You're well enough," she said at last. "Healthy humors flow within your veins. You're melancholic, tho, and I can give you such for that." She went to her shelves and looked from side to side and back again. Eyes lit upon the bottle she desired. I moved to her side to see its contents — a dark green powder.

"What's it called?"

"'Tis motherwort. Just make a simple tonic with some clear water. Drink it down. There is no better herb to take melancholy vapors from the heart, to strengthen it and make you merry and cheerful as once you were."

"You're sure, are you, that I was once merry?"

"Oh, very sure, Madame."

"How so?"

"Just a wee sparkle yet left o'er in those sad eyes."

Purkoy stood under the grey parrot's perch yapping at it, and the bird yapped back in Purkoy's own voice. I picked him up as the old lady tipped some motherwort onto a sheet of parchment, folded it into an envelope and sealed it with some orange wax. I paid her what she asked.

"Come back and see me if you see the signs on him or on your self the same." She opened her door. "Good luck to you, Madame, and Godspeed."

'Twas strange, for I wished not to go. The company of this plain old woman in so humble an abode had warmed me, given me more ease than all the rich comforts of the Court. But I could neither stay nor tell her of my heart's true desires. I took the parchment envelope and then I took her hands. "You are very kind," said I and gently squeezed her spindly fingers with my own. I heard the parrot call "Good day! Good day!" and then I closed the door.

John scrambled down from the driver's seat, helped me in amongst the cushions. Courtesy forbade him asking me my business, but I could see the question burning in his eyes. He climbed up again but before he spurred the horses on, the old lady's door creaked open once again and she bustled forth, smiling with her pearly teeth, almost breathless.

"Madame!" she cried. I leaned out the window and she thrust another parchment packet in my hand. "Something for your pregnancy. A rich potion for kidneys and the liver." I fumbled for my purse but she stayed my hand. "No, a gift from me." And that was all. She turned and disappeared inside her house.

The horses, whipped to go, jolted the carriage forward, and sudden tears were likewise jolted from my eyes. They fell for neither pain nor anger, but for that old woman's rare sympathy for another woman. I pulled Purkoy close to me and was glad for him, but he is poor substitute for the little one I so long to hold.

Yours faithfully,

Anne

4 July 1534

Diary,

Are all men betrayers? Is there no faithful one amongst their sex? Rumor of a plot to poison the Lady Mary with a magick potion, and my self the executioner, made its vicious circle of the Court. Not wishing to give fuel to this false gossip, but needing some intelligence of its origin, I sent out my own spies who like ferrets returned to me with small bits of the lie which I pieced together into an entire beast. The Lady Mary is, as always, the heart of it with her complaints of feeling ill, believing its cause a foul potion in her food. And she, with no taster employed in her meager household, had no recourse but to eat that which was placed before her, or starve. The feet of the animal were all her faithful servants and supporters who ran swiftly with this news from Hatfield Hall to Court. The eyes of the beast were those of the driver, John, who saw and told of my meeting with the crone who spoke of potions at my carriage window. In these days, just place any old woman near a potion and she is surely called a witch. But what of the mouth which gave teeth to this rumor? 'Twas sour surprise even to one so schooled in treachery as me — none but Henry Percy, my old love in whose employ till recently was John the wretched driver.

Percy. Good love and friend who not so long ago conspired with my self in secret so that our past hearts' marriage would never jeopardize my present one. I could at first not believe that he gave rise to this false plot. But I heard the talk told from several mouths, and then when at mass on Sunday past I caught his eye he quickly turned away and would not meet my gaze, I knew the truth of it. I will never know the reason he has turned on me, become my enemy. Perhaps the grey illness of his body turned its icy fingers to his soul. Perhaps he's found a new author for the story of his bitter life — my self. Perhaps some obscure political advantage is his reward for my downfall. I do not know nor do I care to pursue it. I can only make denial of that murderous plot and mend what remains of the tattered fabric of my reputation.

To that end, as well to see Elizabeth, I rode to Hertfordshire and Hatfield Hall. Tho the grounds and gardens are vast and the forested hunting park rich with game, that house I like very little. 'Tis red brick styled in the old fashion, all ugly battlements and turrets, cold and mean within. Methinks if this child had been a son, his royal residence would be much grander.

Keeping my daughter's sweet presence as reward, I gathered my composure and benevolence and sent a greeting to the Lady Mary, requested that she pay a visit and honor me as Queen. I said frankly that if she did, she would be as well received as she could wish, and reacquainted with her Father's good pleasure and renewed favor.

You would think that this girl who yearns so for the King's love, would learn obeisance to that end. But no. The answer to my pleasant invitation came like a slap to the face — a dry note writ in her formal hand that she knew of no Queen in England other than her mother. And that should "the King's Mistress Marquess de Pembroke" be willing to speak on her behalf to her dear Father, she would be most grateful. A cold hand squeezed my heart at her reply.

I called then for Mistress Shelton who overwatches the cursed bastard, and gave her new instructions that insubordination of any sort should be met with equal force of intolerance. "Slap her if you must," I told her. "Let her feel the sting of the Queen's displeasure as she already knows the King's."

With that I took my leave of all unpleasantness and hurried to the sunny nursery rooms where my Elizabeth slept swaddled in the great gilded cradle of estate. Her staff, four score strong, bustled about all in her pleasure — a dry nurse assembling the tiny garments made by several sewers and embroiderers, all manner of grooms and yeomen in their divers labors, three rockers who took their turns at the cradle.

My cousin Lady Bryan who is chief governess of this staff, came to greet me with nursery business of great import, happy for my timely presence. The babe's wet nurse Agnes, who had suckled the Princess since birth, recently suffered from a drying up of milk in her breasts, and a new nurse demanded to be found. Several names were put before me with the women's varied commendations, and Lady Bryan and my self spent good time on these deliberations as the wet nurse's health and her demeanor are of great consequence. She need not be high born, but her family blood must be good, free from any lineage of criminality or madness. Even the meat and drink she takes at the time she gives suck to the child must needs be carefully watched, for the humors of her body do pass to the babe. Finally 'twas agreed that Mary Gibbons of Hampstead would take the place of Agnes and that was settled.

My counsel was sought on another matter — this the coming of the French envoy who would in ten days time arrive to make inspection of the Princess, previous to betrothal with King Francis' third son. Tho the bans will not be spoke for seven years, these diplomats require a measure of satisfaction in their intelligence of the candidate. The men shall view Elizabeth first in very rich apparel in state and triumph as a Princess, and later in her natural state for them to be assured of no defects in her body, as already malicious rumors of the child's deformities have reached all the courts of Europe. Tho I loathe these customs making my daughter little more than royal chattel I have no recourse, and find some measure of joy in knowing she will marry to no less than a Prince of France.

So the fine work of the nursery sewers — garments and bedclothes for Elizabeth's great occasion — were spread before me for my inspection. 'Twas marvellous work and I took much delight in the shape and tininess of those garments, as well as their richness. Pale yellow satin stitched with threads of gold and silver woven into one Tudor rose signifying Elizabeth, hung between two larger Tudor roses for Henry and my self. The gowns were of the finest white silk and gossamer tissue layered over thick with French lace and trimmed with crimson ribbons and rosettes. And the cap, like a tiny crown, was studded all round with tiny diamonds and pearls.

Finally my sweet babe awoke and she was brought to me red faced, squalling heartily. She seemed overwarm in her tight muslin swaddling, so I had the nurse unwrap the binding. Once unbound she was wretched no longer and came soft and yielding into my arms. O, I do love this little girl, perhaps the one truly good thing I have made in my unhappy life. The afternoon was blissful and my only sadness came when it was time to ride for home. I might have stayed longer, but Henry looks kindly on neither my time spent at Hatfield nor the ride there, claiming it difficult and perhaps hurtful to my unborn child. I bow to his wishes face to face and argue little, keeping shrill tones from my voice, but I will not be kept from my Elizabeth and make this quiet pilgrimage as often as I am able.

Yours faithfully,

Anne

22 September 1534

Diary,

Schism with the Catholic Church hangs like a great cloud o'er an already stormy England. Henry's subjects are raw from their compulsory oaths to faithfully and wholeheartedly uphold our marriage without consideration of any foreign authority or prince or potentate, and more oaths rejecting his marriage with Katherine, placing Elizabeth first in the succession to the throne. In cities and in villages they chafe at priests who preach the Pope is no more than Rome's Bishop, and our own Archbishop of Canterbury the highest prelate under God for Englishmen. They do not take kindly to these changes. They are forced — every man and woman, high born and low, to swear on pain of torture, death, dismemberment that they love the "harlot" now their Queen, and deny their King is a tyrant and a heretic.

The Holy Nun of Kent who did at last recant her treasonous prophesies against the King and I was hung at Tyburn, cut down whilst still alive, bowels torn from her belly, body cut to quarters and each displayed in far corners of London. Her death haunts me. I see those mad eyes in my dreams. For her prophesies turned my life's course and tho she'd changed her colors several times since, I still believe those early innocent words to me were honestly proffered, and of divine origination.

Thomas More stubbornly refused the oath in all its parts. To the Act of Succession he will swear but cannot — for his conscience will not allow it — deny the validity of the King's first marriage. Clever man, he danced all round the oath, wishing long life to Henry, my self and our noble issue, but never granted that our marriage was legitimate. And on the subject of the King as most Supreme Head of England's Church, he assuredly refused to swear, using as his argument Henry's own early writings, the "Assertion of the Seven Sacraments," claiming the Pope's authority supreme. That in deed the Pope had placed England's crown upon Henry's head, and could therefore when he desired remove it. Henry was made furious by this reasoning and by More's refusal to comply. He was soon arrested and his present home's the traitor's chamber of the Tower of London.

Henry grieves at More's decision and imprisonment, and questions his own beliefs. But I defy this "conscience" of More's which he holds so sacred and which will surely make a beloved martyr of him should he die of his treason. I ask, what's the good of conscience if it lead you wrongly? A madman might follow his conscience that tells him to murder his wife and children. Should we then forgive him of his crime? More's conscience, which the people hold in such high esteem, tells him that the Pope — a mortal man — is not just the Prince of Rome, but was placed on that throne by God himself, and should therefore have rights to command Kings in far off lands. Surely he is wrong, as Luther's growing army knows. This Pope is a man, born of woman, and has no more of God's ear than any other man or woman does.

Where was More's conscience when he took the post of Chancellor knowing full well that Henry's course would one day make me Queen? Perhaps 'twas in his purse which needed filling to support his ungainly family. And where was his conscience when he, so dependent on Thomas Wolsey for his early advancement, turned on the Cardinal in Parliament with such vicious and merciless claims, that even More's supporters cringed from him?

I see the turmoil caused by Henry's love for me. 'Tis ironic, is it not, that his love is gone, yet England's laws are changed, the King commands the Church and my daughter stands to one day take the throne. When I started on my course I would never have believed such a story. But it is so. And the story has no ending yet. We shall see how it unfolds.

Yours faithfully,

Anne

LIZABETH LOOKED UP from the pile of documents on her desk to watch Robert Dudley, his handsome head bent low over the parchment upon which he was writing with careful quill strokes. They had been closeted alone in her Privy Chamber for the better part of the day, and all of her councillors' pleas for audience had been denied. This was too lovely, thought Elizabeth, to allow her fusty old advisors to break the dreamlike spell she and Robin had cast. When she allowed her mind to loosen from its usual rigid strictures and formal procedures she could, for hours at a time, imagine that she and Dudley were King and Queen, quietly and in sweet harmony attending to the business of State.

"To whom are you writing, Robin?" she inquired mildly of him.

"Lord Sussex, Lord Deputy of Ireland," he replied, still intent on his writing. "I've asked him to send over some Irish horses for your own saddle." He finished with a flourish, then looked up at Elizabeth. "I've said that you have become a great huntress and require especially strong animals and good gallopers. That you are mad for reckless speed and run your geldings half to death."

He smiled at her then from across the room with such warmth that she found herself blushing. These sessions with Robin, which had become frequent during William Cecil's journey to Scotland to negotiate the Edinburgh peace treaty, had lately ended with Elizabeth in Dudley's arms, the high summer days folding comfortably into soft nights. She was quite aware that everyone at court was scandalized, even common folk were gossiping about their queen's indecorous behavior, but she could not bring herself to return to the prescribed way of business just yet. There would be more than enough time for that. And besides, they were accomplishing a great deal during these sessions.

She had overseen the Scottish negotiations, reviewing dispatches Cecil sent her daily and forwarding her impressions and opinions back to him promptly. She had kept abreast of the movements of her ambitious and deceitful cousin Mary Queen of Scots, recently widowed of the young French King Francis and threatening to return to the British Isles with her ridiculous claims to the English throne. And she had studied and amended her councillors' proclamation for currency reform.

Robin for his part had, with his newfound influence as her obvious favorite, attracted followers of his own, and quite as many enemies. He had learned substantially about the machinery of government and her many households, and had offered her good counsel on a variety of matters.

It was true that in the past weeks she'd had little time for activities that did not include her lover. When they were not working as they were now, they rode, hunted, gamed, or otherwise kept private company together. She had made careful effort to avoid discussion with her councillors of her hoped-for marriage to any foreign prince. She had not even read in her mother's diary, for it had become extremely painful to peer into the unfolding doom of Anne's life. But more to the point, Elizabeth's nights were too passionately occupied with Dudley to allow for such private and solitary pastimes as reading the intimate journal.

"I have in front of me an interesting document, Robin," said Elizabeth.

"What is it, my love?" he asked absently.

"'Tis the patent for an earldom . . . for one Robert Dudley," she answered, subduing a smile. For on hearing her words, Robin's ears, nay his entire face and body, had pricked up to battle readiness. Raising Dudley to the peerage, they both well knew, was a certain prerequisite to their marriage.

"I did not know you had had it drawn up," he said, coming to his feet. He stretched languidly and tried to maintain a studied nonchalance. But she knew his heart was racing, and he longed to see the document with his own eyes, feel the parchment between his fingers. Though in love with her Master of the Horse and believing he loved her most ardently, Elizabeth had no illusions about him. Robert Dudley was as ambitious a man as she had ever known, and had come to welcome every gift or property or title she had bestowed upon him.

He made his way across the chamber with the gait she loved — at once so graceful and so manly — and leaned over her shoulder to kiss her bare neck, lingering there with his lips. She wondered briefly if his eyes were on herself or on the patent for his earldom that she held in her hands.

"When will Her Majesty sign it?" he asked with restraint.

"When it suits us," she replied with eminent hauteur, using the royal plural he so despised.

Stung but unwilling to show it, Dudley lifted a lock of her crimped hair off the luminous white shoulder and kissed her there. She turned to him, her small breasts rising from the low square cut of her bodice. He moved his warm lips across their roundness and all the breath seemed to leave her body in a great sigh. Elizabeth's fingers threaded through the waves of his thick brown hair and her eyes closed. She was suddenly lost, lost, and the parchment creating Robert Dudley Earl of Leicester slowly fluttered to the floor.

⁂

Elizabeth hurried through the lush gardens of Richmond Palace toward the stables to meet Robin. He had promised her a brisk ride on the new grey jennet he'd dubbed Speedwell. So eager to see her love, she barely noticed the masses of flowers or smelt the great clusters of pungent herbs that lined the brick walks. She was therefore taken by surprise to be confronted by her Chief Secretary William Cecil standing in the path in front of her.

"My Lord Cecil! You startled me." She motioned for him to come forward to greet her, which he did with all due courtesy but little of his natural friendliness. Elizabeth had learned of Cecil's steely stubbornness the year before when she had hesitated to send the English army to Scotland to support the Protestant rebels. She had given in to his judgment and he had proven correct. Today, besides appearing weary from his journey back from Edinburgh, the stern, angry expression on his face bespoke matters even more serious. And she knew without asking what had prompted his ire. He began to speak without her leave, his voice quivering in the battle between rage and diplomatic restraint.

"I am confounded, Your Majesty. At a loss to understand how things could have deteriorated so badly in my absence," he said.

But Elizabeth was not inclined to make this scolding easy for him. "Things? What things, William?"

"Affairs of state, Madame . . . and what is left of your reputation."

"I have been seeing to the affairs of state, Lord Cecil, as have you in Scotland. I'm delighted with the treaty. We need no longer worry about the Franco-Scottish alliance or invading armies from the north, and have established Protestantism once and for all on the British Isles. As for my reputation —"

"It is said that you have been shut up and scarce seen these last months, so engrossed have you been with Lord Robert."

"'Tis true, I have spent some good time with Robin."

Cecil was quickly losing his composure. "Do you not see how severely your good repute is crumbling? How your chances of making a good marriage abroad are disappearing? Your Scots cousin Mary believes you are poised to marry your horsemaster. The Archduke's father is looking into the rumors of your scandalous behavior. Ambassador de Quandra's slander is even more damaging. He's reported to King Philip that you are a woman ruled entirely by your lusts, a woman of neither brains nor conscience, with a hundred thousand devils in your body!"

"The Spanish ambassador has never approved of me, and believes I am simply a worthless woman until I'm married."

Cecil's silence on the last point instantly inflamed Elizabeth.

"You agree with him, don't you!" She turned and strode away so that he could not see the angry tears that had sprung unbidden to her eyes.

"That you must marry, there is no doubt, Your Majesty," Cecil replied more gently, following behind her. "But that I think you worthless under *any* circumstances you must know is entirely untrue. Your conduct with Lord Robert," — he chose his words carefully — "even if it has only the *appearance* of misconduct, is more serious than you apprehend. And it has badly undermined my position —"

"That is not true," said Elizabeth emphatically.

But Cecil was determined to be heard and continued as if the Queen had not spoken. "— to such a degree that if you insist on retaining the man as your chief advisor, and continue to entertain the idea of marrying him —"

"How do you suppose I should marry Lord Robert, Secretary Cecil?" interrupted Elizabeth. "He already has a wife."

"A wife who is ill, as all at court are aware."

"Do you dare suggest Robin and I are waiting for Amy Dudley to die!"

"Do you deny it, Madame?" he replied quietly.

Elizabeth's neck burned with fury that Cecil had given voice to her own terrible and unspoken desire.

"As I was saying, Your Majesty, if you are determined to pursue this dangerous course, I will be unable to continue in your service as secretary."

"William!" She turned to see Cecil, a miserable expression on his face, his arms hanging impotently at his sides. Elizabeth suddenly felt her senses numb, as though a heavy quilt had been thrown over her head. Cecil's words as he went on seemed dull and muffled.

"I will gladly serve you in any other capacity, Majesty. In your kitchen, your garden . . . I know it is folly to ask you to choose between myself and Lord Robert, and I will not press you for your answer immediately. But if it please Your Majesty, give it some thought in the coming weeks. And advise me of your decision."

Cecil begged her with his eyes for leave to go. With a nod she gave it, and he silently disappeared from the brick walk.

Elizabeth stood straight and motionless as one of the stone pillars in her garden, and she found herself arguing silently with her absent secretary.

Do not make me choose, Cecil, I beg you! I have been so happy. Dudley is a man I trust and adore. Do you not see I have no wish to take to my bed and body a stranger, a rude foreigner? I wish to marry my friend, my countryman, my love. I may do as I please.

I am not some helpless girl, some father's chattel to bargain with and sell as he wishes. I am the Queen of England and by God I will have my way!

Suddenly, as if moving out of a dense river fog, Elizabeth could feel the late morning sun beating down on her uncovered head, smell the riot of fragrances wafting up from the low garden, hear a trio of gossiping ladies as they made their way through the pear orchard. And then a great pain, like a dozen sharp needles piercing her skull, struck her with a terrible force. She reeled from it, sought support with her hand but found none, and almost fell.

"Kat, help me," she whispered almost as a prayer. She knew that the palace grounds were alive with courtiers, yeomen, ministers, and gardeners, but she was terrified of anyone seeing her in a weakened condition. And so by the force of will alone she pulled herself erect. Each foot she placed carefully in front of the other and, fighting for composure as she nodded regally to this gentleman or that lady, made her way into the palace and back to her apartments.

Elizabeth's distress must in fact have been transparent to all, for by the time she arrived pale as a corpse, Kat had the royal bed already turned down. The Queen collapsed gratefully into her mistress's waiting arms and allowed herself to be gently laid down. To all of Elizabeth's confused mutterings, her lady simply murmured, "Rest, sweet girl, rest."

⚘

Three days passed in which the Queen lay abed racked with a fire in her head that seemed to drain all heat from her limbs and belly. She was delirious with pain and cried even as she slept. She called alternately for Robin Dudley and for Cecil and even, Kat was baffled to hear, her mother Anne. The royal physicians were summoned and the portly trio stood, heads together, murmuring their worthless remedies over Elizabeth's prostrate form. Her pulse was taken and pronounced strong. She suffered neither fever nor flux nor pox, but she remained so very ill that in those three days Kat never slept for fear that her dear charge would die with no one who loved her by her side.

Elizabeth opened her eyes in the evening of the third day to find her mistress lighting candles in the stuffy bedchamber to illuminate her night's vigil. She could see how slowly her old companion moved, how heavy lay her eyelids over the tired eyes.

"Kat." Elizabeth's first word after so long a silence was surprisingly strong and clear. Her lady turned with the sound of her name to see the Queen pulling herself up to sitting, alert and clear eyed.

She cried out, "Elizabeth!" and fell on her charge with embraces and copious tears. Kat pushed the damp frizzled hair back from the younger woman's brow and searched her eyes for an answer.

"I'm all right, Kat. I feel well. A little weak perhaps, but nothing that some light food will not cure."

"Lady Sidney!" called Kat, and the closed door opened instantly, for the waiting lady had been sitting just outside it. Mary Sidney entered the bedchamber to find Kat fluffing pillows behind the Queen's back.

"Majesty, I'm so happy to see you improved." Lady Sidney approached the bed. She knelt and taking Elizabeth's hand, kissed it. "Tell me, what is your pleasure?"

"Some rich broth. Make it salty. Sliced pears. And a wet cloth. I stink like a goat."

"Yes, Madame," said Lady Sidney with a smile. The Queen had returned to them with her temper quite intact. She curtsied and hurried to the door.

"One more thing, Mary. When you return, see to it that Kat is put to bed immediately."

"It shall be as you wish," she said and left the room.

"Your Majesty . . ." Kat objected.

But now that the danger to herself was passed, Elizabeth could see exhaustion overtake her friend and engulf her.

"Katherine Champernowne Ashley," she said with a playfully stern expression, "your Queen is deeply indebted to you for your sweet ministrations and utter devotion, but she has given you a royal command, to rest now, and she will tolerate no disobedience in this regard."

"Yes, Your Majesty." Kat inclined her head compliantly and in that moment relinquished control over the Queen's body and gave it back to Elizabeth.

"Now, fetch me the Turkish jar from my table." Kat handed her the tiny container from which she removed a key. "Unlock the chest at the foot of the bed and bring me the claret leather book. Then pull the candles closer to my head."

Kat moved very slowly, her normally sharp mind dulled by sleeplessness. When she placed Anne's diary in Elizabeth's hands she was far too tired to wonder what book it might be that was kept under lock and key at the foot of the Queen's bed.

As she took the leather volume from Kat, Elizabeth murmured softly, "I dreamt of my mother."

"Ah, you called for her whilst you slept."

"Did I?" Elizabeth smiled gently and drifted inward, remembering.

"What was it you dreamt?"

"She was in the high tower at Nonsuch Palace, or I believed it to be her, though I could not see her face as she was illuminated by so bright a light. She was calling out to me, calling my name. 'Come closer, Elizabeth,' she said, 'I have something to tell you.'"

"And what did she tell you?"

"Nothing," said Elizabeth, pulling the diary to her breast. "She had no time, for the castle began crumbling around her, all in chunks of stone and masonry, till she was sitting on a tall stool with the castle walls in a great pile around her." Elizabeth took Kat's hand, its papery skin dotted with flecks of brown. "Go on, let Lady Sidney lay you down. Get some rest. For I shall be back on my feet tomorrow and will need you refreshed by then."

Her waiting lady reluctantly but gratefully removed herself from the Queen's sight. Elizabeth opened Anne's diary and found the place where she had left off. She had woken with at once a terrible dread and a terrible desire — both, to know the certain and intimate details of her mother's piteous fate. It was suddenly clear to the Queen that here in these pages was not only her history but the key to her future. If she were wise she would study the diary and learn from it as a general would study the details of a great battle. Elizabeth knew that she stood at the first of many crossroads, with no plain map to guide her actions save the one she now held in her hands.

She began to read almost greedily, determined to complete the diary before daybreak. Within moments Elizabeth was so engrossed in the pages that when Mary Sidney returned with the broth and the pears, the Queen never even noticed her presence.

12 December 1534

Diary,

I am sore distraught for I have seen a person act so vile and wicked that my own heart aches with it. That person had banished from Court a poor widow forgot by her family, whose only crime was marrying for love and a pregnancy conceived in that union. That poor widow, now happy bride, was Mary Boleyn Carey and that cruel person, her sister — my self.

When I think on it for understanding I see how I perhaps came to such an act of unkindness. My own pregnancy had come to end in a bloody miscarriage but a day before my sister's plight was put before my eyes. I was still abed having yet found no words to tell the King — sore, weak, pitying my self and this bad fortune added to the rest — when I welcomed my Sister back from Calais, only to find her aglow with new life growing in her belly. Bile rose in my wretched throat and before I counted all the consequences, shouted out that she'd disgraced her self, brought scandal to my Court and dishonor to my name. Even blinded by fury I could see Mary's happy face dissolve to shock and tears. She turned to run from my painful presence but like a deadly archer loosing poisoned arrows from his bow, I shot her down with stinging words from my bed.

"Who gave you leave to go from the Queen's presence!" I shrieked. She froze where she stood. "Turn to me, Mary. Let me see the face of an ungrateful sister who dared without the King's permission to give her self away to a simple soldier when there was some good value to be got from a marriage of alliance."

"You must forgive me, Sister, but he was young and love overcame reason. I true believed the world set so little by me, and he so much, that I thought there was no better way but to take him and forsake all other ways, and live a poor honest life with him. Our Mother, Father, even Brother George are cruel against us and have turned their backs on me."

"And so do I!" I shouted then at her. "Get out, I have room for only one fool in my Court!"

Stung as she was by my words she held a proud posture, no doubt bolstered by her husband's love, and backed from my bed-chamber. Sick as I was, sicker still did I become. I cried and raged until I vomited, hating my happy sister no more than I hated my miserable self.

Secretary Cromwell, when I next saw him in his private of-fices, showed me a letter Mary'd writ to him begging him to speak gently on her behalf to Henry, who should likewise speak to me and soften my resistance. She said she knew that she could have a man of greater birth, but never one who loved her so well, nor one more honest. "I would rather beg my bread with him than be the greatest Queen in Christendom," she wrote.

"If I may be so bold as to give advice to you, Your Ma-jesty," said Secretary Cromwell, "I would forgive your sister. She is, after all, your blood . . . and the damage has been done. The King . . ." He paused as tho he had lost his words.

"What about the King?"

"I think he would not like to be bothered with this business."

"Quite so," I told him evenly. I did not say I knew full well the King would find the mention of his old mistress's name of-fensive, nor did I deign to educate him on the great remorse I'd lately suffered on account of my scurrilous treatment of my sis-ter. "Send Mary and her new husband my blessings and the King's as well. And when the child comes we'll send a rich gift so she will know our love's sincere."

"Very good, Your Majesty. Leave it in my hands." As I left Cromwell's apartments I wondered at the spareness and the modesty of his rooms for a man so high in the King's favor. Surely he could have a soft cushion on his chair, fresher rushes on the floor, a few fine hangings to keep out the draughts. Perhaps in his sincere and undivided attention to the King's business, he does neither see nor feel the cold and harsh surroundings.

By that time Henry'd had the news of my miscarriage, and in public was little colder than he'd been before. But in my bed late at night where he had come to exercise his rights — since he no longer came to take his pleasure — I found him rough and crude. He reeked of ale and I could smell another woman's scent upon his body.

"How does my Queen?" he inquired with that particular ugliness of voice which told of his loathing. "We shall try again, Anne, tho your womb seems an uncomfortable place for my sons."

I held my tongue on which hung some bitter words. I spread my legs for him and bore his stinking breath and hateful seed, for this is the bed that I have made and I have nought to do but lie within it.

Yours faithfully,

Anne

24 February 1535

Diary,

Despite my growing miseries my maids and I spent last evening in our cups and laughing very merrily, for the fool I have in my employ — a woman named Niniane — we all like right well. She finds many marvellous ways to make jests of all our woes. Nonsense and puns, bawdy songs with verses that, once sung, we ladies sing along with. She makes unimaginable contortions of her body and her pliable face, juggles, tells ribald stories all complete with accompanying sounds like horses clopping, bells ringing, thunder pealing. Most times and to our great delight she makes men the butt of her jokery, pratfalls and impersonations — feeble brained noblemen, vainglorious fops, clumsy clods and lecherous Bishops. A cuckolded man who'd caught his wife in bed with her lover, she described as looking like a dog falling out a window. We howled with laughter till we cried, but begged the girl for more till she could hardly stand. I paid her handsomely in praise and gold, and bid her stay close to me, for I have troubles multiplying daily and need a respite now and then.

Henry, not content with whores kept in private brothels, even maidens kept above his chambers for satisfaction of insatiable venereal cravings, has again taken Elizabeth Carew as his lover. She seems no passing fancy and they do not hide their amorous liaison from my eyes, in deed flaunt the romance for all the Court to see. Of late this handsome waiting lady wears hung round her throat rich jewels which could only be of royal origin, and a smirk upon her face born in confidence of Henry's protection. I had endured this humiliation several months in silence, then let my rage overtake my reason and commanded Mistress Carew from the Court. Henry heard of it and quickly nullified my order, sending me a harsh message that I had better be content with what he'd done for me, for he would not do it now were it to begin again. O sweet Jesus, this man my husband does humiliate my very soul. To have suffered all that I have as recipient of his unwanted love, and then to be treated poorly as Queen Katherine was! And this is not the end of it.

Henry's now begun to show some fair affection to his daughter Mary. He sent a fine new litter and rich hangings for her rooms in Hatfield Hall. But worse than this, I fear he speaks more lovingly of her than of Elizabeth to his courtiers. Last visit that I made my daughter, I was accompanied to Hertfordshire by a complement of Lords and Ladies not the least of which were Dukes of Suffolk and of Norfolk. We spent a most congenial ride together and I anticipated some happy hours spent within the royal nursery, all these courtiers gathered round the Princess paying homage due her self. But when once we'd come to Hatfield's door and our carriages and horses led away, all but two of my ladies like magick disappeared, and without a word of warning (tho surely was a plan rehearsed) made their way to Lady Mary's chambers there to pay *her* homage! I stood speechless with my remaining loyal ladies trying hard to hide the crimson flush my indignant cheeks were showing. My maids, too, were taken by surprise by this rude mutiny, and in their kind way made light of it, urging me to go directly to my daughter, the very sight of whom they knew would ease my angry disposition.

Elizabeth is not yet two, but bold in spirit and strong upon her tiny feet like a tiny whirlwind. She is a happy child and so beautiful it almost makes me weep. I spoke with Lady Bryan who says my child does suffer with her great teeth which come forth very slowly. I promised I would send nigh some lavender oil to soothe her aching gums and calm her nighttime wailing.

The afternoon which might have then passed pleasantly enough was later marred when I received a most insulting note from Lady Mary, stating her refusal to come out from her apartments, as she did not wish to see me. And when I later gave Mistress Shelton orders that the girl be punished for her rudeness, Henry him self had those orders countermanded.

I confess, where I once shrank from accusations of Mary's poisoning, these days I wonder if her execution is the only end for such a traitorous subject. She and that scabrous mother of hers! Both continue to refuse the oath that each and every person in the land must swear to or face execution. Let God hear me now, I shall be that girl's death and she shall be mine!

Yours faithfully,

Anne

2 March 1535

Diary,

I fear the French have now deserted me as rats desert a sinking ship! My good allies, country of my education, supporters of my marriage, make certain mockery of my friendship. This was made clear upon the coming of King Francis' delegation headed by the Admiral of France and my old friend Chabot de Brion, whom I have received most lavishly in England on his many visits, and in Calais previous to my wedding. We understood one another, this man and I, spoke the same language, held the same thoughts. His prodigious flattery I believed sincere.

On their arrival of this occasion to discuss a royal marriage, tho, Chabot made no attempt to seek an audience with me as he is wont to do, or bring a token of affection from Francis, or even greetings from that King. When Henry did inquire if the Admiral wished to pay his respects to the Queen he replied that he would do so *if it pleased the King*! He abstained from all the revels, jousts and tennis games I'd planned so carefully for him. And when he chanced to see me, he was cold and so ungracious that a strange thought passed thro my mind — that this man was not Chabot at all, but some stranger disguised as him. For I was sore confused by such behavior. Confused, that is, until negotiations opened for the English-French alliance and my daughter's hand in marriage.

It seems that King Francis' loyalty has flown in the direction of Rome. Tho he still grants Henry's marriage to Katherine invalid, Mary, he asserts is still the heir and thus demanded an old betrothal of the wretched girl to his son the Dauphin be fulfilled. Threats were made, yes threats that if the pledge was not honored they would tie the French Prince in matrimony to the Emperor's daughter.

All of these ugly surprises tore at my mind's fabric leaving its edges ragged and frayed, so that at the final feast given for the French emissaries I imbibed too freely, and thus had no guard upon my tongue. Chabot sat coldly at my right making inconsequential conversation and I, in turn, chattered like a mindless girl. Then my eyes caught sight of Henry cross the room catching sight of his beloved mistress. The King was stopped dead, and the look of his face — so fraught with passion and so like the look he once held for me — caused to rise in my throat a sudden bitter laugh which, loosed by wine, became a great unstoppable torrent. Chabot was quite offended and asked whether I was mocking him, which led to even more of my laughter. He spluttered, turned a furious red and rose indignantly to go. I sobered quickly then and held his arm, knowing this momentary lapse of sanity could harm irreparably my daughter's yet endangered cause. Nothing short of truth would, I knew, calm the man and so humiliating my self as I spoke, I admitted seeing Henry's loving actions toward his mistress. I was grateful that Chabot believed my explanation, but I cringed at the pity for me I saw within his eyes.

Upon the Frenchmen's departure Henry sent word that

their proposal would not do, and offered up instead Elizabeth for the Duke d'Angoulême's bride. The delegation sailed with stiff and formal promises of a swift reply. I believed that Henry was as cold as he could be to me, but I was wrong. His eyes after their departure fixed me with a steely stare and he said, "You should pray God, Madame, that their answer comes in your daughter's favor, for what use have I for either of you if not for such alliances?"

Many weeks have come and gone and we wait in vain for their decision. Eastertide is now upon us but I feel no celebration. I make the motions that are expected of a queen — ordering new gowns, planning feasts and masques and special masses — but each day of silence from across the Channel tolls in my head like some dread and heavy bell down an empty abbey corridor. I pray God takes my part in this, for I have never sinned as much as I am being made to pay for.

Yours faithfully,

Anne

14 April 1535

Diary,

My prayers are answered! The French have finally agreed the Duke d'Angoulême shall wed Elizabeth. The marriage shall be negotiated in Calais the latter part of May. And happily I do report my brother George is back in England, his long assignment into France completed. A most welcomed friend to my inner circle, he brings more than divertissement, French songs and ditties, latest fashions, books and new ideas. He brings me love and loyalty that I have sore missed. He pays his Queen and sister so lush a measure of attention that her life has flowered and turned fragrant once again. He and Francis Weston, Henry Norris and Mark Smeaton often join my ladies for late night revelries, music, dancing, gaming, laughing at Niniane's anticks.

I know that God has not been so kind to some men. Several monks of the Carthusian Order who've refused the oath have recently been jailed. Thomas More and John Fisher, too, languish still within the Tower for their refusal to comply. Often Secretary Cromwell visits them, offering every easy way to save face and do as all others have. Even members of More's family have sworn. But he remains so stubbornly opposed that Henry's temper grows daily more fierce upon the subject of his old friend, now enemy. Mayhaps reason will steal upon More suddenly from the shadows of his cold cell, and he will swear to end for once and all so needless an imprisonment.

George often rides with me to Hatfield where he finds his pretty niece growing quickly. Plans for Elizabeth's weaning have been taken up with Master Cromwell, Henry and my self. The Lady Mary still ensconced at Hatfield holds Court with her supporters, not so secret as she supposes, who court her and rally round Ambassador Chapuys. His constant letters to the Emperor are no doubt filled with schemes and plots (all failed) to place her first in the succession.

Have I forgot to say that Clement is dead and a new Pope, Paul III, stands in his place? This man, stronger in resolve by far than doddering Clement ever was, threatens Henry's peace directly with a declaration that for his foul act of marriage to me, he is deprived of his Kingdom, and even a promise of invasion. The King worries little since France and Spain will soon be at war, and thus the Emperor will be so much involved that no invasion could be mounted upon England. And such a war would cause Francis' call for aid, and his alliance with Henry, which would give the King great satisfaction.

So much improved is my mood that some schemes of my own foment inside my head. But I will leave them for another day.

Yours faithfully,

Anne

20 May 1535

Diary,

I am pregnant and new hope grows in me as a spring seed pushes for the light of day. Forgive me, Elizabeth, but my prayers of late are that this child's a boy, Henry's Prince and our saviour. This hope, together with a great need to endure, survive this chosen life, this fate, has born inside my head a master scheme which, once fulfilled, will restore my place and power on the throne. I must make the King love me once again. Find within this worn body and battered heart that bold and arrogant girl whose flashing eyes lured Henry deep within a dark maze of desire, and held him there for six long years. Find pretended lust for that once steely frame now grown mottled, fat and loathsome. But even more than body's passion I must make him know that all his sacrifice and pain in having me was not in vain. That his proud plots and plans, his Great Matter and marriage to me did come to some good, after all was said and done, not merely death to friends, excommunication from the Church and hatred from his subjects. I will think on this a while longer, fix the details of intrigue within my head, for I cannot fail in this.

Niniane, my fool, makes high jest round my pregnancy. Methinks she must have borne children of her own to know with such perfection all the inward rumblings, weird cravings, painful pleasures that condition brings. One evening when she and I were quite alone in my bedchamber she jumped upon my bed and curling small into a ball, became the babe inside my belly, squalling, kicking, quite spoiled and demanding crisp apples, sugared newt's toes and lullabies be sung to him. "I am the little Prince!" he cried (or so she cried for him). "I am Prince and future King and I am tired of the darkness. Bring me light! And sweets! And much jewels and gold, for I am my father's son and desire above all else to be rich!"

Master Holbein has made a drawing of me, unbidden. Tho no one else would say, I knew it most unflattering, my face bloated with pregnancy, hair tucked up in a gable hood. Only Niniane on seeing this portrait cried, "Who is this matronly sow with several chins? Never you, Your swan necked Majesty!" When I said that it was in deed my self, she grabbed the offending picture and danced round the room with it singing a wild tune about Holbein's appropriate punishment for so treasonous an act — being strung up naked by his two thumbs at Tyburn and the offending picture rolled and stuck up his arse. O, she does make me laugh, and in a way so strange brings a fair friendship, for in her bold humor lies Truth. And that is something rare, for few will share the same with me.

All queries that I make of Niniane's own life she turns completely round about and makes jokes of them, keeping her self most private and mysterious. I wonder often on this woman, crude and wild who also shines with much intelligence and goodness. How did she come to this life? Who were her kin? What was her class? Perhaps one day she'll say.

Yours faithfully,

Anne

7 June 1535

Diary,

My star has risen once again, and I am Henry's only sweetheart. He dotes upon me more than ever now, keeping me close by his side in all things. I will tell you how this came to pass. First the child within me brought a healthy roundness to my hollow cheeks and what wrinkles round my eyes and mouth had appeared, I fought with several applications of quicksilver which, tho biting and malignant to the skin, did their wondrous work to leave my face smooth in its appearance. A fine white lead I used for paleness, then a touch of alum for a rosy cheek, and cochineal for lips did make me young and looking lovelier than I had for some time been. Nets and headdresses were put aside. My hair I wore long and unbound as I had in our courtship days. My gowns were all his favorite hues, deep russet, rose, gleaming black and emerald green. Jewels I chose for their compliment to me as well as sentimental value, those which he had given me when our love'd been most in bloom. I paid mightily for divers

French parfums and bathing oils and cremes, so I would float in fragrant clouds wherever I would go.

Thus I presented myself to the King, at first in fleeting moments as I swept across a crowded chamber where he was. No words but some seductive smiles, a sideways glance, a look of admiration for him self. The May Day Revels did provide a sweet opportunity for me to shine. I was cast as Queen of the Spring, my gown a riot of silken flowers. In the masque I danced a graceful sprightly dance and sang a song which all applauded heartily. I was pleased to see the King's gaze fixed not on his mistress, but glowing proud after his wife. When I took my bow I curtsied low in his direction, held his eyes and knew that he was once more mine for the taking. When the dancing had begun he crossed the room to ask for my hand and when we partnered to the galliard his kicks and leaps were like a young stag again. He was happy, I could see this clearly, and so that evening late I waited in my bedchamber and the King came to me.

As I fed him spiced wine before a blazing fire I found what courage I could, and was bold with him as I had been before love and marriage had weakened me. With my hands making soft work upon his temples I told him that if he thought honestly, he'd know that he was more bound to me than man can be to woman. That I had extricated him from a state of sin in his marriage to Katherine, and that without me he would never have reformed the Church. Moreover, in that reformation he had gained all the riches of the monasteries and was now the wealthiest Prince that ever was in England.

He listened close, leaning on the words I spoke, even said "Go on" and so I did. I handed him my hair brush and as he was wont to do when we were young, he brushed my hair for me, long smooth strokes until my hair was as a single bolt of black silken cloth. I told him his virility had given us another chance for our Prince. And then like Master Holbein, I painted a portrait with Henry and my self as allies who stood together on the one side, whilst all the world was drawn as if the enemy; the treacherous Emperor, unfaithful French, belligerent Pope, treasonously stubborn Katherine and Mary who behind his back still try to raise a mutinous army. I said that he and I had been torn from each other by cruel forces and wicked men who could never comprehend the strength of our union. Then I kissed him, rousing both the King and the man within him. He needed no further urging, fairly ripping off my gown, carrying me to bed.

I have known his body lately, so 'twas no surprise that it was corpulent and foul with bulging veins and oozing sores upon his calves and thighs, but those times I had not pretended lust, but turned my face away and let him take his pleasure quickly. Now I summoned all my resolve, opened up my lying heart and made love with him. 'Twas a test of my skill as actor for there is, with all honesty, no shred of real affection left for this beast I call my husband.

Once satisfied the King was most ecstatic, hope welled within his breast for our future, his son, England's glory. He spoke my name again with great love, and I rejoiced silently that by my own hand I had once more changed my fate and with my daughter in my arms, stepped back from that dark abyss which beckoned us to it. Jesus be praised. He is surely with us.

Yours faithfully,

Anne

20 July 1535

Diary,

How is it that so good and learned a man conspires in his own execution? What sense is there to stand so faithfully to one principle against one to which all others conform, that death is his only choice? Confound Thomas More! He is dead now, his head stuck upon a pole on London Bridge keeping company with the heads of John Fisher and those Carthusian Monks. Could he not have sworn the oath and saved his life? And Henry, ah well, he has made a Catholic martyr out of More, all the better for his subjects to rally now around.

My Brother George and Father saw their executions. First

Fisher, lately made Bishop of Rochester by the Pope, was so frail they say they were amazed that so much blood could pump from so skeletal a corpse. But 'tis More's execution which haunts my dreams and waking reveries. The long grey and tangled beard, his exhortations to the headsman not to miss his mark for his poor neck was short. Binding up his own eyes with linen 'fore he laid his sick body flat upon the scaffold, as the block was low and very small. He even made a jest. Told his executioner not to cut his beard, for his beard was not a traitor. That great man, that silly fool lying on his belly waiting for the axe.

When the news was brought of More's execution, the King and I were side by side at his gaming table. His face flushed hot and red and he raged, "God's blood! The honestest man in the Kingdom is dead!" Then he strode from the gaming room and closeted him self for several days.

I swear I will think on this no longer. Push all terrible thoughts from my head, for I am still the Queen and have much high business to attend.

Yours faithfully,

Anne

10 August 1535

Diary,

This grese season Henry's taken his round bellied Queen on summer progress with him and treats her most royally. I stand beside him on the hunting stage as in older days and we watch the deer run, shoot together, drink ale in the crisp afternoon and make more merry than we have in many years.

In the counties Winchester and Hampshire we were shown good and gracious hospitality by our noble subjects in divers manors, castles, hunting lodges. And tho heavy rains robbed us of many good hawking days, no angry mobs of country folk marred our leisure travels. My hope is that this forecasts some new acceptance of their Queen and baby Princess, but my heart says 'tis fear of Henry's heavy hand and forced submission which makes the common people mild.

Still, pleasures of another kind waited round several pastoral bends. The monasteries of Rochester and Dunst, with their treasure hoards of Roman artifacts, lay open for the King's taking. Great heavy crosses made of gold, exquisite tapestries, gem encrusted miters, pillars, goblets for the mass, all obscenely rich and quite unnecessary for God's worship, were carried off to London as plunder by the King's men.

Mayhaps these new riches have turned Henry's head, for he now speaks openly against those great Spanish stones round his neck. "I will no longer remain in trouble, fear and suspense I have so long endured on account of the Dowager Queen and Lady Mary," I heard him say to Suffolk. "You shall see, the coming Parliament will release me therefrom. I will wait no longer!"

I restrained my tongue, for it sounded as tho the King needs no further persuasion toward their execution. Ah, 'twould be a sweet day that those bitter harridans were gone from this world, and my Elizabeth safe from their disaffection. I pray that Henry bears resolves for this as great as was his to make me Queen. If so, our future is assured.

Now lodged at Wolfe Hall in Wiltshire County near to Wales, we are made to feel mightily at home within the Seymour family manor. Thomas and his fertile wife Margaret inspire us with their fecundity, ten living children — five daughters, five sons. Edward has been Henry's Master of the Body some years now, and his sister Jane — quite ordinary and meek — was Katherine's maid of honor. Her brother spoke for her, too shy her self to ask from us a place within the Court. Henry made it plain that it would please him to please Edward, so I will see about a place amongst my ladies for this little mouse.

In all honesty this summer progress pleases me, but 'twill please me even more to hie for home and comforts of my Court. For this child must be fully carried, safely born.

Yours faithfully,

Anne

5 December 1535

Diary,

'Tis beyond all belief and understanding, Henry's late betrayment. He has made a mouse his mistress! My maid of honor Jane Seymour, prim little cunt, is my new replacement. No one thinks she has much beauty, just a plump and undistinguished figure with a voice which you must strain to hear, she speaks so softly. She has no brains to speak of either. But no matter, her brother Edward Seymour does the thinking for her. Henry is besotted in a way I've not seen before, save with his love for me. But how does this plain Jane inspire such a passionate affection from the King? 'Tis Edward's scheme I'm sure, this wretched love affair which will grow his place in Henry's Court. I fear my fickle cousin Francis Bryan, also Nicholas Carew, conspire with him in this plot. Is there no such thing as a loyal courtier? I think not. They have Jane playing my old game of love — tempting Henry with deft teasing, simpering smiles, promises of full submission to the King that lead not to bed but only chaste kisses and promises of many sons.

I admit I've lost all patience with the whore mongerer and cannot hide my loathing. Harsh vituperations fly from my mouth both in private conversation and whilst in public company. When he says "yea" I say "nay," for any contradiction's better now than none. I find new ways to irritate and make a fool of this pompous clod every day, laughing at his silly duckbill slippers, and outrageously bejangled costumes of ever widening girth that cause him to look the size of a wall. He's commanded all his men to poll their heads and grow their beards and so, making use of Niniane's observation, my self announced loudly at dinner that the King was like a bearded billiard ball.

I hurl abuse as well at Norfolk, long my enemy but now brazen with his appalling slander at my back. He's said to have complained I'd spoken to him as one would not address a dog. But Niniane, upon hearing that, claimed my Uncle Norfolk should feel complimented, for I treated my dogs better than most people. To Mistress Seymour who boldly flirts with Henry, sitting on his lap, I gave a smart slap across the face and left a long red scratch.

Henry tolerates my vexatiousness with a strange calm which troubles Brother George, who fears the quiet 'fore the storm. But I am ruled by some hellbent demon whose unleashed frenzy cannot be staunched. What cruel God decided my fate shall be the judge of further punishment, for the gauntlet has been thrown down and now the battle has begun.

Yours faithfully,

Anne

9 January 1536

Diary,

Katherine, once Queen of England, is dead and I am laid low. So violent and unnatural was her end with fearsome vomiting and stabbing pains within her stomach, some say she died of poison. But this is not true, for her only enemies were the King and I, and we are surely not responsible. Henry is beside him self with glee and shouted out with hearing news of her death, "God be praised that we are free from all suspicion of war!" 'Tis true, Katherine's nephew Charles the Emperor will find no reason for invasion now, so long as his cousin Mary's safe from harm, for who can say which way fate will take the throne's succession?

This, then, is why I've taken to my room, my bed, but even there find no solace. 'Tis true I cried with happiness on hearing the report, even made a handsome gift to Master Ellis, the messenger who'd brought it. I rejoiced that Henry had Elizabeth carried here from Hatfield Hall to join the round of celebration mourning, had her dressed in yellow matching his doublet, and my gown, and that he'd come into the room where my ladies were dancing and joined in their wild gaviote, a man transported with joy. But when the King took our daughter in his arms and carried her about from room to room, parading her for all his men to hold and praise, I felt a sure and sudden sickness of the heart. I dismissed my ladies, and even Niniane could not assuage my grieving mind.

For this is what I all at once knew. Katherine's death may be the end of me. Whilst she lived Henry could never divorce me, for that would mean him going back to her. But with the Lady dead and gone the King is free to marry whom he will. You say the King would not divorce me. I say think again! I see the loving way he looks upon Jane Seymour's bland and peevish face. I hear the frequent gossip of his third marriage, which he always fails to contradict.

O Elizabeth, the man who shows off his golden haired and yellow bundle proudly to his courtiers may be the instrument of my destruction, and your own. Pray with me sweet girl in your child's prayers that this babe inside of me's a boy. For good King Harry sees little to commend his family, and less intention to cherish them. Like a great storm blowing inland from the Western sea, I fear he is unstoppable and shall rage with marvellous fury till we all are drowned.

Yours faithfully,

Anne

28 January 1536

Diary,

That which I most feared has come to pass. I have miscarried of my saviour, for the small bloodied flesh expelled from my womb was clearly male.

The great celebration of Katherine's death had gone on for weeks. No mourning black in Court or public was allowed by Henry. Feasts, dancing, masques, even masses were sung in rejoicing, and those who loved the lady mourned in secret under pain of death. A joust was called but far from wishing noise and jostling crowds, I sought quiet privacy, and stayed to my apartments with Margaret Lee and Niniane who entertained us merrily with Chaucer's verse and song.

Then with sudden sounds like soldiers massing at my chamber door which quite alarmed us all, my Uncle Norfolk burst upon our quiet afternoon with evil news. The King lay in the tiltyard dead, thrown from his stallion in a joust and crushed by the mighty war horse fallen on his Majesty's body! The sharp pain of fear pierced my limbs, head, belly and all strength ebbed from my veins. Margaret claimed I grew pale as death and she tried to comfort me. But Norfolk, like some malignant viper, struck at my fragile heart with harsh words. With Henry dead, he said, I was surely lost, for there was no one loyal to Elizabeth and her succession to the throne. If I fought for her, claimed my self Regent, great strife and civil war would sure be England's lot. All this while I mourned the sudden loss of Henry, that loss tinged with unpleasant joy that the beast was dead. Then Norfolk left, not bothering to bow, as tho I was Queen no longer.

Dazed, mortified, reeling with all terrible possibilities I began to tremble uncontrolled. Margaret and Niniane strove to warm me, stay these convulsions, comfort me with kind words, but all I knew was wanting Elizabeth in my arms, for danger danced all round us like some macabre troupe of shadow players. Margaret took her leave, promised she would have Elizabeth brought to me, as well as my few loyal men.

But when they came — Wyatt, Norris, Weston — they brought news that the King lived! In deed, the man had been two hours in a dead faint, but now was back upon his horse with threats to ride again. Well, I took to my bed then for sheer exhaustion of spirit. Tho Niniane found ways to coax some laughter from such perverse occurrences, I grew only more pale and weak. And on the day Katherine was laid to rest, blood flowed from between my thighs and my babe died within my body. The midwife made examination of the tiny thing and said it had the appearance of a male child. This was told to Henry who came to my chambers in a fury even greater than when Elizabeth was born a girl.

He did not shriek at me, but spoke coldly. "I see clearly God does not wish to give me male children." When I said that this was not God's doing, that this premature birth came with news of his own death, roughly handled by Norfolk, he was neither moved nor consoled. He had no pity for my weak condition or my loss — only his — and strode from the room without a backward glance saying he would speak to me when I'd recovered.

Margaret Lee who'd stayed so close and faithful, burst to tears upon his leaving. I thought to comfort her saying I would surely have another babe, but she was inconsolable, speaking her fears to me. All Court buzzed with gossip that Henry now believed he'd been seduced thro my sorcery, and our marriage was null. God, he said, had shown him the truth of this with his failure to allow us sons, and now he meant to make a virtuous wife of Jane Seymour. Sorcery! I a witch! My six fingered hand, the Devil's mark upon my neck, the potions I had used to heal his pains, magick in my fingers that soothed his aching head. These had finally come to haunt me. I saw that my fate was no better than Katherine's, and Elizabeth's no better than Mary's. Banished Queen and bastard child sent to distant bleak houses with no leave to even seek the other's comfort.

My limbs are weak, my heart heavy. I lie abed with no will to leave it. What shall become of us?

Yours faithfully,

Anne

6 February 1536

Diary,

How bitter is this day. My beloved Purkoy's dead. News of his demise was delivered by the King with as much unkindness as false news of his own death was delivered by my Uncle Norfolk. I was praying with my Chaplain Matthew Parker when Henry came exploding thro my chamber door to say that he was off to London for Shrove Tuesday, and that he required me to stay behind in Greenwich. I begged him please to let me join him, for Elizabeth was housed in London and I had need of seeing her. He refused that request and, too, refused to even take a list of measurements for several silken caps I wanted made for her, saying cruelly she had little need for such fine caps, and asking had I nothing better to do with my time than write silly lists of useless things.

My temper flared at hearing such rude sentiments about our daughter, and I chastised him roundly saying his inconsistent love gave others leave to show disloyalty. Even Master Cromwell now lifted his cap at mention of the Lady Mary's name. To this Henry made no reply, at least none that satisfied. He made move to go and I held his arm speaking harsh truths of his new mistress Lady Jane.

"She plays you, Henry, plays you as I used to do. In fact she plays *my* games. I hear she would not take the purse of gold sovereigns that you gave her, would she Henry? Would not soil her virtue nor her honor taking such a gift if she were not first your lawful wife? Are you so blind you cannot see that she has two clever brothers who seek advancement for them selves thro her?"

"Hold your wicked tongue, Madame. Hold or have it silenced for you."

"And how would you have me silenced, Henry? Divorce me? Send me to a nunnery?"

"Do not try my patience, Anne. 'Tis worn dangerous thin."

But I found courage and faced him, held his mad glittering eyes with mine.

"I never loved you, Henry. Never once in those ten years." His mouth quivered but his jaw held firm as I goaded his pride with a coy smile. "Did you think I came to love you? Yes, you did." The color rose in his fat cheeks as I spoke those lying words for truly, Diary, I *had* loved him once for a time, before I gave my self to him. And in Calais, and that winter after. But now I gave him no satisfaction of that love.

"Go and have your horse faced, mealy mouthed girl," I cried. "Have her! But you best remove from your memory all thoughts that Anne Boleyn ever loved Your Gracious Majesty. For she never did. Never."

He fixed me with his terrible stare and in that moment I thought that he might raise his hand and kill me with a blow. Instead he said, "Your dog is dead." And then he smiled. "Pity, since he was surely your most loyal servant." I never saw Henry go, so blinded was I by instant tears. Tears that he had satisfaction seeing he had caused.

Yours faithfully,

Anne

9 April 1536

Diary,

Briefly I believed that all was well again. Ambassador Chapuys had relayed a message from the Emperor that he wished to deal with Henry and my self with hopes of some treaty with him, now that Katherine's death removed a great obstacle from the path to our alliance. That he wished to treat with my self as well as Henry pleased me greatly and bespoke Charles' new respect for me as Queen. And this Spanish scheme pleased Secretary Cromwell mightily, since he of late believed the French were poor and unreliable friends. More than this I think he worried at one day finding England left to stand alone against both Spain and France. And so was planned a round of meetings and festivities with Chapuys at their center.

Henry made no move excluding me from these plans, and I made great preparations for a private dinner in my chambers after mass for the High Lords, with Chapuys as the guest of honor, hoping that some important business might be accomplished at my table. All was well at mass with Bishop Cranmer offering a most politick sermon, and many pleasant smiles returned from Chapuys to my self. But when 'twas time for the Ambassador to repair unto my chambers, Henry slyly routed him and members of the Privy Council to his own apartments and left me presiding o'er some hollow feast whose main course was my humiliation.

In the end the King never did accept Chapuys' terms, for he demanded first that Henry now submit his will to the Pope, and second legitimize his bastard Mary. Cromwell, furious his own careful plans were in a shambles, took his leave and went home ill, where now five days later still he lies. His discomfiture, I fear, is my only consolation in the matter.

These days Henry makes little demonstration of his love for Elizabeth and no pretence at all for me. I think my days at Court are numbered, and several of my ladies dare to speak to me of distant convents where a discarded Queen might find sanctuary.

There is little that consoles me lately. Only Mark Smeaton's sweet music and Niniane's foolishness are balms to my sore soul. A few staunch friends still surround me, Thomas Wyatt, Henry Norris, Francis Weston. Their flattery and flirtation I know to be much less true romantic ardor — for I am no longer beautiful — but more of brave constancy and Courtly love. This kind attention grows in me for them a passionate and most profound love, more deep that what I knew for Percy or the King, and more rare than what I feel toward Elizabeth, for she is tied to me in flesh and blood and body. 'Tis friendship in its finest flower, the gift of one unselfish heart unto another. And for this I am altogether grateful.

I care little for most women as they have always hated and mistrusted me, but Margaret Lee is more a sister than I ever had in Mary. How she dotes upon my self! She is Mistress of the Queen's Body and 'tis her duty to see to my care, but I know she chooses overcarefully the clothing I should wear to be the ones that are to my advantage — color, style and flattering cut. She preens me endlessly, warms my chilly feet and hands and rubs my aching head with such tenderness I am sometimes brought to tears.

And sweet George. No woman had a better brother than I do in him. We share memories of our lives that stretch back in time to childhood days. He teases me still, and in our laughter all care and sorrow of the present vanish magickally. I close my eyes and hear him creeping up the curved stair to my room in Hever Hall where we whispered, lest our childish voices planning great wars and silly entertainments be heard.

I see us in an autumn wood at Edenbridge, he crowning me with a flower wreath, naming me Queen of the Leaves. "Fall to your knees, for I am your Liege!" I would grandly shout, and down would tumble red and gold and orange leaves in their thousands. George would cry, "All powerful Majesty, see how your subjects bow to your command!" Then we would shriek with laughter till our bellies ached with it. Once I was the Queen of England. Now I am only Queen of the Leaves.

Yours faithfully,

Anne

I am a prisoner, Diary, a prisoner in the Tower of London. Woe to me for I am surely finished, accused of adultery, nay treason. For in England adultery practiced by a Queen is treason and treason is death. This is no just accusation to be argued in a court for its fair outcome. No, a distant nunnery will never do, for Henry needs me dead. Mark Smeaton and Henry Norris poor boys, accused of carnal knowledge of the Queen are also in the Tower. 'Tis said that they've confessed to laying with me. Surely they have not for they are honest men and this heinous accusation is altogether false. A lie. Have they been tortured into such confessions? Shall I be tortured too? Cromwell, this must be his scheme. He'd turned on me of late. And he is capable of such a deed as this. I watched him guide the King thro the maze of his divorces from Katherine and the Pope, and into my bed. Those beady eyes. That cruel mouth. I saw the look of him leading that evil delegation into my rooms. Even silent as he allowed my Uncle Norfolk to serve me with arrest, Cromwell's foul presence cast a pall of doom around my head. They took me in the light of day upriver on a rude barge for all to see my disgrace. No friend nor loyal courtier escorted me, only horrid enemies and harridans. Lady Kingston, my aunt the Lady Boleyn, Mistress Coffin whose name so fits her. No kind words could they afford. They stood behind and out of my sight. I felt their eyes on me staring at my neck and I felt my sanity slip from my mind and join with the swirling river currents leaving my brain empty of good sense and reason. O God help me. I think that when I came here I acted badly, not a Queen. I laughed and wept and trembled uncontrollably. The barge brought me to the Tower steps and I grew so cold looking at those grey weeping prison walls I faltered then and fell upon my knees. Lord Kingston, Constable of the Fortress there to meet me caught my arm and said a kind word. I think 'twas kind for I remember little of that time except my asking if I should be taken to a dungeon and Lord Kingston saying no, that I should be lodged within my old apartments, those in which I'd stayed before my Coronation. And I remember too that as I was led to my rooms I saw the Tower's fat raven hop hop hopping cross the green and laughed at its anticks, but in that moment heard the Fortress cannon booming cross the Thames announcing my arrival and saw a wooden scaffold, place of execution. Thomas More, I thought, good Father More. His head rolling upon the green grass and so I cried bitterly. Master Kingston guided me thro my prison door and made to leave. I clutched his arm and cried, Shall I die without justice? He replied the poorest subject the King hath, hath justice. I laughed a mad laugh. He looked on me with pity. I called for a mirror to see how a pitiful Queen should look, but they did not obey my command. I am trapped here. Trapped with these horrid women who taunt me saying all London now rejoices on the street at my arrest and that now the Lady Mary, nay Princess Mary shall take her lawful place in the succession. They hate me but attend me carefully. I know they've been told, Remember all she says, she will incriminate her self further. I know they listen but I cannot hold my tongue. Gibberish spills from my mouth like water from a deep well of fear, calling curses to my enemies that if I die all England should be punished for seven years with droughts and pestilences. Elizabeth, Elizabeth what have I done to you? If I am a traitor then you are naught but a traitor's child. You have surely lost your mother, lost the future crown and mayhaps lost your life. I am to blame I am to blame I am to blame. Sweet girl forgive me. And my Mother. She will die of sorrow. Die as I die. Jesu help me. I am all alone and so afraid.

Anne

13 May 1536

Diary,

I have regained my senses, but the world made clear again is so anguishing a place that I am sore tempted back to madness. They've arrested George my brother charging we were lovers. We, incestuous! I truly wonder at Henry's fierce determination to have this homely woman, that he might make this accusation. Francis Weston and William Breyerton are also named in that way, and now join Mark Smeaton and Henry Norris in the Tower. Even Thomas Wyatt and Richard Page are now imprisoned on these lewd charges. O God, I cannot bear that these good men should suffer from the folly of my life. I beg my gaolers hourly for some news pertaining to my fate, but they feed me only mean bits of gossip meant to give me pain. That Henry nightly floats a barge downriver to the Carews' house where lodges Mistress Seymour, and there all the time making merry, awaits my trial and death.

I have bid Lord Kingston take my letters to Henry and to Secretary Cromwell, but he refuses saying he will take only spoken messages abroad from the Tower. I know the Constable's loyalties lie with Princess Mary and before her, with Katherine, so he will grant me no favors that might restore my power. But I must find a way to make communication with my accusers, serve them with notice that I will not confess to these or any other charges made of lies and of corruption. And remind them all that they will find no honest man to bear witness to these alleged crimes.

I have still had no word from my Father or of him, whether he be similarly charged with treasonous crimes and languishing in prison, or if he is one of my accusers I have no knowledge at all. With a son and daughter so disgraced most men would fold and die of shame. I imagine my Father, if he is not him self implicated, somehow using our downfall to his own advantage.

Of some consolation to me in my miserable confinement is Lord Kingston's niece, a Mistress Sommerville who's come to join the ranks of my gaolers. The Lady is no longer young nor pretty but she has the quietest eyes, and uses them to soothe all those round her. To her uncle and the other ladies' irritation she treats me more than kindly. She treats me as the Queen. I find my self longing for the small moments we are alone so that I may speak plainly and with no fear, and in these times I have leave to write to you. Tho she gives me no false promises of my release from prison or these false charges, she offers me the hope of joy in Heaven should I die, for she swears that she knows no better woman than my self. She gives me other comforts too — reading to me from the Scriptures, letting me speak of my Elizabeth, then telling stories of her own children. And Diary, she brushes my hair. Delights in it. This small service sometimes makes me cry, for she does it so tenderly, so like Henry used to do.

I have had thoughts of asking Mistress Sommerville for some secret assistance taking my letters abroad, but I have not had the heart for this. For I believe she would not refuse, and such actions would place her life in jeopardy for me. Even pleas that Archbishop Cranmer come and hear my confession have been cruelly ignored. I sometimes fear I shall never in my life again lay eyes upon a friendly and familiar face.

Yours faithfully,

Anne

15 May 1536

Diary,

A dream unimaginable has become my fate. I am to die for treason against Henry, condemned by my peers of a great lie. A lie. My husband, my friend and lover of these ten years will murder me most publickly in cold blood . . . and no one will object. How can this be so? How has it come to this, that all the Lords of England have embraced evil so fervently that they would execute one Lady so that her husband might marry another? It might be said that Henry is no ordinary husband. He is the King. The Sun. A God on earth. But I have known him, and the truth of it is Henry is a man, no more no less, placed upon the throne by other men, thro war and bloodshed and the love of power. This is what they know and what their fathers and their fathers 'fore them knew, and they are debased by it. All trappings of Court life, like a spicy sauce which cannot hide the taste of putrid meat beneath it, cannot disguise the base instincts which rule the hearts of England's noblemen.

Today those who have survived this bloodletting sit like hungry vultures perched o'er the carcasses of those who fell. Pairs of black and liquid eyes covet the feast below — the properties of those condemned with me — incomes and rents, tapestries, clothing, furnishings from their great houses — like hunks of gory sinew to be fought over, tugged and torn between so many greedy beaks.

Their families will deny them, for 'tis unwise to love a traitor, even one's own kith and kin. But my Father is not an unwise man, this is well known. Thomas Boleyn will never be taken for a sea captain who refuses to desert his sinking ship. O no, not my Father. They say he stood at the trial of Weston, Norris, Breyerton and Smeaton, helped condemn them of adultery with his child. And it is said that he made offer to stand even at my trial and George's, but in the end was spared the indignity. I think had he been there he would have found us, as all twenty-six of my peers did, guilty as charged. For my Father values his neck too highly to love a traitor. Nay, I give my self more credit than is due. For I think my father *never* loved me. Never even saw me. I was just a girl to use, a clever girl with some beauty and as much willfulness and pride as any man. It galled him, no doubt, that his youngest daughter dared to rip the reins from his iron grip and bestride the reckless stallion that was her own life, ride headlong into glory and disaster. He never loved me.

I must write of my trial for it is part of History now, and tho 'tis dangerous for any living man or woman to see it other than as Henry will have them do, this Court's infamy, its gross injustice must one day be known and surely reviled. My friends had their day before the peers on 12 May and all were found guilty of treason — having carnal knowledge of the Queen and conspiring the death of the King. They are to be butchered horribly as only a traitor or a heretic is punished. Three days after their débâcle came mine.

I was marched from my apartments cross Tower Green to

the grey and ancient battlements of the King's Hall. As I entered I saw 'twas so vast a room that it could and did hold two thousand men and women who had come for the great occasion of a Queen's trial for treason. Jostling there shoulder to shoulder in the stinking, sweltering hall were London's Mayor, its Aldermen, countless courtiers, divers ambassadors from foreign lands with their hunched scribes beside them, country squires and their ladies who had surely begged to come to London for such a spectacle as this, and great swarms of common folk there to see Justice done to the Great Whore whom they had hated for so long.

Throngs parted as I made my way forward. Pretending some imagined triumph, I held my back more straight, my chin more high than I had managed in many years. My ladies, save Mistress Seymour who was fittingly absent, appeared to me as colorful birds arrayed in their finest plumage. But they who had for so long made a pretty, giggling flock round me, stood not together but now perched within the protection of their families or bands of new friends.

Margaret Lee stood clutching Thomas Wyatt's arm with a look that bespoke a rare combination of joy and grief for her brother's recent clearing and release, and my own omnipresent doom. Wyatt looked unutterably sad and I thanked him silently for you, Diary, my most loyal friend of all my days.

Niniane had placed her self in my sight as I passed. And perhaps moved by the pure ridiculousness of the occasion, I chose my jester as the only one to whom I spoke within the crowd. "Niniane," I said and stopped before her. She was right amazed and brought forth a wicked smile. She leaned close to me.

"I think they mean to rename you," she whispered.

"And what name would that be?" said I.

"Queen Anne Lackhead, Your Majesty."

"Then they will have named me most wisely," I said and gave a smile back to her.

"I love you, My Lady," said she. "And you will be sorely missed in this fool's heart."

I walked on. There before me waiting at the bar all robed in rustling scarlet in two long rows, was all the peerage of England, each of twenty-six faces decorated with the gravest of countenances. I saw there among them Henry Percy of Northumberland, pale and pinched and older than his years. At their head upon a high platform, beneath the royal canopy sat not the King (for he had no stomach for this) but my Uncle Norfolk, weighted down with golden chains, a long white staff in hand, the Earl of Surrey, Duke of Suffolk and the Lord Chancellor Audley.

My Uncle made no waste of time and read out with a clear and bloodless voice the charges that I the Queen, for more than three years despising my marriage and bearing malice in my heart against the King, and following daily my fickle and carnal lust, falsely and traitorously by foul talk and kissing, touching, gifts and divers unspeakable incitations, did procure the King's daily and familiar servants to be my adulterers and concubines. Of my brother George was charged that I seduced him, alluring him with my tongue in his mouth and he in mine, and that he carnally knew his own natural sister in incestuous liaison. With the others it was said that I conspired the King's murder, having never loved him in my heart, even promising marriage with one of my treasonous bedfellows after Henry's death. Places and dates were furnished of my lewd crimes, lascivious carriage. It seems that my uncontrollable lusts guided me willy nilly to frequent dangerous indiscretions. I took these lovers several in a night, and less than one month after Elizabeth's birth, and sometimes during pregnancy. To be fair they brought forth some truths — that I had laughed at the King, his clothes and person, that I had ridiculed the ballads he had wrote. But that these should be evidence of my treason made me wonder at their desperation.

All accusations read, I stood to make my own defense, but I was silenced harshly by my Uncle. No witnesses, no testimony on my behalf were to be allowed. These outrageous and irregular proceedings so shocked the onlookers that they stirred noisily with their displeasure crying "Give her leave to speak!" and "Let her show proof!" That moment was, I think, the sweetest I have had as Queen, for I felt the people there were with me. I cannot say that they loved me. Perhaps 'twas only knowing if the King's own wife could be treated thus within a court of law, their lot was much the poorer, and Justice had surely died in England.

So I reined the furious voice that wished to shriek curses at these spineless insects, and only pled not guilty to the charges, asking God to be the witness to my innocence. Then Norfolk made demand from all the Lords who sat upon their benches for a verdict in the case and they, one by one with no choice to make but guilty, so found me. I watched as that single word fell again and again from their corrupted lips, but I was little moved by its repetition . . . except by its pronouncement from one mouth.

Henry Percy faltered 'fore he uttered those syllables that would put to death the only woman he had ever loved. He faltered and I made a challenge of the moment, tried to meet his eye. But like a gauntlet thrown down and never taken up out of mortal fear, he refused my engagement. Just stared straight ahead and said "guilty" more loudly even than the others had.

Norfolk pounded his white staff upon the floor three times and its crashing echoed in the hall, now so still the sound of a dove's wings against the air might be clearly heard.

"Because thou has offended our Sovereign, the King's Grace, in committing treason against his person, thou hast deserved death and shall be burnt here within the Tower of London on the Green, else to have thy head smitten off as the King's pleasure shall be further known."

I heard then a great muttering from the crowd. "Foul play!" "Where's the King, with his new mistress?" "Where's justice here?" and other low curses on this cowardly Court. I might have been marched away without another word had not the mood been such, but my Lord the Duke of Norfolk weighed the intelligence of letting me speak or forcing my silence, and finally gave me my permission.

If ever I owned dignity, 'twas then and there that I knew I must needs make use of it. I kept all trembling from my voice and looked square at each of my accusers in their turn and said, "Gentlemen, I think you know well the reason why you have condemned me is something other than the evidence brought before you today. My only sin against the King has been my jealousy and lack of humility. But you must follow, if not your own clear conscience, the King's. I have prepared my self to die, my Lords, and regret only that men innocent and loyal to Henry must lose their lives on my account." Then I turned to the onlooking crowd, my own subjects who were very still, and let them look upon my face, that which they had for so long reviled, to see the truth of my innocence for them selves, and asked them humbly to pray for me. I let no man touch me as I swept, the Queen of England, from that hall.

Later in my prison rooms Lady Sommerville came and sadly gave report of my Brother's farce they called a trial. She said that he'd acquitted him self with so much grace and wit that most believed he would be freed. But it seems his rage got the best of George and he, enjoying one bittersweet moment of defiance, made publick a charge he'd been forbidden most explicitly to speak — that of Henry's impotence. 'Twas said that I told to my sister in law, and she to George, that the King had neither vigor nor strength for the manly act. This provoked such great whispering, nay laughter from the audience that my Uncle had to call for order. But this moment of contempt, said the good lady, so angered the Lords that it cost my brother his liberty and life. As final punishment we are to be kept until our deaths without the comfort of each other's company.

Finally she told how, with court adjourned, all the Peers were bidden rise by Norfolk and they did — all but one. Henry Percy still sat slumped in his chair quite collapsed and deathly ill. He was carried from the hall by four guards, for all the other Lords had no time to delay with the weak or wounded.

So now I face the flames or if some memory of me should bestir the King's generosity, the axe. I am very tired and pray to find some peace in sleep, but this wretchedly condemned woman's hope to find sweet dreams is naught but a dream it self.

Yours faithfully,

Anne

16 May 1536

Diary,

My friend the Archbishop Cranmer has visited me. I thought, fleetingly, that he had come with my pardon from the King — banishment perhaps to a distant convent. But the only leniency which Cranmer brought this day was painless death. I am not to be burnt, for that was not the King's pleasure. Poor Cranmer — thin as a sword, his nose a great beak and his eyes dull with agony. He smelt of incense as tho he had knelt for hours in a smoky chapel. But his voice was strong and never wavered as he greeted me warmly and managed a smile. But he had little time, and so presently informed me of the mission on which he'd been sent by Secretary Cromwell.

"The King and Cromwell were well apprised of my disposition," he said, "for I had written to Henry after your arrest that I never had a better opinion of a woman than I had in you, and that next to His Majesty I was bound to you, of all creatures living."

"You wrote that to Henry?"

"Of course I did, for it was true."

"It was very brave of you, Thomas."

He cleared his throat. "The King is determined to have this new marriage, Anne, and wants no impediment. Moreover he demands that Elizabeth . . . be named a bastard."

I reeled from these terrible words, as tho struck by a great hand. All my good works on my child's behalf had been in vain.

"So my death is not enough?"

"Just days before your trial he tried once again to bully Henry Percy into signing a statement affirming your precontract of marriage with him. Percy was very weak and ill, but refused. Now the King requires you to furnish proof that your marriage to him self was null and void."

"*I* furnish proof?"

"Yes. You may either contradict Lord Northumberland and claim you did have a precontract with him, or you may inform the King of his affair with your sister, which will place you in too close an affinity for a legal marriage."

"So the King must be informed by *me* that he fornicated with Mary . . ."

"Do not ask me to make sense of Henry's mind. You know that is impossible."

But my own mind was suddenly awash with new possibilities. "If we were never married, Cranmer, then does it not follow that I was never Queen?"

"Yes."

"And adultery in other than a queen is never treason."

"I see the path of your logic, Madame, but it is sadly" — he stumbled on the words — "not the King's desire that you live. He wishes only that Elizabeth be proclaimed illegitimate."

"Tell me, was this Cromwell's plan?"

"Quite so. I have traced it back to the meetings with Ambassador Chapuys on the Imperial Alliance. You remember that when those negotiations broke down Cromwell took to his bed for five days claiming indisposition? I think he must have lain abed planning this scheme, for he emerged from his cocoon like some malevolent butterfly with deadly wings outstretched to enfold his prey. That prey was you, Madame. He gathered your enemies, all the spies in your house, to give evidence against you. He had Mark Smeaton brought to his house on Throgsneck Street on the pretense that the poor boy should play for him. They tortured a confession out of him."

"I thought as much. But why? Why did Cromwell do it? Did he not twist and overwork the law and man's reasoning beyond imagining to make my marriage to Henry possible?"

"You forget he is a butterfly taken up by which ever wind is the strongest."

"Yes, and there is only one wind in England," said I bitterly. "Its name is Henry."

"Remember that Cromwell once spoke fervently for the Imperial Alliance, but when the King came out against it, the Secretary knew he had chosen sides wrongly. There was only one thing left he could give Henry to please him. A new marriage to Jane Seymour. A marriage with no impediments."

"But does Henry honestly wish to see me dead? He loved me once, Cranmer. With his heart and soul he loved me. You know as well as I what he did in order to have me."

"And you know that with a man like Henry the pendulum of passion swings as far to one side as the other. Madame, I fear . . ." He paused as tho the words were too thick in his mouth to fall from it. "I fear if you do not give him what he wants, it will not go well for Elizabeth."

The blood ceased to flow within my veins and I shuddered.

"Would he kill her too?"

"King Henry is capable of great evil, and murdering his own daughter, if it satisfied his need, is conceivable to him. He or his incubus Cromwell could find some reasoning, the same as he found for murdering you. You are a witch, therefore your child is one too. Or perhaps being a bastard will make her marriage prospects dim and the girl becomes expendable, even a liability. Anything is possible. For the King is mad."

"You speak treason, Archbishop."

"If the truth is treason, then I am justly accused."

"I was condemned on a lie."

"As we all know, Madame." He could not bear to look at me for his shame, and stared out the window to Tower Green. But when his eyes lingered and fixed outside and his jaw hardened into a grimace, I looked to see what he regarded so intently. Pairs of workmen carried many raw wooden boards to the center of the lawn and piled them there next to the scaffold where Thomas More had died.

"You asked if the King had no love left for you. I think perhaps one flicker remains in that torch which once burnt so fiercely. He has sent to Calais for the finest headsman on the Continent, so that your execution . . . so that it should be cleanly done."

His words sent a wave of fear thro my body, but when it passed I was calm and could afford a small irony. "Ah, I hear the headsmen from Calais are very good. And I have a little neck. It should be an elegant occasion."

"O Your Majesty!" Cranmer fell to his knees before me, took up my hands and kissed them, weeping bitterly.

"Come my friend, don't cry for me. I think that this ending which seems so cruel and unjust is part of God's plan which may not be well understood by our selves, but perfect in his eyes."

I said this to ease his mind, tho 'twas not the truth in my heart. But it did ease him. Before long he wiped the wetness from his cheeks and I helped him to his feet.

"I am ashamed that you speak the comforting words that should be mine to you."

"Never mind. Bring me quill and parchment and I will write the document that Henry wishes to have." When Cranmer had provided these things I sat and wrote in a confession that I had in deed been precontracted to Henry Percy, and that I was closely related to the King by degrees of affinity with my sister, and also how I had bewitched him and that he was no longer bound by these false ties to me in marriage. I granted that our daughter was illegitimate and then I signed "Anne, Marquess de Pembroke" to the paper. As I blotted the ink most carefully, for there could be no doubt and no mistake on this statement, I asked Cranmer what would become of him.

"I am safe, I suppose. Certain members of the Privy Council called me to the Star Chamber and they made me full aware of my duty to appear as believing your guilt. Lord Sussex made sure to remind me of our favorite prophecy, 'Then will be burned two or three Bishops and a Queen.'"

"As tho you needed reminding you could fall with me."

Cranmer closed his eyes and threw back his head, his lips pressed grimly together. "I deserted you, Your Majesty. But please believe me, it was not of cowardice. You were already lost and my support at such a point was of no account. I must survive to continue the work of the New Church."

"I know, Cranmer, you did well. I shall pray with my last breath that you succeed and that England never fall beneath the yoke of Rome again." He looked unspeakably sad. "Will you ever see your Dutch wife again?" I asked.

"I think not. 'Twas a foolish act, that marriage."

"But you married for love, Cranmer. That is very rare, but never foolish. Mayhaps when Henry tires of your services you might travel again to Holland and see her."

He chuckled at the thought and smiled.

"Yes, mayhaps. Thank you, Your Majesty, for thinking of me at so difficult a moment for your self. I swear I know no one kinder than you."

Then the good priest heard my last confession and gave me gentle penance for my sins. It was time for him to take his leave. As he rolled the damning document and placed it in a pouch he said he would not tell me to be brave, for I was more brave than he could ever hope to be. Then he bid me adieu and said that he would pray with all his heart for my soul. I kissed him then and let him go.

I felt a strange happiness enwrap me, as tho a thick shawl had been thrown upon my shoulders, for the man's presence had been a fine gift to me from Henry, and I knew that I had done all I could do to protect my sweet and innocent child.

Yours faithfully,

Anne

"YOUR MAJESTY!"

Mary Sidney's greeting sliced through Elizabeth's mind like a sword, instantly severing her from the tragedy in which she was so deeply immersed. Anne, Archbishop Cranmer, their final meeting in the Tower all vanished as a parade of cheerful waiting ladies scurried through the royal bedroom carrying pots of steaming water to Elizabeth's bath chamber.

"Come on, up you get!" cried Lady Sidney, unceremoniously pulling back the satin coverlets. "You've been abed for long enough. Your councillors are howling for you, as is my brother."

"How is Robin?" inquired Elizabeth, feeling a bit strange, for her lover had not been in her mind for some time.

"He pines for you, Madame. And whines. Robert has kept well to himself since Lord Cecil's return and your indisposition. Come, let me help you up. Lean on me, for your legs are sure to be weak."

"Where is Kat?"

"Asleep and snoring in the coffer chamber. Last night when I put her to bed amidst the other ladies all laughing and shouting she was dead to the world in three seconds. Even when Lady Benton's pet squirrel crawled right up on her shoulder she didn't stir. The woman was fair exhausted."

Mary Sidney pulled Elizabeth to her feet. Her legs felt like two tall pots of jelly, but after a moment Elizabeth shook off her waiting woman's help.

"Go now. Make sure they add a good measure of lilac oil to my bath. And I will wash my hair."

"Is that wise, Majesty? You have just been —"

"Go."

"Yes, Madame," she said and disappeared into the next room.

There were still more pages to be read but Elizabeth retrieved her mother's diary from between the crumpled linen sheets and replaced it in the locked chest at the foot of her bed. With her thin nightgown fluttering around her ankles she walked, feeling light as an angel, into her bath chamber.

There Lady Sidney oversaw preparations for the Queen's bath, ordering more cold water to the tub, more linen scrub cloths and a sprinkling of rose petals and herbs. Elizabeth saw the steaming water had risen from the copper tub and fogged the floor-to-ceiling mirrored glass. With a final test to the temperature of the water Mary Sidney bade the Queen enter her bath. Another waiting woman pulled the gown over Elizabeth's head and she stepped into the warm, fragrant water.

Several hands began to scrub her pale, tender skin with slow gentle strokes. The steam had softened the air and further muted the voices of her ladies who, sensing the Queen's still weakened condition, kept their usual chatter low and calm. Lavender and herbs wafted round her head. The water lapped round her throat and with the swiftness of a hunting hawk in flight, Elizabeth's mind soared to the Tower of London.

She was inside her mother's mind. Feeling the slenderness of her neck and imagining the headsman's blade as it sliced through the tissue and bone. Wondered if she would feel the pain, see the world for one fleeting moment through the eyes of a disembodied head as it rolled in the grass on Tower Green.

The treachery of men.

The horror of the image drove Elizabeth back to her own thoughts. To her mother's bravery. Anne had fought so long for dignity and control of her destiny. Fighting like a man, a gallant knight, she had through the years confronted and defeated one formidable enemy after another — Wolsey, Suffolk, Clement — only to be undone by her greatest ally.

Ah, the betrayal, cried Elizabeth silently. Henry had fought at

Anne's side for as long as she was strong, as long as she withheld from him that which he desired above all. Her sex. The moment she had succumbed to his advances and, thought Elizabeth bitterly, to the holy estate of matrimony, he had turned on her. Viciously. Suddenly. Sickeningly. He'd punctured the steely armor, impaled the woman he had once loved in the vulnerable place between her thighs.

Elizabeth had neither understood nor accepted the full and poisonous treachery of her father's act until this moment. Henry had loved Anne with a passion so great as to rock the foundation of England, nay all of Christendom. And then when it had served him otherwise, the simple discarding of her was not enough. Elizabeth had always believed what all the others had believed, that Anne had deserved her death, an adulteress and a traitor. Those few who had known of her innocence either were dead or as had Lady Sommerville, withheld the truth to save their own lives. Even Cromwell, who had been architect of Henry's greatest triumphs, had lost his head in the shadow of Anne's disgrace. Now Elizabeth was faced with the spectre of her once beloved father as a faithless whoremonger and a royal beast.

"Lord Cecil has been most concerned, Majesty," said Lady Sidney, breaking Elizabeth's reverie. "He came asking after your health two and three times of a day. He is a most faithful servant, Madame."

Most guilty, the Queen silently corrected her lady. Cecil must have known that his ultimatum had sickened her, and was ashamed. But when next she saw him, she thought, she would be kind to him and gracious, for his motives were pure and in no way self-serving. He believed her love affair with Dudley was injurious to her position and that marriage to him would be a disaster. But just now she must stop thinking on all of it and savor the women's massaging fingers and the fragrant mist swirling around her blessedly pain-free head.

※

The first meeting of the Queen and the Privy Council since her illness had been a brilliant success. Elizabeth had praised her men effusively for the triumph of Edinburgh and, to their surprise, had shown an uncommon decisiveness in the matter of a new tax. There had been a certain camaraderie this day, much easy bantering and some hearty laughter, which Elizabeth found especially delightful. She had charmed them entirely, she thought, and put their minds at ease of her. Even Lord Cecil was in good cheer, though his thin edge of perpetual reserve was a sign that he had not forgotten his ultimatum. And she had not pressed the issue of Robin's patent creating him Earl. There would be time for that. . . .

The afternoon sun angled in low through the leaded glass as the councillors chatted amicably and gathered up their papers to go. Elizabeth was first to notice the nervous young messenger enter and fall to his knees waiting to be acknowledged. She bade him rise and, as if all sensed the importance of the man's mission, the councillors fell silent. The boy cleared his throat not once but twice and then began to speak.

"Your Majesty. I am come from Cumnor House in Devon."

Elizabeth's stomach pitched like a boat in a heavy swell at the mention of Robin Dudley's home manor. She suddenly wished that the young man would disappear as in a conjurer's puff of smoke. But he continued.

"Lady Amy Dudley is dead. She was found at the bottom of the stair by her servants when they came home from the fair. Her neck . . ." The boy faltered over the words. "Her neck was broken, but her death seemed not from the fall. Her headdress was never disarranged. They are calling it murder."

Elizabeth heard the councillors explode with angry oaths and frantic whispering. She struggled for composure.

"Has Lord Robert Dudley been informed?" she demanded.

"Yes, Majesty. A moment ago in the stables."

"Very good." Elizabeth was determined to meet none of her men's eyes, nor allow them to see her cheeks which burned hot and red.

"Someone pay him," she called without turning back to the council, and strode through the double doors.

They know! thought Elizabeth as she waved away the small contingent of ladies who stood waiting to accompany her from the Privy Chamber back to her apartments. She could not at this terrible moment bear their sly glances and false deference. She had to travel what seemed like miles of corridors and hundreds of stairs passing courtiers, guards, and yeomen all of whom, she was convinced, were smirking at her.

When finally Elizabeth entered her Presence Chamber she was shaken to find it fairly crammed with ladies and gentlemen all of whom were strangely reserved and not, as she might have expected under the circumstances, abuzz with gossip. The reason for their reserve, she discovered, was standing in the far corner with his sister, Mary Sidney.

Robin looked pale, his normal robustness now shrunken with palpable fear.

"Out!" cried Elizabeth. "Everyone out!" The room cleared within seconds, so fierce was the Queen's directive. Even Kat, who had been inside the royal bedchamber, now emerged and, knowing better than to ask if she were an exception to the command, followed the others. Only Robin stood alone and very still in the fading afternoon. It was dim, for in the commotion of the moment no one had remembered to light the candles.

Elizabeth moved past Dudley into her bedchamber and he followed silently, closing the heavy door behind him. She prayed that each slow breath she drew into her body would calm her, steady her, allow her a measure of sanity, for she was on the brink of exploding.

"Why?" she said, finally breaking the terrible silence.

"Elizabeth . . ."

"She was dying, Robin. Could you not have waited?"

Dudley moved toward Elizabeth with his arms outstretched to hold her, but she backed away from his embrace.

"How can you think this of me, Elizabeth? There is no proof she was murdered. Only strange circumstances."

Elizabeth watched Dudley closely. She observed every movement of every muscle in his face, the texture of his voice, the tilt of his shoulders. But as desperately as she tried she could not discern the truth or lie of his words.

"Amy was found at the bottom of the stairs. Her neck was probably broken in the fall."

"And now you are suspected," said Elizabeth. "*I* am suspected. Do you not see how this appears? The Queen of England is being swived by her horsemaster. They wish his wife to no longer be impediment to their scandalous affair. The wife is found conveniently dead."

"I did not murder my wife, I swear."

"And do you swear you did not *have* her murdered? Do you swear you did not plant the idea in your trusted servants' minds that you wished above all to be free of her?"

"I will say again. I did not murder Amy. But I will not lie to you. I am glad that she is dead."

"Robin!"

Dudley's last words caused the room to spin and blur around Elizabeth, so that for a brief moment it was no longer her lover that stood before her but her bloated father Henry. The beast. Henry who, dressed in gaudy yellow, mourned her mother's execution by next day marrying Mistress Seymour. He, too, was glad his wife was dead.

The treachery of men.

"Speak truthfully, Elizabeth." Dudley's face reappeared, supplanting her father's ghastly apparition. "You wished her dead, too."

"I will grant I wanted you for myself, but I never wished another woman's blood on my hands."

"I love you, Elizabeth. With all my heart and soul. Be it God or the fates, but they have seen fit to clear my way . . . and I am free to marry."

"No!" Elizabeth clapped her hands over her ears. "Do not say such things!" It was her father's voice again. Glad she's dead . . . free to marry . . . glad she's dead . . .

"Elizabeth." Dudley reached out to the Queen. Her whole body was quaking with cold emotion.

"Please no. Do not touch me." She tried to calm herself, regain her reason. "Just go now, Robin. I think you must retire from Court for a time. There will be an inquest and you'll be found innocent of any wrongdoing." She searched his eyes. "You *will* be found innocent, will you not?"

"Yes, I will."

"Good. Then go to Kew." Elizabeth's mind was racing ahead. "Stay there quietly until you are sent for. Speak to no one of this save Lord Cecil whom I will send with my communications."

"Will you write? If I must be kept in exile from your body, my love, I cannot bear to be far from your thoughts as well."

"I will write."

Dudley fell to his knees before Elizabeth and laid his head amongst the folds of her skirt. She placed her hands on either side of his face and brushed away the tears that fell from his eyes. In this way they stayed for some time until she bade him rise. He stood and, tenderly kissing her fingers, Robert Dudley begged his Queen's leave and backed, trembling, out of her bedchamber.

As brittle as Venetian glass Elizabeth Tudor laid herself down upon the royal bed and commenced to weep. She wept for her mother, her father, for Robin and Amy, for love, for death and all her sweet impossible dreams lost forever.

17 May 1536

Diary,

The King has once again been merciful. My friends and brother have been spared the agony of a slow slaughter. But they are all yet dead, heads severed of their bodies, their once precious blood now only fit to wash an executioner's boots. I could not see the scaffold from my prison window, so I bid Lady Kingston take me to a place to see this monstrous occasion, that which my folly had wrought.

Great crowds gathered for the day's events — whole families carrying picnics, government officials high and low, foreign dignitaries, merchants who had closed their shops in celebration. The scaffold had been built high for all to witness the brutality, and so one by one Norris, Weston, Breyerton and Smeaton took their places. I could not from my parapet hear the final words that these brave men spoke, but learned later none of them betrayed me, only asked for God's mercy and that they should die well.

As George, my dearest brother, came next to the scaffold all quiet went the crowd. Women pulled their children close from sight of the incestuous fiend. A fat man leered at George and licked his greasy fingers, perhaps recalling his sister or his daughter squirming under his repulsive weight. I saw a young gentleman, a green and callow hopeful to the royal Court who, with haunted eyes, watched still as stone. Fear was surely coursing thro his veins, for he saw too clearly the mortal danger in his new profession.

I wished desperately to catch my brother's eye ere he laid down his head, to send him the greatest measure of my love and receive the same in kind to brighten our dark journeys. But his eyes were fixed before him, each movement fraught with dignity, each spare word chosen carefully so that his final act of living might be long remembered as fine and most courageous. Farewells spoke he paused, lifted up his head to see the stark blue sky with great clouds like sailing ships floating by. I was reminded of the blustery day I saw him off on Dover shore to France. I saw again the graceful gesture as his nimble fingers snatched to grab his wind blown cap. Ah, that day had been a happy one with many hopes before us.

My own eyes looking skyward, I had not seen him kneel before the headsman, only heard the sickening thump, the cheers of that rude congregation. So I turned, for I had no wish to see the fountain of my brother's blood wasted on Tower Green.

Lady Kingston watched at my prison door for me, her eyes merciless, her tight mouth a slash between a bulbous nose and thickening chin. Overcome with all the cruelty I had witnessed, and fearing so for my Elizabeth that she might suffer such a fate on my account, I spoke to her beseechingly. I grovelled and repented of the treatment I had shown the Lady Mary, hoping she would take some pity on her tiny half sister, just an innocent with no other friends in life to claim. My gaoler, though cold as stone, agreed to take my protestations in their wholeness to the woman she called Princess Mary. I felt the steel band round my heart loosen its terrible hold and I breathed more easy.

For my death which comes tomorrow in the morning, I must prepare. Jesu, give me strength.

Yours faithfully,

Anne

18 May 1536

Diary,

They have delayed my death another day and tho I think they mean to torture me with small cruelties as this, I am happy for the time which shall be well spent. For today I mean to write to Elizabeth from my deepest heart and for her eyes only. I shall give this book into the keeping of Lady Sommerville, who has promised me that when the time is right she will put it in my daughter's hands.

You have been a true and patient secret sister, Diary. I have writ the whole of my life onto your empty pages. Thro these many years I came to see you as a kind eyed, highborn Lady of a certain age, rich with wit and great intelligence. There you sat, or so I oft imagined, in a sunny window seat poring o'er each new passage, as one friend will read with eagerness a missive from another.

Tho no reply was ever sent from you, I yet received a wealth of invisible riches. As quill met paper some strange alchemy occurred. My Diary worked as Philosopher's Stone to take my memories, dreams, conversations, hopes, fears and scattered thoughts — like some base metals — and turn them into gold. This gold was, I believe, my own mind's enlargement, my soul's enhancement. And for that gift I do thank you with all my heart. Let me leave you, friend, with my last verses.

> O death rock me asleep,
> Bring on my quiet rest,
> Let pass my very guiltless ghost
> Out of my careful breast.
> Ring out the doleful knell,
> Let its sound my death tell;
> For I must die,
> There is no remedy,
> For now I die. . . .
>
> Defiled is my name full sore
> Thro cruel spite and false report,
> That I may say for evermore

Farewell to joy, adieu to comfort.
For wrongfully you judge of me
Unto my fame a mortal wound,
Say what ye will, it may not be,
Ye seek for what shall not be found.

Yours faithfully,

Anne

My darling Elizabeth,

When last I laid my eyes upon your sweet self you were not yet three years old. More beautiful than a painted doll you were, and as toward and gentle of condition as any child I have ever known. I remember that day, for the spring sun streamed blindingly bright thro the nursery windows, and your tiny red satin gown seemed afire in the light as you toddled toward me, arms outstretched. Perhaps you have no memory of those early years but I can truly say, Elizabeth that tho our times together were sadly few, you knew me and you loved me. Loved me with a fierce possessiveness that all thought was strange for such a small child. My lap was your throne and I your only subject. Whilst there ensconced you did demand my full attention, and allowed no interference to our intercourse. You commanded me of which songs to sing, which tales to tell, which places on your neck and ears and feet to kiss and tickle. I so cherished those rare, enchanted hours and hope you have some memory of them, because I must die knowing I leave you a motherless child in a cruel and dangerous world.

All signs say you will never wear the crown of England. Mary may reign and Jane Seymour's issue will surely take precedence, but if I am to die well I must believe that you will one day be Queen. 'Tis not the Nun of Kent's prophecy tells me this, tho I do believe she saw the future truly 'fore she came to be the pawn of powerful men. But I see how the fates have such strange ways of turning suddenly and violently beyond our control. I see you one day ruling England for you have besides my determined blood, your Father's royal lineage behind you.

Tomorrow I die because I lusted not for flesh, but to command my own destiny. This is not a womanly act, I know, but I have oft thought that in this way my spirit is much the same as a man's. In this world a woman is born with one master who is her Father. He rules her life until he hands her to a husband, who rules it till death. Many preachers preach that women have no souls. But some perverse twisting in my self has always kept me from obedience to men. I was but a girl when first I counted my self their worthy opponent. I defied them all — Father, Cardinal Wolsey, Henry. Held my ground like some knighted soldier on a battle ground. Mustered my forces, advanced, retreated, fought many skirmishes, practiced diplomacy, won some great battles. And lost the war.

But except for pain of leaving you, my child, I have no regrets. For I have truly lived as few women are privileged. I have known true love, fought for and won a crown, treated with Kings and Queens and Cardinals. Borne a child. Some say I was a witch, but you have read this diary and know my power came not from Satan.

Methinks my heart first hardened and so grew stronger with the loss of my first love, Henry Percy. I might have withered from that terrible misfortune but instead, like some torn and bleeding bear chained and baited by howling mastiffs in the pit, my ire roused I struck out again and again and lived to fight another day.

Tho I loved my Father faithfully and two Henrys passionately and they did betray me, I will not tell you that all men are betrayers. Some I have known — your Uncle George, Thomas Wyatt, Norris, Weston, Breyerton were good men and true. And I forgive your Father, Elizabeth, and think I understand the strangeness of his mind. For men love that which they cannot have, and hate that which they cannot control. I was both to Henry.

So, daughter, tho I have suffered and shall soon die for this selfish need to rule my fate, I beg of you to do the same. Let no man be your master. Love, lust, marry if you will, but hold apart from all men a piece of your spirit. 'Tis thus that I shall grasp the headsman's block with no regrets and never be afraid of death. And tho before receiving sacrament I shall swear on damnation of my soul that I am innocent of all crimes charged to me, for your sake I shall yield my self humbly to the King's will and ask his forgiveness.

I soon shall die yet I rejoice, for in you a part of me lives on. My diary, which is your ancestral history, is my only legacy. But be assured that this mother's heart is filled with love for you, Elizabeth, and know truly that whilst in Heaven I shall watch tenderly o'er your self your whole life long. Adieu, sweet girl, adieu.

Yours faithfully,

Anne

$\mathcal{W}$ILLIAM CECIL LOOKED UP to see the Queen as she entered the Council Chamber. The sun had barely risen and most of the court was still asleep. But he was an early riser and now he sat alone, lost in quiet contemplation just behind the door, so Elizabeth did not immediately see him. Her unusual demeanor — a kind of determined stillness of the soul, he thought — deterred him from breaking the silence and announcing his presence.

He watched as she moved directly to her desk where lay a pile of state documents and letters, and began thumbing through them till she found the one she sought and held it up before her.

It was then he saw the blade clutched in her long ivory fingers, the glint of steel flashing in the morning sun. She raised the dagger and with short punctuating strokes slashed at the parchment once, twice . . . perhaps a dozen times till it lay in ribbons on the polished wooden floor. When she turned to go she saw her trusted advisor.

It seemed to Cecil in that moment Elizabeth pulled herself yet further erect than her normally proud carriage. She did not smile at him nor did she impale him with an icy expression. She merely acknowledged him with a reserved nod as she passed him on her way out the door.

When some minutes were past Cecil stood and walked to the document lying in tatters on the floor. He bent and lifted the pieces in his hands and laid them on the desk. It only took a few moments to reassemble the page, that which had been destroyed by the Queen's displeasure. It was the patent creating Robert Dudley an Earl.

✵

"Show her in, Kat, and then leave us."

Elizabeth's waiting woman opened the door and, beckoning Lady Matilda Sommerville into the Queen's bedchamber, removed herself from their presence. The old woman's painful curtsy was cut short by Elizabeth's gentle hand on her arm.

"Come," she said. "Won't you sit down with me, Lady Sommerville?"

As they moved to the window seat the old woman's eyes fell on the Queen's silver-topped table where lay a dozen identical embroidered badges — the kind sewn onto the livery of royal servants. She stopped and squinted at them with interest, though she did not dare act so familiarly as to pick one up. Elizabeth, seeing her interest, handed her one of the badges and she brought it up close to her eyes.

The design was a crowned and sceptred white falcon which stood upon a root sprouting white and red roses. The lady smiled.

"'Tis a proud symbol, is it not, Lady Sommerville?"

"Aye, and you honor your mother's memory in using her favorite badge, Your Majesty." She moved to lay the badge down but Elizabeth stayed her hand.

"No, keep it if you wish, as a token to remember us both," said Elizabeth. "Come, let us sit."

They sat together in the window seat overlooking the river, a gentlewoman of much advanced age and the young Queen.

"I wish you to tell me of my mother's death, Lady Sommerville."

The crone sat quiet and still for so long a time staring out at the wherries on the Thames that Elizabeth wondered if she had perhaps not heard the question, or could not answer for the pain of her reply. But finally Lady Sommerville spoke. Her gnarled fingers worried the embroidered badge, her faded eyes seeing again the events of a day many years past.

"The sun was shining so bright and beautiful on that terrible morning. Somehow the Queen, your mother, had found within her poor battered soul a last draught of strength and greatheartedness to see her through to the end. She had us dress her in a simple grey damask gown, low cut about the neck, and we'd put her long hair up inside a linen cap. Though her face was bare of all paint and powder she looked — oh, she looked so beautiful that morning, and so young. And she was smiling, smiling and almost happy. Lord Kingston was unnerved by her demeanor, saying the Queen looked to have much joy and pleasure in death. But I knew 'twas not true, for she did not wish to leave this world or her young daughter, a lamb among the lions.

"She walked proud onto Tower Green. She did not weep nor faint at the sight of the scaffold and the unruly crowd which fell silent at her approach. Even the French headsman from St. Omer was so awed by her pure beauty and calm acceptance of this fate, that he seemed to shrink and waver in his deadly resolve.

"She stepped up the stairs to the platform which had been lowered since her brother and friends' executions, on the King's orders, so fewer citizens could see the death. She looked about confused, for she saw no block. But the executioner — as she handed him the fee for his services — kindly explained that his skill was such that he did not need one. He urged her then to say her piece, so she turned to the gathered crowd and did not flinch from their blood-hungry stares.

"Her voice was strong and unwavering as she said her fare-thee-wells and bid the people pray for her. And then she did as all those who die thusly do, to protect the ones they love — she lied to mightily praise the King her husband, saying that a gentler or more merciful prince there never was.

"Then she knelt, arranging her skirts ever so carefully over her feet and ankles, and tied a blindfold over those lovely, lovely black eyes. The headsman, still wishing to ease her final fear and pain, conceived a clever ruse. Concealed beneath the straw was his sword which he took up in his hands and walked away from her toward the scaffold steps calling loudly, 'Bring me the sword!' In that instant when your mother turned her bandaged eyes toward his voice he wheeled and struck the head from her neck in one bold sweep. The ploy worked. She never knew the blade was coming."

Lady Sommerville stopped, overcome with as much sadness and horror, it seemed to Elizabeth, as the moment of her mother's death.

"As custom dictates, the executioner removed the blindfold from her eyes and held the bloody head aloft for the crowd to see. They cheered, Your Majesty, but if truth be told their hearts were not behind it and few came to dip a rag in her blood as a ghoulish souvenir. She had died so boldly, and their King seemed, just then, little more than a royal murderer of women. Contrary to rumor, the Queen's lips did never move after her head was struck off her body. I can say honestly that she felt no pain and died fully in that instant."

Elizabeth placed her long graceful fingers over the old woman's bony hand and held it there comfortingly, though she could not bear to meet the lady's eyes.

"The other waiting women and myself wrapped her body and her head in a winding cloth. Henry had not seen fit to provide her with a coffin, so we placed both parts in an arrow box, and several men carried it to the Chapel of St. Peter ad Vincula just off Tower Green. There she was laid beneath the choir, and there she remains till today."

The two women sat quietly for a time, listening to the shouts of boatmen on the river. Finally Elizabeth spoke.

"Did you read the diary, Lady Sommerville?"

"Aye. I read every word of it, Majesty. All but the last, which was written for your eyes only."

Elizabeth smiled.

"As you have given me a gift most priceless, I wish with all my heart to give you one of equal value. So please, tell me how I can reward your faithfulness."

The crone thought only for a moment, as though she had known such an offer would be made. "I have a granddaughter, Your Majesty. A sweet child of seventeen. She has never been to court and as she much enjoys the country life, has no ambition to come." The old lady paused again to form her words carefully.

"She loves a young man, the son of a local artisan who himself is apprenticed to his father's trade. He is likewise devoted to her. As custom demands, my son and his wife have made plans to marry their daughter to a toothless old widower to enrich their own estate." She gazed imploringly at the Queen. "It will break the child's heart, Your Majesty, into a hundred thousand pieces."

Lady Sommerville's eyes filled so suddenly with tears that she was herself taken by surprise. Elizabeth pulled a handkerchief from her sleeve and offered it to the woman, who gratefully dabbed her eyes.

"Forgive me," she implored.

"There is nothing to forgive, good lady. I have heard your request . . . and I grant it. I will see that your son and his wife are generously recompensed for the sacrifice of allowing their daughter to marry whom she wishes."

"Oh, Your Majesty!" Lady Sommerville murmured, overcome.

Elizabeth's eyes found her mother's diary where it lay on her bed. "Consider it a gift from . . . my mother Queen Anne."

"She was a great woman, Majesty. As misunderstood as could be. But you should be most proud to have the Boleyn blood rushing in your veins."

Elizabeth helped Lady Sommerville to her feet and saw her to the door.

"You do me a great honor with such an audience as this, Your Majesty."

Elizabeth regarded the woman's world-weary eyes.

"It is you who have done me the honor, good lady. You have returned to me a treasure I had no idea I had lost. And a love I had forgotten I owned."

As Lady Sommerville rose from her curtsy she found herself engulfed in an embrace the warmth of which her old body had never known from man or mother.

"God bless you, child. We are lucky in England to have you for our Queen."

When the door closed behind the woman Elizabeth moved to her bed and reached for the diary. She held the claret leather volume to her breast and closing her eyes, tried with all her mind's power to find within her memory the image of her mother's face, but nothing came.

"Kat," she called, and instantly her companion was at her service. "Call for my barge. I'm going downriver this afternoon."

"As you wish, Majesty. What shall I say is your destination?"

"My destination? The Tower of London."

Devoid of fanfare the royal barge floated downriver in silent grandeur. The afternoon sky was crowded with rolling black thunderheads pierced by brilliant beams of golden sunlight which set the illuminated portions of the river afire. Elizabeth sat on the upper deck quite alone, for she had instructed all her ladies to stay behind, sending Kat into a righteous blather.

"'Tis not fit behavior for a Queen," she'd scolded, "to go off unattended by her lords and ladies. And the Tower. What business have you at the Tower on such short notice, I ask you?"

"My own," Elizabeth had answered mildly, quite unperturbed by Kat's unrelenting bossiness. "My own."

As she watched the sun play upon the waters and between the clouds Elizabeth felt a great calm descend upon her soul. She suddenly felt more well and strong and whole than she had in all of her life. There was urgent business that needed attending. Business that none of her councillors — not even William Cecil — could possibly conclude.

Mother.

The Queen's unceremonious arrival at the Tower wharf had taken the yeomen at the Traitor's Gate entirely by surprise. They scrambled to their feet and snapped to attention, straightening their helmets and mumbling formal greetings as Elizabeth debarked from her barge and passed under the raised portcullis into Tower Green. As she strode alone through the huge courtyard the bald Constable scurried to meet her, still brushing bits of dinner off his black bib.

"Your Majesty, what an honor! Oh, but we were not expecting . . . how can I serve you? . . . careful where you step. You can see that we're replacing this walk, Majesty, and it wouldn't do if you were to slip and fall. Would you care to take my arm?"

"I can see well where not to step, Lord Harrington, though I thank you for the offer of your arm. My wish is to be left to myself. In fact I would be grateful if you would clear the Green of all workmen and guards. I want to be quite alone."

"Alone, Your Majesty?"

Her stern expression was all that was needed to confirm the order. He rushed away shaking his head and so upset by the Queen's unusual command that a toe stuck between two of the flagstone slabs and the man tripped, only righting himself of an embarrassing fall at the last moment. Elizabeth smiled as she saw the masons and the carpenters scatter, watched the yeomen guarding several tower doors and gates learn they were for the moment dismissed from their posts by order of Her Majesty and disappear.

Finally she was alone in the ancient castle yard, the massive walls of the White Tower soaring high above her head. She gazed up at the battlement between the Bell and Beauchamp Towers where she'd taken exercise during her own incarceration. Remembered the dank stairwell and her clandestine meeting with Robin. Remembered how the horror of dungeons with their hideous implements of torture had kept her awake at night, worrying that she might fall victim to the racks and presses, teeth crushers and thumbscrews. The Tower was a place where, once imprisoned, a person could die of fear alone at the thought of his grisly demise. And now she owned it, had no fear of the place . . . or the ghosts of those that had lost their lives here.

Elizabeth approached the doors of the King's Hall and threw them open. She stood in the cavernous and echoing chamber under the great arched ceiling imagining the noisy crush of humanity assembled for her mother's trial. The thump, thump, thump of the Duke of Norfolk's staff on the wooden floor to call the proceedings to order, the scarlet gowns of the Queen's twenty-six peers, and the stink of their fear lest they choose wrongly and incur the King's wrath upon their own heads.

Mother.

She imagined Anne the Queen having mustered the reserves of her courage standing before that court, answering its false and heinous accusations with elegant defiance. Hearing her enemies as well as her once friends proclaim her guilty of treason, adultery and incest. "Condemned by her peers of a great lie."

And yet, thought Elizabeth, her mother had been no saint. By some reckoning her hands had been stained with blood. She'd been reckless and more bold than an Englishwoman had ever dared to be. From her youngest days she'd been willful to a fault, possessed of a wild tongue and temper. She'd been a woman ruled by passion, ruled by ambition . . . but unwilling to be ruled by men.

How odd is the blood, mused Elizabeth. I did never know my mother, had no way to learn from her, yet I mirror her character in so many ways.

So many ways . . . and yet not all. Anne, it occurred to her, had been consistently inspired by anger and revenge. Wolsey. Katherine. Mary. Norfolk. But it had grown and festered, and the evil had eventually turned back upon Anne herself. It was one quality of her mother's, Elizabeth decided, that she would do well to never emulate.

When the Queen emerged from the King's Hall the scattered sun had been completely obliterated by dark clouds and Tower Green was a study in gloom. Though no scaffold was now erected on the lawn Elizabeth strolled to the place where it once had stood, where her mother's lifeblood had stained the May grass. She wondered at how Anne could have come to this place to die so ignominiously. The two men in a woman's life are her father and her husband, thought Elizabeth. Anne's father had, with a breathtaking ruthlessness, used his daughter to his own advantage, and abandoned her when she could no longer serve him.

Anne's husband. There was no doubt that Henry had loved her. But she had been trapped by that love, like a hind pursued by hounds. There had been no way out for her but the chase. Henry had wanted her past all reason, past all caring. When a King desires a woman there is no answer but Yes, Sire. Unless like Anne, she mounts a great challenge. She had proven Henry's most elusive quarry, leading him headlong through dark and dangerous landscapes, making his blood boil for her capture. Still she escaped him, year after year till he was half mad with the pursuit and his failures. But Anne, it need be remembered, was yet the hunted. Prey. With nothing to do but flee or surrender to his love which, as she had always known in her soul, was death.

Elizabeth reflected upon her mother's husband. The man described in her diary as "Beast" was Elizabeth's own father.

I loved, nay adored my father, thought the Queen. He was my

master, my King, my God before God. And now from my mother I learn he was a monster. Oh, 'tis a hard bone to swallow.

He had been cruel and outrageously unjust, but Elizabeth knew that all in her that was Henry she could not dismiss. She had learned perhaps the most important principle of her queenship from him. That whilst she might be kind and generous, seek peace for her kingdom and harmony amongst her men, she must at all times *rule absolutely* or lose the throne that had been so hard won.

Elizabeth shivered, for the gloom was deepening round her. She made her way across the Green to the Chapel of St. Peter ad Vincula and pulled open the heavy, creaking doors. Built in the ancient Norman style, it was small and unadorned. With only a few candles illuminating the nave and sharp incense thickening the air, it was a dark and melancholy place. She knelt briefly under the crucifix at the altar, but did not linger, for what she sought was the choir. The inlaid marble floor showed no indication of what lay under it — the earthly remains of her own mother, murdered at her father's hand. Without warning Elizabeth was overcome with the ache of a longing so powerful it rocked her on her feet. Her mother who had held her, had loved her, had died because Elizabeth had been born a girl, lay all but forgotten beneath her feet, a headless pile of bones.

In the silence Elizabeth strained to hear Anne crying out from her grave. A message, a lesson, a warning. But nothing came to her except a desperate ache in her heart for Robin Dudley. Her dearest friend, bringer of the sweetest sensations, sharer of her boldest fantasies. She could no longer trust him. She could trust no man. If her mother's voice could ever make itself heard Elizabeth was certain it would say, *Never relinquish control to any man.* Then a strange idea began to take shape in her mind. The one man who had natural cause to rule her — her father — was dead. Why on earth should she marry now ... or ever? Willingly surrender the awesome power of the crown to a husband? Would that not make her a great fool?

She stopped suddenly. Am I entirely mad? she thought. What folly am I planning? A monarch who schemes to remain childless and end the greatest dynasty ever to rule England?

She remembered how when she was young she had proudly announced to Robin that she would never marry. He had laughed, told her she was a silly girl. That she was a princess born, and bound to wed. Twenty years had passed. Now she was queen and here she stood contemplating that promise. Had she known even then in her child's heart that love, for a woman, was to be feared?

"Will I never marry?" Elizabeth said aloud, the words echoing in the marble chapel. Never marry? Never bear sons? Never birth a daughter? Hot tears sprang unexpectedly to Elizabeth's eyes. To never have a daughter, who would speak kindly of her, cherish the tokens of her life — a ring, a book, an initialed handkerchief. But no, she forced such sentimentality from her thoughts. What need had she of children? She would be rich with subjects who loved and adored her, who would long remember her glorious reign.

Then like a miracle, the dark of the chapel was pierced by a single renegade sunbeam which streamed in through the clerestory window. Elizabeth was riveted to its startling brilliance and suddenly . . . There! It had been transformed into the blinding light streaming in through the Hatfield nursery windows. There! She smelled the rich scent of spice and musk. There! She heard the gay laugh, the lilting French lullaby. And then in a ghostly vision emerging from the light into clear and brilliant focus were a pair of eyes — alive, deeply black and bewitching. Yes, yes, they were her mother's eyes! Teasing coquette's eyes that could drive a man mad with wanting, a dark sea where his soul could drown. Arrogant flashing eyes where lived a keen intelligence that defied despair. Ever hopeful eyes that sought passion where none could finally be found.

The vision began to dim.

"No!" cried Elizabeth aloud, for she wished fervently to bask for a few moments more in her mother's sight.

The eyes smiled merrily then, and Elizabeth's heart soared, for she could see they were filled with great and unspoken joy, reflecting in them the love of a tiny red-haired girl toddling with outstretched arms into her mother's warm embrace.

"Hold, stay with me, Mother!"

She reached out her hand toward the vision, but the ghostly eyes were fading. They grew faint . . . and then vanished entirely until all that was left was a shaft of light streaming in through the clerestory window. And as a great cloud moved to cover the sun, that disappeared as well.

Elizabeth stood in the chapel still as a statue of the Virgin. The vision was gone, but she had remembered. Remembered and taken within her a piece of her mother's spirit, one that would forever be a part of herself — a second spine to keep her strong throughout the coming years, a second heart to beat within her breast. For she would surely need greatheartedness to be the Queen that the Nun of Kent had clearly prophesied. The Tudor sun who, risen from the belly of Anne Boleyn, would shine as England's brightest star.

Elizabeth turned and swept from the chapel with the strength of destiny at her back, pulling the heavy doors closed with a resounding crash.

Yes, she thought as she strode out into the now sunlit afternoon, I am my mother's daughter. And I shall make her proud.

Acknowledgments

This book is the result of twenty-five years of passionate interest in the brilliant world of Tudor England. My indoctrination began with a pair of novels by Norah Lofts that introduced me to the two female titans of the early sixteenth century, Anne Boleyn and Katharine of Aragon.

When simple interest turned to serious research I gained invaluable knowledge and insight into the life and times of my characters from biographies by Carolly Erickson, Marie Louise Bruce, Elizabeth Jenkins, and Paul Johnson. William Manchester's *World Lit Only by Fire* was my source for understanding Luther and the Protestant Reformation.

I heartily thank my editor, Jeannette Seaver, for her deep understanding of this work; my copy editor, Ann Marlowe, for knowing more about the sixteenth century than I did; and my agent, Kim Witherspoon, for her dedication in finding the book its proper home.

In the personal realm I owe enormous debts of gratitude to several people. My teacher, Deena Metzger, helped me leap the formidable hurdle from screenwriting to novel writing. Billie Morton, dear friend and fifteen-year partner in crime, not only offered the original suggestion that I write this book but dogged me eternally with kind but scathingly honest criticism and with admonishments against missed opportunities. My mother, "Skippy the lionhearted," was the earliest and fiercest champion of my writing career, and remains my greatest inspiration.

To my husband, friend, teacher, and ally, Max Thomas, I owe the most profound debt of love and appreciation. With unfaltering loyalty and graciousness he has supported me physically, emotionally, spiritually, and materially throughout our years together.